Soldiers' Wives

Fiona Field joined the army at eighteen, married a bomb disposal expert at twenty-one and then, at twenty-six, got thrown out for getting pregnant. Her youngest child is a soldier just returned from Afghanistan.

Soldiers' Wives

FIONA FIELD

HEAD of ZEUS

First published in paperback and eBook in the UK in 2014
by Head of Zeus Ltd

9 7 5 3 1 2 4 6 8

A CIP catalogue record for this book is available from the British Library.

Paperback ISBN: 9781781857748
eBook ISBN: 9781781857731

Printed and bound by CPI Group (UK) Ltd, Croydon, CR0 4YY.

Typeset by Palimpsest Book Production Ltd, Falkirk, Stirlingshire

Head of Zeus Ltd
Clerkenwell House
45-47 Clerkenwell Green
London EC1R 0HT

WWW.HEADOFZEUS.COM

For Tim – who came back from Afghanistan
alive and well. Not forgetting the very many
hundreds who did not.

Chapter One

The olive drab army ambulance screeched to a halt, making Private Chrissie Summers, sitting in the back, grab onto the stretcher for support. She felt her heart rate jump as nervous anticipation kicked in. She knew from the emergency radio call that whatever she was about to confront wasn't going to be pretty. Terrorist bombings never were. She flung the rear door open and leapt out onto the ground, and almost gagged as her foot kicked a large mangled and bloody lump. The remains of a leg.

She could hear screaming. She'd never heard a man scream before and the sound was surreally high-pitched. And over and above the screaming, the sounds of the ongoing battle raged. Bullets crackled nearby, there was the thump of a mortar being fired intermittently, and now and again there was the ear-splitting *brrrp* of a machine gun. It was dark and smoky with strobe-like flashes from the weaponry around her and lines of tracers arcing through the night, and Chrissie was terrified. Never in her worst nightmares had she envisaged being in the middle of a scene like this.

'Summers, over here.'

The command from her superior medic who also doubled as ambulance driver, Corporal Phil Johns, brought her attention back to the reason she was there. Swiftly she took in the situation. Three casualties: one was obviously a T1 – the

1

highest priority. He was in a critical state; life hanging in the balance. The guy's leg had been blown off above the knee and blood was gushing onto the ground. Two of his comrades were packing wads of lint against the stump and he had a big 'M' written in felt-tip on his forehead: morphine had been administered. The second casualty had a huge gash down his face, and what looked like a chest wound, and the third soldier was writhing around screaming his head off. He could wait. Chrissie's training had taught her that, in general, the ones who were well enough to make a noise were well enough to take their turn; it was the quiet ones you had to worry about. And the squaddie with the missing leg was silent. Only the pumping blood indicated that he wasn't already dead.

Chrissie stepped over the severed limb and ducked as she ran the several yards across open ground to join Phil by the amputee. She wasn't sure that ducking would make that much difference with the bullets flying about, but her instinct for self-preservation overruled any vestige of rationality.

'Get a tourniquet on this one,' he ordered, 'then get a line in. He needs saline.'

Chrissie busied herself while Phil ran to check the condition of the other two.

The two squaddies moved away from their comrade to allow Chrissie space. As she worked the packing fell off the end of the soldier's leg revealing the splintered end of his femur and the mangled mass of raw meat that had once been his thigh. She felt her gorge rise but managed not to be sick. She worked on, tightening the tourniquet before ripping open a sterile pack to extract a cannula.

'Will he be all right, miss?' asked one of the squaddies.

Chrissie's reply was interrupted by another huge blast

which made her jump out of her skin. She dropped the cannula.

'Fuck,' she muttered. She got another one out of her emergency medical pack. 'Not sure,' she said. She tapped the vein on the back of the casualty's hand. 'We'll get him casevaced to the field hospital just as soon as we can. We're easily within the golden hour. We'll save him if we can.'

Over her head the two squaddies exchanged a look which clearly indicated they didn't share her confidence.

Chrissie finished working on her patient. The tourniquet was tight, the blood had ceased to flow, the drip was in and he was as stable as she could get him in the circumstances.

'Right, you two. Get him on the stretcher and put him in the ambulance.'

She glanced up. She could see Phil was still bending over the guy with the chest wound. She headed for the screamer. Not that he was screaming now, which was a worry.

She knelt down next to him. His eyes flickered towards her; he was still conscious.

'Where are you injured?' She patted his hand reassuringly and checked the name on his dog tag. Private Perkins.

'It's my stomach.' Even though he was whispering through clenched teeth Chrissie could detect his Geordie accent. His forehead was beaded with sweat but she couldn't check his skin colour because he was slathered with cam cream in shades of brown and green; at least she assumed it was cam cream and not dirt.

'OK,' said Chrissie. 'So were you close when that IED went off?'

'Close enough,' he said, his face contorted with pain.

Chrissie noticed that the front of his multicam jacket was dark – but it was all in one piece. If he had a blast injury, why wasn't his clothing shredded? Something wasn't right but she didn't have time to fart about analysing it. 'What's your first name, Perkins?'

'Lee.' He winced, then added, 'And what's yours?'

'Chrissie, and I'm here to help you now, Lee. I'll just see what's wrong and then I'll give you something for the pain.'

'It's not so bad. I don't want you worrying too much over me, bonny lass.' And he smiled at her. Chrissie's heart went out to him. Typical soldier – putting on a brave face, despite everything.

She ripped open the Velcro flap at the front of his combat jacket and reached for the tab of the zip. The fabric, she noticed, was sticky and warm. Lee was obviously bleeding – and pretty heavily. Something still didn't quite add up but she was too involved with his condition to stop and think. She pulled the zip down and as she did so, grey intestines slithered out onto the muddy ground.

'You should have seen your face,' said Phil, grinning broadly over the top of his pint.

'It was a rotten trick to play.' Chrissie was still smarting with embarrassment.

'It wasn't a trick, it was part of the exercise. I thought you would be bound to spot that his combat jacket was completely undamaged and realise you'd been set up.'

Chrissie glowered in response. Around them, other soldiers, still in grubby combats from two weeks on manoeuvres, were also grabbing a quick pint in the garrison bar, winding down by reliving the highlights of the exercise before their evening meal in the cookhouse and then heading off to make the most of a free weekend. The noise was deafening.

'Aw, come on, surely you can't still be angry.'

'Angry? I'm furious. No one warned me it might be that extreme.'

Chrissie slammed her Bacardi and Coke on the bar with such force it slopped over and splashed her hand. They hadn't warned her, either, about how affected she'd be by the plight of the wounded; the false bravado of the soldiers had been something else. She'd been so wrapped up in the exercise she'd forgotten they were all acting, but now she didn't doubt it would be the same for real on the battlefield. And then there had been that last casualty – Lee Perkins. She hadn't been able to get him out of her head since. Stupid, she knew, but that's how things stood.

'Listen, war isn't a game,' said Phil.

'I know that. But I thought I'd at least get let in gently.'

'The lads in Nad-e Ali don't,' said Phil.

Chrissie sighed. 'OK, you've made your point. Maybe I should change trade.'

Phil shook his head. 'You'll be fine. You're a grand combat medic.'

'Really?' Chrissie brightened up a bit.

'Yes, you're a natural.'

'Except when I hurled at the sight of those guts. I knew we'd have some amputees pretending to be recent bomb victims. I was geared up for that, but not guts. By the way, what were they? Sheep?'

'Pig. Local abattoir obliged.'

'Euw.'

'Well, you'd better get used to it. If you go out to Afghan, it'll be for real.'

'I know, I know, I shouldn't have chucked, but it was just a shock. It won't happen again.'

5

Phil stared at her. 'Were you in nursing before you joined up? Is that why you seem to know your stuff?'

'Not proper nursing. My mum was ill for ages and I looked after her. There wasn't anyone else to help.'

Phil nodded. 'That would explain it. So how is your mum now?'

'Dead.'

It was Phil's turn to look discomfited. 'Shit, Chrissie, I'm sorry.'

Chrissie shrugged again. 'It was the only way it was going to end. She had multiple sclerosis so it was always when, not if.' Chrissie knew she sounded quite blasé about the fact that her only known living relative was gone, but she'd had a year to come to terms with her loss. Besides, she'd done her grieving over all the years she'd watched her mum decline. By the time the end had come, it was almost a relief that the hideous illness had drawn to an inevitable close.

'Tough on you, though. It's not what should happen to kids, is it? Not much of a childhood.'

Chrissie nodded. 'It wasn't great.'

And that's an understatement, she thought. She couldn't actually remember a time when she hadn't cared for her mother. All those years of putting her mother's needs first, of never being able to go on school trips, of not being able to join after-school clubs, or the sports teams because she couldn't go to away matches; and then later not being able to go out on the lash with her mates, or go on holiday, or go clubbing, or any damn thing. But of course, with the death of her mother, the state benefits went, and with no job, Chrissie still had no prospect of *living* rather than existing. And for once she wanted to be taken care of. She needed to be fed, housed, clothed and paid, and – she realised one day as she passed the Armed Forces recruiting office – the army was the perfect answer. And they'd said she'd be perfect as a medic. Result.

So here she was, her basic training finished, and now working with a proper army unit; her first real army exercise was behind her and the rest of her life in front of her. And she had every intention of getting as much as she could out of it. Except she had been posted to the medical centre of a UK-based regiment and not out to the field hospital at Camp Bastion, which was what she really wanted. 'Too young and too inexperienced,' was what she'd been told. So she was being patient – except that the exercise she'd just completed had given her confidence one helluva knock. What good would she be on the battlefield proper if she couldn't control her reaction to extreme trauma? Obviously the army had been right in their assessment of her, so she'd have to continue to be patient a little while longer and carry on training till she was ready.

She drained her drink. 'Another beer, Phil?'

He glanced at his watch. 'Best not. Need to get my kit sorted out.'

'That's a point,' agreed Chrissie. 'OK, see you Monday.'

'Indeed you will, but not for much longer after that. I got warned for posting last week – Bastion.'

'Phil!'

'It's all right, it's cool. I'm looking forward to it, really. Proper soldiering, not dealing with hangnails and headaches.'

'Maybe.'

'It's what I've been trained to do, Chrissie. And it isn't as if I've not been there before. This'll be my second tour.'

'When are you going?'

'Soon. A week at work, then pre-ops leave, then...' He made a gesture of a plane taking off with his hand.

'Good luck then.'

'Nah – I'm going to rely on skill and training.'

Chrissie leaned forward and gave Phil a quick peck on the cheek before she slid off the bar stool. 'Even so...'

She walked across the crowded bar, grabbed her Bergen from the pile of identical huge rucksacks in the corner and, staggering under the weight of it, headed out of the bar and took the long route to her barrack block. She could have cut across the parade square and shortened her journey, but she knew if she did, she was bound to get caught by the RSM, and being bawled out by Warrant Officer Class One Jenks was to be avoided at all costs. Regimental sergeant majors across the army were universally feared and hated by soldiers in equal measure. And in her months in the army Chrissie had noticed that most officers didn't mess with them either.

Five minutes later, Chrissie got to the top of the barrack block stairs and crawled into her four-man room, dragging her rucksack behind her. She dumped it at the foot of her bed and flopped onto her duvet.

'Good time?' asked Immi, her room-mate, who was lying on her bed flicking through a magazine.

'Grim,' was all Chrissie could say.

'That bad?'

'You don't want to know the details, but let's just say it made *The Texas Chain Saw Massacre* look like a chick flick. Over and above that, it rained most of the time, it was cold and I am so filthy I probably smell.' She glanced at Immi who was wrinkling her nose. 'Correction, I'm so filthy, I *do* smell and I made a complete prat of myself in front of a bunch of soldiers.'

Immi rolled her eyes. 'What did you do, babe?'

Chrissie shook her head. 'I was sick.'

'Something you ate?'

Chrissie shook her head. 'The rations were fine.' She told Immi about the pig guts.

Immi's face was a study by the time Chrissie finished. 'You're joking me,' she whispered.

'Nope.'

'Gross.'

Chrissie nodded.

'I don't know how you cope,' said Immi. 'I mean, don't get me wrong, I think you're a total heroine, doing what you do, but there's no way I could deal with blood and guts and all that scary shit.'

'The guts *were* a bit epic.'

Immi shuddered at the thought. 'Didn't you ever want a nice cushy office job like mine? I mean, why on earth would you want to spend your life up to your arse in bodily fluids?'

Chrissie thought about it. 'I did some tests and they said I was ideally suited to being a combat medic and I just agreed. And someone has to do it. It's really important.'

She hadn't been able to save her mother's life, that had never been an option, but she could make the difference for others. As far as she was concerned it beat the crap out of being a clerk like Immi. How dull would that be, stuck in an office and shuffling paper?

'Rather you than me, babes.' Then Immi added, 'Makes me glad I was left behind with the rest of the rear party. The barracks might have been like a morgue for the past two weeks but I was warm and dry, and had access to a shower.'

'Is that a hint?' asked Chrissie.

'Well...'

Chrissie wearily dragged herself off her bed, grabbed her dressing gown and a towel off the rail and took herself off to

9

the ablutions. When she returned ten minutes later, carrying her damp, dirty clothes in a bundle, she was clean and scented, although still utterly knackered. She flumped down on the edge of her bed and stared blankly at the wall, trying to summon the energy to find clean clothes. After a bit, she said, 'Is it me or is it still a bit whiffy?'

'I think it's your combats,' said Immi.

Chrissie sighed. She knew it wasn't just the combats she'd taken off – she had a rucksack full of filthy, wet clothing. What she really wanted to do was crawl into bed, not put a couple of loads through the washing machine.

'Sorry,' Immi apologised for pointing out the obvious. 'Tell you what, I'll help you get sorted.'

'Would you?' Immi's kind offer gave Chrissie the strength to tackle the stinking shit-heap that formed the contents of her Bergen. The two girls carried the kit down to the laundry room, bagged two of the industrial machines and loaded them up.

'You're being dead kind,' said Chrissie, as she retied her dressing gown belt. 'Surely you must have got heaps of better things to do?'

'Nah,' said Immi. 'With you on exercise, Keelie away on a course and Gillie on leave I've had our room to myself. I've been able to see enough of Baz to last me a very long time.'

'Lucky you,' said Chrissie. Not that she was envious about what Immi had got up to with her latest – called Baz apparently. Immi bounced from one boyfriend to the next, with barely a pause for breath.

'It's try before I buy,' she'd told Chrissie. 'I'm doing my four years in the army then, when I find a keeper, I'm going to marry him.'

Bully for Immi, Chrissie thought, but it wasn't what she herself had planned. After years of always having to put someone else first, the last thing she wanted was to have to think about anyone else. Nope, no husband, no kids, no commitments, just herself to consider, for as long as possible. Maybe a bloke, now and again, but she certainly wasn't looking for a potential husband – no-strings-shags were all she was after.

They climbed the stairs back to their room where Chrissie began to dress in clean civvies.

'God, you're lucky,' said Immi.

Chrissie paused in pulling a T-shirt over her head. 'Why?'

'Because you always look so healthy and tanned. I'd kill to have your skin colour.'

Chrissie finished tugging her T-shirt into place. 'Really? You wouldn't say that if you'd had the bullying I got at school. Being mixed race isn't just about never having to go to the tanning salon.'

Immi looked sheepish. 'Me and my mouth. I'm sorry. I never thought.'

'Don't worry about it,' said Chrissie, tugging on her jeans. 'And at least I don't glow in the dark!' Immi threw a pillow at her which she caught and chucked back. 'Let's go to Tommy's Bar.' She grabbed a hairbrush and hauled it through her dark curly hair. 'I owe you a drink for all the help you've given me with my kit. After a fortnight of drinking nothing but tea, water, or that revolting juice drink you get in the rations, I want something stronger.'

Immi shrugged. 'I'm surprised you haven't got the shakes. A whole two weeks with no booze? Respect, sister. And honest, babes, you'd have done the same for me. You don't have to buy me a drink.'

Which was true, but Chrissie had made her mind up.

'Can I be a bit cheeky?' asked Immi.

'Sure.'

'There's a girl I've got to know at the hairdresser's – you know, Zoë's?' Chrissie nodded. She'd heard of the place although she'd never set foot in it. 'She's called Jenna and she's having a tough time of it, 'cos she married this squaddie and they haven't got a quarter yet. Her mum lives locally, but she has to share a bedroom with her sister and he still lives in barracks, so her married life has hardly got off to a flying start.'

'So why *did* they get married? I mean, if they can't live together it seems pretty pointless.'

'But if they're *not* married they won't ever qualify for a quarter. It's mad. Anyway, her bloke has been away on some months-long course or other, then he gets back, only to be sent straight off on that exercise. She's been totally pissed off by it all and is really in the dumps. How about we invite her along too? She's nice,' added Immi. 'You'll like her.'

'Won't she want to meet up with her hubby, though? Shouldn't he be back by now?'

'Some of the battalion aren't due back till late tonight, or so I've heard. If he's one of them...'

Chrissie shrugged. 'Why not? The more the merrier. Although I'm not going to make it a late one; a couple of bevvies then I'm going to hit the hay. I'm knackered.'

Immi grabbed her phone and called her friend, while Chrissie lay on her bed and let her mind drift back to the exercise.

Had she enjoyed it? Had real soldiering come up to the mark? She contemplated the previous two weeks. Sure it had been grim, just as she had told Immi. The latrines had been vile, the food had mostly been compo rations, eaten cold out of tins, the weather had been dreary and sleep had been almost non-existent, but that wasn't the whole truth. It had been amazing to be part of something so massive, so organised. There had been a buzz of excitement, a sense of purpose, teamwork and camaraderie, all those things she'd yearned for when she was growing up. All those things that had been so horribly lacking, while her heavy responsibilities made her increasingly isolated from her peers. But all anyone now cared about was how she performed and how she fitted in. And she did. She absolutely did. It wasn't a bit like school when she'd been the only one who could never have a sleepover, the only one who couldn't accept birthday party invites, because she could never reciprocate. Now she was exactly like everyone else – OK, she was still in a minority because of her ethnicity but no one gave a fuck about that. She had the same kit, the same training, the same ethos, the same everything and she loved it. Yes, she'd even loved that exercise, she thought. Maybe it was time to start hoping that the army might consider moving her on to the next stage – putting her training to a real test, not just playing at being a medic on exercise. It was a good thought.

'What are you grinning about?' asked Immi.

'Nothing,' said Chrissie, straightening her face quickly. She didn't think Immi would understand.

'Didn't look like nothing to me.'

'Just pleased to be back and in the warm and dry,' she fibbed.

'Who wouldn't be?' said Immi with a shudder. Her idea of privation was being made to do without straightening irons. 'You all set, babes? And Jenna's coming over to meet us. She sent her old man a text but he hasn't replied. She sounded well pissed off.'

Chrissie rolled off her bed. 'So – we're meeting her there? Ace. There's a Bacardi and Coke with my name on it and I'm going to claim it.'

Chapter Two

The soldiers' bar was packed when they got there, as it always was on a Friday night. Soldiers tended to save Friday and Saturday for getting shit-faced – and stayed comparatively sober for the rest of the week. Smelling of stale booze or swaying with a hangover didn't go down well with the sergeant major at the morning muster parade.

Chrissie sent Immi off to bag a seat, while she squeezed her way to the bar, catching snippets of conversations as the soldiers swung the lamp, with exaggerated tales of their performance on the manoeuvres.

'... so I said to this SAS guy, you're not hard, you're a twat, and he legged it. The big girl's blouse.'

'... then the sergeant major came up to me and he only fucking said I'd pulled Captain Wiggins' chestnuts out of the fire for him. Without me the whole platoon would have been up shit creek.'

'... and this bird was about to drop her trousers for a piss and I thought I was going to get a really good look at her snatch and some stupid fucker goes and lends her his poncho. Where's the fun in that?'

Chrissie grinned as she eavesdropped: soldiers, what *are* they like, she thought. She finally got served with drinks for them both and took them over to where Immi sat in a corner away from the TV and the fruit machines where relative peace reigned. She'd just sat down, when Immi glanced over her shoulder.

'Ooh look, there's Jenna now,' said Immi. '*Jenna*,' she hollered in a voice a sergeant major would be proud of. 'Over here.' She stood up and waved. There was an exchange of sign language. 'She just getting herself a drink,' said Immi.

'Fair enough.' Chrissie looked at the slender back view of Immi's friend as she waved a ten pound note and tried to catch the eye of the barman. She might not be catching his but she turned the heads of every other bloke present with a silver river of hair that streamed down her back and endless legs clad in skin-tight jeans. If the front view was half as good as the back, thought Chrissie, her husband was a lucky man.

Jenna got served, gathered up her drink and her change and tottered over to join Immi and Chrissie. Wow, thought Chrissie when she saw Jenna's face, although it was obviously a high maintenance look. For a start the eyelashes just had to be false. Instantly, Chrissie wished she'd made a bit more of an effort. A lick of mascara and a quick brush of her hair was no contest for this vision of personal grooming now sitting opposite. But although Jenna might look like a million dollars, from the set of her face, it wasn't making her happy.

Chrissie introduced herself and reasoned that maybe she wouldn't feel happy either, if she hadn't seen her bloke for months.

'Jenna,' said her new acquaintance. 'And thanks for the invite.' She put her mobile and her drink on the table.

'No worries,' said Chrissie. 'Nice to meet you.' She smiled at Immi's friend, who smiled back, but with a slight air of dissatisfaction.

'I haven't seen you down Zoë's place.'

'No, well…' Chrissie was spared having to explain that she wasn't really into that sort of stuff, by Jenna's phone trilling.

''Scuse me,' Jenna said as she picked it up. 'Oooh, yes… Lovely… In the corner… Yeah, see you in two ticks, hon.' Her face was transformed by a happy smile.

'Your old man going to make it, then?' said Immi. 'We're going to get to meet him at last?'

Jenna nodded, still grinning. 'I'm hoping that now he's back for a bit, we can get someone to sort out a quarter for us. I'm sick of living at my mum's.'

'I can imagine,' said Immi.

'I mean don't get me wrong, I love my mum, but I can't take her new bloke, Pete. He's a creep – don't know what she sees in him but she says I'm just being a cow. I swear he fancies our Shona more than my mum. It's just the way he sometimes looks at her, and she's only seventeen…'

'That's not nice,' murmured Immi.

'No, it isn't, and I told Mum, but she says I'm imagining it and won't listen. I just hope I'm wrong.' Jenna shuddered. 'And Mum's been tricky about me moving back home – I think Shona got used to having her own room and now she's kicking off 'cos she's having to share and Mum is getting fed up with that…' Jenna sighed. 'But it wasn't my fault my job in London went tits up,' she finished, morosely.

'I didn't know you'd worked there,' said Immi.

Jenna shook her head. 'It was pants, it didn't work out, it was a dream job.' A wistful look came into her eyes.

'So what was it?' asked Immi.

'I got an apprenticeship as a stylist with Marky Markham—'

'No shit!' squealed Immi.

Jenna nodded. 'Straight up.'

Chrissie was at a loss. Who the hell was Marky Markham?

But Immi was impressed so presumably Jenna had landed something good.

'Yeah,' continued Jenna, 'it was a fab job but the pay was shit and the cost of living in London meant I could barely afford to eat. It was a nightmare. It broke my heart when I had to throw in the towel, because half of his clients are like A-listers. I mean I've shampooed some well famous hair – Kylie's, Davina's, the Duchess of Wotserface's, loads...'

'Wow. Fantastic.'

'That bit was but the pay...' She shook her head and sighed.

'That's so wrong,' sympathised Immi.

Jenna snorted disgustedly. 'And unfair. Just because I couldn't rely on the bank of Mum and Dad. There were two other apprentices but they were from like Epsom and Kingston,' her voice dripped with sarcasm as she said the place names, 'and it didn't matter to them if their pay was crap. Mummy and Daddy bailed them out.' She rolled her eyes. 'Like my mum, with Shona and the twins all still at home, could do the same for me. And it didn't help that Scuzzy Pete was out of work at the time and sponging off her, so there was even less chance of her having any spare cash.'

'Oh, hon, that's so unfair.'

'Wasn't it just,' said Jenna, looking angry and upset in equal measure. Then she tossed her beautiful hair defiantly. 'Gotta move on though, and I'm going to show everyone. One day I'm going to be a bigger and better hairdresser than Marky Markham.'

'Go, you,' said Immi. She leaned over and put her hand on Jenna's. 'And you know what? I totes believe in you.'

'Thanks. I'll be living the dream soon; got the gorgeous husband, I'll soon have the house and then all I need is the salon and I'll be on my way. I'm already in with a load of the officers' wives, who can afford the sort of prices I'd like to charge. And talking of gorgeous hubby...' She waved. 'Over here, babe,' she called.

'Nice one,' said Immi, *sotto voce* to Chrissie, as they both clocked the gorgeous hubby – which he certainly was. 'No wonder Jenna's missed him, anyone would.' Immi was right; any girl with a pulse would want to keep this Zac Efron lookalike – thickly lashed eyes, level brows and smiley mouth – close to her. But it wasn't just dark eyes and white, even teeth; this guy was tanned, tall and fantastically built. Frankly, thought Chrissie, he could be the British Army's poster boy.

He hooked out a chair at their table with his foot and sat down, leaning over to give Jenna a kiss. Jenna instantly wrapped her arms around him and gave every impression she was trying to eat him.

Immi and Chrissie both turned their attention to their drinks. They'd sunk a good half of them by the time Jenna came up for air.

'Hi.' Immi extended her hand. 'I'm Immi, what's your name?'

'Nice to meet you, Immi, I'm Lee Perkins,' he answered, in a heavy Geordie accent.

Chrissie's drink fell out of her hand and dropped onto the table where the glass shattered and sticky Bacardi and Coke spilled across the polished wood before splattering onto the floor.

'Fuck,' she exclaimed.

'You want to be careful about saying that, bonny lass,' said Lee lazily. 'Some soldiers might take it as an invitation.'

Well, I wouldn't say no, thought Chrissie. God, he was gorgeous without his cam cream on, the most fanciable bloke she'd ever met in the flesh and she felt an instant and instinctive surge of raw lust, despite the fact she knew he was Jenna's husband. So she kept her face turned away from him as she raced off to the bar to get a replacement drink, and a damp cloth and dustpan to clear up the mess. She hoped to God that Lee hadn't recognised her because, looks or no looks, if he was like most soldiers she'd encountered in her nine months in the army, he'd tell everyone about what he'd done and how she'd reacted. She'd be a laughing stock – a medic who couldn't cope with the sight of blood. OK, it had been worse than that, but, as Chrissie well knew, soldiers weren't fussy about the honest truth when it came to a good anecdote. But thankfully, when she returned to her table Lee and Jenna were once again engrossed in each other.

'What's up with you?' asked Immi, as Chrissie got busy with clearing up the mess.

Chrissie felt her face flushing. 'Nothing,' she mumbled, not looking up.

'Nothing, my arse,' hissed Immi. 'What do you know about Lee?'

'*Nothing*,' protested Chrissie more loudly. Did Immi *really* want to know that her mate's husband was the soldier who had had a few kilos of pig guts strapped around his waist a couple of days earlier? That this was the guy she'd honked over? Probably not. And, even if Immi did, she couldn't be trusted not to open her mouth and say something daft. No, least said, soonest mended... or something.

'When he said his name you jumped like you'd been stung.'

'No, I didn't.' God, why couldn't Immi give it a rest?

Immi raised her eyebrows and shrugged. 'Have it your way. Anyway, it doesn't matter; it isn't as if he's available. More's the pity.'

'You can't blame him for going for Jenna, though,' Chrissie said. 'She's very pretty.'

'So she bloody should be, given that she works in the beauty industry. All that access to all those lovely products. Have you ever thought of having your hair coloured?' said Immi, examining the ends of her rich chestnut hair: this week's colour of choice.

Chrissie shook her head. 'It's just so much faff. And you keep having to have the roots done or it looks rank. Frankly, I'd rather go for a decent run than spend hours having my hair dyed.'

'You could do it yourself.'

Chrissie shook her head. 'You know what a prat I am when it comes to stuff like that. I'd mess it up and end up with green hair, or something. Can you imagine what the boss would say?'

Their platoon sergeant was nearly as ferocious as the RSM and another person to avoid getting on the wrong side of. Outlandish hair would be certain to press Sergeant Wilkes's buttons.

'Oh, get a room,' murmured Immi, as Lee and Jenna started snogging again. 'You know, from what Jenna's told me, she'd barely met Lee before she got him up the aisle. I mean, I know looks-wise he's quite a catch, but I can't see why civvies like Jenna want to date soldiers, let alone marry them. They're never around, they're always in fights—'

'On the other hand,' interrupted Chrissie, 'they've got money in their pockets and some girls have a thing about blokes in uniform.'

And this last was, Chrissie knew, one of Immi's reasons for joining. In fact, as far as Chrissie could see, Immi's *only* motivation, given the amount of time she spent chatting up the male soldiers. All the other things the army might provide – comradeship, sport, excitement – Immi ignored. While Chrissie had been picked for the battalion athletics team and had hopes of getting into the hockey team, Immi only just managed to scrape through her annual fitness test and threw a strop if she was made to do anything that involved leaving the comfort of her clerical job in the 1st Battalion, the Hertfordshire Regiment's orderly room. The thought of rushing round battlefields like Chrissie might have to, picking up wounded soldiers, was Immi's idea of hell on earth.

Lee extricated himself from Jenna's grasp. She was a beautiful girl, no doubt about that, and he knew they made a smashing couple – 1 Herts' very own Posh and Becks – but just sometimes he wished she could be a little less full-on. He was getting fed up with all the leg-pulling his comrades dished out to him about being married – suggesting that he needed Jenna's permission for everything: blowing his nose, taking a dump... and snogging like this in Tommy's Bar wasn't going to help matters any.

'I can't stay long,' he told her.

'Lee! I've barely seen you for weeks, months even. Just the odd poxy weekend.' She pouted. 'It's not fair.'

'It'll be better when we get a quarter. I'll go and see the new boss as soon as I can. I've heard on the grapevine he's a sound bloke. And he's married, so he should be sympathetic.' His new platoon commander had only been posted in to the company at the start of the exercise, so Lee hadn't encountered him yet, but the rumour was that he was OK.

'We could still go somewhere tonight,' wheedled Jenna. 'Come on, sweetie,' she cooed, putting her hand on his crotch and giving the bulge there a gentle rub. 'You know you want to.' She rubbed harder. 'Doesn't your genie want to come out and play?'

Lee removed her hand. 'Jenna, I'm knackered.'

'Just a quickie? Please. Just for me?'

Lee relented. Why not? Shit, if he was getting all the flak for being married, he might as well make full use of the benefits. 'Oh, OK then. Get your coat, you've pulled.'

Jenna leapt up with a squeal of delight. 'Oooh, Lee Perkins, I do love you!'

They said a hurried goodbye to Immi and Chrissie before pushing their way through the crowds of soldiers in the bar, ignoring the lewd gestures, the catcalls and the 'we-know-where-you're-going' comments, and back into the fresh air.

Ten minutes later Jenna was struggling up the uneven path behind the barracks in her high heels while Lee marvelled that she could walk in them at all, especially over this rough terrain. Finally she declared they'd gone far enough not to be tripped over by other couples from the barracks also in search of some privacy, although Lee suspected that her shoes had more to do with this than their distance from the camp.

'Come here, you,' said Jenna, turning Lee to face her. She gave him a deep probing kiss, as he wrapped his arms around her and pulled her tightly against his lean body. They were well away from the paths and byways where keep-fit fanatics might be out on an evening run, and oblivious to the scents and noises of the twilight, being utterly absorbed in each other.

Then Jenna drew back and took the poncho that Lee had in his hand, unfurling it with a deft flick of her wrist on the ground.

'Come on, Lee,' she said as she knelt on it. She lay back and began to unbutton first her thick jumper and then the top she had on underneath.

Lee hunkered down next to her and gazed at her body.

'Look, sweetie,' she said, propping her naked top half up on an elbow so her breasts jiggled tantalisingly, 'much as I'd love to spend the whole night posing for you, it's bloody cold and I'm about to get frostbite. So get your kit off, there's a love, and get on with it.'

As chat-up lines went it wasn't wonderful, thought Lee, but he was used to obeying orders and anyway, it was what they were here for. Besides, she did have a point, it was perishing. In a matter of seconds he had his shirt off and trousers down and was lying naked next to Jenna with his multicam combat jacket over the top of them for extra warmth. He felt her hand slide down his torso and then onto his hip. Slowly, he could feel her fingers tiptoe over his skin towards his cock. In the afterglow of the sunset and the lights from the barracks reflected off the autumn clouds, he could see her smiling at him.

'You warm enough now?' he whispered as he brushed his thumb over her nipple. Jenna shivered, but Lee wasn't sure whether it was from desire or the cold.

'I will be in a minute.' She gave a naughty giggle as her fingers finally lighted on his penis, which instantly responded. She kissed his nose.

Lee slid his hand between her legs and, finding her deliciously wet and ready, plunged in and began his rhythmic thrusting. Beneath him, Jenna squirmed and made obligingly encouraging noises, and Lee pumped deeper and harder until Jenna made some little yips of delight as she raked her fingernails down his back. A minute later Lee came too and he collapsed, spent and trembling on top of her, his body slick with sweat.

'Thanks, babe,' said Jenna, panting slightly. She kissed his nose again and gave him a gentle shove.

Lee rolled off her, but stayed snuggled up close. 'Say if you feel cold,' he said quietly as he gave her a cuddle. It had hardly been an ideal shag, but better than nothing, and Jenna seemed happy enough, which was all that mattered.

'Well...' said Jenna.

'You want to go back in the warm?'

Jenna squinted at her watch. 'Maybe I should be getting home soon. Mum'll have a go at me if I wake up Shona, so I can't be too late. God, I so can't wait till we get a quarter.'

'We've got a long weekend coming up. I thought we could go and see my mam.'

'Your mum? You sure?' Jenna sounded wary. 'She wasn't happy about you and me getting hitched.'

'It's time to build bridges. Besides, she's had time to get used to the idea now.'

'You sure?'

'Jenna, I'm twenty-three. I've my own life to live. Mam's got to get used to the idea that I love her, I always will, but I'm putting you and me first now.'

Jenna didn't look convinced. 'I suppose. But on top of her not wanting you to sign up and join the army... I mean, she has got reasons to be mad at you, like getting married when you knew she was dead against it.'

Lee pulled on his T-shirt. 'Then it's time she got over it. When she gets to know you properly she'll see exactly why I fell for you, and as for that other business – just because Dad got killed in Iraq doesn't mean it's going to happen to me.'

But that was the main problem. His mum had been against him joining; she'd lost her husband because of the army and Lee was her only son. It had taken him till he was twenty-two to get the courage to go against her. It was that, or die of boredom in civvy jobs. And, having defied his mother once, it had been easier to do it a second time when she'd expressed her doubts about Jenna's suitability as an army wife. She might have got used to the fact that Lee was in uniform, but she was still very sniffy about his missus.

'You can't blame her for wanting to keep you safe.' Jenna leaned forward and gave him a kiss, tactfully glossing over the fact that she had a mother-in-law who disliked her. 'I don't want anything to happen to you either. So – have you actually asked her yet if we can stay? Because I'm sure I can get away if she's OK about it. Zoë owes me a weekend off. Didn't seem any point in asking *not* to work Saturdays when you were away.'

'I'll ring her tomorrow.' Lee stepped into his trousers and then zipped them up.

'And while we're up there, you can show me what Newcastle has to offer.'

Lee gave her a slow smile. 'It'll have to be during the day. There's a double bed in the front room and frankly I'm planning on spending as much time in it as possible.'

Jenna gave him a friendly shove. 'You soldiers are all the same – and I should know!'

For a second Lee felt a tiny stab of jealousy. Then he manned up – pretty girl like her, of course she'd have had a few previous boyfriends. And why not?

He walked her back to where her car was parked and watched as she drove away towards her mother's little council house, the other side of the garrison. It was that little runabout that had brought them together in the first place; it had been broken down at the side of the road, just beyond the barrack gates. Jenna had been standing beside it in the rain looking helpless and Lee, returning from a night out with the boys, had offered to have a look at it for her. Two minutes later he'd found the lead that had disconnected from the battery, fixed it back on again, and his reward had been a date, which had developed into a helter-skelter ride into marriage.

There were times when Lee couldn't quite believe how fast it had all happened. Six months ago he'd just finished basic training and had been posted south to this unit, and all he'd had in mind was doing some proper soldiering; now, here he was, married with a wife and responsibilities. And a mother who was less than happy about everything. Lee sighed. The bridge he would have to build needed to be about as big and solid as the Tyne Bridge.

He made his way back to his barrack block. His thoughts turned to Jenna's two mates who had been with her when he'd arrived at Tommy's Bar. He was sure he'd seen the coloured girl somewhere before. Of course, there weren't that many girls who worked with the regiment, so they tended to stick out. Jenna's mate Immi certainly did – in *all* the right places. But the other girl – Chrissie, was it? – wasn't nearly so obvious, although she was pretty in an understated way. Big brown smiley eyes. Then he remembered. The last time he'd seen those big brown eyes they hadn't been smiling, they'd been full of worry, because she thought he was about to die. She was the medic. She was the nurse who'd hated his guts.

He was still chuckling when he reached his room.

Chapter Three

Down the road from the barracks, in a quarter on Omdurman Avenue, Maddy Fanshaw wearily surveyed the overflowing boxes and packing cases that littered the sitting room floor. It was a nice quarter, much nicer than the one she'd just moved out of, so she couldn't complain.

Actually, she thought, she bloody could. It might be bigger, brighter and more modern than the last house but it still had dreary fawn carpets and hideous stretch covers on the issue three-piece suite, and the paint was chipped and peeling, the kitchen units tatty and the cooker electric. She hated electric cookers. And Seb... Seb wasn't around and she was knackered and...

She dashed away a tear. Feeling sorry for herself wasn't going to get things done, but there was so *much* to be done, she thought despairingly: the unpacking, the getting straight, and Nate to look after. Maybe if he wasn't colicky, she'd cope better. Maybe if her husband hadn't been away for a whole fortnight, it wouldn't seem so impossible. It wasn't his fault and she knew she was being horribly unfair, but there was a small bit of her that blamed him for the state her life was in right now.

OK, so getting posted very suddenly, just three months after she'd given birth, hadn't been something anyone had planned or expected, but Seb going off immediately on some regimental exercise the minute he arrived in his new job, leaving her to cope with the house move alone, had almost been the last straw.

'Not to worry,' he'd said cheerfully. 'It'll be much easier without me underfoot, getting in the way.'

And because Maddy had never moved house before, she'd believed him. And when she'd realised just how ghastly the process was, there was no chance of dumping Nate with her parents for a few days while she dealt with the worst of it as they'd already swanned off on their annual cruise.

'If only you'd warned us,' said her mother on an expensive satphone call from somewhere in the Pacific, 'we could have fitted our dates around you.'

Maddy thought bleakly that she'd only had three weeks' notice herself, so that had never been an option. She tried to gee herself up with thoughts of the pioneering women who'd schlepped out to India or trekked along the Oregon Trail, but they hadn't had to cope with army cleanliness inspections of the houses they had left behind. The realisation had just deluged her in more feelings of self-pity.

But Seb would be home tonight, he'd lighten the load. Except, she thought, as she looked at her watch and saw that it was nearly nine, where the hell was he? She was sure he'd said they would get back to the barracks mid-afternoon and here it was, well into Friday evening and still no sign.

Maddy longed for supper and bed, but she had no doubt he expected to come home to a tidy house and a happy smiling wife. And, more than likely, some food, but she didn't want to cook twice – once for herself and then again for him. Or maybe she ought to go ahead and eat and not wait any longer? God, she was too tired even to make a decision about that. She leaned back in the armchair and let her eyes close. Just five minutes...

'Hello, sleepy head.'

Maddy jumped, and her eyes snapped open as she was catapulted instantly into wakefulness. She hadn't heard the front door open. Feelings of utter happiness swept through her, just at the sight of him, banishing her earlier ones of resentment.

'Seb!' She jumped up from the chair and threw her arms around his chest. Even though she was tall – five feet eight – she only reached his shoulder. 'Seb, darling, welcome home. I didn't mean to be asleep.'

'Asleep? You were snoring your head off,' he said with a grin. 'I'm surprised the neighbours haven't complained.'

Maddy snuggled into his embrace, ignoring the grungy smell of his combats. 'The neighbours are too nice to do that. Well, the ones I've met are.'

'That's good to hear.' Seb let her go and swung his huge Bergen off his back and dumped it on the floor – adding to the chaos. 'How's Nate?'

'Colicky.'

'Still?'

What did he expect – that she'd found a magic cure for that on top of doing everything else? Her resentment, egged on by physical exhaustion, seeped back. 'You've only been gone a fortnight, Seb,' she grumbled, not adding that it had felt like a bloody sight more, what with one thing and another.

'Yeah, but I thought it was called three-month colic.'

'I'm not a bloody miracle worker.' Maddy said this a bit more tersely than she intended.

'I'm sorry, sweetie, I didn't mean...'

'No, and I didn't mean what I said. Just a bit short in the

sleep department still.' She smiled. She adored Seb; she adored every bit of him from his floppy blond hair to his size thirteen feet; she adored his dark brown eyes and his gorgeous, kissable mouth and his wonderful, sculpted pecs. And she adored him despite his absences and commitment to his job, and his bloody rowing, which ate into weekends and spare time. 'You're late.'

'I know. There was so much to do when we got back. You know how it is.'

Maddy did. She'd heard the mantra often enough: that a good officer looked after his horse first, his men second and himself last. And, she'd noted, way after that, way, *way* down the pecking order, came his family. She tried not to mind; Seb had explained to her exactly what army life would be like, he hadn't pulled his punches, but Maddy had signed up regardless. And there *were* good bits, lots of them, but the bad bits were beyond shit.

He leaned towards her to kiss her. She could smell beer.

'Have you been to the mess?' she accused, her hazel eyes flashing with annoyance.

'A swift half with the lads. Honest, that was all. Just to unwind a bit, before I came home. It's all been a bit full on and we only got back about an hour ago.'

Maddy battened down her irritation that he hadn't come straight back to her. Why shouldn't he have a drink with the lads? Except when was the last time she'd been able to go out with her friends? Not since Nate had arrived – not once.

She swallowed down a lump in her throat. God, what was the matter with her? Seb did *not* want a tearful wife as a welcome present. 'Do you want something to eat?' she offered, pulling herself together.

'Too knackered at the moment. I tell you what I would like, a hot bath and a large Scotch. And then probably bed.'

He did look knackered, Maddy conceded. Even more tired than herself, and that was saying something. They were like a pair of zombies. 'The exercise was tough?'

Seb nodded. 'Pretty tough. The lack of sleep just grinds you down after a bit.'

As if Maddy didn't know. And she'd been at it for three months; Seb had suffered for just two weeks. But she didn't say so. Feeding in the middle of the night – night in, night out – and coping with a baby who cried relentlessly when he was awake, wasn't half so hard as running about playing soldiers, was it? She could have done with someone to run her a bath now and again and bring her a stiff drink, but had it ever happened? She sent Seb off for his bath while she poured a large Scotch, which she took up to him. He was already stripping off his noxious clothes when she appeared in the bedroom. Beneath his combats his skin was grey with grime and fatigue.

'Don't fall asleep in the bath,' she instructed. 'I'll be up in fifteen minutes to check you haven't.'

'Yes, ma'am,' said Seb with a grin.

'And clean the bath after you when you get out. It'll be revolting.'

She had gone downstairs and motivated herself enough to make a stab at unpacking a few more bits and pieces, when she heard a knock at the door. She thanked any god listening that whoever it was had had the sense to knock and not ring the doorbell, which might have woken Nate.

'Caro! How lovely.' Which was a lie. Not that Maddy wasn't happy to see her new neighbour – Caro *was* lovely from what she'd seen of her. Certainly she was more acceptable than her only other visitor so far – Mrs Notley, the commanding officer's wife. She had called around the day after Maddy had moved in. Maddy had barely got the door open before she'd barged in and taken stock of what she'd seen. Or, at least, that's what Maddy had assumed she'd been doing. With Nate screaming, it had been difficult to hold a conversation.

'And I won't hold you up,' Mrs Notley had almost shouted to be heard over Nate's cries. 'I just popped by to make sure you've settled in OK.'

It would have been patently obvious to anyone that Maddy hadn't and that she was struggling, but the 'popping in' obviously wasn't going to come with an offer of help. Mrs Notley wasn't wearing pressed jeans and a Boden shirt, topped off with immaculate hair and make-up, with the intention of rolling up her sleeves and getting her hands dirty. In fact, thought Maddy, Mrs Notley was here to tick a box on her list of jobs to be done, and to make sure this new wife knew who the boss's wife was.

'It's colic,' Maddy explained, as Mrs Notley (no invitation to call her by her first name, Maddy had noticed) raised an eyebrow in her son's direction.

'Poor you,' said Mrs Notley. 'I was lucky, I've had four children and not one suffered.' But there was no doubt in Maddy's mind that Mrs Notley didn't think *luck* had played a part at all. 'Still,' she'd breezed on, 'colic or no colic, I've no doubt you can't wait to get stuck into regimental life.'

Maddy tried hard to arrange her expression into something that might be taken for enthusiasm rather than horror.

'Unless,' continued Mrs Notley, with a hint of a sneer, 'you're going to be one of these career women.'

Shit, thought Maddy, since when did having a job and earning money become socially unacceptable? She'd heard that in some circles the only acceptable career for an officer's wife was supporting her husband's, but she'd never really taken it seriously. But now... sheesh, how last century was *that*? She grabbed Nate out of his chair while she tried to think of an ambivalent answer.

'Mrs Notley...' She paused, waiting for the 'call-me-whatever' invitation. Nope. 'To be honest, right now I can't think of anything beyond unpacking and Nate's colic. He's only a few months old,' she added, although wasn't it obvious, especially to someone who had had four kids?

'But soon you'll be *raring* to get back into harness. And as soon as you are, I am sure you'll be *dying* to make yourself useful as a regimental wife.'

When I do get any energy back, I'm going to be *raring* to earn money and *dying* to do a proper job, thought Maddy desperately. Fuck being a volunteer drudge for the regiment. But she had an awful feeling that the sentiment was going to be unacceptable. Mrs Notley might have managed to be the Perfect Officer's Wife, while she'd been popping out kids like peas, but all Maddy could cope with right now was getting through each day.

Still, she thought, pushing the last nightmare visit into a corner, this was Caro at the door, not Mrs Bloody Notley, so she slapped on a smile and tried to look welcoming.

'Hon, this is a big ask,' said Caro, 'but Will is back and wants feeding, and I'm out of bread. The kids ate the last for their tea and the Spar is shut. Any chance you can bail me out?'

Thank God, thought Maddy, a sensible request, not something that was going to require a huge personal sacrifice of either her time or her career prospects or both. 'Good grief, yes. It's not a big ask at all, I've got at least one loaf in the freezer, if not several.'

Caro followed her into the house as Maddy went to find the bread. 'I see you're still battling with the move,' she said, looking at the piles of kitchen equipment still waiting to be put away.

Maddy returned with the loaf. 'I'm being pathetically slow, aren't I?' She knew of some wives who could get a house completely straight in just a few days.

Caro flashed her a smile. 'Absolutely not. In fact I think you're doing wonderfully well, considering you did the move on your own with a tiny baby.'

'Why is it that us wives always seem to end up doing it? The men seem to have to be in their new post before we can leave the old house, or go straight off on an exercise the instant we arrive.'

'They plan it that way,' said Caro, giggling. 'Actually, I shouldn't joke, they probably do!' Maddy handed over the loaf. 'Thanks,' said Caro. 'I'll bring you a replacement in the morning. Seb back?'

Maddy nodded. 'Home and already in the bath with a large drink.'

'Just like mine. I'd better go and wake him before he dissolves.'

Maddy shut the door behind Caro and slumped. She heard movement upstairs. Seb must be out of his bath. She offered up a little prayer that he didn't want food or to tell her all about the exercise and that he just wanted to collapse into bed, because then she could do that too with a clear conscience.

She unpacked another few items and then, bugger, the bathroom door opened and shut followed by the thump, thump of Seb's feet on the stairs. Could he make any more noise? she thought, irritably.

'Whah, whah...'

That was all she fucking needed. She waited for Seb's footsteps to stop and go back upstairs to get Nate but, no, he carried on.

'The baby's crying,' he said, entering the sitting room in his dressing gown.

Maddy stumbled past him, fighting back tears of exhaustion and frustration. 'Of course he's fucking crying,' she snapped. 'It's all he does when some prat wakes him up!'

She ignored the look of hurt on Seb's face. Tough. Maybe next time he wouldn't barge about like a sodding elephant.

The next morning, while Nate grizzled in his bouncy chair, Maddy tackled another box of possessions. Every now and again she gave the chair a gentle push with her toe to keep it in motion, which stopped Nate's muted wails escalating into full-blown screams. Seb was, as always on a Saturday morning, down at the gym doing a punishing fitness routine, and although Maddy had dropped a heavy hint that she could do with a hand around the house instead, he hadn't picked up on it. She tried not to feel annoyed as she unwrapped more crockery and found space in the tatty kitchen units to store them. She had known how much he adored his rowing when she married him, only back then she hadn't been left holding the baby. Literally.

The doorbell rang as she slammed a cupboard door shut and, scooping Nate out of his chair, she went to answer it, hoping that it was Seb back early.

'Caro.'

Her neighbour waved a loaf of bread. 'Here you go,' she said, thrusting it at Maddy.

'You didn't have to, honest. It was only a loaf.'

'But, having cleared my debt, I am now free to borrow

again, and next time it might be something really important, like gin.' Caro grinned. She looked down at the baby in the crook of Maddy's arm. 'And who do we have here?' She rubbed her finger across Nate's cheek and was rewarded with a wail. 'Oh, sorry, didn't mean to upset him.'

'Don't worry,' said Maddy. 'Nathan cries at everything.' She tried hard to smile.

'That's not a nice thing to do to your poor mummy.' Caro looked up at Maddy and clocked the dark circles under her neighbour's eyes. 'Tell you what, how about a tea break. I bet you've been busy all morning and up since sparrow's fart.'

Maddy considered the endless bloody boxes that still needed seeing to and then thought, sod it. 'That's a brill idea.' She flung the door wide. 'Come in, just excuse the chaos.'

She led Caro into the kitchen and, still carrying Nathan, she began to fill the kettle one-handed.

'Let me,' said Caro. She gently took Nathan from his mother and dandled him on her lap. Nathan, for once, didn't start bawling. 'No husband?' asked Caro.

'Fitness training,' said Maddy as she plugged in the kettle.

Caro raised an eyebrow.

'He rows for the army,' explained Maddy.

'Oh, so he's the guy who nearly made the Olympics,' exclaimed Caro. 'I heard on the grapevine that the regiment was getting some amazing athlete.'

Maddy shook her head. 'I think the story you heard has got a bit exaggerated. I don't think that was ever really on the cards, although a couple of his rowing buddies made it. He was out in Afghanistan when the selection process took place, so he was never really a contender.'

'If he was in Afghan in 2012...' She counted up on her fingers. 'So when he came back...?' She looked at Nate.

'Pretty much. We only planned to get married, not start a family, but hey.' Maddy shrugged and then grinned. 'It was quite a honeymoon. Tea?'

'Please – milk, no sugar. Still, you must be delighted.'

Maddy nodded enthusiastically, but she felt she was trying to convince herself as much as Caro. Of course she adored Nate – she just thought she'd adore him even more if she could get a whole night's sleep. She shoved teabags into a couple of mugs.

'I've got two boys, two and four,' said Caro. 'They're out with their dad at the park right now. Tell you what, why don't I take Nathan home with me for a couple of hours, which'll let you get on in peace? It wouldn't be any trouble, honest.' She gave Maddy a winning smile.

Maddy was utterly torn. Jeez, yes, she could do with a break but, firstly, she barely knew her neighbour and secondly, Nate was hardly easy, so it seemed a crap deal for Caro. And what on earth would Seb say if he came home to find that she'd palmed his first-born off on a virtual stranger? As she stirred the mugs she weighed up the pros and cons.

'Caro, that's really, really kind but I can't.'

'No worries. The offer is genuine though, and there if you need it.' She leaned forward and posted Nate back into his bouncy chair and set it in motion before taking her tea.

'Crikey,' said Maddy. 'He isn't yelling.'

'So, while peace reigns, why don't I tell you about the camp?'

They sipped their tea and Caro gave Maddy a list of facilities, from the nearest surgery to a decent washing-machine repairman. 'And then there's a pretty good Wives' Club.'

Maddy looked blank.

Caro shook her head. 'Surely you had a Wives' Club at your last posting?'

'Might have been one, but I wasn't much of an army wife. I worked almost right up to the moment I had Nate and then we moved. I didn't join in much.'

Caro looked at her. 'So it's all change for you: new house, new baby, no job?'

Maddy nodded. 'In a nutshell.'

'Do you want to go back to work?'

'Ideally, but I don't think there's much call for biochemists around here. And Mrs Notley won't approve if I do.'

Caro shook her head. 'Sod her. She's the least of your worries if you want to have a career. Frankly, the biggest hurdle is moving every couple of years. By the time you've found a job, you'll probably only hang on to it for about a year or so and then you'll be off again. It makes your CV look a bit odd – a bit busy, shall we say. Anyway,' she continued, brightly, 'in the meantime you have no excuse not to come to the Wives' Club. Next week it's a talk on making Christmas cakes and you'll score a Brownie point with Mrs N just by showing your face.'

Maddy tried to look enthusiastic – Christmas cakes? Already? – and would she get drummed off the patch if she just bought one? And did she want one of Mrs Effing Notley's Brownie points? But then Seb might want her to collect a few. God, this army game was a nightmare, thought Maddy. She thought she'd just *married* a soldier, not joined up herself.

'Right,' said Caro. 'What else do you need to know?'

'Has Mrs Notley got a Christian name?'

Caro snorted and rolled her eyes. 'Ann, but no one uses that. If you get really well in with her – dinner party invitations and that sort of shit – you might, *might*, get asked to call her Mrs N. Even Julia Frenchay, the garrison commander's wife, isn't as stuffy, and her husband is a brigadier, not just a poxy lieutenant colonel.'

Maddy nodded. 'So she really *is* stuffy – it's not just me.'

'Oh no. So you've met her then.'

Maddy nodded. 'She waltzed in here a couple of days after I'd arrived; took one look at me, Nate and the state of the house and, from what I could see, decided I was a lost cause.'

'That's Mrs N. But don't worry, she doesn't think anyone can match up to her standards, so you're in good company with almost all the other wives – well, the junior ones anyway. Some of the major's wives try and compete. So, what else should I tell you about? I know, hair! There's a nice hairdresser run by a woman called Zoë. She's got a really great stylist called Jenna and if you ask Jenna nicely and quietly, she'll do home visits. It makes life a lot easier, I can tell you. Probably a good idea if you get your hair done with her first at Zoë's, because, if you don't get on, you're not committed to anything; but she hasn't made a mess of my hair yet.'

'Thanks for the tip,' said Maddy. She ran her fingers through her rich chestnut hair. 'I really need a good cut. What with my old job, then Nathan and the move, I haven't had my hair done for months. God, the idea of a bit of pampering...'

'Well, take up my offer of babysitting Nate and get yourself down there.'

Chapter Four

On Sunday, Chrissie finished sorting out the last of her kit from the exercise, got her uniform ready for Monday morning and, with little else to do to fill her day, took herself off for a run. She loped through the barracks, past the officers' married patch, then the soldiers' one, and on down the road that led to the nearest town. She planned to run round the ring road and then over the hill to the rear of the barracks and in through the back gate. Five miles, she reckoned, and not too much of a challenge.

She jogged on at a steady pace, her iPod plugged into her ears, her thoughts roaming randomly, paying attention to the light Sunday morning traffic and her surroundings only when necessary. She reached a set of traffic lights that would allow her to cross a busy junction and was jogging on the spot as she waited for them to change. She leapt out of her skin when she felt a tap on her shoulder. She spun round, ripping her earphones out, ready to confront whoever it was.

'Lee!' Despite the fact that her heart was already pumping from the run, it still quickened with pleasure at seeing a friendly face.

'Thank God,' Lee panted. 'I thought it was you. I've been trying to catch up with you for ages and then suddenly I thought I might have been chasing a complete stranger. That would have been embarrassing.'

The lights changed. For a second Chrissie didn't respond, while she assimilated the fact that Lee – gorgeous, hunky Lee – had chased her. *Her!* Then she remembered; he was *Jenna's* gorgeous, hunky Lee. Oh well.

The insistent beeping of the crossing brought her back to the real world.

'Come on,' she said, not wanting to miss the brief opportunity the little green man offered them to get across. They jogged over, strides matching, and continued along the pavement towards the town.

'You run really well,' said Lee.

'For a girl?'

Lee laughed. 'No, for anyone.'

'Thanks.' Chrissie accepted the compliment and felt herself lighten up. 'I ran for the battalion in the five thousand metres in the inter-unit cup.'

'Impressive.'

'I don't think there were any other female contenders from 1 Herts,' she answered truthfully.

They ran on some more in silence.

'Jenna doesn't run, then?' asked Chrissie.

Lee guffawed. 'Jenna? You must be joking. Her idea of a workout is turning the pages of a fashion mag. Don't get me wrong, she looks after herself...'

'But not in this sort of way.'

'No. And she couldn't do the stuff you do.'

'I couldn't dye hair,' Chrissie countered. No, she thought, working in a hairdresser's would be like being buried alive.

'You could if you were trained.'

'Maybe.'

'It takes a lot to cope with blood and guts.'

Chrissie slid a sideways look at him at the word *guts*.

Had it been deliberate? She caught Lee staring back at her, one eyebrow lifted. Yes, it bloody was.

'It was a rotten trick, that,' he said.

'So you've known all along who I am.'

He nodded.

'You won't tell anyone else, will you? I mean, I think it's just you, me and Phil who are in the picture. I am so embarrassed at making a fool of myself like that.'

'Hey.' Lee looked at her as they ran side by side. 'You had a funny turn, that's all. You got over it, carried on, did your job. There's nothing to be embarrassed about there. The whole incident was designed to test the medics to the max.'

'Maybe. But being sick over a casualty isn't in the Patient Treatment Handbook.' As she said it, she was aware that he'd remembered her from that incident, had deliberately caught up with her today, and was being really kind about how she'd made such a prat of herself. Nice guy, she thought. *Jenna's* nice guy, she reminded herself again. Anyway, even if he wasn't spoken for she didn't want a relationship, did she. Right? Right!

They'd reached the edge of the local town. 'Where now?' asked Lee.

'Around the dual carriageway and then back over Brandon Hill.'

Lee's eyes widened. 'The long way?'

'Why not? Race you.' And with that she shot off. She was several hundred yards on before Lee caught up with her.

'Jeez, Chrissie,' he panted. '*You* might be able to run like Paula Radcliffe, but I'm no Mo Farah. Slow down a bit.'

Chrissie slackened the pace a little. 'I like to delude myself I'm like Jess Ennis.'

Lee glanced at her. 'Good shout.'

'Don't be daft.'

'Jess is well fit.'

'Yes, *she* is.'

'So are you.'

'Thanks.' For a second she hoped he was referring to her looks, rather than to her athleticism, but then reality kicked in. Of course he didn't think she was fit in the 'good-looking' sense, not when he was married to the luscious Jenna. She changed the subject. 'Immi says you've been away on a load of courses.'

'The old platoon commander thought I had potential, so I've been away a lot, getting some education and stuff that I'll need, if I get promoted. Got to hope this new guy, Captain Fanshaw, thinks the same.'

'I'm sure he will.'

'And then, just before the exercise, I tried SAS selection.'

'No!' Chrissie was hugely impressed. 'Really? How did you do?'

'Failed. I went down with flu. One minute I was doing well, tabbing up the Brecon Beacons, the next I was being stretchered off with a temperature of 104.'

'No way. But you must have felt shite long before then.'

'I did a bit, but I thought they'd just put me down as some sort of malingering loser.'

'So it was a *genuine* case of man flu.'

Lee nodded. 'And if I ever get a head cold, I will *never* say I've got flu. Flu is evil.'

'And you're running already? Shit, you're well hard.'

'I'm not running *well* though, am I? My fitness took a real knock. And that's why I wasn't much cop on the exercise and got to lie down and play almost dead.'

They ran in silence for some time, till they reached the

base of Brandon Hill. The path up it was narrow, so they ran in single file to the top. There Chrissie stopped.

'I'm not,' she said, panting heavily, 'quite as fit as I thought I was, either. No chance for fitness training on exercise.'

'Well, if you want a running buddy…?' offered Lee. 'I mean, I need to get myself back in shape again too.'

'Really?'

He nodded. 'I'd like it. Most of the lads in my platoon want to lie in their pits at weekends. It's nice to find someone who wants to do running other than in a squad being beasted by a PTI. And I like to run on sports afternoons too.'

'Brilliant. When we get back to the barracks we can swap mobile numbers. Jenna won't mind, though, will she?' asked Chrissie. Running was hardly like dating but, even so, she mightn't be overly happy about her husband spending time with another woman, no matter how innocently.

'Jenna? God, she doesn't even surface till lunchtime when she isn't working.'

Which didn't exactly answer Chrissie's question, but was a good enough response to shut her conscience up. But not before she noticed that the prospect of running with Lee gave her a real buzz.

Sunday segued into Monday and the rude awakening which came with reveille and the early morning run. Immi rolled out of bed, groaning and moaning about the unfairness of being expected to do PT at six thirty in the morning, long after Keelie and Gillie, who had both returned to barracks the night before, had already got dressed and left. It had taken five solid minutes of Chrissie haranguing her before she'd finally emerged, still complaining, from under the covers.

'I don't know why you always bitch about this, it's part

of the job description,' countered Chrissie, as she threw on her tracksuit and stepped into her trainers.

Immi glowered as she hauled on her sports kit. 'It doesn't mean I have to like it. Anyway, not all units are like this one – why did I have to be posted to one where the CO is a fitness fanatic?'

Chrissie shook her head and glanced at her watch. 'Hurry up, Immi. We're going to be late.'

Reluctantly, and still muttering, Immi followed Chrissie out onto the parade square where the troops were all gathered, lined up in their platoons and by company. Most were jogging on the spot, in an effort to keep warm, as the October morning was distinctly nippy. Just as Chrissie and Immi fell in, the RSM and the CO appeared.

'Shit, we cut that fine,' whispered Chrissie. Arriving after either of these two equalled 'late' and would result in extra duties being awarded on the spot.

The RSM bawled out the commands to bring the parade to attention before he handed over to the PTIs who were to lead each company on a squadded, three-mile run. HQ Company, Immi and Chrissie's one, and which also included the CO and the RSM in its number, was the first to lead off.

'At least we won't die of hypothermia, now,' said Chrissie, slapping her arms against her sides as she ran, to get her circulation moving.

'No, I'm going to die of a combo of stitch and exhaustion,' gasped Immi.

'You can't be tired yet – we've only run a few hundred yards.'

But Immi was already panting too hard to answer. By the time they got to the mile point, Immi was stumbling with fatigue and she and Chrissie, who was trying to urge her mate to keep going, had fallen almost to the rear of the squad.

'Keep up,' screamed a rasping voice.

Chrissie looked behind her. Sergeant Wilkes was pounding after them. 'Come on, Immi,' encouraged Chrissie once again, but she could see it was hopeless. There was no way Immi was going to be able to complete the three miles. Obviously with most of the regiment away on exercise the previous two weeks, there had been no formal PT and Immi had taken advantage of that to bother even less than usual with her fitness levels: fitness levels which had always been borderline and which were now completely below par.

'I can't,' sobbed Immi, as she finally gave up. 'I've got to stop. You carry on.'

Chrissie nodded and ran on while Immi gave up and took the instant bawling out from Sergeant Wilkes. The words 'extra duties' floated after Chrissie, as she raced forward to catch up with the rest of the squad. Putting on a spurt she not only caught up with the squad but eased her way to the front, passing the CO and the RSM as she did so.

Maybe the RSM was in a foul mood (and when wasn't he? It was as if it was in the job description of RSMs always to be in a foul mood) or maybe it was the sight of a woman – a *woman* – passing him, but he halted the entire squad and made them start performing press-ups. Once they'd all, including Chrissie, given him fifty, he then found a steep side-track, and made everyone run up and down that a few times; naturally he and the CO were observers rather than participants. By the time he'd finished with HQ Company, a number of soldiers were being sick in the gutters and the rest were either red, or ashen with exhaustion. Even Chrissie had her hands on her hips, her legs apart and was bent at the waist as she gulped in lung-fuls of air.

While she was doing this, the other soldiers loped past, Lee amongst them. He shot Chrissie a look of sympathy – having the RSM give you a hard time was no fun.

A couple of minutes later the RSM ordered HQ Company to start running again.

'And if no one beats me back the entire company will be confined to barracks for the next week and you can forget the long weekend,' he shouted, fresh as a daisy, to the still-gasping troops. 'Understood?'

'Sir,' came a ragged and lacklustre response.

'*Understood?*'

'Sir!' roared back the sixty or so soldiers.

The RSM, not having performed press-ups or having been beasted up and down the hill, set off at a punishing pace. Soon most of the soldiers were lagging behind. Every now and again, Warrant Officer Class One Jenks would run on the spot and harangue the lagging soldiers 'to get a grip and put some effort into it' but most of his troops were too shattered to respond. There were only a few soldiers, Chrissie included, who were able to keep up with him. It wasn't any sort of spectacular fitness that gave her the impetus, but the certain knowledge that he wanted her to fail – and she wasn't going to give him the satisfaction. In her limited experience of the army, she had found that there were some male soldiers who still didn't accept that women might have equal skills and fitness, and she was pretty sure the RSM was one of them. Her determination to prove him wrong was giving her a boost better than steroids or blood doping.

With about half a mile to go, and with the several hundred soldiers who had just been allowed to get on with their training run without any intervention from the RSM in sight, Chrissie kicked for home, in a move Jess Ennis or Paula Radcliffe would have been proud of. The RSM responded and managed to catch up with Chrissie, shooting her a look of smug triumph as he passed her. Chrissie kicked again and drew level with him. By now they were starting to pass the other soldiers, the ones still running in something resembling squads.

'Go, Chrissie,' cheered a voice from the ranks. Lee.

The RSM gritted his teeth and made another effort to beat Chrissie, but she was spurred on by her lone supporter.

Other soldiers picked up on Lee's support and began to cheer Chrissie on. It wasn't that they wanted Chrissie herself to win, they wanted the RSM to lose. Even if he'd been racing Osama bin Laden, Stalin and Hitler, they still wouldn't have cheered Mr Jenks. The cheering reached the ears of the soldiers who had already completed their three-mile run and were starting to drift to their barrack blocks or homes for a shower, and they stopped to watch the spectacle of Chrissie and the RSM, pounding, neck and neck, along the road to the regimental guardroom.

The cheers, coupled with the knowledge that, if she lost, HQ Company would forfeit their long weekend, gave Chrissie the impetus she needed, and with a final, superlative effort she made it back, through the barrack gate and onto the parade square twenty yards ahead of Mr Jenks. The soldiers erupted.

She wanted to lie down she was so knackered, but pride kept her on her feet while she gulped air.

'You may have beaten me this time,' gasped the RSM, as he stopped beside her and shot a vitriolic look at the cheering troops. 'It won't happen again.'

Chrissie wasn't sure if it was a threat or a promise, but

she didn't care; she was too exhausted to care about anything, except not throwing up or passing out.

Lee, who had seen her cream past, was lost in admiration, as were most of the soldiers from Chrissie's company who pounded onto the parade square over the next few minutes, amongst them the CO, who was stunned to discover that the RSM had met his match.

Colonel Notley came to a halt next to his RSM. 'Don't tell me you were beaten, Mr Jenks.'

'I was, sir.' A lesser man than the CO might have quailed at the tone of the RSM's voice.

'And by a slip of a girl.'

The RSM glowered.

The CO turned to Chrissie whose chest was still heaving. 'Well done... er...'

'Summers, sir.'

'Yes, well done, Summers. Good effort.'

'Thank you, sir.'

'I think your efforts inspired the troops. HQ Company came home in a cracking time.'

Chrissie wondered if they had just chased after her and Mr Jenks out of curiosity. She didn't feel inspirational. But she did feel quite proud that she'd rescued the company's long weekend. It was a good feeling.

The CO drifted off to talk to some of the other NCOs and an admiring group formed around Chrissie.

'Well done,' said Lee, 'you were amazing.'

And Chrissie felt ridiculously happy to have his approval and her good feeling got even better.

'So how many did you get?' asked Chrissie. She was still puffed even though she had recovered sufficiently to climb the stairs, albeit very slowly, to her barrack room where Immi was already showered and now dressed in combats rather than PE kit.

'Five and extra PT for four weeks,' she replied glumly. 'And then I have to pass my BFT or it'll be more of the same. Honestly, Chrissie, I'm a clerk, I bash keyboards all day. Why do I have to be super-fit to open a filing cabinet?'

Chrissie grabbed her towel. 'Tell you what, suppose I have a word with Sergeant Wilkes and see if she'll let me take you for extra PT? I mean, I know I'm not a PTI but she's knows I'm fit.' She didn't add that the whole regiment knew that now. 'And you and I could have a bit of fun together as we work out. How about it?'

'You'd do that for me?' Immi was genuinely astounded.

Chrissie nodded. 'But you've got to promise me you'll make a proper effort. Just 'cos I'm not some hairy-arsed PTI doesn't mean you can take advantage. I'll expect you to graft – *and* pass your fitness test. First time.'

Immi nodded eagerly. 'I will, promise.'

'I'll make sure you do, if you make the effort too. So, to make sure, we're going to start with a session in the gym this evening.'

'This evening!' squeaked Immi. 'But we did a run this morning.'

'*I* did a run this morning,' countered Chrissie. '*You* did a bit of a jog and then gave up.'

Immi gave in. 'Five thirty, at the gym?'

'See you then,' acknowledged Chrissie, as she went off for a shower, leaving Immi looking both apprehensive and miserable. Chrissie decided, as she showered, that she wouldn't be too hard on Immi for the first session – that would come later.

*

Chrissie and Lee's paths crossed again the following Wednesday.

'Look,' said Immi, nodding towards the serving counter in the cookhouse. 'It's Jenna's bloke.' She waved. 'Coo-ee. Lee.' He turned and saw them. 'Budge up, Chrissie, make a space for him.'

They watched Lee grab a plate of spaghetti bolognese and head their way. He had a broad grin on his face.

'Hello, girls,' he said as he sat down.

Immi simpered at him. 'Hi, Lee.'

Lee pushed his plate off his tray, sorted out his drink and cutlery and began to tuck into his meal. After a couple of forkfuls he paused and looked at Chrissie. 'I was hoping to run into you. What are your plans for this afternoon?' On Wednesday afternoons, all soldiers who didn't have specific tasks or duties to carry out were expected to take part in some sort of physical activity for an hour or so at the very least.

Immi shrugged. 'Thought I'd go into town and get some new jeans.'

Lee laughed. 'I don't think the army rates shopping as a sport.'

'It is if you do it right,' said Immi, unabashed. 'Besides, I'll be doing a session in the gym with Chrissie this evening, because she's on a mission to get me fit so she's cutting me some slack now.'

'And,' interrupted Chrissie, 'I want to go on a proper run and if Immi tags along I'll only get as far as the barrack gate.'

'Harsh but fair,' admitted Immi. 'So I'm going to do some extreme shopping.'

'Trust me,' said Chrissie, 'if it was an Olympic sport, Immi would medal.'

Lee smiled at her. 'So you're going running?'

'That's the plan.'

'Want company?'

Immi's eyebrows rocketed skywards. She glanced from Lee to Chrissie. She narrowed her eyes. Was there something going on there? Nah, there couldn't be, not when Lee had Jenna.

'Yeah, why not,' said Chrissie. 'How far do you want to go? Five miles? Ten?'

'Ten miles?' squeaked Immi. 'But that's... miles,' she finished, lamely.

Chrissie laughed. 'It's not so far. We should be back in an hour and a half.'

Immi fanned herself. Jeez – ten miles, that was just showing off. So maybe this pair just got a kick out of running. Weird. She picked up her empty plate. 'Right, I'm going to change and catch the bus. As it's sports afternoon and because I'm on extra PT, I'll go upstairs and sit on the top deck. How's that for exercise?'

She waggled her fingers in farewell, leaving Lee and Chrissie discussing a possible route.

The two were about halfway around their planned route, loping along at an easy pace, their strides matching. They were both puffing slightly, but weren't out of breath. Their trainers slapped the tarmac of the pavement rhythmically, as the cars on the road beside them swished past. A fine drizzle was falling: enough to make the ground greasy and their hair and clothes damp, without it being so wet as to be completely miserable.

'This feels easier than last time,' said Chrissie. 'I must be getting back on form. My self-imposed mission to get Immi fit is having an unexpected advantage for me. Mind you, I spend more time trying to make her do an extra ten reps here and there than I do on the fitness machines myself.'

'I've been down the gym in the evenings, too,' said Lee. 'I've got to work on my stamina and endurance.'

'So you're determined to have another go at SAS selection?'

'Got to be done.'

'What about Jenna? I mean, those guys are never home; they're always getting sent off to some dodgy place or other. Won't she mind about being left on her own for half the year?'

'I'm sure it's not as bad as that. And she knows it's my ambition. She'll be cool about it.'

Chrissie shrugged. What did she really know either about Jenna or the SAS? 'If we go along here,' she said, pointing to a sign indicating a bridle path, 'we can avoid running along the dual carriageway. It's a shade longer but quieter.'

They turned off and began to run along the new route – a disused railway line which had the advantage of being straight and pretty level, but sadly the surface was mostly hardcore and sand, and because of the recent rain it was far from smooth. Push bikes had chopped deep grooves into it, horses' hooves had gouged out dents, and just sheer wear and tear had left big potholes. And the wet conditions made the whole path slippery and treacherous. They jogged along it for a couple of miles, both trying to ignore how rub bish the surface was, but both knowing there had to be an easier way back to the barracks – one which didn't involve trip hazards and endless puddles.

'This is such a bad idea,' said Chrissie as she jumped another puddle and slipped on landing. Her arms flailed as she just managed to keep her balance.

'It's crap,' agreed Lee. 'Let's get off it at the next opportunity.'

'Well, that can't be too soon,' said Chrissie as her foot slithered again.

They continued to jog along, past the dripping, sloe-laden branches of the blackthorns, and the brambles and the nettles which hemmed them in like barbed wire and made any prospect of leaving the path almost impossible.

'There's a bridge up ahead,' said Chrissie after a few more minutes. 'If it crosses a road, maybe there's a chance we can find a path down the embankment to join it.'

'Good call.'

They puffed their way up the slight gradient which had raised the old railway up to the bridge. There the pair paused and looked over the parapet.

'I know where we are,' said Chrissie. 'Isn't that the Swan?' She pointed to a pub garden just visible behind a tall hedge a couple of hundred yards away.

Lee nodded. 'And look, steps,' he said. To their left, where the brickwork of the bridge stopped, there were some rough and uneven steps made out of old sleepers which led down the almost vertical embankment to the lane below.

'Come on,' he said. He tramped through a gap in the dense, soggy undergrowth and began to pick his way down the treads. Gingerly, Chrissie followed. Each step was either a different width or a different height from its predecessor, and that, coupled with the slippery conditions and the steep gradient, made the descent truly treacherous. Ahead of her she saw Lee make it to the safety of the road below and because she was watching him, she missed her step and caught her foot in the wooden riser which stood proud of the tread. With a cry of fear, she felt herself plunge towards the wet tarmac. Lee whipped round and just managed to catch her.

The shock of the fall left Chrissie feeling wobbly and she clung to him to steady herself for a second, while the trembling in her legs stopped and her heart rate returned to something like normal as the jolt of adrenalin left her system. She looked up into his face, inches from her own.

'Thank you, Lee,' she panted.

'No worries, lass,' he replied, looking into her eyes. 'You gave us a bit of a shock, there.'

Chrissie felt her heart do an odd little flick-flack and somewhere deep inside, muscles she hardly knew she had squeezed tight and sent a shiver of pleasure right through her. Swiftly, she pulled herself out of his arms. Whatever she was feeling was wrong on every level: wrong because she didn't want a boyfriend; wrong because he was Jenna's husband; and wrong because no bloke ought to be able to make a girl feel like that just by holding her.

She bent down to retie a shoelace while she got herself under control, then, that done, she stood up and said, 'Right, race you back to the barracks,' and shot off before Lee could respond. He caught up with her after about a couple of hundred yards, but Chrissie pushed the pace to an extent where they had no breath left for talking. By the time they got to the guardroom, they were both shattered.

Chrissie collapsed onto the steps by the barrier, her head between her knees, her breath coming in ragged gasps, her shoulders heaving.

'That,' said Lee, also gasping, 'was one well hard run. Thanks, Chrissie.' He hauled in a juddering lungful of air. 'We must do it again.'

But Chrissie had already made her mind up; she was going to avoid Lee at all costs. Footloose and fancy free, that was what she wanted her life to be for the foreseeable future, and she wasn't going to tempt herself, or providence. And anyway, he was a married man and completely off limits.

'We'll see,' was her lukewarm response. 'I think I'm pretty

tied up for the next few weeks.' And if she wasn't, she was going to find ways of making sure she was.

'But surely Wednesdays...?' said Lee.

'I've got some sports events lined up,' Chrissie lied. 'Netball.' She'd bet her last penny that Lee wouldn't know anything about netball and still less about which of the women in the battalion made up the team.

'Oh well.' He sounded really disappointed. 'See you around.'

Chrissie nodded but in her head she was thinking, No you won't.

Chapter Five

Maddy looked about her sitting room with an expression of satisfaction on her pretty, heart-shaped face. Finally, one room straight, she thought. She was just about to celebrate with a cup of tea when the doorbell rang. Cradling Nathan in one arm, Maddy went to answer it.

'Caro! You must be psychic, I was just about put the kettle on.'

'Hi, Maddy, hiya, Nathan. No, I've not come to scrounge a cuppa, I've come to take you and Nathan out.'

'Out?'

'Wives' Club.'

Maddy noticed Luke in his buggy behind Caro. Not for the first time she thought how startlingly like his mother the boy was, with his blond curls and stunning, navy blue eyes and ready smile. 'But we're not ready. I mean, I hadn't planned...'

'So? We're talking Wives' Club here, not dinner at the CO's house. Get Nate into his outdoor togs, grab a nappy bag and let's go.'

Maddy glanced through the dining room door to her left and saw the tissue and newspaper spilling out of the boxes, the piles of crockery still to be put away in the sideboard, and wavered.

'If you don't get it all squared away today,' said Caro, following her neighbour's gaze, 'no one is going to die.'

Then Nate let out a wail.

Maddy sighed. 'But it's not fair to inflict a colicky baby on other mums.'

'Like everyone else's is perfect – and they cheerfully inflict them on the rest of us. Look at Philippa's kids.'

Maddy shook her head. Who was Philippa and what about her kids?

'You've not met Edward and Josh? No? They live at number thirty.' Maddy was none the wiser. 'Well,' continued Caro, 'just keep them at arm's length when you do. Not that you'll want them any closer as the pair always have about a yard of green snot hanging down their faces. I mean, why their mother hasn't taught them to blow their noses...' She shuddered. 'And then there's Olivia. I've never known a child throw a tantrum like she does. Skweems and skweems and skweems till she's sick,' she said, quoting from *Just William*. 'So little Nate, here...' she plonked a fat kiss on his cheek, 'is an angel in comparison. Just like my two, obviously. But then I might be a teeny bit biased. So come on – pull your finger out.'

Maddy gave in and tugged Nate's all-in-one off the peg by the door. 'Can you stuff him in that?' she asked Caro, handing her the garment and the baby. 'I'll just get his kit together.' Maddy raced upstairs to grab Nate's nappy bag and as she did so, she realised that she was looking forward to getting out and meeting the other wives.

Five minutes later the two women were pushing their buggies along the road towards the community centre, an old senior officer's quarter which had been converted for use in this new role. Nate didn't seem to be too happy about the outing and was grizzling.

'Maybe this isn't a good idea,' she said to Caro, horribly

aware that his cries were quite noisy even out in the open; in a confined space they'd seem even worse.

'Of course it is,' said Caro. 'As if anyone has had a baby who has never cried.'

'And I suppose the colic will pass. Won't it?' she added hopefully.

'Should do. In a previous existence I was a nanny, and I never looked after a baby that suffered beyond about four months. It's not called three-month colic for nothing. It'll pass, honestly. By Christmas, this will all be a memory.'

Maddy didn't listen to what Caro said about the colic – all she heard was that Caro had been a nanny. So that explained why she was so brilliant with Nathan, which only made Maddy feel even more inadequate. 'You must think I'm a complete moron – the way I am with Nate.'

Caro shook her head. 'God, of course I don't. He's your first, and they don't come with an instruction manual. And, let's face it, having to move almost straight after giving birth has hardly made things easier for you – or him. I think you're an absolute trouper.'

'Really?'

'Really.'

They reached the community centre and parked their buggies at the edge of the dozen or so other ones that littered the drive to the big house. Maddy unclipped Nate's car seat from the frame of the pushchair and lugged it in through the front door while Caro took off Luke's restraining straps so he could toddle in after her.

Inside the house the hubbub of women's voices almost managed to drown out Nate's cries. Maddy picked him out of his seat and unzipped his suit before stripping the bulky outer garment off him and popping him back in.

Then she hooked the handle of his seat over her arm like a handbag.

'Come and meet everyone,' said Caro, holding open a door and ushering her into the main room. Around the walls were a couple of dozen dining room chairs, while in the middle of the floor was an impressive array of toys and a number of small children, mostly playing contentedly. Caro nudged Maddy and whispered, 'Spot Josh.'

Maddy looked at the kids on the floor. Oh, yes, she could see in an instant exactly what Caro had meant. Yuck.

'Now then, let me introduce you to a few people and then I'll get us both a coffee.' She made a beeline across the room to a thirty-something woman in a tweed skirt and sweater. 'Maddy, I don't think you've met Seb's OC's wife – this is Susie whose husband is Seb's boss. Susie, this is Maddy Fanshaw, wife of the famous Seb Fanshaw – you know, the rower – and her son, Nathan.'

Susie looked impressed. 'Oh my God, Mike told me we had a superstar joining our company. He's the guy who nearly made the Olympics, no?'

Maddy had long since discovered that wives in army circles seemed to be defined by their husband's status and rank and, although it still rankled, she'd learned to accept that her previous existence as a biochemist and an Oxford graduate counted for nought. She was also faintly amused to hear Susie use the phrase 'our company'. Since when had Mike Collins shared command of B Company with his wife, she wondered? Oh well, thought Maddy, she'd better try and be nice to her while Caro was off getting them both a cup of coffee. She didn't know much about the army, but she did know that pissing off her husband's boss's wife was probably not a good thing.

'You'll have to join the babysitting circle,' said Susie.

'Babysitting circle?' Maddy put Nathan and his chair on a nearby coffee table and flexed her arm to relieve the stiffness. Nate was no lightweight.

'Just about every married patch has one – the mums all get tokens for twelve hours' free babysitting from the other mums. We pay each other for babysitting in tokens – double tokens after midnight – and earn them back by repaying the favour. Easy, cheap and a fab way of getting to know other mums with kids. You don't have to join if you don't want to,' added Susie, although her tone of voice seemed to imply that this wasn't really an option.

'It sounds great,' said Maddy hastily, hoping she sounded sufficiently enthusiastic, because she couldn't envisage ever again having the energy for an evening out with Seb. If she watched the news at ten she was staying up late.

'We've got a meeting at my place shortly. I'll pop the details through your door. You can get to meet the other mums, see who you'd like to entrust with Nate. Make sure you come along.'

Maddy resisted the temptation to snap a salute and say 'yes, ma'am'. It really wasn't an invitation but an order.

'And I'll come round to see you soon – help you get settled in, answer any questions, sort you out with some committees you might want to join, that sort of thing.'

Committees… oh dear God, as if she didn't have enough on her plate with a colicky baby, a recent house move and Seb's rowing training.

'Anyway,' said Susie, 'I mustn't monopolise you.' And she drifted off. Maddy had the feeling she'd escaped because there was someone else more interesting or more worthy of Susie's attention.

Caro returned with their coffees. 'Can I assume that Susie's sorted you out with babysitting?'

Maddy nodded. She was still feeling shell-shocked. 'That's one way of putting it,' she murmured.

'Excellent. But you can always ask me, if you need to have an hour or so to yourself. I mean it,' she added. 'I love babies, so it would be a real pleasure.'

Maddy took a sip of her coffee. 'Caro, promise me that, if you see me turning into some clone of Susie, you'll shoot me.'

Caro laughed. 'She's not that bad.'

Maddy raised her eyebrows. 'No?' She recounted her conversation. 'Honestly, what with her and Mrs N, I've got this feeling there's some sort of operation they do on wives once their husbands get to a certain rank, to insert a set of khaki genes into them. Don't these women want to do anything except advance their husbands? I've heard of career wives, but this is ridiculous.'

Caro nearly choked on her coffee. She looked about her. 'I see your point. It's not universal though.'

'No?'

'Honestly. I'm modelling myself on a woman I met in Tidworth when we had a posting there. She came to my door when I'd just arrived, introduced herself as Lizzy and promptly invited me to a lunch party the following week. "Do come," she said. "I've invited everyone in this road." So I said, "What, even the old farts in the big houses at the posh end?" She just giggled and said that it was come one, come all, so she could hardly not invite them or they'd feel left out. Then she thrust an invite in my hand and told me to ring if I found I couldn't make it. It was only when she'd gone and I read the invite properly I realised she was Lady Mayhew, wife of General Sir Edward Mayhew, the GOC, chief of the old farts.'

'And she giggled? Really?'

'Truly she did. Told me later she thought what I'd said was a hoot. So I'm going to be like her, when I finally have to grow up, and not be stuffy and pompous. Not,' she added, 'that Will'll get to such dizzying heights, but I still don't want to become like Mrs N.'

'Oh, me neither,' said Maddy with feeling, casting a glance in the direction of Susie and Mrs N, now both in earnest conversation. 'Caro?' she asked.

'Hmm?'

'You know what you said about casual babysitting?'

Caro nodded. 'Of course.'

'Could I ask a huge favour? I mean...'

'Spit it out.'

'You know you offered to have Nate, so I could get my hair cut?'

Caro nodded. 'And I meant it. Go and ring them now, Zoë's number is on the noticeboard in the hall. Book an appointment with Jenna. Pick any day except next Thursday, as my mother-in-law is coming for the weekend and I'll *have* to blitz the house.'

'Really?'

'Yes, I really *will* have to do housework. Rumours of me being a slut are all true, but this time I'm going to have to knuckle down.'

Maddy giggled. 'That's not what I meant and you know it.'

'Just phone them. Now!'

Maddy disappeared into the hall to find the list of numbers for the garrison facilities. Just as she left the room Nathan began to cry again.

'Go,' said Caro, picking up the baby. When Maddy returned, Nathan was giggling.

'Laughter, not tears – that's a first. You are a genius,' she said, although she felt a tiny twinge of jealousy that Nathan was being such a perfect baby for Caro and not for her. She pushed the thought aside. 'Tomorrow, ten o'clock,' she said. She held her hands out for Nate, who Caro passed over. It was nice to cuddle a happy smiling child for once.

'Perfect. Drop Nathan around any time. Now, come and meet Philippa, before we all have to pay attention and learn how to make Christmas cake – not that I'm going to; that's why we have Sainsbury's. Honestly, if God had meant me to crochet my own sandals and be an earth mother, He wouldn't have invented supermarkets. And don't worry, despite the snotty kids, Philly is one of us and isn't the least bit khaki-minded.'

Maddy smiled happily. She was really glad Caro had cajoled her into coming to the Wives' Club and that she was getting to know more of her neighbours. Life was going to be so much easier with a bunch of friends she knew she could lean on if necessary – even if some of them did have khaki blood running through their veins.

Lee waited outside the Dismounted Close Combat Trainer, feeling happy that he was going to be spending the second half of the morning playing on what was essentially an enormous video game. And knowing he was going to be busy was going to take his mind off Chrissie. Why had she had that sudden change in attitude? What had he said? Or done? It didn't add up. One moment she'd been dead keen to run with him and now... Over the past few days he'd sent her texts, asking if she was up for a run sometime during the following week and hadn't had an answer to one of them. He was worried that he'd done something to upset her. He hoped he hadn't because he really liked her. He tried reassuring himself with the thought that she might have lost or broken her phone, but he knew that was unlikely. Lee sighed and pushed the worries to the back of his mind as his section corporal arrived and unlocked the door to the indoor laser range.

The twenty or so guys in Lee's section filed in behind the corporal who flicked on the light switches, went to the control panel to the side of the screen and began selecting the program. While he did that, Lee's section took up their firing positions, grabbed their weapons and waited for the instructions.

'This is the way to spend time on the range,' said Lee's neighbour, Jack, who was lying next to him on the firing point.

'Because it's where the deer and the antelope play?' asked Lee.

'Twat,' said Jack, grinning all the same. 'Who wants to be on a real range in real weather, when we can be tucked up in here in the warm and dry?'

'Listen in,' shouted the corporal, interrupting all conversations. 'Twenty rounds at the target, in your own time. Fire.'

In front of each firing position the screen showed a line of Figure 11 targets, the standard army target used on training ranges everywhere: a cartoon of a ferocious-looking soldier, charging forwards, bayonet fixed and with an evil snarl on his face. The lads picked up their electronic SA80 rifles and began firing at the screen, just like they were playing on a giant Wii. Each target showed realistic bullet holes as and when the soldiers scored a hit. Once all twenty electronic rounds had been fired from all the guns, the picture changed, new instructions were issued and they began firing again. This time they weren't aiming at static targets, but at completely realistic video footage of enemy troops thundering over open ground, hell-bent on annihilating Lee and his mates.

Even though Lee knew that this was all make-believe, that it was just a computer-generated image, he found his heart rate rocketing and sweat breaking out on his back and under his arms. Ten minutes later, the exercise was over and Lee felt drained. Suddenly he completely understood how Chrissie must have felt in the hellish exercise involving the fake injuries and make-believe traumas. No wonder it had all been a bit much for the poor lass.

The scenario on the screen changed to a different battle scene and once again his section had to fight for their lives, while the computer scored who made the most direct hits on the available targets. By the time Lee's section had finished their training session on the DCCT, and they'd been given their scores – 'Well done, Perkins, good shooting' – he felt wrung out. On the other hand, it was lunchtime so plenty of time to recover before the afternoon session on helicopter recognition.

Lee made his way out of the warm comfort of the DCCT range and headed for the cookhouse. As he collected his chosen meal of steak pie and chips he saw Immi sitting at a table on her own.

'Mind if I join you?' he asked as he plonked his tray down.

'Be my guest.'

Lee hooked a chair out with his foot. 'No Chrissie?'

'Nope.'

'Is she on leave?' asked Lee innocently.

Immi shook her head. 'No, I don't know what she's getting up to, as she's working all hours down at the medical centre. I hardly see her these days except for when she's yelling at me in the gym, or making me run up and down Brandon Hill. Honestly, that woman's a sadist.'

'So why's she so busy?'

'Search me. If she isn't working, she's out training with one sports team or another. Is there any sport she doesn't want to play?' Immi shook her head in bewilderment. 'And when she's not doing that, she's trying to get me through my BFT, but then I'm too knackered to chat. Honestly, even though we share a barrack room, we spend half our time communicating by text. In fact,' she pulled her phone out of her pocket, 'I've just had one telling me to meet her at the gym this evening again.' Immi sighed. 'I know she means well but I wish she wasn't so sodding keen. I only need to pass my fitness test, not set some sort of world record.'

'So her phone's not lost?'

'Lost? No, why should it be?'

'No, no reason.' But Lee suddenly lost interest in his steak pie. Chrissie was blanking him. He just wished he knew why.

Chapter Six

Maddy sat in the upholstered plastic chair in front of the mirror in Zoë's salon and gazed at her reflection. Then she raised her eyes to look at the hairdresser.

'So,' said the woman who Maddy now knew to be Jenna, 'just a trim, is it?'

'A bit more than that. Could you take a couple of inches off at least? I haven't been able to get my hair cut for months.'

Jenna picked up a clump of Maddy's hair. 'It's a lovely colour, Mrs Fanshaw.'

'Thanks, and do call me Maddy.'

Jenna grinned at her in the mirror. 'Yeah, well,' she leaned in and lowered her voice. 'You have to be a bit careful round here. Some of the wives can be a bit snotty, if you know what I mean. Wearing their husband's rank and all.'

Maddy knew *exactly* what Jenna meant. 'You don't have to worry about anything like that with me, Jenna. I haven't a clue how the army works – apart from having to move house constantly.'

Jenna let Maddy's hair fall again. 'It'd be nice to *get* a house in the first place. Me and my Lee have been married for months now and we've still got nowhere to live. I'm still with my mum.'

Maddy shook her head. 'But that's rotten.'

'Tell me about it. Anyway, best we get on...'

Thirty minutes later Maddy's hair was washed, dried, sleek, shining and cut into a flattering bob. For the whole time it had taken to revamp Maddy's hair, the pair had chatted away like old buddies – their shared army experiences creating an instant bond; from their husbands' duties to their worries about overseas tours, to the possibility of compulsory redundancies, to the attitudes of their fellow wives and to how they saw the next few years panning out, they ran the whole gamut. Finally, Jenna misted Maddy's hair with spray.

'There, all done.'

Maddy gazed at her new image. God, it was such an improvement. Whatever the cost, it was going to be worth it. And she'd made a new friend. All in all, it had been thirty minutes very well spent.

Jenna held up a mirror behind her head so she could see how it looked from the back.

'Perfect,' said Maddy happily. 'You're a miracle worker. Caro Brown said you were a star.'

Jenna smiled at her. 'You mates with Caro?'

'Neighbours. She's looking after my baby, otherwise I'd have had no chance to escape for a bit of pampering.'

Jenna glanced about her and then leaned in again. 'I do home visits,' she said quietly.

Maddy nodded. 'Caro said,' she murmured back.

'She's got my mobile number. Just give me a ring and I'll pop round next time you need a trim.'

'Thanks.' Maddy could tell from the way Jenna was keeping her voice low that her boss had no idea one of her stylists was pinching her customers but, glancing around, the place was pretty busy. And having Jenna come to the house would just make everything so much easier.

She paid her bill, collected her coat and tipped Jenna. 'I'll be in touch,' she said quietly, as she shrugged her thick mac on.

'Great,' said Jenna. 'Maybe when you need your next hair appointment, the army will have pulled its finger out and I'll have a quarter of my own too.'

'I'll cross my fingers and, as I said earlier, I'll see what I can do to help,' said Maddy as she left. She was going to have a word with Seb about Jenna's quarter. She was sure he'd know what buttons to press – after all, they'd got a house with no trouble at all, so presumably he could do the same for one of his men.

Jenna yawned as Lee found a parking space on the road near his mam's house and reversed his Ford Focus into it.

'Tired?' he asked Jenna.

'It's a sod of a long way to come just for a weekend,' she said.

She glanced across at the clock on the dashboard display. Nearly midnight. And although Newcastle had a lot to offer in the way of nightlife – far more than the town nearest the garrison – she wasn't best pleased to have been dragged up here, because she and Sonia weren't, and never would be, soulmates. Beyond loving Lee, they had absolutely nothing in common, and staying for a long weekend with her mother-in-law was hardly Jenna's idea of a fun time.

Lee yanked on the handbrake and switched off the engine. 'Come on, let's go and say hello to Mam.'

Yes let's, thought Jenna, with no enthusiasm.

Lee grabbed the holdall from the back while Jenna undid her seat belt and got out of the car. The pair walked along the row of identical Victorian terraced houses to the one that had been Lee's childhood home. Well, his home after his dad had been killed in the first Gulf War and he and his mam had had to leave army quarters and find a place of their own. Not that he remembered that as he'd only been two at the time.

Sonia Perkins had obviously been looking out for them because as they approached the house she flung the front door wide and launched herself at Lee, her corkscrew perm bouncing about almost as much as her ample bosom.

Bloody hell, thought Jenna, you'd think he'd been gone for years not just a few months since his summer block leave. She also wondered how a woman who was as broad as she was tall – and she was only about five feet – could have produced a son who topped six feet and was built like a whippet.

Finally Sonia stopped hugging her son and admiring how fit he looked and turned to Jenna. 'Hello, Jenna,' she said, not bothering to fake any warmth or affection; her mouth pursed like a cat's bum and her beady eyes were cold and unsmiling.

Two can play at that game. 'Sonia,' she replied, not even bothering with any form of greeting.

They glared at each other momentarily before Sonia bustled back into the house, exhorting them to come in while she got the kettle on.

'I'd rather have a proper drink,' whispered Jenna to Lee.

'We'll make a night of it tomorrow,' Lee murmured back as he shut the front door behind them.

They followed Sonia into the front room which Jenna always thought looked like a mausoleum with pictures of Lee's dead dad everywhere, and the glass cases containing his cap and medals. She stared at the mementoes: his dad's old cap and Sam Browne; his regimental group photos with the 1 Herts' crest on the thick cardboard mount that backed the pictures. Not for the first time she wondered if it was entirely healthy that Lee had joined his dad's old unit. Although it explained why a Geordie was in a southern regiment. She shuddered. No, definitely not healthy, she thought. Lee following his dad and his mum not being able to let go of the memories and move on. Jenna sat in silence while Sonia grilled Lee about life in the battalion, his prospects, his chance of promotion, until Lee pointed out that it was very late and that he and Jenna had had a long day.

'Silly me,' said Sonia. 'You should have said earlier. I've put you in the front room.'

And just as well, thought Jenna, as the back bedroom is a single. But she was sure that Sonia had hated making up the double bed for them and would have much preferred to have had them sleeping in separate beds despite the fact they were legally wed.

Leaving Sonia to switch off the lights, Lee and Jenna made up the stairs to their room.

Jenna shut the door firmly and pulled Lee to her. 'I don't care what you say, Private Perkins, you and me are going to test the springs of this mattress to the limit. Do you realise we haven't shared a double bed for months?'

'So why are you wasting time bumping your gums? Get your kit off and get that gorgeous arse of yours into bed.'

On the Tuesday, Lee mentally acknowledged that if he achieved nothing else in the next few weeks, he had to get himself and Jenna a quarter. Over the long weekend she'd managed to leave him in no doubt that living as they were was completely unacceptable and no way to start a marriage. Of course he'd realised it for himself but he hadn't realised quite how desperate she was to escape from her mother's and be independent.

'It's all right for you, Lee,' she said as they'd walked into

Newcastle for the promised night on the lash, 'you *have* escaped. You've got a job, you've got your own bit of space and you live miles and miles away from your mum. Don't you see, I want that too?'

'I suppose.'

'So make a fuss. The army can't chuck you out for wanting what you're entitled to.'

Lee wasn't so sure but he was between the proverbial rock and a hard place. If he didn't make a fuss, he might lose his wife, but if he made himself unpopular with Captain Fanshaw by banging on about his need for married accommodation, he might scupper his promotion chances and his career. However, he had to make at least a token effort for Jenna's sake, he thought, as he shouldered open the swing door to the company offices and made his way along the corridor to Captain Fanshaw's office. The door was open and his boss was in. No time like the present. Making sure his beret was on properly, Lee knocked on the open door.

Seb looked up. 'Perkins, isn't it? What can I do for you?'

Lee saluted. 'Sir, can I have a word?'

'Course. Come in, shut the door and take a seat.' Seb pushed the papers to the side of his desk and looked at Lee as he took his beret off and pulled up a chair.

'The thing is, sir, Mrs Perkins is getting a bit agitated about us not having a quarter.' The truth was, she was fucking livid, but Lee didn't think the boss would appreciate him being so blunt.

'I know,' said Seb. 'She spoke to my wife about it at the hairdresser's. My wife's been bending my ear about it ever since.'

She had? Bugger. 'I didn't know, sir,' said Lee. 'I'm sorry, sir.'

'It's not your fault, Perkins.' Seb grinned at Lee. 'Women, eh?' Lee nodded. 'To be honest, Perkins, my hands are pretty tied. After my wife told me about what Mrs Perkins had said, I checked with the housing commandant and he tells me you've got almost no points, you don't have any kids, you haven't yet been on an operational tour and so you haven't been separated from your wife for any significant length of time. All of which means you can't expect miracles.'

Lee nodded. 'That's what I told the wife.'

'But she is still giving you a hard time.'

Lee nodded again and shrugged. 'Never mind, sir. I promised her I'd mention it to you, and I have. Thanks for your time, sir.'

He got to his feet and put his beret back on his head before he saluted snappily, turned and left.

Once outside he let out a long sigh. He wished Jenna had told him that she'd already bleated to the captain's wife. Women!

Seb got up and shut the door, then he rang Maddy.

'I've just had your mate Jenna's husband in here, bending my ear about quarters,' he complained. 'I *told* you getting matey with a soldier's wife would cause trouble.'

'Oh.' Seb could tell from Maddy's guilty tone that she knew she was in the wrong. 'Sorry,' she added contritely. 'I only said I'd have a word with you. I didn't promise her that you could do anything.'

'Maddy, I can't buck the system for him. And you're *not* Lady Bountiful. You can't magically solve their problems, so stop acting like you can and making promises you can't keep. Don't get involved and don't go meeting trouble halfway. He and his wife'll just have to wait their turn, like everyone else.'

'We had no problem getting a quarter. It doesn't seem fair,' said Maddy, crossly.

'I'm an officer. It makes a difference.'

'Well, it shouldn't. What happened to the classless society?'

'Anyway, if Mrs Perkins comes whining to you again—'

'She did *not* whine.'

Seb sighed. 'Whatever. If she mentions it to you again, say you can't help and neither can I. Understand?'

'Yes.' She sounded sulky, but Seb wasn't going to apologise. She'd interfered and she shouldn't have.

'See you at lunchtime.'

'Bye.' She disconnected immediately.

Seb threw his mobile onto the desk. He had a feeling that Mrs Perkins was going to be trouble. Shame, because Lee was a great soldier, and a wife who caused ructions might stop him getting on as far as he deserved. He stood up and walked to the orderly room. In the corner, behind the chief clerk, was a bank of filing cabinets containing the soldiers' documents for the whole company. He scanned the paper labels indicating which letters of the alphabet were stored where.

'Can I help you, boss?' said the clerk. He didn't like people messing about in his orderly room, even if it was his superior officer.

'No, Chiefy, I can manage thank you.' Seb hauled open the correct drawer, rifled through the large buff files till he found the one he wanted and then sauntered back to his office.

Twenty minutes later he'd read all there was to know about Perkins, including his application to transfer to the SAS, endorsed enthusiastically by his predecessor – interesting, as it showed just what Perkins' potential might be – and a scribbled note about Jenna Perkins, who had been the direct cause of a number of drunken fights between soldiers in Tommy's Bar because she'd been over-liberal with her favours. Or that's what the inference was. It seemed to confirm what Seb thought: she was trouble.

Chapter Seven

By the time Chrissie finished for the day at the medical centre, she was bushed. It wasn't just the workload – the day after a long weekend was always busy with soldiers who had got into fights or scrapes after three whole days of boozing, which was how infantry soldiers tended to spend their down time – no, her thoughts had been in turmoil all day as she'd come to a decision over the weekend and had been turning it around and around ever since, trying to work out how mad it would be to volunteer for the field hospital at Camp Bastion.

In some ways it seemed the perfect way forward for her: potentially it could be brilliant for her career; it would expand her horizons – after all, she'd never travelled anywhere; and it would get her away from Lee. She had found herself thinking about him far too much, a situation which really wasn't helped by him texting her pretty often, wanting her to run with him. And she wasn't going to risk doing that again, not after the way she'd felt last time. So the easiest way of dealing with the situation was to just avoid him, and if she could get herself out to Afghan, avoiding him would be a piece of piss. Besides, if she didn't go to Afghanistan soon, she might never get the chance, especially if the army really did pull out when they promised they would. Career-wise, too, she needed that experience.

But, and it was a big *but*, would she be accepted, if she

did volunteer? It wasn't so long since she'd been told she was too young and inexperienced. Supposing the army was right and she couldn't cope with witnessing real, life-changing and horrific injuries? How would she feel if she got turned down? And was she bonkers to even want to put herself through what was bound to be a traumatic experience? Weighing up all the pros and cons had preoccupied her all day. It was hardly surprising that even the MO had noticed that she hadn't been concentrating. And wasn't it amazing, she thought, how knackering the combination of being preoccupied *and* working was.

Wearily, she clambered up the stairs to her room and threw herself on her bed. Immi was already in the room.

'Wassup?' said Immi.

'Knackered.'

'Too much of the sick, lame and lazy?'

Chrissie yawned. 'Something like that.'

'Are we running tonight?'

Chrissie shrugged. She knew she ought to; Immi's fitness had come on in leaps and bounds, but somehow she just couldn't face it this evening.

'Tell you what, Immi, why don't you go on your own?'

'What?'

'You've got to be able to motivate yourself, Immi. I won't always be around to make you go.'

'You're not planning on jacking the army in, are you?' Immi sounded aghast.

Chrissie sighed and shook her head. Quite the reverse. 'No, but, you know... postings, things crop up.' She shrugged. 'You've got another two years to do before you can get out – if you want to – and one or other of us is bound to move on in that time.'

'Suppose.' Immi looked far from convinced. 'But it'll be so tough to keep going, without you to push me.'

'Take your iPod and get on with it.' Chrissie's voice had a sharper note to it than she intended. 'I'll run with you tomorrow,' she promised, to take the sting out of her words.

Immi came and sat on Chrissie's bed. 'What is it, babes? More than just a bad day at work?'

Chrissie sighed and rolled over to look at her best friend. 'Sort of.'

'Want to tell me about it?'

Did she? 'Not really.'

'Man problems?'

'Not really. It's complicated.'

'Come on, tell Aunty Immi. A problem shared and all that bullshit.' There was a short pause. 'Shit, you're not having an affair with the medical officer?'

Chrissie shook her head and grinned. 'No, I'm not having an affair with *anyone*. And before you get the thumbscrews out, why don't you fuck off for that run and give me some peace and quiet.' In fact she'd had plenty of peace and quiet since she'd seriously started to think about volunteering for Afghanistan and she hadn't got anywhere in three days. Another hour was hardly likely to make all the difference.

'I can take a hint.' Immi started to change into her running kit. 'Mind you, if it *is* a bloke giving you the runaround, my advice is dump him. There's plenty more fish in the sea.'

'And you can have your pick, Ims. I really just want to think about me and my career for the next few years and not worry about anyone else.'

Immi stopped pulling on her tracksuit bottoms. 'Sweetie, you can shag blokes without having to worry about them. Love 'em and dump 'em. Trust me, I know.'

Chrissie giggled. 'That's what I love about you, Ims – you're so shameless!'

'I know. Good, isn't it?'

'I think I need to learn from you.'

'Then you've come to the right place.'

The next morning, Maddy, with Nate in his buggy and loaded up with his nappy bag and emergency supplies, wandered along Omdurman Avenue towards Susie's quarter. Caro had cried off the babysitting circle meeting, citing an imminent visit from her mother-in-law and the need to do a massive shop for supplies – 'Mainly gin, to get me through it.'

Maddy still felt she hardly knew anyone on the patch and was a little apprehensive about rocking up on her own, but Seb had told her to man up and so here she was. Tentatively she rang the bell and was assaulted by a shattering wave of noise as the door opened.

'Sorry, it's bedlam,' said Susie, looking flustered as she ushered Maddy in.

Susie might have *looked* flustered but everything else about her was immaculate, from her blond hair tucked into a natty French pleat, to her beautifully manicured nails, to her crease-free linen shirt over her pressed jeans. Mrs Middleton couldn't have looked neater or tidier. Maddy was instantly conscious that, in contrast, her appearance left a lot to be desired. Maybe she should have changed into a clean top after all, but she hadn't bothered because she knew Nate would only dribble onto it the instant she picked him up again.

It certainly was bedlam, though, as Susie's sitting room was far too small for the ten or so toddlers. Surrounding them, sitting on a mix of chairs, were mothers off the patch, some of whom Maddy vaguely recognised, most of whom she didn't.

'Coffee?' offered Susie.

'Think I'll give it a miss,' said Maddy, wondering about the wisdom of juggling a baby and a hot drink.

'It'll calm down in half an hour. Lots of the mums have to fetch kids from the playgroup at about eleven thirty and those that don't, go home to get lunch ready.'

Susie clapped her hands and got some sort of order in the room, so she could introduce Maddy. The other wives greeted her with smiles and waves and some words of welcome, as Susie reeled off their names.

'Don't worry,' said one of the wives, who Maddy thought might be called Jenny – or was it Penny? 'You've got ages and ages to get to know us. That's the thing with regiments: our husbands may get posted out now and again to staff jobs but they always end up back here.'

Back here? Constantly? Oh joy, thought Maddy, but she smiled brightly. She knew she was being unfair; there was nothing wrong with her neighbours – shit, she hardly knew them – but did she really want to spend the rest of her life surrounded by the same people, people who would judge her on her ability to throw a dinner party or chair a committee? She suddenly had a vision of lab rats scurrying round, their behaviour monitored by Mrs Notley and Susie, and suppressed a slightly hysterical giggle. She sat on a vacant chair and jiggled Nathan, who was grizzling softly on her lap, as she listened to the conversation which now resumed around her. As far as she could tell they were discussing the best way to get mud and cam cream out of combat kit.

Shoot me now, thought Maddy, is this what life holds for me? Is this to be the highlight of my days, gathering laundry tips? She thought back to her time at Oxford and conversations she'd had with fellow students. Never once could she remember anyone swapping household management advice. The smile on her face became more forced. This wasn't what she'd envisaged when she'd agreed to marry Seb. When they'd been dating, it had seemed to be all summer balls, dinner nights and glamorous men in uniform. Not this. Not for the first time in recent weeks she wondered if she'd made a dreadful mistake.

Then, as Susie had predicted, the mothers pretty much left en masse to get other children from the playgroup or kindergarten, before preparing a meal for their menfolk. Maddy rose and made a move to escape. Nate had finally drifted off to sleep and was temporarily silent, and Maddy felt that if peace lasted a little longer she might get a few of Seb's shirts ironed, before he came home for lunch.

'Hang on,' said Susie. She rummaged through a pile of papers, stuffed behind the clock on the mantelpiece. Maddy noticed the number of invitations wedged by their corners into the frame of the overmantel mirror. No wonder Susie ran the babysitting circle, she must be constantly out and, when her daughters were back from prep school, in need of childcare. Susie found what she was looking for and handed it to Maddy.

'Your tokens,' she said. 'Plus a list of the circle members, telephone numbers, number of kids, that sort of thing.'

Maddy opened the envelope and glanced at the sheet. If nothing else, it would be a useful aide memoire as to who lived where on the patch. She stuffed it back in the envelope.

'Thanks.'

'Stay to lunch.'

'That's really kind but Seb's expecting me back.'

'Ring him. Tell him to have lunch in the mess. He'll probably be happy to pretend he's back there, living in.' Susie must have seen the expression on Maddy's face. 'Sorry, that came out all wrong. I didn't mean he might be regretting getting married but it's a big step for the lads when they move out of that all-boys-together atmosphere and have to grow up.'

Frankly, Maddy didn't think Seb had really grown up. She still felt a nagging irritation about the way he'd abandoned her and Nate when they'd moved house and sometimes it seemed as if she was his personal scout now, the way she picked up after him, did his laundry and had his meals ready on demand. Fuck it, she thought, fuck his shirts, she *would* stay to lunch and if they didn't get done, *he* could iron them. Even if Susie did intimidate her more than a little it would be nice to make another friend on the patch.

Seb seemed very relaxed about Maddy's decision when she phoned him. Then he said, *sotto voce*, 'Good move, getting in with the boss's wife. You could offer to have her round to ours for lunch, too. Never does any harm to be friends with the OC and his missus.'

He was right, of course, but Maddy preferred to have friends just because they got on, not for ulterior reasons.

Susie bustled about in her kitchen, which Maddy noted with interest was just as shabby as her own.

'Just soup and bread. Wine?'

Maddy shook her head. She might gag for a gin in the evening, but she tried not to drink during the day, except very occasionally at weekends. 'No thanks,' she said.

Susie stopped in her tracks. 'Just one, surely?'

'No, really.' She looked at Nate, who would provide the perfect excuse. 'I'm still breastfeeding. Maybe something soft?'

Susie rummaged in a cupboard which, as far as Maddy could see, was mainly used for storing tonic water, and emerged with a bottle of elderflower cordial.

'Perfect,' said Maddy. Susie poured it into a tumbler and added a couple of ice cubes.

'You don't mind if I do?' said Susie, whisking a bottle of white out of the fridge and cracking off the screw top. She filled a large glass to the brim. 'Now then, what can I tell you about army life and the patch...?'

Maybe it was the wine that loosened Susie's tongue, but after a while Maddy felt that she was hearing just a little too much gossip about the other wives. Which was frankly disturbing because it made Maddy wonder what the hell Susie would say about her and Seb. For instance, Maddy wasn't really sure she needed to know quite what a bad influence Susie thought Caro was.

'She's very relaxed with some of the senior wives,' said Susie. 'Too relaxed, if you know what I mean. Doesn't do the right thing – or she does it in the wrong way. And she doesn't support Will properly.'

Which made her sound more like some sort of truss, thought Maddy.

'Will won't get promoted much beyond major, with such a loose cannon in his corner.'

But was promotion the be-all and end-all? Susie had intimated it was and that she was sacrificing everything for Mike's future prospects, but looking at the lines of discontent etched into her face and having heard the complaints she'd already made about the moves and sending her kids off to prep school, Maddy wondered if it was really worth it. Surely, she thought, there had to be a compromise. But on the other hand she knew Seb was fiercely ambitious; she didn't think he'd be too impressed if he found her to be more of a hindrance than a help. He'd probably cheer if she became more like Mrs N or Susie, a prospect which frankly frightened her.

When Maddy got away she was even more worried about what she'd taken on by becoming an army wife. The previous evening, when her parents had phoned to announce their safe return from their holiday, she'd admitted her doubts to her mum, but her mum's response had been that it was probably just a touch of the baby blues and she'd snap out of it once Nate started sleeping through the night. But what if it wasn't just that? What if she wasn't cut out to follow the drum?

As she strolled home, she wondered if she could really face the next thirty years of being a regimental wife, of bracing up, getting on with it and toeing the line. Her thoughts were interrupted when a little blue Corsa screeched to a halt beside her. The passenger window wound down and the driver leaned across and yelled 'Coo-ee' at her.

'Jenna.'

'You look like you've lost a quid and found a penny,' said Jenna.

Maddy forced a bright smile. 'No, just miles away. Honest.'

'I was hoping to see you. Just been round at Caro's cutting her boys' hair. Anyway, I wanted to thank you.'

'Thank me? What on earth for?'

'We got a quarter. Lee's just phoned and told me. And I know it was down to you.'

'No, it wasn't. Truly, it must just be the luck of the draw.'

'Get away with you, I know you pulled some strings. Anyway, I won't keep you but I owe you one for this.' And with a cheery wave and a puff of exhaust fumes, Jenna's car zipped away.

It wasn't me, thought Maddy, it was just luck. If Jenna knew what Seb had said to her about being some sort of do-gooding Lady Bountiful trying to solve the soldiers' problems she'd know that nothing was further from the truth.

Another thing she'd got wrong, she thought morosely, as Nate started to cry once more. Crap as a mother, crap as a military wife...

At least, though, Jenna was happy. Like she had been a few months ago. Disconsolately, Maddy wondered how long it would last.

Chapter Eight

It was about eight o'clock that same evening when Chrissie and Immi cruised into Tommy's. Immi had decided that Baz was yesterday's man and wanted to find a replacement. It frankly baffled Chrissie how Immi managed her love-life so none of her ex-boyfriends ended up hurt or resentful about being dumped. So far, they'd all seemed to accept that their fling with her was over and harboured no hard feelings. She had no idea how Immi handled her exes, but it had to be with fantastic skill. Respect.

'And besides,' she said, as she dragged Chrissie out of their room, 'as you told me you're not having an affair with anyone – your very words, Chrissie Summers, so don't deny it – we might find someone for you. No!' She held her hand up, as Chrissie was about to protest. 'No one for the long term, but if you ask me, you need taking down off the shelf and giving a good dusting.'

Chrissie laughed. 'Not such a bad idea. I've got some nooks and crannies that need a bloody good seeing to.' Besides, it might take her mind off how she felt about Lee.

It was quietish when they got to the bar, but experience told them that it would be much busier in just a short while.

'So, what are you drinking?' asked Chrissie. 'Lager top?'

Immi nodded. They got their drinks and headed for a table in the centre of the room.

'No point in being invisible,' said Immi, plonking herself down in full view of both the bar and the main door. She looked about. 'Christ, fuck-all talent in at the moment, though: spotty Jack and his mates from B Company and a bunch of baby new recruits. Still, we might as well give it an hour – see what the cat drags in.'

'Jack's not so bad,' said Chrissie. 'He mightn't be a looker, but he's good company.' Immi gave Chrissie a very doubting look. 'He is, honest.'

'If you say so, hon.'

A roar of laughter rocked the room.

'Told you,' said Chrissie.

'Told me what?'

'That he's funny.' Chrissie picked up her drink, grabbed Immi's arm and hauled her to her feet before dragging her mate over to where Jack was.

'Hi, guys,' said Chrissie.

'Hiya, Chris,' said Jack, his face beaming with pleasure at the sight of her. 'And who have we here?' he asked, gazing Immi up and down.

'Someone way out of your league,' said one of his mates.

'Hey,' said Jack, grinning, 'I only want a name, not a phone number and a hot date.' Despite his acne, he had a great smile and brilliantly blue eyes.

Chrissie wondered if Immi mightn't reassess him when she got to know him a bit better. Certainly Chrissie herself had, when they'd met on exercise and he'd managed to raise her morale after a particularly gruelling and rain-soaked day. Mind you, she thought, honours were even. Once he'd lifted her spirits out of the doldrums she managed to trade joke for joke with him.

'Jack, this is Immi,' said Chrissie.

Jack introduced them to the rest of his pals: Doug, Bonzo and Chewbacca – who was tall and hairy – then said, 'We were talking about weddings.'

Immi, who had been taking a sip of her lager top, nearly choked. 'Blokes? Talking weddings?'

Jack looked at her steadily. 'I know this must be an alien concept to you ladies but unless you're batting for the other team, and something tells me you aren't,' he gave Immi a lewd wink, 'you're going to need a guy waiting for you at the altar otherwise your big day isn't going to go exactly to plan, is it? So yes, guys *do* know about weddings and we've even been known to take an interest in them.'

'I *know* that,' said Immi a bit petulantly, 'but I thought most guys would rather run a mile than get involved with any actual planning.'

'So are you one of those metrosexuals, then, Jack?' asked Chrissie.

'God yes, of course I am, aren't I, guys? Haven't I been telling you all the importance of getting your back, sack and crack waxed?'

'You have?!' asked Immi, believing him and impressed, being a slave to personal grooming herself.

'Want to see?' said Jack, his hand starting to unzip his flies.

Again the lads around him exploded with laughter and even Immi could see the funny side.

As the laughter died down, Chrissie said, straight-faced, 'Actually, I do. I've never seen bald balls. I'm asking purely out of medical interest, you understand.'

Jack gave Chrissie a long look, before he tugged on his flies again.

'Hang on,' said Chrissie, as she rummaged in her handbag. 'I just need to get my magnifying glass out.'

Once again, the blokes erupted with laughter.

'So,' asked Chrissie, when things had calmed down a bit, 'what aspect of weddings were you lot finding so riveting?'

'It was just weddings generally. I've been invited to Terry Gibbons's... know him?' Jack asked Chrissie.

'Can't say I do,' said Immi, trying to get involved in the conversation. She tossed her hair about a bit for good measure, to try to get the lads to notice her.

Much as Chrissie loved Immi, she knew that her best mate was a bit put out by not being the centre of attention. Jack and his mates weren't the sort to be swept off their feet by a pretty face, long legs and a mass of chestnut hair, they were much more into personality and wit. And, bless Immi, she was a great friend and kindness itself as well as a looker, but when it came to razor-sharp repartee she wasn't going to be able to compete with the present company. Oh well, she'd get over it.

'Terry from the cookhouse?' said Chrissie.

'That's him,' said Jack.

Immi stared at Chrissie. 'How come you know just about everyone in the battalion?'

'Because I'm always sticking needles into people or checking their pulses or dishing out painkillers, or getting them to piss into bottles, or something else utterly wonderful. Your involvement with soldiers is just their names on documents and you hardly get to meet anyone. Trust me, if you worked in the medical centre you'd get to meet *everyone* – and get to know more about them than you really want to.' She turned back to Jack. 'So what about Terry's wedding?'

'Nothing really. We were just saying that's another good bloke who won't be allowed out to play on a Saturday night.'

'You cheeky bugger,' protested Chrissie, slapping Jack

playfully. 'Women don't shackle their blokes like that and you know it.'

'No, the single ones don't but something happens when they get that gold band on their finger,' said Jack. He glanced over Chrissie's shoulder. 'And here comes a case in point.'

Chrissie spun round to see who Jack was talking about.

A voice carried from the doorway across to where they were standing. 'For fuck's sake, Lee, it's a dump. I mean, I'd rather stay with my mum, and that's saying something.'

Coming into the bar were Jenna and Lee. Something had rattled Jenna's cage, and she was making it quite plain that she wasn't happy. Chrissie felt a guilty rush of blood colour her face because given the way she'd been blanking him for days now he was the last person she wanted to see. Not, she thought, that with his wife with him he could really ask her why she hadn't answered his half-dozen texts. No matter how innocent they were, she didn't think Jenna would be thrilled that her new husband was busy sending messages to another woman.

As she watched Jenna stalk across the floor she saw her turn on Lee again.

'So you're going to go right back to Captain Fanshaw and tell him it's not good enough. I mean, he doesn't live in a crap house like this one, does he?'

'Uh-oh,' said Jack in a low voice. 'I don't think Private Perkins is going to be getting lucky with his missus tonight. It looks to me as if she's going to be tearing up his nooky ration book any minute now and no mistake.'

Jenna turned back towards the bar and caught sight of Chrissie and Immi. She headed straight for them.

Whatever was going on between Jenna and Lee, Chrissie could just tell she and Immi were going to be asked to get involved. Chrissie took a step sideways, putting Immi in direct line with Jenna, thus making it easier to escape if she wanted to.

'You'll agree with me, won't you?' said Jenna.

'Agree with you about what?' said Immi.

'About my crap house,' said Jenna.

She was stopped from going into detail by Lee asking a little sheepishly if it was OK to join them.

'The more the merrier,' said Jack. 'And it's your round, by the way.'

Lee rolled his eyes. 'Fuck off, Jack,' he said, with no malice. However, he turned to Immi and Chrissie. 'Another drink, girls, while I'm getting one for me and Jen?'

'We're good, thanks,' said Chrissie, feeling horribly awkward, and taking another pace away.

Immi gave Lee a wink. 'Actually, we're not good, we're sensational,' she joked.

'Aren't we all, hon,' said Jenna. 'Wasted on soldiers.' She gave the boys in the group a cheeky smile.

'In which case,' said Lee, 'you can get your own.'

'Only joking,' said Jenna, hastily. 'I'll have a rum and black.'

Lee turned to the bar to get the drinks for himself and Jenna. Chrissie used the opportunity to escape completely and resume her conversation with Jack. She really didn't want to spend the evening with Lee, when she'd spent the past week or so doing her utmost to avoid him.

'So, Jack... Terry's wedding?'

Jack shrugged. 'Actually, nothing much to tell. I just don't know why people go to all the fuss and expense of a big full-on church do when you can nip down the register office and be out in time for when the pubs open – job done.'

'And I thought the last of the romantics had already died,' said Chrissie, shaking her head.

The group laughed. Chrissie saw Lee cast an envious glance in their direction. Talking about his new house obviously wasn't pressing his buttons. Poor guy, she thought.

'Chris has got you bang to rights,' said Jack's mate, Doug.

'Look, all I'm saying is that weddings cause a lot of hassle all round and they cost a mint and not everyone enjoys them. I was at one a month or so back and my stepdad's nephew bawled and yelled so much that he had to be taken outside till he calmed down.'

'Didn't he want to get married?' asked Chrissie, deadpan.

Once again the bar erupted and once again Lee glanced longingly across at them.

'You don't sound happy, Jenna,' said Immi, ignoring the hilarity behind her. 'What is it that's crap, exactly, about your house?'

Jenny blew down her nose noisily. 'Pah! Everything. We got a message from the housing commandant today that we've finally got a quarter. So I go and have a look at it, only from the outside, of course, but even just looking at the front I could tell the place is a dump.'

'Really?'

Jenna shook her head. 'The garden is a mess, the outside paint's all flaking and when I looked through the windows the curtains and carpets are vile. I mean, they're orange. Orange! Honest, Immi, if you paid me I wouldn't want to live there.'

'It can't be that bad, surely?' said Immi.

Jenna wrinkled her perfect brow. 'You have no idea.' She listed several further inadequacies to do with the house which included the size, the lack of garage and the fact that the neighbours had small children.

'I dunno,' said Immi. 'I've got a few friends who live down on the patch and their houses aren't so bad. And you've got to accept there's going to be kids. Run a strimmer round the garden, put up some nice pictures, a couple of rugs and some cushions—'

'I know how to decorate a house,' said Jenna cutting in. 'I'm not stupid. But this one needs knocking down, not tarting up.'

'That's me told,' murmured Immi to herself.

'So,' said Jenna, 'I want Lee to go to Captain Fanshaw and get it sorted out, but he won't. And we've been told that if we refuse the quarter we go to the bottom of the waiting list again. I mean, where's the justice in that?' She glared at Immi, daring her to contradict.

'I know some of the quarters aren't exactly show houses,' ventured Immi. 'But they're a start.'

'Not the sort of start I want. I mean, I've seen Caro Brown's house and Maddy Fanshaw's and they're OK. Well, not what you'd pick for yourself, but at least they're nothing to be ashamed of. But ours... gah.'

'But they're officers' houses,' said Immi.

'What difference should that make?' she countered, angrily.

'Hel-*lo*,' said Immi, 'but have you seen the officers' mess? Silver candelabra, oil paintings on the wall, mahogany dining table – and look at this.' Immi waved her hand around to indicate Tommy's Bar. 'Fruit machines, laminate floor, plastic chairs. Officers are toffs and we're peasants.'

'Well, I'm not standing for it. I'm as good as them.'

'Please, Jenna,' said Lee. 'Please don't cause trouble. It won't be for ever and, as Immi said, it's a start. At least we get to live together. And the longer we're married, the more points we get, so the next time we move we'll qualify for a nicer house.'

'Oh yeah, and when do you think we'll be moving? The regiment's been here for years. I don't want to live in that shit-hole for years more.'

'Then live with your mother, because that's the alternative. Is that what you'd rather?'

'No. Lee, babe, I didn't mean that.'

'No, well, that's what it sounded like to me.'

There was a short embarrassed silence.

'Come on,' said Lee. 'We came here to have some fun, not talk about rubbish army housing.' He cocked an ear towards the other group in the bar as yet more laughter rang out. 'Chrissie and Jack have got the right idea; they're having a great time by the sound of things.'

'I suppose,' said Jenna, sulkily. She took a swig of her drink. 'But I ain't happy about that house, Lee. It's not fair and that's that. Just because you're a private doesn't mean you're less of a person than Captain Fanshaw.'

'Maybe we could have a bit of a party when we move in,' said Lee. 'Get our mates to come along and help us sort out the garden in exchange for a few bevvies. Hey, guys.' Lee raised his voice to get the attention of Jack's group. 'If I provided beers and some nosh how would you feel about coming over to mine one Saturday, to help bash my garden into shape?'

There was a general murmuring of assent, but with various conditions regarding the amount of beer and the quality of the scoff.

'Chrissie?' said Lee, noticing she'd remained silent.

'I do a lot of duty weekends at the med centre,' she said swiftly. 'And when I'm not on duty, I might be involved in sports matches. I don't get much free time.' She turned away towards the main group again.

Lee looked disappointed, a look that wasn't lost on Immi. 'Oh. That's a shame… it's just…' he said, half to himself.

'*Just* what, Lee?' said Immi, naughtily. 'You *just* want free medical cover, in case someone gets injured hacking through that jungle the army calls your garden.'

Lee shook his head. 'It's nothing. It's just I reckon, if Chrissie pitched up, then Jack and Doug and that lot would be sure to as well.'

'She's certainly popular,' agreed Immi, failing to hide a faint note of envy as she stared at Chrissie.

'She is that,' said Lee, following her gaze.

'Hmm,' said Jenna, her eyes narrowing slightly as she looked at Chrissie and then at Lee.

Chrissie glanced over her shoulder and saw Lee staring at her and her stomach did that lurch again, like it had when he'd stopped her falling down the railway embankment. And then she saw the expression on Jenna's face. Fuck – had Jenna guessed how she felt? Surely that just wasn't possible. Well, sod that, she was *not* going to fall for a married man, no way, and what's more, she wasn't having a married man, or his missus, get the wrong idea about her. In that instant she made her mind up: she'd go and see Major Rawlins, the medical officer, first thing in the morning and volunteer for Bastion.

Chapter Nine

Lee signed the documents listing the existing damage and faults with the quarter and the inventory of the items he and Jenna had been loaned as a get-you-in pack, and Major Milward handed over the keys.

'We'll be sending barracks services around to replace the shelves in the kitchen. I can't promise exactly when that'll be, but we'll give you a few days' notice so you can make arrangements to be here for the contractors.'

'I understand, sir, thank you.'

'And as I said, I know the carpets are shabby, but this quarter isn't scheduled to have new ones for another couple of years.'

Lee wondered how he was going to explain that to Jenna. It didn't help that as well as being orange, which Jenna had already clocked, they were generally skanky. But it was a substandard quarter, so their rent would reflect that, and they were lucky to get anything – or that's what the housing commandant had said. He wasn't sure that Jenna was going to agree, though. There were worrying patches of mould in the bathroom, the paint was marked and shabby throughout, the kitchen looked ancient and there was no double glazing. The place was going to be a mission to heat, but on the bright side, he and Jenna would both be out at work all day and at night they could snuggle together in bed. Maybe if he put it to Jenna like that she wouldn't go off on one. Maybe.

Major Milward expressed his hope that Lee would be happy in his new home and left. Jenna, waiting in her little Corsa on the road outside, almost barged him off the path in her haste to get in and see *exactly* what they'd been allocated.

'Wait,' said Lee, as he stopped her on the doorstep.

'Is it so bad you don't want me to see it?' said Jenna, suspiciously.

'No, hon.' Lee swept her into his arms. 'I just want to do this,' and he carried her inside.

'You daft bugger, Lee Perkins,' said Jenna, nuzzling his neck as she pushed the front door shut behind them. She kissed him on the cheek as he put her down, before she said, 'So what's the worst then? What's this house like?'

Lee pursed his lips. 'We-ell.'

'That bad?'

He quickly shook his head. 'No, not so rank. And it is a place of our own. And Major Milward said we could give it a lick of paint if we wanted.'

'So it's a dump.'

'No. And we can have Christmas here, together, in our first home,' offered Lee.

She gave him a hard stare, and pushed past him into the little sitting room. 'You are kidding me,' she said, looking around.

'It's not that bad. A nice rug—'

'Don't you "nice rug" me. This carpet is disgusting. What the hell happened there?' Jenna pointed to a large dark stain.

'The major said it was red wine.'

'Really?' It was obvious Jenna thought it was no such thing.

'They've been professionally cleaned, so whatever it *was*, it's just a stain *now*.'

'Hmmm.' But she was off into the tiny dining room, which got a sneer, and then through that, into the kitchen. She stood in front of the cooker, with its solid electric plates. 'Bloody hell. I can't cook on that!'

Which was news to Lee because, as far as he knew, Jenna couldn't cook on *anything*. Or at least that's what her mum had said. Lee looked at the electric oven – was it so bad? It was sparkling clean, whatever age it was, but Jenna's look of horror was unmistakable. 'We'll buy a microwave.'

But Jenna was moving on. She'd gone back into the hall and was heading up the stairs.

'So where's the third bedroom?' she asked Lee when he caught up with her.

'What do we need that for?' Lee was at an utter loss. A bedroom for them and one spare for anyone who might care to stay – what on earth would they do with a third?

'So where are all my clothes going to live?'

'Your *clothes*?'

'Well, they're not going to fit in there!' Jenna waved a hand at the two wardrobes in the main bedroom.

'Why not?' He could get his kit into half of one of those and still have room to spare. Jenna could have all the rest of the space and the other wardrobe.

Jenna just rolled her eyes and sighed. 'Lee, have you any idea about women's wardrobes?'

Lee shrugged, completely bewildered.

'Well, trust me, we need space.'

'What, a whole bedroom's worth?'

'A walk-in wardrobe's worth.'

Lee wondered for a second what planet Jenna was living

on. There was no way she'd had that in her mum's council house. His face must have reflected his thoughts.

'At the moment half my stuff is packed in boxes in my mum's loft. I thought when we got our own place I'd be able to get properly organised. I'm so fed up of never having any space just for me. I'm sick of making do.' She stopped and shook her head.

Lee felt a rush of sorrow. 'I'm sorry, babe,' he said. 'Maybe in the next place.'

'Yeah, well...' She opened the door to the bathroom and shut it again. 'I suppose I should be thankful we've an indoor toilet.' She turned away quickly from Lee, but not before he could see a tear glistening in her eye.

Jenna sat on the army issue sofa in the sitting room and stared at the stain on the carpet. Zoë had given her the day off, to move in and get straight, so she didn't have to rush. Lee, however, having completed the march-in, had had to go back to work, leaving Jenna to unpack the two suitcases she'd brought from home, make up their bed and put away the china and cutlery they'd been issued with by the army in their get-you-in pack. She sighed as she looked at the scruffy orange carpet, the drab, unlined curtains at the window that didn't quite go with the carpet – but then what would? – and the dreary magnolia paint on the walls.

Yup, it was a dump. She supposed she ought to be grateful to have a quarter; she wasn't the only girl on the council estate desperate to get away from living at home with her mum. Heck, she had mates with a couple of kids who still couldn't get a place of their own. But that didn't make this place any less scuzzy. She made up her mind – she might have been given a dump, but it didn't have to stay that way.

She'd make something of this place, make it habitable at the very least.

Revitalised, she went out to her little car and dragged in the two big suitcases which contained enough possessions to keep her going for a week or so. Next, she lugged into the house two bin bags full of bedding and towels, followed by her portable TV and DVD player, and finally, she brought in the box of hair care products that she had pinched over the months from Zoë's and which she used on her private clients. By lunchtime, her clothes filled both the wardrobes in the main bedroom, the bed was made up, her hairdressing stuff was arranged neatly in the spare bedroom on the chest of drawers and the TV was on in the sitting room, filling the house with banal daytime chatter.

Jenna looked around. It was still a dump, but at least now it was *her* dump. Her stomach rumbled and she glanced at her watch: lunchtime. She walked the hundred yards to the Spar to grab a sandwich, and while she was there, she also bought a notebook and pencil. Returning to the house she walked around it, eating her lunch and making notes as she went. By the time she'd finished, she had a plan. She decided not to tell Lee what she had in mind just yet; she'd need to get a few quotes from local workmen first.

The doorbell rang. Jenna wondered who it might be. When she opened it, she saw an unknown young woman and a small child on the doorstep.

'Hiya,' said the stranger. 'I'm Sharon and I live next door. And this,' she said as she stared fondly at the slightly grubby toddler, 'is Gary. I named him for Gary Barlow.'

Like I care, thought Jenna. But she had the sense not to voice her opinion. 'Hi,' she replied. 'Jenna.' She stuck her hand out and her new neighbour shook it.

'You got a kettle and everything?' Sharon asked.

Jenna nodded. 'All sorted, thank you.' She could tell Sharon was angling for a cuppa but Jenna still had stuff to do. And she looked at the kid with the mucky hands. Her house might be a dump, but it was a clean dump and it was going to stay that way. The last thing she wanted was some snotty kid making a bad situation worse.

'My husband's in C Company,' said Sharon.

'Mine's in B.'

'Do you think they'll know each other?'

'I really don't know.' I really don't care. But she smiled, as best she could. 'I'm sure we'll find out.' Jenna glanced pointedly at her watch. She wanted to get the ball rolling with her plan, and Sharon was holding her up.

'I know you from somewhere, don't I?' said Sharon, ignoring Jenna's hint.

'You might do. I work at Zoë's.'

'That's it. It's going to be well useful having you as a neighbour. You'll be able to cut Gary's hair for him.'

Huh, Sharon could think again – unless she was planning to pay the going rate. 'Yes, well, I mustn't keep you.' Jenna started to shut the door.

'You must come round to mine – have a coffee. Bring your kids, maybe.'

'No children.'

'Yet,' said Sharon archly.

'Ever,' said Jenna firmly. She pushed the door further shut. There was an ear-splitting scream. She looked down. Fuck, the brat's fingers were in the hinge. She flung the door wide as Sharon started screaming too, just to add to the bedlam and chaos. What was she screaming for? She wasn't hurt. Jenna checked out Gary's fingers; they looked a bit odd, a

102

bit wonky, but they were still all attached and there wasn't any blood.

'How could you?' screeched Sharon, grabbing Gary away from Jenna and throwing her an evil look as she did so.

'It wasn't my fault.'

'Why didn't you check?' Sharon was on her knees, cuddling a still shrieking Gary.

'How did I know he'd shove his fingers in the way?' retorted Jenna, angry at being blamed. She hadn't asked them to visit. 'It was an accident. I didn't mean it.' She did feel a twinge of guilt; the kid was obviously hurt, but how was it her fault?

But Sharon was now ignoring Jenna and trying to soothe her son. Another mother, passing with a couple of kids in tow, stopped.

'What's up, Shaz?'

'Jenna here slammed the door on little Gary's fingers,' snapped Sharon.

'No, I didn't. I shut the door and Gary's fingers got caught. I didn't *slam* it.'

The other woman looked from one to the other, taking in the situation. 'Here, let me look.' She too knelt down by Gary and gently had a look at his hand. 'The thing with babies' bones is, they're soft.' She rubbed Gary's head. 'Just a nasty shock, I think, and nothing broken.'

Sharon glared at Jenna. 'No thanks to you.'

'I'm sorry,' said Jenna, meaning it. 'I'm sorry Gary got hurt but I really didn't mean to do it. It was an accident.'

Sharon still looked angry, so Jenna gave up. And then she noticed just how much snot the lad had produced. Euw. No way was she *ever* going to have kids. Shit and piss at one end and snot at the other.

Still cradling the injured toddler, Sharon got to her feet and, ignoring Jenna, walked off, accompanied by her Samaritan friend. Jenna returned indoors, and this time she did slam the door.

Rubbish house and a rubbish neighbour. Could life get any worse?

Chapter Ten

'Can you come to my office for a moment?' said the MO.

Chrissie put aside the stack of soldiers' medical records that she had been refiling after morning sick parade and followed Major Rawlings along the corridor. He closed the door behind her and took his seat behind his desk.

Chrissie swallowed nervously. Uh-oh, what had she done?

'Take a seat, Summers.'

Chrissie perched on the edge of the chair to one side of the desk, feeling a little more relaxed. Soldiers about to be bollocked didn't get to sit down.

'I've been thinking about your request for a posting, Summers.'

For a fortnight? He'd been sitting on her application for a whole fortnight, while she'd been on edge, wondering if it would be rejected. Well, thanks a bunch, sir. It's just my life and career you've been messing with. Instead she said, as evenly as she could, 'Yes, sir.'

'And I've just finished reading the PXR for Exercise Autumn Armour.'

He'd lost her. 'PXR?'

'Post exercise report.'

'Oh, good.' She hadn't a clue what she was supposed to say to that. Did he want a prize for good work? And his point was...?

'I was particularly interested in how the medical team performed.'

Oh, well, that was that, then. Given how she'd been useless, when confronted with a hideously traumatic injury (and it had only been a *fake* one, not even the *real* thing), there was no way anyone was going to want her on the front line. More of a liability than anything else. She waited for the bad news.

'Corporal Johns spoke highly of you.'

'Phil did? Sorry, sir, Corporal Johns did?' Chrissie couldn't keep her stunned surprise out of her voice. She didn't think her immediate superior rated her very much at all – she knew he'd always been nice to her, but that was just because he was a nice guy. Even he had been less than impressed when she'd honked over Lee.

Major Rawlings smiled. 'Why the surprise?'

'Oh, no reason.' If it wasn't in the PXR, then she wasn't going to blow it now, by telling him. 'So does that mean you're going to recommend me for a posting?'

Her boss nodded. 'But not just yet.'

'Oh.'

'I thought after Christmas, so you can spend the holiday with your folks and then we'll think about it in the new year.'

'That's very thoughtful of you, sir, but I don't have any family.'

'What, no one?'

Chrissie shook her head. 'Not that I know of. My father is an American airman who disappeared off the scene before I was born – I don't even know his name, as it doesn't appear on my birth certificate, and my mother was an only, like me, and she's dead. And as for grandparents... I haven't a clue.'

Major Rawlings shook his head. 'I'm sorry, Summers. I had no idea.'

'No reason why you should, is there, sir? It isn't tattooed on my forehead. But it does mean that Christmas and stuff like that doesn't play a big part in my life.'

'I can see that. Even so, regardless of your personal circumstances, I'll need a replacement for you. Corporal Johns is already out there, so I'm short-staffed as it is, and the Manning Office has informed me that there is a shortage of fully trained combat medical techs. The ones they've got have already been earmarked to go straight to Bastion. Until they can post someone in to replace you, I'm afraid I can't release you.'

'But I will be allowed to go.'

The MO nodded. 'In due course.'

'I'll have to be patient then, won't I, sir?'

'Let's hope it's not for too long.'

You and me both, mate. On the bright side, Lee had finally given up texting her, so that was one less thing to worry about. Immi had passed her BFT, so that was another. All in all, if she got this posting, life was looking pretty good again.

Seb Fanshaw sat on a chair in the adjutant's office.

'And it's got to be someone from my platoon?' he said.

Andy Bailey, the battalion's adjutant and thus Lieutenant Colonel Notley's right-hand man, leaned forwards across his desk. 'That's what the commanding officer said. Of course, if you want to go and argue the toss with him...'

'No, no, of course not.'

'Thought not. But 2 Herts is having a nightmare of a tour; they've lost fifteen men so far, killed and wounded, and they've only been there three weeks. They can't expect to operate effectively unless they're brought up to strength. The

TA can provide some of the replacements immediately, on a temporary basis, but we've got to find the others for permanent deployment in the new year. And the CO said we can't ask for volunteers to step forward as battle casualty replacements. He knows the ones who are likely to do it and they may not be the most appropriate candidates.'

Seb nodded. 'It's just it's a tough call. Not made any easier by the fact I haven't had a chance to really get to know all my men yet.'

'That won't wash with the CO. You've been here well over a month; he'll just want to know what you've been doing.'

Seb sighed. 'I'm on the case,' he said defensively.

'I'm sure you are.'

'But the first couple of weeks was that exercise. With everyone cammed up to the eyeballs, putting names to faces was fucking hard.'

'You'd better come up with a better excuse than that, if you don't want the CO to read you your fortune. It's all very well being the rowing hero, Seb, but you're not at university now, and just spending your long vac being a soldier. This is the day job as well, now.'

Seb put his hands up. 'I know, I know, and forget what I said. I'll find you a likely candidate. Promise.'

He picked his beret off the desk and returned to his own company lines and his office. Dispiritedly he sat down behind his desk and wondered how to start making the choice. As if he didn't have enough on his plate. Maddy seemed to be in a permanent grump, Nate never seemed to stop crying, his rowing training wasn't going well and now this. He held in his hands the fate of one of his soldiers, and the weight of responsibility was heavy. But this was one of the things he'd trained for; this was why he was an officer, why he got paid more than a soldier – making tough decisions came with his job description.

He rolled his chair across the floor to the noticeboard and unpinned his copy of the nominal roll. So, who should go? He flicked over the first page, which listed the NCOs, and turned to the second sheet of blue copier paper. He ran his finger down the list of twenty or so names. Not the guys with kids, he thought. And maybe not the married ones. No, that was unfair; the unmarried ones still had girlfriends, mothers, sisters...

There was only one fair way to do this. He shut his eyes and jabbed his finger at the paper. He opened his eyes again. Perkins. Perkins would be going to Afghanistan. Seb thought about it and realised that, in fact, this was the perfect choice; Perkins was one of the few guys in the battalion, and probably the only guy in the platoon, who had never done a tour there. If he really had the potential to get promoted, it was essential he did a tour there first; there was no way he could command respect from other soldiers who had been out there several times if he had no actual combat experience himself. Perkins it was, then.

It was just Mrs Perkins that niggled Seb – how was she going to take the news, and what spanners would she chuck into the works, once she'd heard it?

'You're going where?' shrieked Immi. She put down her knife and fork, pushed her lunch away from her and glared at Chrissie.

'Bastion.'

'Why?'

'Because I'm a combat medic. Because I volunteered.'

Immi shook her head in disbelief. 'You did what?

Volunteered? For Bastion? But it's dangerous, you stupid moo. Rule one of being in the army is never, *ever* volunteer for anything. If you learned nothing else at basic training, surely you learned that. And you not only volunteered, but you volunteered for Bastion, and it's dangerous out there. And hot in the summer, freezing in the winter, and did I mention it's dangerous? Oh, and it's dangerous, fucking dangerous.'

Chrissie put her hands up. 'I know, I know, but I won't be on the front line. Well, not much.'

'Not *much*!' Immi's voice rose to a bat-squeak. 'You shouldn't want to go near the front line *at all*.'

'Yes, I know. Let me guess, it's dangerous. But I'm a soldier.'

'You're a *woman*!'

'And?' Chrissie glared at Immi. She'd thought she would be glad for her, not reacting like this. 'I want to help people, make them better.'

'Well, you won't be doing that with a bullet in you.'

'Who says I'll get shot?'

'People do out there. That's what happens – or worse. What the fuck is wrong with the cushy job you've got here?'

Nothing, but it wasn't enough. She needed to push herself, test herself, and Afghanistan mightn't be a holiday destination but it was abroad. She'd never been abroad, hell, she'd never even been in a plane. And in a year or so, Afghan wouldn't be an option. And not long after Afghan came off the list of possible postings so would Germany. What then – join the army and see Colchester and Catterick and maybe Salisbury Plain…?

'It's just something I want to do.'

Immi's eyebrows shot up. 'Like you're so good with trauma. I remember what you told me happened on that exercise.'

'That was a one-off.'

Immi snorted. 'Says you, but you haven't been able to put the theory to the test since, have you? Giving people anti-tetanus jabs and stitching up the odd cut is hardly dealing with T1 casualties, now, is it? And what happens if you're wrong?'

'I'm not.'

Immi softened. 'Look, hon, I don't want to see you upset or hurt. It's awful out there. You'll have to deal with dreadful stuff, soldiers blown to bits, people dying, ruined lives. And the conditions are rank and...' Immi's eyes filled with tears.

Chrissie took her friend's hand. 'It's my job,' she said gently. 'It's what I signed up to do. And the war is going to go on whether I'm there or not, and the soldiers, guys like Baz or Lee or your...' She couldn't remember the name of Immi's latest.

'Tom,' supplied Immi, helpfully.

'Your Tom, are still going to get hurt. So if I can do something, *anything*, to stop just one of them ending up in a wheelchair, or dead, then I want to.'

'I suppose,' said Immi. She sighed. 'So when are you going?'

Chrissie shrugged. 'Dunno. When they can replace me.'

'No one can replace you,' said Immi. 'And that's the truth.'

Nate's colic was finally on the wane and he sometimes went a couple of hours without wailing, so Maddy was making the most of this window of peace and quiet to whizz to the supermarket and get a few essentials. She pushed his buggy past the shelves and freezer units, hoping inspiration would strike about what she could feed Seb for supper. Obviously, if he was going to be rowing over the weekend – and when wasn't he? – it had to be something laden with carbs and calories. Bangers, mash and beans, she wondered. No, they'd

111

had that only last week. She peered at a chiller cabinet full of ready meals, lost in thought, and hoping for a brainwave.

'Hiya, Maddy.'

She spun round. 'Jenna. Lovely to see you.'

'Your hair's still looking good,' said Jenna.

'Isn't it? And have you moved into your quarter yet?'

'Yesterday.'

'Lovely.'

Jenna's face darkened. 'Not really. It's a dump.'

'Oh. I'm sorry.' Maddy knew full well that army quarters weren't fantastic, but dump was a bit harsh, wasn't it?

'Lee says I'm making a fuss and it's not too bad, but he's used to living in trenches and all.'

'Well, they don't object to you making the odd improvement – a coat of paint a nice rug or two—'

Jenna held her hand up to stop Maddy. 'Don't you start. Sorry, but if one more person tells me that a few scatter cushions will make all the difference...'

'Oh.'

'But I'm going to make improvements all right. I've got plans. And the place might be a dump, but I still reckon I can make something of it.'

'Really?'

'Yeah. If I rip the bath out of the bathroom and put a shower in instead, I can fit a backwash unit and set up in hairdressing.'

'But you can't do that!' Maddy was stunned.

'What's to stop me?'

'Well... there's regulations.'

'Oh yeah? But we pay rent. It's my house now.'

'I don't think the army'll see it like that.'

'Like I care.'

Maddy was about to say, 'Well, you should,' when she stopped. This wasn't her business. She wasn't to interfere, Seb had told her straight, and he'd be livid if he found out she'd offered advice to a soldier's wife again. There was no way she was going to do anything that Seb might think was out of line for the platoon commander's wife. She couldn't face another argument. She was still not getting enough sleep, although Nate was much better than he had been, and Seb was working all hours, so they were both knackered. If they started arguing, God only knew where it would end. So, instead, Maddy said, 'Good luck.'

'Cheers. And when it's done, you can be my first customer. I owe you that much, at least. On the house.' She smiled at Maddy.

'Great, thanks.' Well, that was something. Then she had a rethink. Of course she wasn't going to get a free hairdo. There was no way the army was going to let Jenna carry out her plans. Ever.

Seb walked back from Battalion HQ to his office. The adjutant had approved his selection of Private Perkins; they'd checked with Manning and Records and, as far as the army's main human resources office was concerned, there was nothing in Perkins' records to prevent him from going. So this was it: this was the moment when he would have to break the news. No matter that the poor bugger, after months of waiting for a quarter, had finally got one and had just moved in with his new bride, he was the one who was going. The phrase, 'If you can't take a joke you shouldn't have joined,' jostled to the front of Seb's brain. Only this wasn't much of a joke.

He shouldered open the swing door to the company offices

and pulled his beret off his head. He passed one of the clerks as he made his way to his office and asked him to send Perkins to see him. Might as well get this over and done with.

'You sent for me, boss.'

Seb looked up and saw Perkins peering round the door. 'Come in, take a seat. I've got some news. There's no easy way to tell you.'

Perkins' face went white as he staggered a little shakily to the chair. 'It's not me mam, is it?'

'Your mother? Good Lord, no. God, sorry, I didn't mean to give you a scare like that.'

'Oh, as long as it isn't her, then that's OK.'

'No, this is just army business. I'm warning you for posting.'

'Posting? But I've only just got here. I've only just got me quarter, like.'

'I know but you're needed as a battlefield casualty replacement and you're going to be temporarily transferred to 2 Herts.' Seb studied Lee's face. Was he pleased, apprehensive or what? Soldiers might join the army knowing the job description would probably involve combat, but not everyone relished the prospect, when it became a reality. 'So how do you feel about it?'

'Don't rightly know, sir. It's all a bit left field. I don't suppose the wife's going to be too happy.'

'I'm afraid that's the penalty they pay for marrying a soldier.'

'I think she already thinks there have been too many penalties and not enough perks,' said Lee drily. 'When am I likely to go?'

'You'll be sent on some pre-ops training. You'll have to

have medicals, jabs, that sort of stuff. If you haven't made a will, then you should, especially now you're a married man.'

'OK, boss, I get the picture.'

'Sorry, Perkins, but it's best you face up to the realities.'

Lee stayed silent.

'Any questions?'

'Yeah, you still haven't told me when I'm off.'

'Probably after Christmas. You're also entitled to some pre-ops leave; take Mrs Perkins away somewhere nice, maybe.'

'Thank you for the advice, sir. Is that all?'

'Seems like quite a lot to me, Perkins.'

He stood up to go, then turned. 'Just one thing, sir.'

'Yes?'

'Why me? I mean, I'm not being difficult but you know, with a new wife and all and some of the guys are single...'

'You're the only one in the platoon who's not done a tour.' Seb didn't tell him it was also the luck of the draw.

'Fair enough, sir. I think the wife'll be more understanding if that's the reason.'

Seb hoped for Perkins' sake she was. Somehow, from what he'd read, and heard on the grapevine, he doubted it.

Chapter Eleven

After duties that evening, Lee walked slowly back to his quarter, wondering how on earth he was going to break it to Jenna that he was off to Afghanistan in a few weeks' time for at least three months, maybe longer. He had really mixed feelings about it, but he didn't think Jenna would see anything but the downside of it all; that they'd only been married a few months, the army had dragged its heels over giving them a quarter, and now they had they were being split up again. How were they supposed to make a go of married life with that sort of shit going on? She wouldn't listen to what he said about it being important that he did an operational tour if he wanted promotion. He couldn't expect her to understand that – she was a hairdresser not a soldier. Thank God she had a job, he thought. At least that would give her a focus each day – something to think about, other than what he might be getting up to and what he might have to face.

He'd already decided to play down that he was quite excited about the prospect of going out there. Combat – that was what he'd been trained for, that was what he'd joined the army to do; but all the same, now the reality of actually fighting was right there, it was a bit of a facer. He knew it wouldn't be the same as playing soldiers on the DCCT range or having a shoot-out on Call of Duty – there was no reset button out in Afghan, no extra lives to be had at the click of a mouse button. And it didn't help matters that 2 Herts had had so many casualties so far. It made you wonder, he thought, whether they were unlucky or careless. Christ, he hoped it was the former. He really didn't relish being in a multiple with some moron for a boss, who had no idea about tactics or risk.

He walked past the turning to the bigger, swankier officers' quarters with the cherry trees on the lawns that fronted the houses and with the Land Rover Discoveries, the Passat estates and the nippy Minis parked in the drives, and continued along the main drag through the garrison to the smaller, shabbier houses, where the soldiers lived, the ones with the Corsas and Mondeos outside.

How, Lee wondered, had Jenna ever thought they would get a house on Omdurman Avenue? But if she'd seriously thought she was going to live in a gaff like Captain Fanshaw's, no wonder she'd been disappointed when she saw their final allocation. She'd get used to it – it wasn't so bad, and it would be better when she'd made friends with the other wives.

He arrived at his house. There was a white van parked outside. What was going on? He was just about to put the key in the latch when a bloke in brown overalls barrelled out of the door, almost knocking Lee down.

'Sorry, guv, didn't see you there,' was all he said, before he jumped into his vehicle and sped away.

'Jenna,' called Lee as he went inside.

'Hi, babes,' she said, coming down the stairs.

'Who was that?' Lee pulled his beret off his head and dumped his combat jacket over the banisters. Jenna picked them both up and hung them on the hooks behind the front door.

'Just the plumber,' said Jenna.

'What's wrong? The housing commandant didn't tell me there was a problem. Well, except for those shelves.'

'Oh, it's nothing, just routine maintenance. Just as well I was in, really,' she said lightly.

'Yeah.' But he wasn't really listening. He was still wondering how to break the news to her. 'Look, Jenna, how about we have a cuppa?'

Jenna gave him a hard stare. 'Something up?'

'Sort of.'

'If it's about that kid yesterday, it wasn't my fault.'

'Kid?'

'Oh, it was nothing. A woman and a toddler came round and the kid got its fingers in the way when I shut the door. I said sorry.'

Lee shook his head. What was she on about? 'No, it's nothing like that.' He moved into the kitchen and filled the kettle. 'It's sort of bad news.'

'Not your mum?'

Lee shook his head. 'No, me mam's fine.' He busied himself getting a couple of mugs out of the cupboard.

'Then what is it? Spit it out.'

'I'm being posted.'

'Posted?' Jenna's voice reflected her opinion – she was *not* happy. 'They can't fucking post you. We've only just got a house. They can't expect us to move out when we've only just moved in.'

Lee put a hand on her arm. 'You can stop here – we're not going to have to move house. I'm going to Afghan.'

'Afghan,' Jenna whispered.

'Yeah. The lot out there – 2 Herts – are having a hard time; you've seen the news.'

Jenna nodded.

'Well, they need a few extra guys to make up the numbers, like. And I'm the one. I'm going.'

The kettle boiled and clicked off, but they both ignored it.

'Why you?'

'I wasn't with 1 Herts when they did their last tour. I'm one of the few guys who's not been, which makes it my turn.'

'But we've only just got married.'

'That's not the army's fault.'

'I won't let you go.'

'Jenna, love, it's me job.'

She turned away from him and got the tea bags, chucking one into each mug, then she poured on the water. Suddenly she slammed around. 'Why aren't you fighting this, Lee? Why aren't you telling them to go and pick someone else?' She stared at him. She held his gaze for a few seconds, then she said, 'You want to go, don't you?'

'Jenna, I said it before, it's me job. It's what I do.'

'You'd rather fight the Taliban than live with me. That's it, isn't it?' Her voice wobbled.

'Don't be daft.' He took her in his arms and gave her a cuddle. 'And I'm not going tomorrow.'

'When, then?'

'After Christmas, they reckon.'

The fight seemed to go out of Jenna. 'I suppose we've got a bit of time together before you go. And Christmas.'

'That's the spirit, lass. We'll get me mam down from Newcastle, we'll get your mam and the rest of your family over, and we'll have a right good time.'

'I suppose.'

Lee gave her a kiss. 'Now, let's get that brew sorted.'

*

'What's up, Seb?' asked Maddy, when Seb finally came through the door at gone seven. He looked careworn.

He gave her a kiss on the cheek as he shed his combat jacket and beret. 'Same old, same old. How's Nate?'

'Same old, same old,' retorted Maddy.

'So is he in bed?'

Maddy pointed at the clock on the hall wall. 'What do you think? Gin?' Even if Seb didn't want one, she was gagging for a drink.

'Please. I am going to have to learn to escape from the office earlier, if I want to see him before we pack him off to boarding school.'

Maddy thought about suggesting he gave up rowing at the weekends, but knew she'd be on a hiding to nothing there. Sometimes, she thought crossly, as she sloshed gin into two glasses, she might just as well be a single mum. And if she was she wouldn't have to cope with all the army crap on top of everything else. She followed the gin with tonic and sighed. She was being unfair – again. But she turned to Seb, handed him his drink with a smile, and said, 'Well, that's something to hope for.'

They went into the sitting room, cleared of Nate's toys and tidied ready for Seb's return, and snuggled on the sofa while they both sipped their drinks.

'Something smells good,' said Seb.

'Chicken in barbecue sauce and mash.'

'Hope there's lots. I'm starving.'

When wasn't he? 'Heaps.'

Seb lapsed into silence and looked glum again.

'Come on, Seb, you look like you've got the world on your shoulders.'

He sighed. 'Not really, just I had to make a tough decision today.'

Maddy waited from him to continue, but the silence stretched on. Finally she said, 'Is it a state secret, or can you tell me?'

'No, it's not a secret, and I expect you'll find out soon enough – the patch grapevine being what it is. It's your mate Jenna Perkins' husband.'

'She's not my mate,' said Maddy swiftly. 'Just because she did my hair doesn't mean we're best friends.'

Seb gave her a look which seemed to imply he didn't quite believe her, but Maddy ignored it. Least said, soonest mended and all that crap.

'Anyway,' continued Maddy, 'what about him?'

Seb told her what he'd done.

'Bugger,' said Maddy quietly. 'That's not going to go down well. Why him?'

Seb told her.

'Even so – they've only just started married life.'

'Shit happens, Maddy.'

'Jenna isn't going to like it.'

'But it isn't up to her, is it?'

No, thought Maddy. Wives just don't enter into the army equation *at all*.

'Anyway,' said Seb, 'I've got a letter for you.'

'Me?'

'Think it's an invite.' He fished in a pocket in his combat jacket and pulled out a cream envelope. 'Here you are.'

Maddy took it and ripped it open. She scanned the contents.

'And?' said Seb.

Maddy sighed. 'Susie wants us to go round to hers for supper.' She turned to Seb. 'I suppose we've got to go, haven't we?'

Seb nodded. 'When?'

'A week Saturday. Whoopee.'

October morphed into November, Christmas trees began to appear in shop window displays in the local town, festive songs were back on radio station playlists, the weather took a turn for the worse and the annual call for volunteers to be on duty over the impending holiday was met with the same annual silence. Everyone knew that any soldier who misbehaved over the next few weeks would get awarded extra duties, which would be scheduled into the roster for the crucial period, thus neatly sparing anyone else the bother. And, consequently, the RSM had his eagle eye open to nab anyone who so much as breathed out of turn.

It was Immi who first fell foul of the RSM. It was one of those ridiculously balmy late autumn days of blue sky, full sun and no wind. The sort of day that, in spring, makes everyone think that summer is just around the corner and, at the end of the year, makes everyone rush out in shirtsleeves for one last chance to grab some rays before wanting to hibernate for months. Immi had sneaked out of the back of Battalion HQ for a crafty ciggy and was leaning against the wall of the office block, eyes shut, relishing the sun on her face.

She was brought back into reality with hot breath on her face and a voice yelling at full blast, 'Whatthehelldoyouthink you'redoingyouhorriblesoldier?'

Aghast, she snapped open her eyes and stood up straight; she knew that voice. And there was the RSM, his puce, angry face inches from hers, his piercing eyes screwed up in rage.

'Sir?' squeaked Immi, dropping her fag on the ground in shock.

'Pick that up,' he screamed.

She did.

'I'll have you for littering and being improperly dressed,' he hollered, his face still uncomfortably close to hers, his pace stick now being jabbed into the ground.

'Sir?'

'What do you think you're doing, outside, without your beret on?'

'Having a smoke,' said Immi, before she could stop herself.

'Are you being insubordinate? I can *see* you're having a smoke.'

'Sorry, sir.' Immi was at a loss what to say. Tell the truth – she was doomed. Say nothing – she knew it would be even worse.

'Dispose of that,' the RSM jabbed at the nearly burnt-out cigarette, 'and report to my office in five minutes, in the correct uniform.' He stormed off.

Immi sagged. Jeez, just her luck. She took a last, deep drag on her ciggie, resisted the urge to light another one to steady her nerves, and returned to the office. Feeling wobbly, she grabbed her beret and made her way to the RSM's lair at the end of the corridor.

Timidly, sick with nerves, she knocked on his door.

'Enter.'

She did, marched in front of his desk and marked time, till he told her to halt. She hoped he couldn't see that her legs were trembling as she stood rigidly to attention.

'Cooper, you're a shambles.'

'Yes, sir,' she answered, although his accusation made her livid. She always looked immaculate in uniform.

'Outside, headdress off, lounging against a wall, smoking.'

OK, she'd been on NAAFI break so smoking was allowed,

but she was guilty of lounging. And she hadn't been wearing her beret. But he was still well unfair.

'Yes, sir.'

'I can put you on a charge and your platoon commander will make a decision as to your punishment, or you can accept mine.'

Immi knew her military law. The worst she could expect was seven days' restriction of privileges, or possibly an admonition from Lieutenant Bates, whereas the RSM would award her extra duties – and she knew what that meant. With bravado belied by her shaking knees, she said, 'I think I'd rather go in front of Sir Bates, sir.'

The RSM leaned across his desk. 'Really. So I prepare the charge sheet and I say you told me to "fuck off". That's gross insubordination, whichever way you look at it. And no extenuating circumstances. Sir Bates can't deal with that, can he? So then you'd be on OC's orders and it'd be an entry on your regimental conduct sheet, and that wouldn't be good for your promotion prospects, now, would it?'

Immi swallowed. 'But I didn't say that, did I, sir?'

The RSM raised his eyebrows. 'Got a witness?'

She was beaten. She knew where this was going. 'How many extras, sir?'

'Let's be fair. Let's call it four.'

'Thank you, sir, very fair.' Immi blinked. She was not going to cry in front of this bastard.

'So you're volunteering to be duty clerk from the twenty-third of December to the twenty-seventh. Dismissed.'

Struggling to control her tears at the absolute sodding unfairness of it all, Immi returned to her desk.

Chapter Twelve

Despite the fact that, for Immi, Christmas was effectively ruined, she had plenty of events prior to the actual holiday at which she wanted to look good and the first of these was Remembrance Sunday. While it could hardly be classed as a social occasion, just about every soldier in the garrison would be present for the annual parade which was held in the huge sports hall. And if she was going to be there with around the best part of one thousand soldiers it stood to reason she needed to look her best, so she booked an appointment with Jenna. Anyway, given the timing, her roots should last for most of the rest of the party season and she could have them touched up over what remained of the Christmas break, ready for the New Year, and unless the odds were *totally* stacked against her, she wouldn't be on duty for that.

As Jenna started painting her hair with the gloopy dye mixture, Immi asked her about her quarter.

'It's pretty minging,' Jenna admitted, 'but Lee says that once he starts getting promoted, we can expect something better. On the bright side,' she added, leaning into Immi and lowering her voice, 'I reckon I'll be able to run a nice little business from it.'

'But you can't do that – there's regulations.'

Jenna stopped slathering dye into Immi's hair. 'Don't you start. Lee and I pay rent, it's our house, we can do as we like. Especially if my customers don't go bleating to the authorities.' She stared at Immi in the mirror. 'Anyway, I'll be able to do your roots there for half what it costs here.'

Which Immi found quite tempting. Not that she minded paying to have her hair look good, but no one in their right mind would pass up a bargain.

'So will you work here still?'

'I think I might have to.' She started painting the dye on Immi's roots again. 'Dunno how many clients I can take with me. I mean, I expect my regulars to follow me.' She gave Immi another significant look. 'I've already had a couple of plumbers in, to give me quotes for installing a backwash unit in the bathroom.'

Immi couldn't keep a look of utter bewilderment off her face. 'But what if the battalion gets posted? I mean, you might have to move at any time, and it'll cost a fortune to put it back how it was.'

'Pah. Move? Why would the army want to do that to us? It'll just be like a game of musical chairs. If they move 1 Herts out, someone else'll just have to be moved in here, so that'd be bonkers, wouldn't it? Anyway, as soon as I've made a decent wedge, I'm going to open my own salon proper.'

'But what about Zoë's? I mean, if you're in competition…'

'What about this place? Honestly, I mean, look at it. Who the fuck still thinks that wood-panel effect wallpaper is stylish?'

Immi looked around the salon. Maybe it was pretty dated, but the quality of the styling was good, which was what counted.

'A bit of competition would shake this place up no end,' continued Jenna. 'Just because she's got a captive market, Zoë has stopped caring. Well, I'm about to change all that.'

Immi didn't doubt that Jenna would, but she had a horrible feeling that it mightn't end well, for neither Jenna nor Zoë. She changed the subject. 'What are you and Lee doing for Christmas? It must be quite exciting having the first one in your own house.'

'We've got Lee's mum coming down.'

It was obvious from the look on Jenna's face that she wasn't wildly enthusiastic about this.

'Problem?'

'She doesn't like me – doesn't approve.'

'That's tricky.'

'It's 'cos Lee is an only. He could have married Pippa Middleton and she'd have still had an issue, the mean old cow.'

'That's going to make Christmas interesting.'

'It's going to be a 'mare. I'd have me mum over to give me a bit of support but what with her, Pete, Shona and the twins there's no way we could fit them in, not for a sit-down meal, so Christmas Day it'll be me, Sonia and Lee, God help me. Of course, we'll see my family Christmas Eve. We'll pop over to take pressies and have a drink. Anyway, nuff about my plans, what are you doing?'

'I got spammed for extras. The RSM caught me smoking and had a go at me. It was extras, or go on a charge.'

'The bastard.'

Immi nodded.

Jenna finished touching up Immi's roots and began peeling off her plastic gloves. 'So, I need to leave this to develop for twenty minutes. Can I get you a magazine, or a tea, or anything?'

Immi opted for the latest copy of *Hello!* and a tea, and settled back to relax, while the dye got busy and worked its magic.

She was engrossed in an article about Kerry Katona when Jenna came back and took her to the basins to get her hair shampooed.

'I was thinking,' said Jenna, as she began to rinse the colour out of Jenna's hair. 'With you stuck here too, how about you coming over to ours? I mean, we can't manage another five but one person... well, I don't like the thought of you being stuck in barracks on your own. That'd be minging, and anyway, it'd be nice to have a mate to have a laugh with – I won't be getting any with Sonia. I know you're on duty, but you'd still be on the base. Would you be allowed?'

'God, Jenna, that's sweet of you. I'll have to ask the chief clerk but I can't see anything really urgent happening on Christmas Day and, as long as all the other duty staff know where to find me and I've got my mobile switched on, there shouldn't be a problem. I'll get back to you.'

'You do that. It'd be great to have you there. If Lee's mum starts kicking off, it'd be nice to have someone on my side.'

'Oh fuck,' said Immi as a thought struck her.

'What's up? The water's not too hot, is it? I didn't get shampoo in your eyes?'

'No, nothing like that. It's just...' This was tricky. How could she ask if her mate Chrissie could come along? Christmas dinner was a pretty big deal and asking if someone who was almost a complete stranger could join in was huge. Especially when Jenna had already said space was tight.

'Come on,' said Jenna, 'spit it out.'

'It's my mate Chrissie.'

'What about her?'

'She's an orphan.'

'She's a *what*? You're kidding me.'

Immi shook her head.

'Straight up? Really? No mum or dad?'

Immi didn't say *obviously, that's the definition of an orphan.* 'Not a soul in the world.'

'Bugger me. What, not even a brother or a sister?' Jenna stopped lathering Immi's hair and began to rinse the shampoo out.

'No one. And with me on duty, we were going to make the best of a crap situation together.'

'I know this Chrissie, don't I? Coloured girl, yes? The one who was having a right laugh down at Tommy's, the day Lee and I got our quarter?'

Immi nodded. And didn't add, *the one you caught Lee staring at more than he should have.*

'Yeah, I remember her,' said Jenna thoughtfully. Immi didn't ask what it was that she remembered. There was a pause then, 'Why not bring her along too? The more the merrier. Mind you,' she added as she switched off the water, 'I can't guarantee how the food will be. I've never done nothing like cook a turkey before.' She slopped on a palmful of conditioner and began to massage it into Immi's scalp.

Immi felt herself relax as Jenna's fingers worked the lotion deep into her hair. 'Chrissie can cook. Or at least she says she can,' said Immi. 'I bet, in return for a proper Christmas blow-out, she'd give you a hand.'

Jenna's hands stilled. 'Immi, you're a fucking genius and I love you. You get Chrissie to say yes to helping and I'll provide you with your bodyweight in vodka, because if I've got Chrissie to help, I might just be able to impress Lee's mum for once! Make her think I'm not a complete dead loss.'

'Jen, I'm sure she doesn't.'

'Wait till you meet her. In the meantime, we have a plan.'

*

129

'So what do you think?' said Immi. 'Isn't it the best solution you've ever heard?' She bounced up and down on her bed in their barrack room.

But Chrissie wondered how she could break it to her friend that it was far from wonderful – in fact, it was terrible. She still felt guilty about the way she'd treated Lee, and then there was her awful suspicion that Jenna had thought that Lee fancied her. Of course it was bollocks, of course he didn't, but she still remembered that look on Jenna's face. If Jenna thought that, then spending a whole day with her and Lee was hardly going to be a picnic. But what excuse could she possibly use not to take up the invitation? She wasn't even rostered to be on duty; she was going to be stuck in barracks because she had nowhere else to go, so why on earth *wouldn't* she want to take up the offer?

'I don't know,' she protested. 'I hardly know them. They don't want a stranger hanging about on Christmas Day.'

'I want you there, babe, and anyway, you're not a stranger. They've met you a couple of times. We'll have a blast, and I promised Jenna you know all about cooking and everything. She's relying on you to be there, 'cos she's never cooked a turkey before.'

'I'm not *that* great in the kitchen. I'm called Chrissie, not Delia.'

'I think you'll be a whole heap better than Jenna. Does she look like the domesticated type to you?'

Chrissie thought about Jenna's nails, hair extensions and false eyelashes for a nanosecond and decided that Immi probably had a point. But whether or not Jenna could cook, it didn't have any bearing on whether she could face spending pretty much a whole day with the pair of them. And if she admitted to Immi the real reason, Immi would probably wet herself laughing. Which was worse – spending Christmas with the Perkinses, or telling Immi she suspected that Jenna thought Lee fancied her?

'Oh, come on, Chrissie. What's the alternative – us and a bunch of deadbeats in the cookhouse? The duty officer trying to cheer us all up with a few choruses of "We Three Kings"? At least this way we get to slob out, watch some TV, and pretend we're not having a crap time. And if you don't say yes, then I can't, either, because I couldn't bear the thought of you being on your own.'

Oh great, the guilt card, thought Chrissie. How could she turn this offer down now, without looking a total cow? 'Can I think about it?'

Immi looked at her, bemused. 'Why? What is there to think about?'

'I hardly know them, Ims. A few drinks down Tommy's don't make me and Jenna bosom buddies.'

Immi's forehead creased. 'Don't you like her?'

*No, I don't think she likes m*e, but she couldn't say that. 'Immi, I don't know her well enough to like or dislike her.'

'Then this is the ideal opportunity to get to know her better. I'm sure if you spend some time with her, you'll see how great she is.'

Chrissie considered her options – and there weren't any. And perhaps she was wrong about Jenna's suspicions. In fact, she was sure she was. Lee, fancy her? Of course he didn't, not when he had Jenna. 'OK, cool,' she said. 'Tell Jenna she's really kind. And if she wants some advice about the turkey, I'll be happy to help. Just one thing, though.'

'Yes?' said Immi.

'You've got to promise me not to mention to anyone that I might be off to Afghan soon. I don't want to put a

131

downer on the day and stuff like that always does. I know I volunteered and I'm happy to be going, but that's not the point.'

'If that's what you want, babe, that's what you can have.' Immi bounced across the room and gave her best mate a hug. 'Ooh, Chrissie, I was so pissed off about not being able to go home, but now I think we're going to have so much fun.'

Chrissie raised a smile for her friend.

'Won't we just.'

Jenna was in the kitchen heating up a couple of ready meals when Lee got back from a long run.

'Hiya,' she called from the kitchen. 'How was the run?'

'Knackering.' He appeared in the kitchen doorway, red and sweating.

'Get yourself showered, Lee Perkins. When you've done that, I've got some good news.'

'Tell me now, lass.'

'Not till you're decent.'

Lee tramped upstairs, stripped and then threw himself under the shower nozzle suspended over the bath, once again wondering why the army didn't join the twenty-first century and bung proper cubicles in their quarters. He hauled on a pair of clean trackie bottoms, a T-shirt and a hoodie, before thundering downstairs again.

Jenna was just dishing up two reheated chicken jalfrezis and rice and was opening a packet of ready-cooked poppadums.

'So, what's the good news?' asked Lee, as he pulled a chair out from the kitchen table and plonked down on it.

Jenna pushed his plate across the table to him. 'We're going to have a bit of a party here at Christmas.'

Lee forked up some curry. 'Really?' he asked, before shovelling the food in.

'Yeah. We've got Immi and Chrissie coming over. We'll have a right good laugh.'

'That'll be nice,' he said, slightly indistinctly through a mouthful of food. 'But I thought you said we didn't have room for visitors. I mean, why those two, if your family can't come here?'

'Because there's only two of them and five of my lot. Anyway, do you really want Scuzzy Pete here?'

Lee chewed his food and agreed it was a better option. Although mention of her name made him wonder, yet again, why Chrissie had been avoiding him for weeks now. He'd not seen hide nor hair of her for ages and he still worried about what he'd done to upset her. It must have been something serious but he still didn't have a clue. Maybe he'd find out over Christmas.

A lightbulb moment struck him: maybe she had a bloke – that would explain it. If she was all involved with a new boyfriend, it might be difficult to explain about running with him. For a second he felt a sting of jealousy. But why should he? She was free to do what she liked. It was nothing to do with him, and anyway, he had Jenna.

'So why are those two stuck here?' he asked. 'Haven't they got homes to go to?'

Jenna explained their circumstances. Then she added, 'But this is the good bit – Immi also says Chrissie can cook. She's going to help me with the lunch.'

'Mam could do that.'

'Your mum is coming to us for a nice break. She doesn't want to have to roll her sleeves up and get busy in the kitchen.'

Lee stared at Jenna. Well, this was a turn-up. She wasn't

usually so interested in his mam's welfare. But maybe things were easing off. Maybe that weekend up in Newcastle had improved things. He hoped so.

'She'll probably want to lend a hand, though,' said Lee.

'Well, I insist that she doesn't,' said Jenna firmly.

Lee backed off. He loved his mam and he loved Jenna; he wasn't going to get involved. Besides, wouldn't it be better if the two women worked things out between them? 'Just one thing, though, Jenna. I still haven't told me mam I'm off to Afghan in the new year. I don't want her worried by the news over Christmas; I don't want her upset. So let's not mention it, eh?

'If that's what you want, hon, of course.'

Chapter Thirteen

'Come on, Maddy, or we're going to be late,' called Seb from the front door where he stood, impatiently jingling his keys.

Maddy rolled her eyes and gave Philly an apologetic smile. 'So, as I was saying, if Nate doesn't settle, just ring me. He should, his colic is so much better but...' She shrugged. 'Honestly,' and she lowered her voice, 'I'm not that sure I really want to go to Susie's and I won't mind if I have to come home.'

'It'll be fine,' said Philly. 'There'll be lashings of drink, you can be sure of that, and she's a pretty good cook.'

'So I've heard.' Maddy sighed. 'I'm just not sure I can bear an evening of playing competitive army wives.'

Philly giggled. 'It's only for a few hours. Just lie back and think of England.'

'Maddy!' called Seb again.

'Got to go.'

'And don't rush back,' Philly called after her, as Maddy left the house. 'I need the tokens.'

Despite Seb's prediction that they were going to be late, the Fanshaws arrived at Susie and Mike's house at seven forty, which Seb declared was bang on time. Apparently army punctuality – five minutes early is 'on time' – was different when it came to social occasions. As if to underline the point they could see two other couples approaching the path to the Collinses' house from the opposite direction.

'Oh, fuck,' groaned Maddy in a low murmur. 'Mrs Notley.' She felt Seb stiffen beside her.

'Best behaviour, then,' he muttered in her ear. 'No getting slaughtered.'

Fat chance, thought Maddy, knowing that on their return, if Nate awoke, she'd be the one who would have to cope.

With all three couples arriving more or less simultaneously, there was chaos in the narrow hall as coats were shed and carted upstairs and Mike tried to take orders for drinks and introduce Maddy and Seb to Alan Milward, the housing commandant, and his wife, Cath. Finally, the four couples made it into the cramped sitting room, drinks were distributed, Susie excused herself, 'must see to dinner', and a conversation began amongst the men, discussing the chances of England in the Six Nations Rugby, and amongst the women, discussing the running of the thrift shop. After a while Maddy stifled a yawn. The conversations moved on, but still only seemed to range over boring parochial topics. Maddy pretended to be interested by injecting the words 'yes', 'no' and 'really' at intervals while she wondered how Philly was getting on with Nathan, and how soon it would be possible for her and Seb to leave once they'd eaten.

Susie reappeared and announced that dinner would only be a few more minutes and suggested to Mike that their guests might like a top-up. Given the size of the gins that had been poured first time around Maddy realised that Philly hadn't been exaggerating when she said there would be lashings of drink. To be on the safe side Maddy opted for just tonic this time. She had a feeling it was going to be a long evening. After a while, Susie disappeared again and Maddy, sitting near the door to the kitchen and only half listening to the current conversation about boarding schools, heard Susie's exclamation of horror.

Oops, thought Maddy.

Susie popped her head round the kitchen door. 'Mike, darling, there's a bit of a hitch.' She flashed a smile at her guests. 'Nothing to worry about, just a teeny little delay. Maybe, you'd all like another drink, just to keep you going.'

Mike got the hint and reached for the gin – again. Blimey, thought Maddy, everyone's going to be shit-faced before we even sit down.

Through the gap in the door she could see Susie frantically filling a kettle and then measuring rice into a pan. The silly moo had forgotten the rice. Maddy did a swift calculation and reckoned it was going to be at least another twenty minutes before they ate. Dear God, and it was already nearly eight thirty.

Finally, when Maddy's stomach was beginning to rumble audibly, they sat down to vichyssoise. She tucked in gratefully, thankful to have something to start mopping up the gin.

Mike sloshed wine into his guests' glasses. Seb shot Maddy a warning glance which implied that they should both take it steady. Maddy thought that given the amount of gin Seb must have already drunk it was probably a bit late for him but she was happy to comply. A broken night *and* a hangover held no attraction.

By the time the stroganoff made it on to the table the steak was barely edible – although, to give Susie her due, the rice was perfect – but Maddy was pretty sure she was the only one who noticed how chewy the beef was. The number of empty bottles on the sideboard was reaching epic levels and still Mike was pouring with a liberal hand. Maddy felt her eardrums were about to bleed from the racket of the conversation which was getting more and more raucous and less and less logical or rational. By the time they got to the coffee, mints and brandy stage Maddy knew she was the only sober person in the room by a country mile – even Mrs Notley seemed to have the glassy stare and lopsided smile of the fairly pissed.

Finally, well after midnight, the party began to break up. Maddy felt almost catatonic and she could see that Seb was in a similar way – but his state was entirely caused by drink whereas hers was caused by boredom. Through the open door to the kitchen Maddy could see the chaos that reigned in Susie's kitchen and didn't envy her having to cope with clearing that mess up along with coping with a hangover. And with a panic, Maddy realised that at some stage she would be expected to reciprocate the hospitality. As she left, she glanced at the bottles on the sideboard: fifteen – and she hadn't had more than a glass or two. Bloody hell.

Once again, Maddy wondered if she was really cut out to be an army wife.

Just over a week later Maddy walked into the officers' mess in time for the post-Remembrance Service curry lunch. She'd opted not to go to the service itself, because there was no way Nate could be guaranteed to be quiet for the two-minute silence. His colic was almost completely over but he could still cry loudly and lustily if the fancy took him, which it had for most of the TV broadcast that Maddy had watched instead. But now the solemn bit was over, no one would mind so much if he was vocal at a social occasion and anyway, thought Maddy, if his cries got too much, she could just take him home. As she entered the big, red-brick Edwardian building she was greeted by a smell of curry, underlaid by a faint whiff of furniture polish and the smell of damp dogs. Army officers, she'd discovered, liked dogs and in every mess she'd been to since she'd known Seb, there had always been half a dozen lolling around somewhere. What was it with officers and their dogs? Maybe, she thought wickedly, they liked the idea that, even if their troops weren't always slavishly obedient, their pets were. Which was probably why army officers didn't keep cats.

She hung up her coat and went to find Seb, hauling Nate's buggy over the thick pile of the dark maroon carpet, past a couple of chocolate labradors sprawled under a side table and onwards towards the hubbub. That level of noise had to indicate the bar, which was where she fully expected her husband to be. This was her first visit to this mess and she felt a little nervous.

She found an open door halfway along the main corridor and the volume of noise climaxed. She peered in, looking for Seb or any familiar face. Maddy wasn't normally shy but she felt out of her depth in this gathering of uniformed officers and smart wives. She spotted Susie and – oh, bugger – Susie spotted her. And Maddy still hadn't written a 'thank you' letter for that dinner party. Her face flared with guilt over this social faux pas. She resolved to rectify things as soon as she got home.

'Maddy,' she called. 'Do come and join me.'

Another order, thought Maddy. She parked Nate's buggy in a corner, unclipped his carry chair and headed over. Even as she arrived she got the distinct impression Susie was looking past her, to see who else was entering the room.

Maddy was about to gush something appropriate about the *lovely* dinner party when Susie said, 'Drink?'

'What? Oh, yes, please.' She would have liked a good belt

of Dutch courage, but she decided that, on balance, keeping her wits about her on this first foray into the mess might be a good idea.

With a deft wave of her hand Susie signalled to a mess waiter.

He looked expectantly at Maddy. 'Orange juice, please,' she said.

'And your husband's mess number?'

'What?' said Maddy.

'For his mess bill,' said the steward.

Maddy shook her head.

'Put it on Major Collins's,' said Susie. 'Number seven.'

'Very good, ma'am,' said the steward as he left.

'As a rule, battalion officers don't buy each other drinks,' said Susie, 'but we can make an exception in this case. No Seb?'

We? Did Susie think she was a battalion officer? 'He said he was going to meet me here,' said Maddy. 'Can't think what's happened to him.' The steward reappeared with her drink on a silver salver, and she grabbed it gratefully.

Susie's eyes, she noticed, continued to flicker over her shoulder while they made small talk. At least, this time, the small talk didn't seem to involve laundry or the thrift shop, thought Maddy. Naughtily, she began to play Officer's Wife Bingo and ticked off the conversational topics she'd come to recognise: house moves, tick; boarding schools, tick; housing standards, tick; and 'when we' – as in 'when we were in...' plus the name of a previous posting. Oooh, Cyprus, double points scored for *that* one. She was just about to award herself full marks when Seb appeared.

'Sorry to have been so long,' he said, after he'd greeted Susie. 'Got caught by the CO.'

'I am so sorry,' said Susie, looking relieved, 'but do excuse me. There's someone I must see. Been trying to catch her all week.'

'No, please…' murmured Maddy. As Susie left, she watched her make a beeline for Julia Frenchay, the garrison commander's wife. At which point, Caro, Will, Philippa and a bloke Maddy could only assume to be Philippa's husband all pitched up too. It was almost as if they'd been waiting for Susie to push off.

'How about we make up a table together?' said Seb. 'That's OK with you, isn't it?'

'Fantastic,' said Maddy.

'Glad to see you getting on with Susie,' said Seb.

'Which reminds me, Susie paid for this.' She waved her half-empty glass at Seb. 'Or, at least, she put it on her husband's mess bill.'

'It's probably a drop in the ocean on Major Mike's bill,' said Caro.

Maddy remembered the empty bottles, lined up after the dinner party. 'Well, I suppose all that entertaining, the dinner parties…'

The others in their group fell about.

'God, no, that's not that reason,' said Caro. 'It's Susie. Unless the rumour mill is completely wrong, she gets through a couple of bottles of gin a week, at least. Don't ever ring her up after seven o'clock, if you want a sensible answer.'

'Or you can,' said Philippa, with a naughty giggle. 'It's quite funny.'

Maddy stared at them, astounded. 'But… but I thought she was the perfect army wife.' And then she remembered the glasses of wine Susie had had at lunch after the babysitting meeting and the kitchen cupboard stacked with tonic water and the fact she'd forgotten to put the rice on. Suddenly, what Philly had said made sense.

'Oh, she is… up till tea time,' said Seb. 'Want another?' He looked at Maddy's now empty glass and beckoned to a steward.

'You'll be pleased to know this is neat orange. I won't let you down and get a reputation – well, not today, at any rate.'

'Believe me, sweetie,' said Caro. 'You're really going to have to go some to get into her league. And that's why she tries to be so fucking perfect before the sun goes over the yardarm – she's got to redress the balance.'

The steward appeared and took the order for the drinks for the group, before sliding away again, through the press of mess members crowded into the room.

After he'd gone, Maddy stared at the others. 'But… I mean, what about Mrs N? Surely, if Susie's trying to be the perfect wife…' But then she remembered that Mrs N had also been pretty pissed at Susie's dinner party.

'Mrs N's not much better,' confirmed Caro. 'Army wives tend to get driven to the bottle.' She turned to Will. 'Don't we, darling?' Will didn't answer but gave everyone a wink. 'Anyway,' continued Caro, 'Susie can be relied upon not to get pissed in public, only in the relative privacy of her own home, which is all that matters, as far as the army is concerned. Of course, if that changes, Mike's career…' She drew the side of her hand across her throat. 'Or, he'll dump her.'

Maddy's eyes widened in horror. 'Really?'

'Why do you think the army's divorce rate is like it is?' asked Philippa. 'Wives either get fed up with the moving, their crap job prospects, sending their kids away to school, the shit housing, the separation and the rest and kick *it* into touch, or their husbands get fed up with their wives bitching about it and kick *them* into touch.' She made a meerkat squeak. 'Simples.'

The steward reappeared with a tray of drinks.

'So drink up,' said Seb when everyone had got one. 'Gin makes it all seem so much better – unless you administer it in industrial quantities.'

'Cheers,' they all said as they clinked glasses.

Maddy glanced across the room at Susie and Mrs N. Who would have guessed? And yet another path trodden by some army wives she'd do well to bypass herself.

Maddy stared at the battalion's forecast of events which Seb had brought home the previous day. There was no doubt about it, the countdown to Christmas had started. The battalion diary was a succession of parties for each of the companies: the Warrant Officers' and Sergeants' Mess Christmas Draw and Ball; the Wives' Club Christmas Bring-And-Buy; the Officers to Sergeants' Mess Drinks; the soldiers' Christmas lunch; the Officers' Mess Christmas cocktail party plus sundry other get-togethers and fund-raisers. In the last couple of weeks before the twenty-fifth itself, it seemed to Maddy that for most people associated with the battalion (and not just Susie and Mrs Notley) life was going to consist of recovering from one hang-over before sinking enough alcohol to ensure the next one.

Over a lunch of tomato soup and toast, Maddy broached the question of Seb finding time to babysit his son while she went Christmas shopping.

'Oh, Mads. Must I?'

'Seb! And how else is Christmas supposed to happen?'

'Internet shopping?' he asked hopefully.

'Don't be silly. I haven't a clue what to get lots of people. I need to browse about the shops to get ideas and I can't do

143

that with Nate in tow. And Caro has got Will to promise to take the boys, so we can go together. Please, Seb.'

'I know but...'

'He's your son too, Seb.'

Seb sighed. 'When?' he said wearily.

'Next Saturday.'

'But the Officers to Sergeants' Mess Drinks is on Friday.'

'So? It's a lunchtime do; you're not planning on getting so pissed you're going to be out of the game for the best part of twenty-four hours.'

'No, but...' Seb looked at her pleadingly. 'And if I don't have a hangover, I thought I'd go rowing training.'

'Seb,' she said, a little more sternly than she meant, 'when was the last time I asked you to look after Nate? Is it too much to ask that you don't get shit-faced on Friday?'

Seb looked woebegone. 'But this is a once-a-year event.'

'So it'll happen again next year. Please, Seb, it's not so much to ask.'

'OK. All right. I'll do it.' He threw his spoon back into the bowl, spattering soup across the table.

Maddy thought she'd never heard anyone give in with such bad grace *ever* but she wasn't going to back down. Just for once, she needed to make Seb realise that marriage wasn't a one-sided affair and she had rights in the partnership too, just as he had responsibilities – and one of his responsibilities, just occasionally, was looking after his son. And having asserted herself she felt pleasingly empowered. Maybe she'd try pushing the boundaries again – once Seb had got over the shock of her standing up to him this time.

The Warrant Officers' and Sergeants' mess was rammed. It was barely possible to see the red, swirly carpet because of the press of people standing around in the main bar, and it was with huge difficulty that the waiting staff circulated with trays of wine and beer to keep pace with demand for drinks. The noise was ear-splitting.

Seb bent his head close to his chief clerk's to try to catch what he was saying. It wasn't just the noise that made it difficult to hear what Chiefy was saying, the fact that his words were a bit slurry didn't help matters.

'… and I'm telling you, bossh, you're the besht platoon officer I've worked for.'

'Thanks, Chiefy,' said Seb. He stumbled slightly and the dregs of his drink slopped in the bottom of his glass. 'You're not so shabby yourself.' He threw his arm over his chief clerk's shoulder, in a gesture of manly friendliness.

'Aw, get away with you. Here, let me get you another one.'

Seb shook his head and tried to focus on his watch. Was it half past three or a quarter past six? Nope… he couldn't see clearly. Bloody stupid watch dial.

'Come on, sir, one for the road.'

Should he? Aw, where was the harm? And he didn't want to hurt Chiefy's feelings. It would be rude not to accept. Anyway, Maddy wouldn't mind if he was a bit late, would she? She'd understand.

Across the crowded bar, Seb could see the RSM and the CO both standing on their heads, trying to drink pints upside down. There was one thing you could say about the senior NCOs – they sure knew how to throw a party.

'Oh go on, Chiefy,' said Seb, belching slightly. 'Why not?'

'And a whisky chaser? It is Christmas, after all.'

'That's one helluvan idea. Thanks, Chiefy.'

*

145

The next morning Maddy sent a text to Caro: Seb is dying how is will? Despite Seb's truly epic hangover, the prospect of a day out with Caro was hugely cheering and, no matter how shit her husband felt, Maddy wasn't going to change her plans. Hangovers weren't fatal and Seb would just have to man up – as he was wont to encourage others to do.

She hummed happily while she made two mugs of tea and found a rusk for Nathan to chew on. She spooned sugar into one mug – good for hangovers, she'd heard – found a pack of aspirin in a kitchen cupboard and, promising Nate she'd be back in a jiffy, she ran upstairs to deliver tea and painkillers to Seb.

She wrinkled her nose as she entered the room; it reeked of stale beer. She thumped the tea down on the bedside table and put the packet of pills beside it.

'You'd better hope these work miracles, because I'm going out at ten. Nate just may fancy a nap then but if he doesn't, you'll have to entertain him.'

She ran back downstairs again, before Seb could protest, just in time to hear her phone chirrup the incoming-text alarm. She picked it up.

Will also dying tee hee. See you later.

Maddy giggled. Today was going to be fun, and after weeks and weeks of almost no free time she reckoned she really deserved a day out. And a bit of last-minute Christmas shopping with Caro was just what the doctor ordered. No doubt Seb and Will would get together at lunchtime and have a hair of the dog and moan about the unfairness of wives leaving them to deal with kids *and* hangovers.

For the first time since she'd arrived on the patch, she felt really upbeat; maybe she had turned a corner, as her mother had predicted she would once Nate was sleeping better and his colic cleared. Maybe being an army wife wasn't so bad. She had a gorgeous, fit husband (when he wasn't dying with a hangover), she had a roof over her head, she was surrounded by neighbours with similar-aged kids and it was Christmas. Maybe, she thought as she went to meet Caro, maybe it was time to think about being more than just a mother. Maybe it was time to think about getting her own career back on track. It wouldn't go down a storm with Seb – or Mrs Bloody Notley – but her degree from Oxford didn't deserve to go to waste and she had her own life to live. Surely wanting to make a success of her own life wasn't such a big ask? Although she had an awful feeling that maybe it was – or it would be to Seb.

Chapter Fourteen

Christmas Day dawned cloudy, grey and overcast with a hint of drizzle. It was one of those quiet, dreary winter's days that would normally make people's spirits sink: too warm for there to be any chance of it snowing and thus turning dull, drab, dark winter into a magical wonderland but, equally, too damn raw and cold to make it pleasant for kids to play outside on their new toys. But, at first light, none of the wives on the various patches around the garrison paid much attention to what the weather was up to, as they were roused by alarms signalling it was time to haul themselves out of bed, switch on their ovens and get the turkeys ready to go in.

In her quarter, Jenna groaned as her alarm went off. For a while she lay in bed wondering what sort of stupid idea it was to buy a twelve pound turkey that needed getting in the oven at silly o'clock, so everyone could sit down for Christmas lunch at one. What was wrong with having a lie-in and everyone eating at four in the afternoon?

'Because, if we do that,' Lee had said, 'we'll all be pissed on Bacardi and vodka.'

Jenna supposed he had a point, although she reckoned on having a skinful of bevvies by lunchtime because, if nothing else, it might be the only way to survive the visit from Lee's mum. Shit, that woman was a pain. It wasn't that she ever said anything really disapproving, but Jenna could just tell from the look on the sour old bat's face that nothing Jenna did was good enough. She'd sniffed at the quarter – like Jenna had deliberately picked the worst one just out of spite – she'd turned her nose up at her bedroom, and the look on her face, when Jenna had made a lasagne with jars of tomato and cheese sauce, had been a classic. So she didn't cook every last thing from scratch. Who the fuck did, in this day and age? Well, Nigella Bloody Lawson did for the cameras, but Jenna wouldn't mind betting that as soon as the TV crew buggered off she was just like every other woman in the country and banged ready meals in the microwave at every opportunity. Since when was taking a cookery short-cut a crime? But Sonia obviously thought it was. Today, however, the old bat was going to get proper roast turkey and all the trimmings, and she could shove that in her pipe and smoke it.

Spurred on by the thought that she'd show Sonia Perkins a thing or two, Jenna slipped out of bed, grabbed her dressing gown and stuffed her feet into her slippers, before padding downstairs. She switched the kitchen light on, waiting a few seconds as it hummed and flickered, before she took from the kitchen drawer the instructions that Chrissie had written out for her. Jenna read them through once again and then turned on the oven. Chrissie had told her not to worry and that she'd be over mid-morning to help with the meal, but that it was essential Jenna got the bird in the oven first thing, and she'd written down exactly what Jenna had to do before she arrived.

While Jenna waited for the oven to get to the right temperature, she got the turkey out of the fridge, wrestled it into a roasting tin and covered it tightly with tin foil. When the little red light went out, she heaved the whole lot into the still-sparkling oven – the ready meals she mostly dished up hadn't sullied its pristine condition – and slammed the door. She slipped back upstairs to bed, hoping to God nothing held Chrissie up, as she didn't have the first idea about how to carry on with the meal after this stage.

When Chrissie and Immi arrived later, it was obvious to them both that Jenna had already made a start on the vodka – and although she wasn't yet pissed, she soon would be. Sonia Perkins was glowering at her from her seat in the sitting room and Lee was looking nervous as he tried to keep the peace between the two women in his life. Immi and Chrissie handed over a few little gifts and were each given a present from under the tree.

'Oh, choccies, lovely,' said Chrissie, opening hers. Immi had the same and the two girls were both genuinely touched to be included in the family event. However, from the way Jenna was swirling the ice cubes around her now-empty glass and from the look on Sonia's face, Chrissie realised that if the rest of the day wasn't going to go tits-up, she needed to take action and fast.

Muttering things about basting the bird, she dragged Jenna into the kitchen and shut the door. Immi, thankfully, got the hint that Chrissie had taken charge of the damage limitation exercise and began chatting to Sonia and Lee about Newcastle, which she had visited once and luckily could remember enough about her trip to make conversation.

'Sit down, Jenna, you're going to have a cup of strong coffee, just as soon as I can make it,' Chrissie ordered, pushing Jenna onto a kitchen chair before putting on the kettle.

Jenna sulked and looked pointedly at her glass, but Chrissie ignored her, concentrating instead on flicking open the cupboards to familiarise herself with this new kitchen. She'd found mug and coffee by the time the kettle boiled and then made a cup of strong, black instant, which she passed to Jenna.

'Here.'

'Must I?' said Jenna.

Chrissie gave her a hard stare. 'If you don't want your first Christmas to be a complete disaster, yes, you must.' Then she softened. 'Look, I can see your mother-in-law might be tricky—'

'Tricky?!' squawked Jenna.

'—but this is Lee's Christmas, as well. If you love him, shouldn't you try to make it a lovely day for him? Upsetting his mum won't achieve that, now, will it?'

Jenna sighed and nodded. 'It was getting me through it, though.'

'Get pissed over lunch by all means, I expect we all will, but just stay off the voddies for now, eh?'

Meekly Jenna sipped her coffee, while Chrissie whirled around the kitchen, peeling potatoes and carrots, preparing sprouts, and starting to make the bread sauce. Every now and again, she gave Jenna a simple task to do, like washing up a few utensils, or wrapping cocktail sausages in strips of bacon. By the time elevenses came round Jenna was virtually sober and Sonia was smiling again. Chrissie wasn't sure the situation would last the whole day, but at least they might get through lunch before things reverted.

With the turkey and all its trimmings safely cooking and a reasonable atmosphere now reigning, Chrissie allowed Jenna to re-join the other three in the sitting room. Delicious smells wafted after them through the door.

'So, where did you learn to cook?' asked Sonia, bestowing a warm smile on Chrissie. Chrissie realised with relief that she and Immi had Sonia's approval. That was one hurdle cleared.

She explained about her childhood.

'That's not fair. That's no life for a bairn,' said Sonia.

Chrissie shrugged. 'You have to make the best of what you've got. And I knew no different. It was OK.'

'Hmm,' said Sonia. 'It's a shame others don't look at life like that.' She sent a look in Jenna's direction.

Bugger, thought Chrissie, Jenna was still in the doghouse.

Lee obviously realised it too. He jumped up. 'Well, I think it's time we had a glass of bubbly to get the celebrations going.'

'It's a bit early yet,' said Sonia.

'It's Christmas,' insisted Lee.

'Sounds like a great idea to me,' said Chrissie, hoping that, as she'd found favour with Sonia, her opinion might prove to be significant.

'Oh, well... if you insist,' said Sonia.

Lee went into the kitchen and there was the sound of a champagne cork popping. A couple of minutes later he re-appeared with a tray of brimming glasses.

'I think we ought to toast Chrissie,' said Lee with a smile. 'To the chef.'

'A bit premature for that,' said Chrissie. 'It might be pants.'

'I can tell a born home-maker when I see one,' said Sonia. 'And I know that turkey is going to be fine. You'll make a grand wife for someone, one day.' And she shot another look at Jenna. Luckily, however, Jenna was too busy chugging back her fizz to notice or care.

By three o'clock in the afternoon, across the garrison, all the presents had been exchanged, crackers had been pulled, the turkeys had been cooked, carved and eaten and most of the occupants of the quarters across the patch were full to bursting, as were the dishwashers, for those lucky enough

152

to have them. Outside in the streets kids, high on excitement, additives and sugar, belted about with their new toys, supervised by fathers who mostly seemed to be nursing a glass of port or a can of beer, while the mothers finished clearing up.

At the top end of Omdurman Avenue, the Collins household was deathly quiet. Mike and Susie were snoring, and drunkenly comatose on the sofa, while their two girls, back from boarding school, had taken themselves up to their bedrooms to watch inappropriate and illicit DVDs they had obtained, and enjoy uninterrupted access to their dad's laptop, Facebooking friends, friends who didn't go to their hugely expensive prep school, friends they knew their mother would disapprove of.

Further down the road, at the junior officers' end, Maddy and Seb had collapsed in a heap on the sofa, while Nathan dozed in his bouncy chair. Maddy's parents, who wouldn't be denied their first grandchild's first Christmas, had taken themselves up to bed for a snooze, full of turkey and a shade too much Veuve Clicquot and Pinot Grigio.

'Do you think Nate had a good time?' asked Maddy, as she lay, knackered, against the cushions, exhausted from the early start and the slog of cooking the meal, then cleaning the kitchen and dealing with the leftovers.

'He had a lovely time, hon. We all did.'

Maddy snuggled closer to Seb and gave him a kiss of thanks. 'Bung the TV on. I feel like watching something mindless.'

Seb picked up the remote and the television flicked into life. The Queen's Speech had finished, a couple of predictable films were already halfway through, and Seb continued to slowly trawl through the channels waiting for something to pop up that appealed to both of them. The BBC twenty-four-hour news channel appeared.

'Is the world still turning?' asked Maddy dozily, as she yawned deeply and contemplated a little zizz instead.

But Seb was reading the banner drifting across the bottom of the screen. 'Fuck,' he said.

'What's the matter?' Maddy jerked awake.

'Another load of casualties for 2 Herts,' said Seb.

Maddy read the banner herself and saw the words *Their families have been informed*. She felt her eyes filling with tears. 'And to be told on Christmas Day.'

'I don't think Christmas would make it any worse,' said Seb.

'But if those poor buggers have kids...' She could hardly bear to think about it. Numbly, still having to make an effort not to cry, she watched the red ticker-tape continue to scroll across the screen with the news of the 2 Herts casualties. The phrase about the families being informed was the signal to every other army relative in the land that, although the news was grim for someone, they weren't about to get the knock at the door with awful news of their nearest and dearest. Maddy knew, only too well, how the army handled this; Seb had put her in the picture when he'd been out there. First, when a soldier was reported having sustained a life changing injury, or worse, all personal communications between soldiers and their families got shut down under something called Operation Minimise, so the bad news couldn't leak out accidentally. Then, the soldier's next of kin got a personal visit from an army officer, probably accompanied by the families officer or a padre, and then once the immediate family had been told and they'd had the chance to tell anyone else who ought to know, then the press got put in the picture too. She remembered vividly how her heart had raced when her phone had rung at unexpected times, scared witless that this was a call from Seb's dad, passing on some ghastly news. It hadn't happened but she hadn't forgotten the anxiety she'd felt.

Suddenly, even though the news affected no one that Maddy knew personally, she couldn't find it in her heart to feel very jolly any more.

Over at the Perkinses' quarter, things had been extremely jolly but that had now degenerated into all-out chaos and hardly anyone was in a state to focus on world events. The mauled turkey still sat on the dining room table, while Immi had utterly forgotten she was duty clerk and, soused in fizz and Bacardi, had passed out on the floor. Jenna was in a similar state and was out for the count on the sofa, and Sonia, no better than either of them, was snoring heavily in one of the armchairs. Only Chrissie seemed relatively sober, but that was in comparison to those who patently weren't. But at least she was still upright, awake and both her eyes faced front.

She stared around the room – even Lee had his eyes shut. Now was a good time to make a move. She'd carried out her side of the bargain and helped Jenna cook a more than passable Christmas lunch. Now she wanted to escape. She'd just make sure everything was cleared away – the least she could do – and then she could bugger off. She began to take the turkey carcass out into the kitchen.

'Sit,' said Lee, opening his eyes, 'you've done quite enough.'

'If this bird doesn't go into the fridge, it'll all be wasted. You can't mess around with poultry. And anyway, I'm just having a bit of a tidy up.'

'There's no need,' said Lee.

'It's the least I can do. I've had a lovely Christmas, much better than if I'd had lunch in the cookhouse, and as soon as I've done this, I'm going to push off.'

She didn't want to stay and chat. She didn't want Lee asking any awkward questions about why she'd been blanking him. What could she say? That she was ridiculously attracted to him and was avoiding him where humanly possible, because it was so horribly wrong? Yeah, like that was a conversation she wanted to have. No, best to just light out and duck the issue. She carried the remains of the turkey through to the kitchen, where she rummaged in Jenna's cupboards and drawers till she found the foil and began to wrap it around the leftovers. Lee followed behind her and leaned against a worktop.

'It can wait,' he said.

'Maybe. But it's time to go. I've had a wicked time, though, thanks to you and Jenna. You've been dead kind.' But she spoke to the counter, not to Lee. She didn't trust herself to look at him.

'And our Christmas would have been crap without you. Jenna wouldn't have had a clue what to do, if you hadn't shown her.'

'And so, what about your mother?'

'She and Jenna would not have made a good team.' Lee shrugged. 'But they both had a grand time and Mam thought you were a superstar.'

Chrissie thought that Sonia should have been thinking that about Jenna, not her. She concentrated on getting the turkey swaddled in foil, embarrassment preventing her from making eye-contact with Lee.

She jumped when she felt his hand on her wrist. She snatched her arm out of reach, sending the turkey platter skidding away from her.

'Stop and keep me company,' said Lee.

'I can't. I have to get back.'

'Immi's the one on duty, not you.'

'I know, but I've things to do.'

'On Christmas Day?'

She picked up the bird. 'Open the fridge, Lee.' She would make sure the turkey was safely put away and then she'd leave. Thankfully, Lee did as he was told.

But when the big, heavy plate was safely on a shelf and she'd shut the door, she turned round and bumped straight into him. He was standing right behind her. Chrissie leapt back, but bounced off the fridge.

'I'm done,' she said, as calmly as she could before she pushed past him, grabbed her coat off the peg in the hall and legged it back to her barrack room. She didn't want to feel this way about him; she didn't want to feel this way about anyone. She wanted to get on with *her* life, on *her* own with no responsibilities other than the ones that came with *her* job. She told herself, yet again, that she didn't want the likes of Lee, or anyone else, worrying about her, or caring about her, and she didn't want to have to worry, or care, about them.

And thankfully, according to the MO, and if the Manning and Records Office didn't change the postings' plot, her replacement was due in to the battalion the first week of January, and shortly after that, she'd be off to Afghanistan and thousands of miles from Lee or any other complications.

Chapter Fifteen

Lee arrived back from taking his mother to the local railway station.

'I'm back,' he called as he got through the front door.

'I'm stripping the bed,' answered Jenna from upstairs. She sounded sulky, but then housework did that to her. Lee did his best to help when he could – after all, they both had full-time jobs, so it was only fair – but, however much he did, it never seemed quite enough. He wondered how she'd cope with every-thing on her own when he flew to Bastion in a couple of weeks.

'You took your time,' she added, coming downstairs with an armful of bedding. 'And I've been thinking, before you bugger off to Bastion, you can buy me a washing machine. I won't have time to muck about in the garrison launderette, when I'm on my own.' She dumped the washing at the foot of the stairs.

'Yeah,' said Lee, 'good shout. We'll get one organised, as soon as the shops are open again. We might even get a bargain in the sales.'

'So how was your mum?'

Lee had promised Jenna that he'd wait till he took his mam to the station before he broke the news about his posting. 'She cried.' Jenna rolled her eyes. 'Jenna, it's not as if she hasn't had to face this before. Dad went off to the first Gulf War and didn't come back.'

'Then she shouldn't expect lightning to strike in the same place twice.'

Did she mean to sound quite so heartless, or was she trying to be optimistic? It was difficult to tell sometimes. He gave her the benefit of the doubt. 'I promised her that if you heard bad news, you'd ring her first.'

'Don't talk like that, Lee, and stop being such a drama queen. Loads of soldiers come back in one piece and you know it.'

Lee bit back his retort that loads didn't – but then he realised that Jenna was trying to show him she was going to be strong while he was away and he wasn't to worry about her. Actually, it was a comfort to him that he was pretty sure she'd cope. Lots of soldiers' wives did, he knew that, but then there were the stories of the ones that didn't. You didn't want to be worrying about how your loved ones were doing, when you really ought to be keeping your mind on your own safety.

'Anyway,' he said, 'she wasn't happy, but she was well pleased I didn't spoil Christmas by telling her earlier. And she said thank you for giving her a nice break and such a grand Christmas and a lovely feast.' OK, that last bit was a lie, his mother had said to thank Chrissie about the turkey, but Lee wasn't going to make matters worse between the two women in his life by giving Jenna yet more ammo to fire at his mam.

A week later, the washing machine was bought and installed, and Lee was getting ready to go for a week's pre-ops training, before his deployment from RAF Brize Norton. He had his kit packed in his Bergen, his helmet was strapped on top, his day sack was ready and all he had left to do was to report to the Q stores to be issued with his body armour and dog tags, and then he was straight on the transport to the exercise area in south Wales, where his training course would take place.

Jenna was waiting for him as he came out of the stores, hefting all his kit. He was surprised at seeing her there.

'Jenna, I thought you'd be busy at the salon. And anyway, we said our goodbyes this morning.'

'I couldn't let you go without a last kiss goodbye,' she said, throwing her arms around Lee's neck and kissing him long and hard.

The Land Rover driver, waiting to take Lee to his pre-ops training, leaned on the horn.

'Come on, mate, I ain't got all day,' he yelled out of the vehicle's window.

'Gotta go, hon,' said Lee, disentangling himself.

Jenna stepped back. 'You just make sure you come back in one piece, Lee Perkins. Love you.' There was a tear glistening in her eye.

'Love you too, Jen,' said Lee, as he threw his kit in the rear of the Rover and then climbed in the passenger seat.

As they drove out of the barracks he saw Chrissie standing near the medical centre chatting to someone. He longed to ask the driver to stop so he could say goodbye to her too, but then realised he was being ridiculous. She'd made it quite plain over Christmas that she didn't want anything much to do with him – so why would she suddenly care now? Even if he was going to Afghan.

Maddy looked in the mirror and realised that the neat bob Jenna had given her had now almost grown out and her hair was looking a mess again. Despite the fact that she knew Jenna would come to the house, the thought of getting away on her own for a bit of pampering for an hour was more appealing. Predictably, when she'd asked Caro to babysit, she'd offered to look after Nate for nothing.

Jenna seemed to be looking pretty chipper, which surprised Maddy. Seb had warned her that Lee was about to deploy to the Middle East any day now.

'How are you doing?' Maddy asked solicitously.

'Fine,' Jenna said happily, as if she didn't have a care in the world, helping Maddy into a gown and sitting her down in front of a mirror.

'How's your husband?'

'Oh fine,' she said airily. 'Now, about your hair.'

Maddy was a bit stunned. But then, perhaps Jenna didn't want to talk about it.

For a couple of minutes the two women discussed exactly what Maddy wanted, and then Jenna took her over to the basins for a shampoo before she got busy with the scissors.

'I've got the plumber coming round in the morning,' said Jenna, chattily.

'Poor you,' said Maddy, tucking in the towel a little more firmly to stop an errant drip trickling any further down her neck.

'Why poor me?'

'Well, it's always a pain when something's wrong with your heating, or hot water, isn't it?'

'Oh, nothing's wrong. I'm having that backwash unit I told you about put in my bathroom, so I can finally get my own business up and running.'

'You're what?!'

'Like a proper salon. I'm having it done properly. It's not a lash-up and it's costing a mint. Of course I couldn't do it when Lee was around. He kept stressing about rules and regulations and such. I mean, like anyone'll really care.'

They probably will, thought Maddy, when they find out. The housing commandant, for one, would certainly have an opinion, and Maddy didn't think it'd be favourable. There was no way the authorities wouldn't find out, especially if Jenna touted for business, which she'd have to do if she wanted any.

'So what are you going to say to Lee, when he gets back and he sees what you've done?' Maddy was agog to know how on earth Jenna thought she could get away with her plan.

'It'll be a done deal by then. Besides, I reckon I'll be making enough money for him not to care.'

Again Maddy bit her tongue. Once Lee was back, and assuming Jenna hadn't already been evicted, the army would probably expect Private Perkins to get his wife to toe the line. And if he couldn't get her to behave, Maddy didn't think Lee would have much of a career – if he had any career at all.

While Jenna carried on washing and then styling Maddy's hair, Maddy tried to thrash out the problem of whether or not she should tell Seb about Jenna's scheme. By the time she was paying her bill, she decided that she was going to pretend she knew nothing about it. She didn't want to be involved and, if anyone asked, she was going to deny Jenna had ever told her a thing about it.

Chapter Sixteen

Chrissie looked at her movement order as she stood on the concourse of Oxford station. In her multicam and with her Bergen, day sack and helmet, she drew the odd curious stare, but she was too busy checking how she was going to get from Oxford to RAF Brize Norton to notice. She didn't mind having to make her own way to the airbase. The Army had sorted her out with travel warrants and details of what trains and buses she had to catch, which made more sense than tying up a vehicle and driver for a whole day just for her. Anyway, as a private soldier travelling alone, there was no way she would have rated such luxury. She read the piece of paper again and then asked a member of the station staff the way to Gloucester Green – which was where her bus to Brize left from.

He took her to the entrance and pointed her in the right direction.

'Going overseas then, love?' he asked. Just about everyone in Oxfordshire knew that the RAF base was where most of the air-trooping happened.

'Afghanistan.'

The railway employee gave her a kind smile. 'Then you take care,' he said, with genuine feeling, as she hauled the heavy load onto her shoulders, trying not to stagger as she did so.

She made her way down the steps, across the taxi rank, past the hundreds of parked bikes and up the road towards the main coach station. Dusk had long since fallen and a brisk wind cut through her uniform, making her shiver despite the exertion of lugging her kit.

There was a bus waiting at the stand when she got to the right stop and gratefully she climbed aboard, handed over her travel warrant and then dumped her baggage in the luggage rack. Wearily, she slumped into a seat. She might be fit, but she wasn't powerful, and her military kit weighed almost as much as she did.

Mindlessly, she watched the other buses come and go from the coach station until, with a throbbing roar, the engine started and they were off. They made their way along the roads of Oxford, past the pretty and ancient stone fronts of the colleges, the pavements packed with students, off for an evening out with their mates, hurrying, heads down against the January weather. Then they drove out through the residential outskirts and onto the A40 towards the Cotswolds and the air force base. Once on the open road, the bus rattled along at a cracking pace, speeding along through the monochrome countryside, lit by a nearly full moon, between the ploughed fields and bare winter trees, past bedraggled livestock hunching miserably in their meadows, with their backs to the chill wind that blew down from the north. Chrissie wondered what it was going to be like in Bastion. Immi had told her it was miserable in winter. But wasn't it in a desert? Weren't deserts hot?

When Chrissie saw the sign off the dual carriageway to RAF Brize Norton, she felt a frisson of apprehension. As the bus slowed and turned off the slip road, the reality that in a few hours she would be heading off to a war zone kicked in. She knew her training was good, she knew she was up to the job, but she couldn't help wondering how she would feel after months of dealing with desperate traumas. Her very recent weeks of pre-ops training had made Exercise Autumn Armour look like a walk in the park.

Once again, amputees had acted as casualties, with lashings of theatrical gore and raw meat applied to their stumps to simulate terrible injuries. Added into the mix this time, though, were pig carcasses with appalling gunshot wounds for the trainees to treat, while, as before, bullets and explosions cracked off around them. What with that, darkness, driving rain, bone-numbing cold, and the soldiers' realistic screams for help, the training had morphed into some ghastly, Dante-esque vision of hell that had left Chrissie feeling physically and emotionally wrecked. Thankfully, she'd not once thrown up at what had confronted her but, the instructors told them, the pressure of their training was *nothing* compared to the experience of a real battlefield.

She'd heard stories about people who had suffered mental illness as a result of their tours. Not for the first time since she'd volunteered, she wondered if she would be strong enough to cope. Suddenly she felt very alone and very scared. What had she got herself into?

And then the bus passed the sign that said *Repatriation Car Park* and her heart missed a beat as she thought about all those poor soldiers who had wound up being carried off the back of a C17 in a flag-draped coffin, watched by grieving relatives. She gave herself a shake – her job was to do her best to prevent that from happening. She was going out to save every life that it was possible to save. And as long as she did her best and worked her hardest, then she mustn't blame herself for those whom she couldn't help. She had to hold on to that thought: it might save her sanity.

The bus driver obligingly dropped her at the main gates and, laden once more, she staggered over to the guardroom to show her ID card.

'How far to the terminal?' she asked, already feeling knackered.

'About half a mile, love.'

She smiled to cover up her sense of despair. Half a mile! She put her ID card back inside her combat jacket, shrugged her Bergen higher up onto her shoulders, grabbed the rest of her kit and set off. She wasn't going to give anyone, let alone the RAF, the satisfaction of seeing her beaten by the distance, or the amount of kit she was carrying. However, when she reached the car park in front of the terminal and found a luggage trolley, she nearly wept with relief.

'Thank fuck,' she muttered, rolling her Bergen off her back and letting it fall with a crump onto the trolley. For a second she felt as if she were floating, but then the ache in her spine and shoulders kicked in as she straightened properly and eased them. She was absolutely knackered and even the *thought* of pushing her bags was too much for the moment, so she sat next to her luggage while she got her breath and her strength back.

An unmarked white coach rolled to a standstill a few yards away and began disgorging thirty or so soldiers. Efficiently, some of the men unloaded their own Bergens and bags from the coach's hold, while others brought over trolleys and formed a human chain to load them up.

'You all right?' one of the guys called over to Chrissie. 'Want a hand?'

'I'm fine,' she lied and stood up to prove it. She began to push her own kit towards the huge, hangar-like terminal.

'Chrissie?'

She stopped dead. She knew that voice. Slowly she turned around. 'Lee?' She stared at him, her heart thundering.

'What the fuck are you doing here?' he asked.

Chrissie stared at him, trying to make sense of what was happening. Was this someone's idea of a sick joke? She had volunteered for Bastion to get away from complications like Lee and here he was. All the same, she felt a kick of happiness: his friendly face meant she might still be scared, but at least she wasn't alone any more.

'But...' Her mind and feelings were in such a muddle, she could barely string a sentence together. She stopped, then a thought struck her. 'What do you mean, what the fuck am I doing here? More to the point, what the fuck are *you* doing here?'

'I'm going to Bastion – BCR.'

Chrissie's jaw slackened. This *was* a sick joke. 'Battlefield casualty replacement? Bastion? But you can't be.'

Lee tugged at the sleeve of one of his comrades. 'Hey, Mac, where are we going?'

Lee's mate Mac looked at him as if he were bonkers. 'Afghan, you twat.'

Lee grinned at Chrissie. 'Now do you believe me?'

She nodded. 'So am I.'

'*You?*'

She nodded again.

'Why?' he asked, his brow creased in incredulity.

'Because I volunteered.'

'But why?'

'Because I wanted to.'

'You coming, Perkins?' Mac interrupted.

'Yeah, right with you.' Lee looked from Chrissie to Mac and back again, as if wondering who had priority for his attention. 'Here, hang on,' he said, apparently arriving at a decision. He stopped Mac from moving on, hauled Chrissie's stuff off her trolley as if it was a couple of feather pillows, and split it between his own and Mac's trolleys. 'Don't say squaddies don't know how to behave like gents,' he said. Then he gave Mac a nod and they moved off, Chrissie with them.

Together, the three of them made their way across the car park and up the ramp to the terminal. Inside the doors there was a small waiting area, with a few chairs and tables for people meeting any arrivals, a little coffee shop, a couple of vending machines, and then to the right was a corridor that led to the massive hall which was the check-in area. In many ways it was very like a normal civvy airport, except here everyone was dressed in multicam combats. They joined the queue of other soldiers waiting to be processed.

'Bloody hell, Perkins,' said another soldier. 'Have you pulled already?'

'Fuck off,' said Lee amiably. 'This is Chrissie. She's a combat medic.'

'Cool.' The guy stuck his hand out. 'Nice to meet you, Chrissie, I'm Tim. And if Lee doesn't want to pull you, can I?'

Everyone laughed, except Chrissie. She was still reeling from the shock of seeing Lee.

The soldiers shuffled forwards, yard by yard, while the RAF movements staff checked names and documentation against the manifest. When they finally made it through, they were herded towards the big departure lounge with floor to ceiling windows which looked out towards the runways and taxi areas and the massive grey C17 aircraft, lit by huge floodlights, which sat nearby waiting to take them all to the war. They weren't due to take off for a very long time, not until the small hours of the morning, but, this being the military, everyone had to be there and accounted for, way ahead of time.

Their Bergens had been checked through to be loaded onto the aircraft, leaving them with their day sacks, helmets and body armour. They joined the rest of the troops in the hall, who were doing what soldiers always do, given the opportunity: making themselves as comfortable as possible, using their day sacks as pillows and grabbing a kip. Lee, Mac and Tim were no exception, and wasted no time in getting their heads down. Chrissie sat on one of the seats and watched the slumbering shapes on the seats and the floors.

How could they be so relaxed? she wondered. She herself was taut with apprehension and, unless things went horribly wrong, no one was going to shoot at *her*. But for these boys, being shot at was part of their job description, along with risking your life and being blown up. She wondered which of these guys, about to fly out with her, would be coming back injured, or worse. As she looked at their young faces, she felt tears form and the back of her nose start to prickle. Hurriedly she blinked and looked out of the window. She mustn't think like that. Strong and professional – that was what was expected of her. She'd managed it in the pre-ops training, and she'd coped with the countless gruesome injuries she'd had to deal with. So given that she was now officially 'tough', it wasn't going to do anyone any good if other emotions turned her into a snivelling waste of space. Brace up, she told herself.

The time for take-off drew nearer. Chrissie, unlike her male counterparts, unable to sleep, watched what was going on outside. The tailgate had been lowered off the huge Globemaster aircraft, a vast jumbo jet-sized aircraft, with high wings and four monster engine pods suspended underneath, and lights glowed from inside its enormous maw. It was a warehouse with wings, she thought idly, and wondered how on earth such an enormous structure could be held up by air. She vaguely knew about aerodynamics and the theory of lift, but it still didn't seem possible. She watched the dozens of pallets of kit and supplies get pushed up the rollers on the ramp and lashed into place in the cavernous body of the plane by RAF loadmasters. A couple of vehicles had also been driven on, and Chrissie was starting to wonder how the hell they were going to fit on all these people as well.

Despite her own anxiety about the journey, Chrissie was just beginning to feel her own eyes droop with tiredness when there was a tannoy announcement ordering the assembled troops to prepare for embarkation. Around her, the slumbering shapes began to stir, collecting their stuff, yawning, stretching, cracking jokes as if they were about to board a cross-channel ferry. Once again, Chrissie felt her heart jump. This was it.

The doors from the departure hall were thrown open, and the soldiers shuffled forward, once again, to pass through them, out onto the concrete, and head towards the giant plane. No air-bridge for boarding here, at Brize Norton. The straggling lines of troops walked up the ramp, into the enormous tube that was the body of the C17. Two corridors were left either side of the cargo, to allow passage to the front of the aircraft, which was kitted out a bit like a civvy plane, only with some significant differences. There were seats ranged down the sides in line and also rows of seats in the middle. If you focused on the seats in the middle, you might just be able to kid yourself this was a holiday flight. But the instant you took your eyes off those, there was no way this could be an ordinary airliner:

there was a cavernous space above the seats, but no overhead lockers, no neat plastic panels to cover up the bleak metal skin, no portholes with twee curtains or blinds, no TVs in the seat backs, no tray tables, no carpet, no galley, no smiling stewards to welcome you aboard. Not that Chrissie had ever flown before, but she'd watched enough episodes of *Airport* and *Come Fly With Me* to know what was what. This might be her first ever flight, but vicariously she'd been around the world. And no way had any airline she'd got to know through the TV had *green* lighting in the cabins. Green was weird. Green was *wrong*. It was all quite surreal, Chrissie decided as she followed Lee to a free row of seats in the centre.

She took her cue from the others and shoved her helmet, day sack and body armour under her seat, before sitting down and buckling up. Somehow, she thought, as she looked about her, she didn't think she was going to be pestered by cabin crew trying to flog her overpriced sandwiches or duty free.

'You OK?' asked Lee.

Chrissie was agonisingly aware of his presence next to her. For fuck's sake – she'd volunteered for Bastion to get away from him, and now here he was, closer than ever. How ironic was that?

'Fine,' was all she said. She was going out to Afghanistan to do a job, not to be mates with guys on the ground. She didn't want to be worrying about anyone but herself while she was out there, least of all Lee, and she was going to try not to get any more friendly than was absolutely necessary, before he deployed to work with his multiple and she did some proper nursing.

She jumped at the sound of some clunks and thumps, but realised it was nothing to be worried about when she heard the low whine of a jet engine being fired up. The noises were repeated three more times, until all engines were running, and then there were a few rattles and shakes, and suddenly she realised that the plane was moving. They were off and taxiing towards the runway.

'We're off,' said Lee.

'No shit, Sherlock,' said Chrissie with feigned calm. She felt her muscles get more and more tense as the huge plane lumbered along the taxiway towards the end of the runway, bouncing gently as the wings flexed when it passed over the slightest bump. She felt it turn through ninety degrees, pause, then move forward, and as it turned again, the whine from the engine increased to a bone-shaking, mind-numbing roar and then the plane began to hurtle forwards. Chrissie felt herself being thrust back in her seat as the acceleration increased and then zoom, the bouncing stopped as the plane took to the sky and its natural element.

'Next stop, Afghan,' said Lee. 'In the meantime, I think I'll get my head down.'

Chrissie knew what he was suggesting was wise, but she reckoned she was far too wound up to follow suit. Even so, with nothing to look at and precious little to do, she shut her eyes and, like all the soldiers around her, she was soon dozing too.

Chapter Seventeen

The aircraft intercom bing-bonging woke Chrissie. She glanced
at her watch which glowed weirdly in the green cabin lights.
Nearly twelve. No, that couldn't be right because she hadn't
changed her watch to Afghan time. Oh well, whatever, it was
the middle of the night, she thought, only with no portholes
to provide a clue, it could have been midday. It was odd not
to be able to see out. Not that she had any idea what it *would*
be like to see out from a height of thirty thousand feet, but
it had to be better than what she was experiencing right now.
She promised herself a nice holiday to somewhere exotic when
she got back – if she got back. She put that thought out of
her mind: of course she'd get back. Maybe Cyprus would be
nice. They'd had a stopover in Cyprus and had been allowed
off the plane. The air had been warm, the sky blue, and she'd
spotted real oranges growing on trees. But, although they'd
stopped for ages, they hadn't been allowed out of the terminal
at the RAF base before they'd finally re-embarked for the
last leg. She'd had no chance to see anything other than the
terminal itself, a glimpse of a lagoon and those oranges. Yes,
she thought, sun, sand and sea would be a treat to look
forward to – assuming she hadn't had enough of sun and
sand by the time her tour was over.

Anyway, they must be almost about to arrive. It had been
explained to them during the in-flight briefing that for

security reasons they would be arriving in the middle of the night.

'So we can't see how shit-scared the pilot is,' quipped the squaddie who had cast himself as the in-flight entertainment.

Never mind the pilot, thought Chrissie to herself. She reckoned she wasn't going to be too cool about landing in a war-zone herself.

Bing-bong went the tannoy again, just to make sure everyone was awake. Then: 'Ladies and gentlemen, I am sorry to disturb your sleep, but this is to tell you that in a few minutes we will be approaching Camp Bastion. Please don your body armour and helmets. When you have done that and are safely strapped back in your seats, we will black out the aircraft and begin our descent. For those of you who have flown this route before, you know what to expect. For those of you who haven't, please be assured that neither I, Squadron Leader Foulkes, nor my co-pilot, Flight Lieutenant Gurney, have a death wish. The manoeuvres we will be taking are well within the airframe tolerances and designed to minimise any possibility of a surface-to-air enemy attack. If you think you might be prone to motion sickness – and even if you don't – it might be wise to have a sickbag on standby. I hope you enjoy the ride.'

Chrissie's eyes met Lee's and she was almost grateful to see a flicker of worry in his. 'What manoeuvres, what tolerances?' she asked him. 'What the fuck did he mean?'

'Haven't a clue, but we'll be finding out shortly. But I *think* he was trying to tell us the wings aren't going to fall off.'

Chrissie gazed at him, open mouthed. 'Wings? Fall off?' she squeaked. 'Thanks, Lee.'

They got their body armour on and fastened the straps of their combat helmets. A couple of minutes later, they were plunged into darkness. Chrissie held her hand in front of her face. Nothing. She touched her nose with her fingers. Not a sausage. When they said blackout, they meant it. Her heart rate began to increase. She had a feeling this was going to be scary and was glad she was clutching a sickbag in her other hand.

Then the plane tipped forward. This hadn't happened when they went into RAF Akrotiri. That had been a gentle glide and her ears had popped intermittently. This was something else entirely; this wasn't a descent, this was a nosedive. Shit, she thought as they plunged, planes weren't meant to fall out of the sky like this. OK, little nippy fighters might do this sort of thing – she'd watched *Top Gun*, she'd seen them strut their stuff – but a huge, fuck-off transport job, a block of flats with wings attached? No way!

The noise of the engines seemed to block out all other sound but, even so, she clenched her teeth to stop herself from screaming as the plummet continued. Then the plane banked violently to the right, followed by a roll to the left. So far in her life Chrissie had experienced just two take-offs and one landing, but even she knew this was way beyond normal. And she didn't care what the pilot had said about tolerances, the wings *were* about to fall off, or maybe they already had. Maybe this was how it had felt on the 747 that had crashed on Lockerbie. S-h-i-i-i-t.

A sour whiff of vomit made Chrissie's stomach churn even more. She clutched her bag and the plane jolted and jounced and continued to dive. At this rate they'd hit the deck any second now. Surely. They'd been plunging earthwards for what seemed like hours. The pilot had lied; he *was* a kamikaze terrorist and they were all doomed. The jinks and jerks seemed to get worse, if anything, as did the smell of sick, and someone was screaming. The engines didn't block out all sound as she'd thought they might, and Chrissie was thankful she'd managed to keep herself under control. But just as she thought that, her resolve crumbled, fear got the better of her and she began to cry. She didn't want to die, but still the nightmare continued, and now it had got to a pitch where she didn't care if it ended in oblivion. Live, die, what the hell: she just wanted peace and an end to this mind-numbing terror.

Then, with an extraordinary change, the aircraft suddenly levelled out, the ducking and weaving stopped and about thirty seconds later, she felt the thump of the undercarriage hitting the ground. They'd landed, she thought. They hadn't piled in nose first. They'd survived. Her sobs changed to a near-hysterical giggle of relief and, just as the lights came back on again, the build-up of adrenalin in her system got the better of her and she hurled.

'Nice one,' said Lee.

But Chrissie didn't care, she felt too weak, too wrung-out and too shaky to give a flying fuck. She fell silent, as the tannoy boomed again.

'Welcome to Afghanistan.'

'And you are – welcome to it,' said the duty comedian in response.

Chrissie raised a wan smile and folded down the top of her bag. She wiped her mouth.

'At least you didn't do it all over me this time,' said Lee, giving her arm a squeeze. 'And you weren't alone, trust me on that. There were big strong men squealing like five-year-olds.'

Chrissie was sure this was a lie, but it made her feel less of a wuss.

'Please remain in your seats, with your seatbelts fastened, until the aircraft has come to a complete stop. You have arrived in Camp Bastion, where it is three o'clock local time.'

She'd made it to Afghanistan. Relief, coupled with gratitude that Lee had been so kind and understanding, all became too much for Chrissie and she burst into tears again.

As Lee's flight was touching down in Afghanistan, Jenna was standing in the middle of her almost-complete bathroom and surveying it with undiluted pleasure. The plumber she'd given the work to had done a grand job. She ran her fingers over the black, sparkling counter surrounding the backwash unit, which was now positioned where the bath used to be. There was a space behind it for her to stand. On the wall above it were some contemporary stainless steel shelves, which sparkled in the light of the inset spots on the ceiling. The glass and stainless steel shower stall in one corner gleamed, and the toilet was discreetly placed in the other, so as not to be visible to her clients while they were being shampooed. She could disguise the fact that this was actually a bathroom, not a pukka salon, up to a point, but even Jenna had understood that it would not be possible, given the design of the house, to put the loo anywhere else.

The bill had been horrendous, but she reckoned that by the time Lee was due back from his tour, she ought to have earned almost enough to repay the money she'd taken from his deposit account. Well, more fool him, for leaving his password and key information kicking around. Besides, when she'd managed to pay the cost of this conversion off and save up a bit more, she was going to invest in a proper salon, with a tanning studio and a nail bar, maybe on the High Street in the town. She didn't want just army wives; she wanted everyone one to come to Jenna's. She'd show Zoë how to run a business; she'd coin it in. Marky Markham move over – Jenna Perkins is coming through. And when she'd made it she and Lee would be able to move out of this poxy box the army called a house and into something much nicer.

Moving away from the counter, she ran her fingers down the piles of black fluffy towels stacked on the shiny shelves. They hadn't been cheap either, she mused, but she wasn't going to make do with the thin, cheap crap that Zoë inflicted on her clients. Honestly, some of them were so rough it was like trying to dry the ladies' hair with sandpaper.

On the opposite wall, on another set of gleaming shelves, were the salon products she'd 'liberated' from Zoë's over the past several months. She'd been careful to collect the colours and products she used on her existing clients – clients she was relying on to remain loyal to her. She knew she'd have to invest in more stock, but this ought to improve her profit margin for a month or two. Or – a thought struck her – allow her to undercut Zoë significantly. It might be better to do that; after all, no one could resist a bargain, could they?

She went downstairs to her sitting room, now transformed by a huge cream rug which almost completely covered the hideous orange carpet. Once Lee's pay had filled up the bank account again, she'd invest in some new furniture, too, so her ladies had somewhere nice to wait for their appointments. But even she knew she couldn't afford such an extravagance just yet. Cream leather, she thought, would be perfect in due course. And a flat screen TV. Lee would love it when he saw it. He'd be so proud of her, getting a business up and running and making the house nice. Fancy making a fuss over some silly rules and regulations; he'd change his tune, when he saw the money she was making. Now all she had to do was print some leaflets and tell everyone in the garrison that she was up and running.

She got her laptop out. As she cut and pasted pictures into the template she'd already designed, she wondered if she ought to tell Zoë she was leaving, or leaflet all the quarters first. Or maybe she ought to give Zoë a week's notice and get the leaflets out while she was working her notice period. That way she could slide from her job to her new venture. Yes, that was the way to do it.

Chapter Eighteen

'You fucking little underhanded cow,' shrieked Zoë.

Jenna stood her ground. 'Don't you talk to me like that,' she hissed right back.

'I can talk to you however I bloody like. This is *my* salon.'

The two faced each other like warring cats, claws ready to strike, eyes blazing; if they'd had tails, they'd have been all fluffed up like bottle-brushes. Around them, by the basins, in front of the mirrors, the other customers and stylists watched the row, agog.

'Call this a salon?' sneered Jenna. 'I've seen better appointed public toilets.'

'I've no doubt you have – it's where sewer rats like you hang out.'

'Bitch,' screeched Jenna.

Across the salon, Immi, waiting to have her roots done, was trying not to laugh. She couldn't wait to get on Facebook and relay the details to Chrissie. Poor Chrissie had sounded quite down when they'd managed to Skype the previous evening.

When she told Chrissie that she'd heard that Lee was out in Afghanistan too, Chrissie had just said, 'Really.'

'You search him out, Chrissie.'

There had been a deep sigh. 'Immi, Bastion is a place the size of Reading.'

'But it'd be nice to see a friendly face.'

'Maybe.'

Immi had ended the call worrying about her friend. Anyone else would have jumped at the chance of meeting up with an old friend in a new posting. Maybe it was long hours and a grim job that had made Chrissie sound so down. Anyway, a blow-by-blow account of what was happening in the hairdresser's was bound to give Chrissie a good laugh. She switched her attention back to the fight.

Jenna, incensed by another insult from Zoë, picked up a hairbrush and hurled it at her adversary. Zoë had the good sense to duck, as the Mason and Pearson whistled past her head. It missed Zoë, but connected with the mirror directly behind her. The glass shattered into a spider's web of crazed fragments.

'Get out,' screamed Zoë, whipping round to take in the damage. 'Get out!'

'Like I'd want to stay in this dump, anyhow.'

Jenna marched to the staffroom, gathered her coat and bag and stormed out, slamming the glass door behind her with such force that Immi wondered for a second if that mightn't shatter, too.

The silence following Jenna's departure lasted a full thirty seconds before the stylists turned their hairdryers back on and a low hubbub of chatter resumed.

And it all might have been quite entertaining, thought Immi, except that her roots had been booked in with Jenna. No hairdo for her today, then.

'Sorry about that,' said Zoë, sweeping across to Immi as if she'd just dealt with a spilt drink, not a very public falling-out. 'I think we might have to rebook you, if that's OK.'

'It'll have to be,' said Immi, grateful that at least Jenna hadn't actually started on her hair. With all the other stylists busy, goodness knew what would have happened if one half of her roots had been dyed and the other half hadn't. She followed Zoë over to the desk by the door. She wondered when, with a member of staff gone, Zoë would be able to fit her in again. Her roots were really on the limit. If Zoë couldn't fit her in soon, she'd have to have a go at doing them herself. On the other hand, maybe she could still get Jenna to do her hair this morning. Presumably she'd gone home and wouldn't have anything else to do. Maybe she'd be glad of the business: her first customer.

Immi made an excuse. 'I'll ring. I need my diary.' That way, if Jenna couldn't fit her in this morning or over the next couple of days, she hadn't burned her boats with Zoë.

Still chuckling about the scene she'd just witnessed, Immi set off for the soldier's patch and Jenna's quarter.

'Hiya,' said Jenna, when she opened the door. 'Come to gloat?' She might have been full of bravado at Zoë's, but she looked pretty deflated now.

'No! I have not. I want you to do my hair.'

Jenna brightened a little. 'Straight up, no kidding?'

'Of course.'

'You'd better come in, then.' She opened the door wide and let Immi in.

'Cor.' Immi whistled. 'This is really nice. Such an improvement.'

Jenna perked up even more. 'Like it? I'm going to get a couple of cream leather sofas to match the rug.'

'Lee must love this.'

'He's not seen it.'

'Nice surprise for when he gets back.'

'That's not the only surprise. Come and have a look at this.' Excitedly Jenna led Immi up to the bathroom.

'Shit a brick,' said Immi, when she saw the alterations.

'Good, isn't it?' said Jenna, mistaking Immi's reaction for total approval.

'Yeah,' said Immi, unable to conceal the doubt in her voice.

'You don't like it?'

'Of course I do, but this is a quarter, Jenna. I mean, apart from the fact that it must have cost a bomb, there's rules.'

Jenna sighed. 'Rules, rules, rules. It's always fucking rules.'

'But this is the army.'

'*I'm* not in the sodding army. Why doesn't anyone realise that?'

Immi bit her tongue. No, Jenna wasn't, but Lee was; although, as she wanted to get her hair done, perhaps this wasn't the time to point that out.

'Anyway,' she said, brightly, 'whoever did this did a lovely job. Love the black and silver. Classy.'

Jenna was instantly mollified. 'Nice, ain't it? And so much better than Zoë's. That's a dump, if ever there was one.'

Immi sat in the chair in front of the basin while Jenna swathed her in a plastic protector. 'Roots?'

'Please.'

Jenna got busy mixing the dye.

'So how did Zoë find out about this set-up?' asked Immi.

'I think I told her.'

'You did what?'

'I know. Can't believe I was so stupid. Mind you, she'd have found out sooner or later, but I was hoping to stay working at hers for a little longer – until I'd got going properly.'

'So why the hell *did* you tell her?'

'I didn't, not exactly. I leafleted the patches and the local area, so I must have dropped one through Zoë's front door. I mean, I never thought... Anyway,' shrugged Jenna, 'I got the last laugh. See this lot?' She pointed to the shelf of hair-dressing products. 'I nicked all of them from Zoë's, over the last few months. Stupid cow never noticed.'

But Immi wasn't sure that Jenna *had* got the last laugh. Zoë wasn't *that* stupid, and she reckoned that she would find a way of getting her own back. This wasn't just going to end with that cat-fight in the salon. Immi would put good money on this being a fight to the death.

The rain hammered down onto the already sodden ground, splashing into the muddy puddles and onto the grey sand, bouncing off the tent roofs, dripping off the vehicles while the damp, chill air insinuated itself into every corner of the tented city that was Camp Bastion. In the background was the permanent roar of planes and helicopters taking off, landing and taxiing, bringing in supplies and replacement troops and taking out the lucky guys who had finished their tour of duty and the not-so-lucky ones leaving on stretchers, or worse.

Chrissie raced from her sleeping quarters across the wet ground, jumping the deeper puddles, splashing through the shallow ones, to the field hospital. Every now and again, she looked up to check she was still heading in the right direction and not about to cannon into another person, also dashing, head down, for shelter. She caught a glimpse of a vast C17 as it took to the skies and almost instantly disappeared into the cloud that lowered over the camp. She'd only been in Bastion for a week and already she was wondering if volunteering had been such a bright idea.

It wasn't just the long hours, the injuries that she had to deal with – real injuries now, not fake ones made of plastic, wax and stage make-up – the lousy weather or the less than ideal living conditions: it was the homesickness. And even Chrissie knew that this was a bit rich, as she was one of the few inhabitants at Camp Bastion who really, truly, had no home. Whatever else Bastion was, it wasn't home – or anything that approximated it. No matter that it had been blinged up with KFC and Pizza Hut, nor that there were huge tents with computer games and big screen TVs getting satellite programmes streamed in from BFBS, it was still a surreal place. And she missed Immi, she missed seeing grass, she missed seeing people out of uniform, she missed being able to catch a bus to go shopping... she missed ordinary life.

And now she was missing Lee. She'd promised herself they wouldn't become friends but since their arrival together the previous week, he'd been a rock and *not* being friends with him had just been out of the question. For a start he'd surreptitiously passed her a hanky to dry her eyes and blow her nose before too many of the other squaddies cottoned on to how frightened she'd been on the plane. Being sick could easily be put down to the rough ride, but crying...? She'd get the piss ripped out of her for that. Then he'd helped her with her kit, when it had finally been unloaded off the flight, and escorted her to her temporary quarters.

'How are you feeling?' he'd asked, as he dumped her Bergen on her camp bed.

She'd smiled. 'Why? Scared I might honk again?'

It was Lee's turn to laugh. 'Well, you've got previous.'

'I'm fine,' she'd said.

'Good. Immi'd kill me if she thought I wasn't taking care of her bessie mate.' And he'd leant forward and given her a big hug. 'Now get some kip. We've got to be up in a couple of hours. I'll save you a place at breakfast.'

She and Lee were billeted quite close to each other for the first few days, while they, along with all the other soldiers new to theatre, underwent induction training. Obviously Lee's training was longer and more detailed as he was going to be out in some camel compound in the thick of the action. Chrissie, on the other hand, might never see beyond the airbase, but she still needed to be aware of the threats and tactics and the latest intelligence. Plus she also needed to be taught the basics on how to keep healthy and hydrated, when the temperatures started to soar again, as they would in just a matter of weeks. After three days, Chrissie was moved to her more permanent accommodation near to the field hospital, but Lee still saved her a seat in the cookhouse at meal times and treated her to an occasional can of Coke in their off-duty moments. And in those off-duty moments she kept a weather eye out for Phil because he had to be some-where in the place, but their paths didn't cross. Not that it was so surprising as, with each day that passed, Chrissie began to get a handle on just how enormous the camp was.

It was a couple more days into their RSOI training – Reception, Staging and Onward Integration – that they were walking back from the training centre and a gust of wind whipped up the gritty, sandy surface right in front of them, producing an instant dust devil. Despite the fact they both managed to shield their faces from the worst of it, Lee got an eyeful of muck.

'Jeez,' he exclaimed as his eye streamed. He put his hand to his face.

'Don't rub it,' ordered Chrissie, grabbing his hand and yanking it away.

'Shit, Chrissie, it canes.'

'Just keep your eye shut. Try not to move it in its socket

too much, you don't want to scratch the cornea. I'll clean it for you as soon as we get to the NAAFI.'

She grabbed his arm and led him between the rows of tents to the NAAFI, where she sat Lee down on the nearest chair and grabbed a plastic bottle of water and a clean paper table napkin from a dispenser.

She stood beside him, looking down. 'Put your head back,' she told him. Then she gently lifted the lid of his left eye and held it open with her finger and thumb and poured in the water. She could see the grains of sand being flushed out as she did. She got Lee to roll his eyes up, down and side to side, to check she'd rinsed all the debris out. 'That should do it.' She noticed her hands were trembling. Why did he have this effect on her? It wasn't natural. Or maybe, more worryingly, it was. 'That was just like the scene from *Brief Encounter*,' she joked to cover up her emotions.

Lee mopped his wet face with the serviette and blinked. 'It certainly feels a lot better. Still a bit sore though.'

'Bound to be.'

'And *Brief Encounter*? What the fuck's that?'

'An old film, black and white. One of my mum's favourites. A couple meet when she gets grit in her eye at a railway station. The bloke, a doctor, gets the dirt out with the corner of his hanky and they fall in love.'

'And he gets his leg over and they live happily ever after.'

'No. They're both married to other people.'

'So, no shag?'

Chrissie shook her head. 'No, no shag.'

'That's a pity,' said Lee, staring at her with a disconcerting intensity. 'Especially if they'd really fallen for each other.'

Chrissie looked at her feet. 'They had,' she whispered. 'But perhaps it was for the best.'

And it was later that evening that Immi had Skyped her, making Chrissie feel even more homesick. Homesickness that was compounded by the need to tell Immi a bunch of lies, after Immi had told her that Lee was out there too and they ought to seek each other out. Like she was going to admit to Immi just how much they were already seeing of each other, knowing full well how close Immi and Jenna were. No way!

Four days later, their encounters, brief or otherwise, came to an abrupt end when Lee's RSOI training ended and he was moved out to join his new multiple somewhere out in Nad-e Ali.

'Drop me a line or two, when you get the chance,' said Lee. 'Tell me what's going on back here.'

'Of course,' said Chrissie brightly. 'And you look after yourself. Watch where you are putting your size twelves, eh? I don't want you cluttering up any ward I happen to be working on.'

She said it casually, but inside she was terrified for Lee. Unlike him, she'd already seen the results of what IEDs could do. The lads seemed so gung-ho when they talked about going to their patrol bases, but the two she'd been treating, casevaced back, injured and limbless, their lives changed for ever, had minds that were as shattered as their bodies. The thought that that might be Lee's fate sent ice coursing through her blood.

Chapter Nineteen

Maddy was manoeuvring Nate's buggy out of her quarter when Caro called across to her from her own.

'You off out?'

'Just going along to the Spar for a few bits and pieces. We need some fresh air and as it's not pouring for once...' She gestured at the sky.

'Fancy a bit of company?'

'Sure, why not.'

'Perfect. Give me a second to get Luke ready. He's been a menace since he woke up and I need to wear him out to calm him down. It's that, or give him to Barnardo's. They're always after donations, aren't they?'

'I think they prefer cash,' said Maddy, grinning.

A few minutes later they were strolling along the pavement towards the little shop that served the married patch. Luke was alternately running ahead or lagging behind, so their progress was rather erratic.

'Ooh, look,' said Caro. 'There's Jenna. I want a word with her.'

'What are you after – an appointment?'

'I thought she could do a talk to the Wives' Club.'

'Oh.'

'You sound surprised.'

'Well...' said Maddy.

'You've got reservations.'

'I dunno.'

'Come on, spit it out,' said Caro, grabbing Luke's arm to stop him running into the road. Maddy stopped pushing the buggy and faced Caro.

'It's just, she's in Seb's platoon and I've been hearing rumours.'

'And?'

'And she's not exactly popular. There seems to be some resentment that she's set up in direct competition to Zoë.'

'There's no law against healthy competition,' said Caro.

'But she's really undercutting her. She doesn't have much in the way of overheads, so she can make her prices ridiculously low and there's wives who don't think that's fair.'

'I suppose.'

'And she seems a bit too upbeat about her husband being in Afghanistan. I mean, she doesn't have to sit around in sackcloth and ashes, we all know life has to go on, but I've heard on the grapevine that some of the wives are questioning whether she cares a jot about her husband. To be honest, I thought that myself, when I had my hair done the other day.'

'That's a bit harsh. She's probably just putting a brave face on it.'

'Maybe.' But Maddy knew exactly how she'd felt when Seb had been over there. She'd been able to function after a fashion and she hadn't become a complete basket case but even so, she certainly hadn't bounced around as if she didn't have a care in the world – which was what Jenna seemed to be doing.

They carried on walking to the Spar. The automatic doors swished open as they approached and a wave of noise buffeted them. Screams, screeches and obscenities rolled out of the door. Nate's face crumpled, Luke's eyes widened and the two mothers craned forwards.

'What the hell...?' said Caro.

They both peered in. By the tills they could see Zoë and Jenna having a proper, full-on cat-fight, skin and hair flying.

A burly sergeant in uniform had got between them at some personal risk and was trying to prise them apart while the Spar staff and the handful of other shoppers present looked on, stunned.

Finally the sergeant managed to part them.

Zoë tossed her hair back and smoothed down her skirt. 'And next time, you slag,' she panted, 'I'll get you good and proper.'

'Yeah? You and whose army?'

'The whole fucking garrison, that's who. No one likes you, Jenna Perkins. You're a ho, we all knew that, but now they think you're a lying, cheating, devious slapper too.'

Jenna launched herself again at Zoë, but the sergeant just managed to hold her back, and Zoë swept out of the supermarket, leaving Jenna hurling insulting epithets after her.

Maddy looked at Caro. 'Still want to invite her to the Wives' Club?'

Caro looked defiant. 'Frankly, I feel sorry for her. She's trying to make her own way and the system seems to be against her.'

Maddy clenched her jaw to stop it dropping. 'You can't be serious?'

'I can. If anyone needs a leg up it's her. Especially if Zoë is bad-mouthing her around the garrison.'

'But no one will come.'

Caro shook her head. 'No? I'll just put "local stylist" on the posters. By the time they find out it's Jenna, it'll be too late. I can't see them making a dash for the door, once they've paid their subs and got their tea and bikkies.'

Maddy followed Caro into the little shop thinking that Caro might have misjudged things completely. And Susie's words about Caro being a 'loose cannon' floated back to her. But she was the new kid on the block so what did she know?

Lee was in the watchtower in the corner of the compound, looking across the Neb Canal. Below him, under the scaffolding of this makeshift sangar, were the mud walls of the compound; behind him were the basic living quarters that the soldiers had rigged up for themselves; and in front of him was the twenty-metre-wide canal. On either side of the canal were the high, grey berms, raised dykes which had a road running along the top. Beyond the berm, on the far side, were more compounds occupied by Afghani families and their livestock, and behind that were the bare fields waiting for the next poppy crop. Squinting through the telescopic sight on his gun and trying to ignore how cold he was, Lee scanned the compounds on the opposite bank and then the trees that edged the far side of the empty field. Freezing rain was hammering down yet again – he was soaked to the skin – but he knew it wasn't just the cold that was making him shiver. The hot intel was that the Taliban in the area had acquired a sniper rifle, with a range of almost a kilometre. For all he knew, the cross hairs might be on him right now. It was a sobering thought, a thought that made him hunker down lower behind the wall of the sangar. Not that it would do much good. He doubted the planking would stop a high velocity bullet; it'd more than likely just make it tumble so that, when it hit him, it would cause all the more damage. He told himself to stop thinking like that and instead keep his eyes open for the slightest sign of movement in his current field of view.

Below and behind him, he could hear the banter of his colleagues. There was a discussion about what they were going to do with the compo rations, to make them slightly less dreary. The consensus seemed to be to add curry powder to the tins of stewed beef. Lee groaned. Not curry again. Jenna might be a shit cook but at least she bought a variety of ready meals. It's a shame, he thought, that Chrissie wasn't here to look after them; she'd be able to create something original out of the army's rations. He remembered the slap-up Christmas dinner she'd produced, and his mouth watered at the thought.

Concentrate! he told himself. He was here to do a job, not think about Chrissie. And he shouldn't be thinking of her, anyway.

Except he did. All the time.

He glanced at his watch; nearly six. Not long now till the end of his stag. Johnny would take over from him just before nightfall. Lee quite liked the dark out here. For a start, the stars were epic. Here, in the desert, the nights were the darkest that Lee had ever experienced and, consequently, the sky was completely coated with little pinpricks of light. Until he came out here he had no idea just how many stars there were. But the second reason he quite liked the dark was the soft glow of faint orange light on the horizon – Camp Bastion. There was something very comforting about having a tangible reminder of its presence, when you were stuck out in the back of beyond, surrounded by a lot of hostility.

The corner of his eye caught a movement, and he swivelled to look at what had got his attention. A small boy and a donkey were walking along the flat ground: nothing to worry about. He turned back to the line of trees several hundred yards away. If he were a sniper, that's where he'd hide to pick off a British soldier.

He heard footsteps on the ladder behind him.

'Hey, buddy,' said the voice of Johnny Flint. 'My turn now. Much happening?'

'Fuck all. A kid with a donkey is just about to walk past.'

'Rush hour, then.'

Lee grinned. 'That's about the size of it. Still, I suppose it's better when it's quiet.'

'Dunno. Makes you wonder what they're plotting.'

Lee took a swig of his water. 'So aren't *any* of the locals friendly?'

'To your face they are; all smiles and "*salaam alaikum*", but you just know that if the Taliban move in to the area, they'll probably want to change sides. The Taliban make the locals offers they can't refuse, and they don't bother with rules of engagement, either.' Johnny gave a hollow laugh. 'Actually, they don't bother with any fucking rules.'

Lee moved so Johnny could position himself behind the gun and then made his way down the ladder to the main compound. Water dripped off the rectangles of camouflaged waterproof fabric that had been lashed up to provide shelter from both the rain and the sun. It made him appreciate just how gleaming Bastion had been. It might have been Tent City, but the bogs flushed and there was running water. Here, the only running water was a stream that ran across the compound every time it rained heavily, and the only sign of civilisation was the interminable puttering of the diesel generator which fed their comms equipment. *Basic* didn't come close when it came to describing their conditions.

Still shivering, Lee decided to skip his meal and head straight for his bed space, which was a two-man tent, hard-up by the compound wall. He peeled off his wet clothes and hung them from a makeshift washing line strung from a couple of scaffolding poles, which held up yet more cam netting and tarps for shelter. Lee was certain his kit wouldn't dry before he had to put it on again, but he had dry clothes to wear in his sleeping bag. More important to sleep in comfort than to have that luxury on stag. Besides, it was much easier to keep alert, if you weren't feeling too cosy.

He decided to get his head down and try to grab some zeds. He was on duty again tonight, and then he'd come straight off his watch and go out on patrol at first light. Still, he wasn't going to complain, not even to himself. It wasn't as if he'd joined the army on a whim.

He pulled on a dry T-shirt and shorts and then his softie suit, which was like pyjamas made out of a duvet, and then climbed into his sleeping bag. Cosy at last, he thought, although both his softie suit and his bug bag already smelled less than fresh. He wondered how bad they would get by the time his tour was over. Minging, probably.

Lying down on his camp bed, he pulled his day sack out from underneath. He rummaged around till he found a chocolate bar he knew to be in there and the letter that had arrived this morning. Post was sporadic, he'd been told, and reality bore this out. If there was room on the supply run, they'd sling the postbag on too. If not, it stood to reason that water, food and ammo were more important.

Dear Lee, he read as he chomped on the Crunchie. *All is well here, although the place seems pretty dull and boring without your ugly mug cluttering up the joint. Work is the same old, same old with nothing much of note to report.*

People come and go. I've got a new neighbour, although you'd expect that given the turnover around here. She seems nice enough and we haven't fallen out yet. I'll try and send you some mags next time I write. Which would you prefer – lads' mags or cars? Or maybe something else. The shop here stocks a variety of stuff. Is there anything else you need? Let me know and I'll send that too. You look after yourself and I meant what I said about your size 12s. Watch where you're going. Best, Chrissie xx

Two kisses? Habit or significant? Part of him hoped for the latter explanation, although his head told him it was more likely the former. They got on – well, if he wasn't already married, he'd have liked it to be more, but no point in contemplating that. And Chrissie's letter was, at the moment, the only one he'd received. No word yet from his mam, or Jenna. Of course, the post from the UK was bound to take longer. There were probably several letters on the way, he reasoned. He just needed to be patient. He slipped the letter back into his day sack, finished his snack and snuggled down to get forty winks. But it was Chrissie he was thinking of, not Jenna, as he drifted off.

Chapter Twenty

'Summers.'

'Yes, boss,' Chrissie answered. She finished writing down the patient's temperature on the chart at the end of the bed, gave the soldier an apologetic smile and turned to give the doctor her attention.

'How's it going?' asked the colonel.

'Good, thanks, sir.'

'Settling in OK?'

Chrissie nodded. 'Getting used to it. I've almost stopped hearing the noise of the helicopters.'

The colonel grinned. 'I know what you mean.' The sound of helicopters was the soundtrack of the base: starting up, winding down, hovering, landing, taking off. There was never a minute of the day without the clatter and the accompanying high-pitched whine of the engines. 'And talking of helicopters, I'm looking for a volunteer.'

'What for?' asked Chrissie warily. She might have volunteered to come out here to Bastion but, like all soldiers, she didn't readily put herself forward for other duties outside her job spec.

'The MERT team.'

'Oh.' Well, that would be something different. The medical emergency response team were the medics on standby to fly in a Chinook to scoop battlefield casualties off the ground and rush them back to the hospital. The Chinook they flew in was kitted out like a full-on A&E, so the treatment could be started as soon as the soldier was on board. The golden hour gleamed a little brighter and was extended a little longer with this facility.

'You'll want time to think about it.'

'A little,' Chrissie conceded. Wanting to save lives was a no-brainer, but Chrissie knew that it wasn't the safest option. OK, so Bastion had incurred attacks, guys inside the huge camp had been killed, but the MERTs flew into raging battles. They had protection from the Apache attack helicopters that accompanied them, and they flew with armed troops on board, who deployed on landing, to protect them on the ground, but Chinooks were still bloody big targets and had been shot out of the sky before.

'How long?' asked the colonel. 'Only we'll need a replacement on the MERT by the end of the week. If you say no, I've got to nobble someone else.'

Chrissie made up her mind. She wasn't a heroine, but she didn't have any dependents. If anything happened to her, there wouldn't be any knock-on. No kids left motherless, no grieving parents, no husband or fiancé to mourn her. Anyway, she quite fancied a ride in a helicopter. 'I'll do it.'

'You sure?' said the colonel.

Chrissie nodded. 'Why not? I've had a really quiet life. It could do with some pepping up. A bit of excitement might be nice.'

'Brilliant. And if it's excitement you're after, you'll be sure to get it. Go and see Major Tomlinson, he'll brief you. You know where to find him?'

Chrissie certainly did. The MERT teams had their own space at the far end of the field hospital, the end nearest the helipad. There they waited for the calls to come in with the details of the casualty to be rescued. While the pilot raced for the chopper and got it started, the team grabbed the necessary medical supplies. Happily they spent a lot of their time being bored, but the trouble was, it wasn't *enough* of their time.

She finished her immediate duties, got permission from the ward sister to go and talk to the MERT team, and slipped down the tented corridors of the hospital to where the standby team hung out. She went into the rest room and introduced herself to Major Tomlinson.

'Welcome aboard, Summers,' he said, shaking her hand. 'A willing volunteer being worth ten pressed men and all that baloney.'

'Yes, possibly,' said Chrissie.

'Hi, Chrissie.'

She spun round. 'Phil!' She was genuinely pleased to see him. A ready-made friend and a familiar face and, finally, their paths had crossed.

'Don't sound so surprised. You knew I was here.'

She laughed. 'I know, I know, and I did try to find you to start with, promise, but there's so much going on, I sort of forgot.'

Phil's face fell. 'You forgot me? I am well insulted.' He stepped back and smiled. 'It's good to see you here, Chrissie.'

Chrissie felt a surge of pleasure at being so welcomed. 'Thanks.'

'So,' said Major Tomlinson, 'let's get back to your briefing, shall we?' But it was said in an easy tone. He, too, seemed pleased that the new addition to the team appeared to be such a welcome one. 'You know how we work?'

'The basics, obviously.'

The major reached behind him and picked a pad off the table. 'You've seen one of these before – a nine-liner?'

Chrissie scanned the pro forma. It was a checklist of nine details required when the request for a casualty evacuation was radioed in. Stuff like how serious the injuries were, how many patients, how they were going to locate the pick-up point and another six other details, including the consideration of whether or not they might have to operate under hostile conditions and the like. 'Only in training. I've not seen a real one filled out.'

'Lucky you,' said the major grimly. 'After you've been with us a week, you'll start wishing you'd never seen one at all.'

Chrissie wasn't quite sure what to say to this, so she kept silent. She just hoped she'd made the right decision and it wasn't one she'd regret later.

'Your mate Jenna has been causing trouble again,' said Seb, as he walked into the kitchen at lunchtime.

Maddy stopped stirring the soup and sighed. How often did she have to tell him? 'She's not my mate. Anyway, what's she done now?'

'She had another slanging match with Zoë. This time in the Spar.'

'I know, I was there.'

'You were *there*?'

'I was popping to get some bits and pieces when Zoë stormed out with Jenna yelling some choice phrases after her.'

'You didn't tell me.'

'I didn't think it was that important.'

'But she's the wife of one of my soldiers.'

'I didn't think you wanted me to get involved.'

'Maddy, there's a difference between getting involved and telling me stuff.'

'I'll remember next time.' She knew she sounded sulky and petulant but she'd been much more worried about Caro's mad plan to invite Jenna to talk to the Wives' Club and the trouble *that* was likely to cause, than she had been with the spat in the Spar. And she couldn't tell Seb about Caro's scheme, because he'd tell Will and Will'd probably get cross with Caro and it would all be *her* fault.

'Anyway, I don't suppose there'll be a next time,' said Seb. 'I can't see how Jenna's business will fly, if Zoë's got it in for her.'

'Doesn't that make you feel a bit sorry for Jenna?'

'It isn't as if she's invested anything in her venture. She hasn't got a proper shop like Zoë, has she?'

'Salon,' corrected Maddy automatically.

'You know what I mean. Whatever she's doing, it's a bit tinpot in comparison. Stands to reason.'

'And it's not a tinpot business.' Shit. She hadn't meant that to slip out.

Seb looked bewildered. 'What do you mean?'

'Nothing.'

'Maddy?'

She couldn't meet Seb's eye.

'Maddy, if you don't tell me yourself, I'll find out. What's Jenna been up to?'

'She's had alterations done to her quarter,' mumbled Maddy.

'She's done what?' Seb's bewilderment turned to anger in a heartbeat. 'You knew this and you didn't tell me?'

'You didn't want to know,' retorted Maddy, now equally angry, although mostly with herself for letting the cat out of the bag. Nate, on the floor in his bouncy chair, looked startled at the outbursts and screwed his eyes up ready to cry. Maddy hunkered down beside him and gave him a kiss. He gurgled instead. 'I asked you if you wanted me to find out what she was up to and you told me "not to meet trouble halfway". Your *exact* words, Seb.' She stared up at him belligerently. 'You made it perfectly clear I wasn't to get involved or interfere.'

'Yes, but I didn't know she'd done *that*!'

'You didn't *want* to know,' she repeated, as she got to her feet again and went back to stirring the soup.

'So what's she had done, exactly?'

'She's got a proper hairdressing basin in her bathroom. And she's had the bath taken out and a shower put in.'

Seb's jaw hung slackly. 'She's what?'

'You heard,' said Maddy.

'And she's got away with it?'

Maddy shoved away the uncomfortable thought that Jenna would have continued to get away with it, if she hadn't got such a big mouth. 'I don't suppose her customers want to rock the boat. She's bloody good as a hairdresser.'

'Just because her customers don't want to rock the boat doesn't mean what she's done isn't against regulations.' Seb ran his hand through his hair. 'Why hasn't someone bubbled her? And how come no one noticed the work going on?'

'I gather she just told her neighbours her quarter needed the bathroom refurbed and they believed her. Some of them were a bit jealous – said their bathrooms were grotty and needed doing – but we all know how the system works. That generally it's never *your* turn for the new carpets or curtains, it's the turn of the person who moves into your quarter when you've gone. You know, jam tomorrow.'

Seb nodded. 'And her neighbours just accepted her story?'

'Come off it, why on earth shouldn't they? Who on earth would be mental enough to have that sort of work done on a quarter? Of *course* all her neighbours thought it was pukka.'

'I can't ignore this – not now I know. I'm going to have to tell Housing.'

'Must you, Seb? She's only trying to run a business. Can't you turn a blind eye? Please.' What had she done? Her sense of guilt went off the scale. Even if she'd changed her mind about Jenna and didn't much like her these days, even if she thought she was out of order, the woman didn't deserve this.

He shook his head, as Maddy put two bowls on the table and poured in tomato soup. 'Not now. How can I deny that I know, now that I do? Sorry, Maddy, but the shit is about to hit the fan. And in the meantime, I think it'd be better if you didn't have anything to do with Jenna – including getting her to do your hair. I think this is bound to cause trouble and let's try not to get involved, eh?'

God, thought Maddy, now she couldn't even choose where to get her hair done. Bloody army. But over and above her annoyance was that thick layer of guilt. Never mind what Zoë might have threatened to do to scupper Jenna's business, she had done it for real.

Jenna was sitting in her swanky lounge, her feet up on the cream leather recliner, taking it easy. Business had been building up slowly and this morning had been her best day of trading yet. She'd had appointments all morning, she'd taken the best part of two hundred quid and, if things kept up like this, in six months or so she'd be able to pay off the cost of the bathroom and the other improvements she'd made to the quarter. Of course, when she'd run out of the products she'd filched from Zoë's, her overheads were going to go up, but she reckoned she'd still be able to undercut the bitch. She wasn't paying proper business rates on the property, nor was she intending to pay income tax. Cash in hand, who was to know what she earned? No VAT either, come to that.

She was flicking through one of the glossy mags she kept there for 'her ladies', when there was a violent banging on her door. She jumped. She didn't have any appointments for another hour. Who on earth was this? Whoever it was was certainly impatient, she thought grumpily, as she got off the recliner and made her way to the door.

'Yes?' she said to the major standing on her doorstep. She thought she recognised him from somewhere.

'Mrs Perkins?'

She nodded.

'I'm Major Milward, the housing commandant.'

Ah yes, the guy who'd done the march-in.

'May I come in?'

'I suppose.' Uh-oh, she thought, with a frisson of anxiety. She could guess what this might be – all those sodding regulations she'd been warned about.

'Good. I don't think our conversation is one to be held in the open.'

And that just confirmed her fears.

She opened the door wide and let the officer in. She could see him taking in her improvements to her sitting room. And that was all legal, wasn't it? she thought belligerently. There was nothing in the army's sodding rules that said you couldn't have your own furniture, if you wanted it. And who wouldn't? The stuff they issued you with was gross.

'Mrs Perkins,' began the major. He sounded very formal.

Time for the charm offensive, thought Jenna. She had nothing to lose and if she could get him on her side, it might make the difference. 'No need to be so formal, is there? Call me Jenna.' She bestowed him with her very best smile.

There was a beat. 'Mrs Perkins,' resumed Milward, 'this isn't a social call. I believe you are running a business from your quarter.'

'Not really,' she lied smoothly. 'I do a bit of hairdressing for friends. There's nothing wrong with that, is there?' She looked him bang in the eye.

'If I believed that was *all* it amounted to there'd be nothing wrong with that. But it doesn't, does it?'

'Who says?'

'That's irrelevant.'

'It bloody isn't. It's that Zoë, isn't it?'

Major Milward shook his head. 'Not Zoë.'

So who had bubbled her? She would give her back teeth to find out.

'So are you?' probed Milward. 'Running a business?'

'No.'

Milward got up and headed for the stairs.

'Hey, where are you going?'

'I need to use your bathroom.'

Jenna ran to stop him but he was already halfway up the stairs. 'Bugger,' she muttered under her breath. She returned to the sitting room to wait for him. It wasn't long before she heard his footsteps descending again.

'Just what on earth did you think you were doing?' he said, as he entered the room.

'Why, what's the matter?' She turned her big blue eyes on him, the picture of innocence as she well knew.

The major looked a little nonplussed. 'Surely Private Perkins told you about the terms of your tenancy agreement?'

'We'd only just moved in, when they sent him to Afghan.'

Charm hadn't worked, so she decided to try another tack. She blinked rapidly, to get rid of imaginary tears.

'But you can't do what you've just done!'

'What?' Keep up the innocent act, she told herself, as she wiped away another non-existent tear.

'The bathroom.'

'What's wrong with it?'

'What's wrong with it?' Milward was quite red now. Jenna wasn't sure if it was anger, or the embarrassment of dealing with a crying woman. 'Everything.'

'But it cost a fortune,' she whispered. She wasn't lying about that.

'And I've no doubt it'll cost a similar amount to put it back to exactly how it was. And that's what you'll have to do. There will be no choice, do you understand?'

She managed to squeeze out a real proper tear. 'But... but...' She let it roll down her cheek. 'What a waste of money. Lee'll kill me.'

'I'm sorry, Mrs Perkins.'

Jenna fled into the kitchen. She leaned against the tatty counter and sobbed theatrically.

'I'm sorry, Mrs Perkins, I really am,' said the major from the doorway. Not that he sounded it. There was an embarrassed silence, while Jenna kept up the crocodile tears. She wondered for a second if she mightn't be overdoing it.

'Would a cup of tea help?' Milward offered.

Perhaps she wasn't – she racked up the sobs. She could hear him clattering around, filling the kettle, looking for mugs. She wasn't going to help him out, why should she? Bastard. Finally, things calmed down, the kettle boiled and she could hear water being poured into mugs. She let her sobs subside a fraction.

'Come on, Mrs Perkins,' Milward said cheerily. 'Things will look better with a cup of tea.'

Jenna doubted it, but as she had no intention of converting her bathroom back – they couldn't make her, could they? – she might just humour him, to get him off her case. After all, she was a civvy – what could the army do to her? She could pretend to stop hairdressing, she could tell him she'd given up her business and, unless he kept an eye on her twenty-four-seven, how would he know?

Except of course her bloody neighbours might grass on her. That Sharon woman had never liked her and would probably kill for the chance to drop her right in it. No, thought Jenna, she had to be more devious. What she needed was Milward on her side.

Milward put the two mugs of tea down on her table and took a seat on one of the sofas. Jenna sat next to him. Not too close, she didn't want to be too obvious. She might only be a private's wife and a civvy to boot, but she was also a woman, and a woman who generally got her own way. She eyed Milward up: short, tubby and balding. Jenna bet her bottom dollar that he hadn't had a woman take an interest in him in a couple of decades. Well, his luck was about to change.

'Thank you for being so kind,' she said, giving him a damp, doe-eyed stare from under her lashes.

'Well, I haven't been, not really,' he blustered.

'Making tea and everything. I didn't mean to cry. It's just… it's just…' She sniffed. 'What with Lee being away and everything and I've been so worried about him.' She smiled weakly. 'I thought if I had something to do, to take my mind off everything, it'd make life a little easier.' She sighed. 'Looks like I won't have anything to help me now.' She allowed two fat tears to roll down her face.

'I know how tough it is,' said the major.

'No, you don't,' said Jenna. 'You have no idea. You've never been the one left behind, have you?'

'Well… no.'

'Exactly. I'm a nervous wreck. Look.' Jenna held her hand out, making sure that it trembled convincingly. She used the opportunity to move a few inches closer to Major Milward. 'I don't sleep properly, I'm losing weight.'

'Can't the doctor…'

'Hopeless.' She shrugged for emphasis. 'It's the loneliness at night. That's the worst thing.' She gave the major a significant look followed by a coy smile. 'And if I don't have a job, I won't even feel tired. I'll never get to sleep, all by myself.' She inched closer again so she was almost touching him. 'You could make an exception for me, couldn't you?' she breathed, staring at him. 'I'd be so grateful.' She put her hand on his leg.

Major Milward leapt to his feet, hitting the coffee table with his knees and making the tea slop over the sides of the mugs.

'I've got to be going. You must cease trading forthwith.' He fled the room, and the house, slamming the front door behind him.

Fuck – she might have misjudged that one.

Chapter Twenty-One

Lee adjusted his body armour and then strapped his helmet on. The rain of the previous few days had stopped and now the weather was bright, but cold.

'Day four hundred in the Big Brother house,' he said to Johnny, deadpan in his Geordie accent, 'and the housemates are making the most of the fine weather.'

'Ha ha,' said Johnny, who was loading a magazine into his SA80 rifle. 'And that's too close to the truth. Just like them we're shut up in a compound, surrounded by hostile strangers. The only difference is the inmates might get sex.'

'And booze,' said Lee morosely.

'And you shouldn't joke about the weather.'

'Why not?'

'Good Taliban fighting weather,' said Johnny.

Lee paused and swallowed. 'Great,' he said with bravado he certainly didn't feel. It wasn't that he was scared, but no one in their right mind wouldn't be apprehensive about going out on patrol, with the possibility that they might get killed or injured. 'Let's hope we get to slot a few first.'

'Assuming they don't get us before we can.'

Lee concentrated on clipping up his chinstrap. 'No chance,' he retorted with more false confidence. He hefted his Bergen containing ammo, medical supplies and water – lots of water – onto his back. The other soldiers were equally laden with other necessities: more ammo, more first aid kits, comms equipment, more water. Some of them had filled their pockets with boiled sweets from the compo rations to give to kids they might encounter. 'Hearts and minds,' Johnny had said, as he'd raided the food store for the goodies. 'Maybe if we're nice to them, the little buggers will be less inclined to kill us when they grow up.'

Lee wasn't convinced. The British had fought here in the nineteenth century and had had their arses kicked – twice – then the Russians had had a go in the twentieth and they'd lost, so why on earth did anyone think it was going to end with tea and medals all round for the allies in the twenty-first? Still, his not to reason why, his just to do and...

Let's not go *there*, he thought.

Sergeant Adams, in charge of their multiple, gave the order for the big metal door to the compound to be opened, and the ten-man patrol made their way out in single file. Johnny slung his rifle over his shoulder and switched on the Vallon mine detector. He wouldn't start sweeping for IEDs till they got over the Neb canal; the area around the compound was too closely monitored for the enemy to have any chance of laying an ambush on their doorstep, but once they got behind the compounds on the far bank, that was when the danger really started.

'It's like going for a heavy night on the lash, isn't it?' said Johnny over his shoulder, as he moved forward.

'How do you work that out?' asked Sergeant Adams.

'We might get legless.'

The multiple laughed, as did Lee. The gallows humour was in such poor taste it really was quite funny, and he couldn't help himself. But even so, he felt his heart start to accelerate. He had been here for several weeks now and the fear at the start of each patrol was just as intense as it had been on his first one. He wondered if the others were cacking it too. Not that it was a question he could ask. The others would rip the piss out of him if he admitted how he felt, no matter that they might be in the same state. Johnny led the way, followed by Sergeant Adams and then Lee, with the others following on.

The metal bridge built by the sappers was about a hundred yards down the canal, and they could pretty much relax till they got to it and crossed over. Despite the fact that it was chilly, the sun was bright in the clear blue sky and the effort of walking with sixty kilos meant that Lee broke into a sweat as he climbed up the berm. Or was it nervous tension that caused trickles of perspiration to run down his spine? Like all the soldiers he kept his head moving, scanning for movement, looking for a glint of sun on metal, checking for any sign of the enemy.

Nothing – or rather nothing that he could spot.

The patrol tabbed on down the berm, across the canal bank and onto the bridge. If there was a sniper out there they'd be sitting ducks here – no cover, nothing. Swiftly they ran over it with Lee's adrenalin reaching epic levels. Now things could get really dodgy. On this side of the canal, the locals could be intimidated by the Taliban. And, worryingly, it was suspiciously quiet. If there were kids kicking about, playing in the dust or tending goats, you could be pretty sure that there was no chance of an ambush. The locals knew when it was safe and when it wasn't, and if it wasn't, they kept their children away from the danger.

Lee reached to the back of his belt kit and undid the straps of what the army coyly called 'tier two' personal protection, which was designed to protect his tackle, should he get his legs blown off. The soldiers called it the combat codpiece or the armoured nappy but, whatever its name, it did wonders for morale. The idea of being an amputee was bad enough but being an impotent one was far worse. Knowing that his knackers were safely tucked away behind some serious protection was a big comfort. He pulled the front of the nappy-shaped piece of kit between his legs and attached the clips at the side, then he carried on walking, although his level of vigilance had racked up again. His nuts might be safe, but the rest of him was pretty exposed, and there was no point in meeting trouble halfway, as his mum liked to say. Keeping a sharp lookout, he also concentrated on putting his feet exactly where the sergeant had placed his.

The object of this patrol was to go and meet the head man of the next village. They had a couple of 'terps' tagging along with them so when they got there they could discuss a proposal to de-mine the village square, which the Taliban had booby-trapped thoroughly. None of the multiple had more than a few words of Pashto at best, so it was essential to have local interpreters with proper language skills to help out. If the head man, the malik, agreed to allow them to go ahead with the de-mining, it would bring some semblance of normality back to another little community as they would be able to trade and re-establish their market. Well, that was the theory, Sergeant Adams had told them. Lee and Johnny were sceptical. What was to stop the Taliban rocking back in the future and buggering it up again? They couldn't be there twenty-four-seven to prevent it. But if it made the Brass back at Bastion happy, then who were they to argue?

Except, of course, the meeting had had to be arranged, so there were a number of people who now knew exactly where this patrol was heading for – and it was perfectly likely that not all of them would be happy for the soldiers to arrive. That was another thought that Lee put to the back of his mind.

At the edge of the bare field behind the compounds ran an irrigation ditch, bordered on each side by reeds and some scrappy trees. They headed for that, Johnny sweeping his metal detector in an arc in front of him, while everyone else followed assiduously in his wake. At the water's edge they all jumped in. IEDs didn't function when waterlogged, so the water might be freezing and smelly, but it provided safety for the moment.

They trudged through the water to the next field, which was full of uncut maize. The ditch pretty much dried out at this point, but the maize provided another safe route for the next few hundred yards, or at least Lee reckoned it did, as he looked about him. Surely it would be difficult to bury a device and not noticeably disturb the crop, and a sniper would find it hard to get a bead on the patrol moving through the densely planted stalks? He began to relax a little.

They were halfway across the field when a shot rang out. So much for being safe from snipers. Lee dropped as if he himself had been wounded and his heart rate went mental. No one yelled 'man down', indicating an injury, but instantly there were shouts and commands from the more senior, experienced members of the patrol. For a couple of seconds it seemed as if chaos reigned while the patrol tried to identify the direction of the shot.

'Bravo one four,' bellowed the radio operator into the mic. 'Contact, wait out.'

Lee and the rest of the patrol began to leopard crawl through the tough maize stalks, heading, as near as they could tell, towards where the shot had been fired. Despite his fear,

Lee's training had taken over, together with the most powerful feeling that he couldn't let his mates down. The stony soil jagged into his knees and the dry leaves of the corn had razor-sharp edges which slashed at his bare hands, but he ignored the discomfort, as he ploughed on. After a couple of minutes, he could tell he was nearing the edge of the field. He slowed down; the last thing he wanted to do was barrel out into the sniper's line of fire. Carefully, he peered through the stems.

Lee jumped out of his skin, as a machine gun rattled off next to him.

'Ten o'clock, in the treeline,' yelled one of his colleagues.

Lee swivelled, as another bullet cracked past, this time very close. He didn't see where the bullet went, but he was pretty sure he could identify where it was coming from. The crack-thump of the shot had almost no discernible time between the two parts. The crack was the supersonic shock wave in front of the bullet as it passed by and the thump was the ordinary sound wave of the rifle actually being fired, which followed – like the flash and bang of lightning and thunder. The closer together, the closer the proximity. This crack-thump had been almost simultaneous; the sniper could only be about a hundred yards ahead.

Lee lay as still as he could and peered through the stalks, to try to see a movement. This guy, if he was still in the area, was either stupendously brave or stupendously stupid. How on earth could he possibly hope to survive, when the odds were ten against one? And the odds had just got shorter: Lee could hear the radio operator sending coordinates for some air support. Lee hoped to God the map reference was correct. He did not want to be picked off by some trigger-happy Apache pilot, mistaking him for the sniper. In this thick vege-tation, he had no doubt that they would be relying on thermal

214

imaging, and his signal would be just the same as the other bastard's. The glow from his body heat on the screen would look no different – human was human, no matter if you were a terrorist or not.

Trying not to let his growing feeling of apprehension get the better of him, he lay as quietly as he could, waiting to hear the sound of the approaching chopper. And after a few minutes, because he knew what to listen for, he heard it: barely more than a whisper in the distance. And then, from out of nowhere, the earth a hundred yards ahead of him exploded. The bang was monumental, and the ground Lee was lying on shook and trembled. Lee had had no idea that the Hellfire missile had been launched, and neither would the sniper. One moment he would have been lying there, trying to get a squaddie in his sights, and the next – oblivion. Clods of earth, stones, bits of tree clattered down and, if it had been a direct hit on the gunman, Lee didn't care to think what else.

'All clear,' said the radio operator after a quick exchange with the Apache pilot.

Feeling very shaky, Lee rose to his feet, staggering once again under the weight of his pack.

'What you done, Perkins?' asked the sergeant.

'No idea what you're on about,' said Lee.

'Your leg.'

Lee glanced down. The left leg of his multicam trousers was torn and his knee underneath had a cut, pouring blood. 'No idea, Sarge. Must have cut it on a stone or something, in all the excitement.'

'Get it washed and put a dressing on it.'

The rest of the patrol waited while Lee took off his Bergen, rolled up his trousers and sorted out the worst of his cut.

After slathering it in antiseptic cream and putting on a dressing they were ready to set off again.

'You keep an eye on that, Perkins,' ordered Sergeant Adams. 'I don't want to have to send you sick, understand?'

But by the time they got back to base that evening, it was obvious that that was exactly what they were going to have to do. Lee's knee was very painful, to the extent he could hardly walk on it, plus it was red and swollen and pus was oozing from the cut. Their medic took one look at it and declared that he didn't think he had strong enough antibiotics in his kit.

'Besides, boss, there's a chance the infection might spread. If he gets septicaemia it could all go shit-shaped really quickly.'

'You'll be going back tomorrow on the supply truck,' said Adams. 'Fucking waste of space you are. Battle casualty replacement means you're supposed to replace the guy that got injured, nor bring us a new injury to cope with. Tosser.'

Chapter Twenty-Two

Seb stared at Major Milward across his desk in his office in stunned silence. Finally, he said, 'You're joking.'

'Nope. God's honest truth. The woman actually made a pass at me. I mean, if putting your hand on someone's thigh counts as a pass – and it does in my book.'

Seb just managed to choke back the question, 'Why you?' He'd met Jenna, he knew what a stunner she was, and Alan Milward was *not* babe-magnet material. But then he thought of the note on Perkins' file about Jenna having caused fights in Tommy's Bar. The inference had been very clear: she was free with her favours and not too picky about who with, but Alan Milward...?

Seb brought his thoughts back to the main problem. 'But did she agree to cease trading?' he asked.

'No, but I gave her an ultimatum.'

'Is she likely to abide by it?'

'I don't think she'll be doing hairdressing from her house. Even Jenna Perkins isn't that stupid. She can earn money from hairdressing in the wives' own homes, I can't stop that, but I *can* stop her from trading from her quarter.'

'I suppose that's fair,' said Seb.

'To be honest, I'd have probably turned a blind eye to it, if it had just been a bit of illicit hairdressing, but she's made unauthorised alterations to her quarter. Straws and camels' backs and all that.'

'And then she made a pass at you.'

'Indeed. Don't think I'll be telling Cath about that last bit.'

Not if Alan Milward had any sense, thought Seb. He remembered meeting Cath at Susie and Mike Collins's dinner party and the word 'formidable' had been invented for her.

'But I could mention to Cath,' continued Alan Milward, 'that Jenna mightn't be the best person for the officers' wives to go to, if they want to get their hair done. I'm not going to let Jenna Perkins get away with this.'

'Isn't that a bit draconian?' asked Seb, forgetting he'd effectively told his wife exactly the same.

'She broke just about every rule in the book. Plus she's done her damnedest to undercut Zoë. I had her complaining to me, only the other day, that there is no way she can compete with Jenna if Jenna isn't paying business rates, or VAT, or anything like that. I'm sorry, Seb, but that woman is a liability and she's going to be real trouble.'

'Fair enough,' said Seb.

He couldn't argue with Alan's assessment. Hadn't he come to much the same conclusion himself? However, he wasn't convinced that Alan would be able to put an end to the problem of Mrs Perkins. 'And what are we going to do about her behaviour towards you?'

'My word against hers, but next time I'll take a woman with me, as a chaperone. I'm pretty certain I'll be going back there. There's going to be a family breakdown to deal with before too long, if that's the way she goes about getting herself out of trouble. Can't see this marriage going the distance, can you?

Seb sighed. Perkins was a bloody good soldier and deserved better than this. The last thing he needed, while he was on an operational tour, was to be distracted by problems at home.

'There's a mate of yours, just come in,' said Major Tomlinson, as he entered the ready room where the crew waited on standby. He saw Chrissie's eyes widen in fear and quickly added, 'Minor injury. Nothing to get too excited about.'

'Who?' Chrissie had made friends other than Lee and Phil since being out in Bastion, but the nature of the place was very transitory. Soldiers arrived, did their initial training and then went into Helmand; the people based in Bastion came and went, so she wasn't very close to anyone outside of her MERT and as far as she was aware, everyone in that was alive and kicking.

'Chap called Perkins,' said the major.

'Lee?' Her heart gave a little bounce of pleasure at the thought of seeing him again.

'If that's his name. Got a message to say he's asking for you.'

'Really?'

'The Lee Perkins you vommed over on exercise?' asked Phil Johns, joining in the conversation.

'The one and only,' said Chrissie.

'And he still wants to talk to you?' Phil's face was a picture of incredulity.

Chrissie nodded.

'Must be a head injury,' said Phil.

Chrissie threw her paperback at him. 'Fuck off,' she said amiably. 'Can I go and see him, boss?'

Tomlinson nodded. 'Of course, except if they call Op Minimise while you're away, I want you straight back here.'

Chrissie nodded back. She knew the form well enough now. Op Minimise might well presage a call-out for themselves, and no one would thank her for delaying their departure when minutes, even *seconds*, counted.

'Anyway,' asked Phil, 'what's Perkins doing here? 1 Herts are still tucked up in Kent.'

'He's a BCR for 2 Herts. Want to come with me? Talk man-talk with him: football and crap like that. He'll probably find it more interesting than me banging on about the shortage of soft loo paper, or the lack of Mills & Boons in the camp bookshop.'

Phil laughed at that and arched an eyebrow. 'Not sure I'm the best person to talk about footie, but I promise I'll do my best. Besides, I could do with a leg-stretch. You sure?'

Chrissie nodded, why not? Besides, she didn't want Lee thinking there was anything between them other than a casual friendship, even if her own emotions were doing their level best to undermine her resolve.

The pair made their way through the labyrinth of corridors to the non-acute ward. Lee was in a bed near the entrance. He had a drip in his arm, but other than that he looked remarkably fit, for a hospital case.

'Hi, Lee,' said Chrissie. His face brightened as she pulled a chair out by his bed and sat down. 'This is my mate, Phil. You two have met before – he's the guy that sorted me out, after I was taken poorly by the guts on that exercise. Remember?'

Phil stuck his hand out. 'Hi, Lee.'

Lee looked from Chrissie to Phil before he shook it. 'Hi,' he grunted.

'So, what's the matter?' asked Chrissie.

'Infected leg.' Lee flipped off the sheet covering his leg, and Phil and Chrissie peered at his wound. The cut had been stitched but it was still a very angry red and the skin around his knee was inflamed. Between the sutures were yellow beads of dry pus.

'Nasty,' said Chrissie.

'Better than it was,' said Lee, pragmatically. 'And on the bright side, I've had a hot shower, food that isn't compo, a shit in a proper lav and a night in a proper bed.'

'Worth the injury, then,' said Chrissie. She tried to ignore the feelings that were surging through her. I am *not* interested, she told herself firmly. 'How's Jenna?'

'I got a satphone call through to her last week, from the compound. I'm hoping to Skype her while I'm here.'

'That'd be nice. I spoke to Immi the other day, who bitched about being bored. I told her to get her arse out here – that'd stop any of that bollocks.'

It was Lee's turn to laugh. 'Can you imagine Immi and all the blokes here?'

Chrissie chuckled. 'Let's not go there.'

'Who's Immi?' asked Phil.

'A clerk in Battalion HQ,' said Lee. 'You must have seen her around the barracks. Brunette, long legs, big blue eyes...'

'Sometimes brunette,' said Chrissie. 'She changed to that from blond and before that she was a redhead.'

'Oh, her,' said Phil. 'Yes, I know her. Not really my type, though.'

'Really?' said Chrissie archly.

'Not my sort at all. I can see the attraction, though.'

'You must be one of the very few blokes in the battalion who doesn't dream of getting into her knickers. And one of a small group who haven't succeeded,' said Lee. 'Myself excluded. Happily married bloke and all that.'

'Hey,' said Chrissie, 'I know she's got a bit of a reputation, but that was harsh.' But she laughed because although Lee had exaggerated hugely about Immi, it was quite funny.

'Sorry,' said Lee, not looking as if he was in the least.

Chrissie changed the subject. 'When will you be fit to go back?'

'A couple of days, at the most. As soon as they're sure I'm clear of any infection, that'll be it – back on the next supply truck.'

An alarm sounded over the tannoy. All movement and conversation on the ward stopped and attention was swivelled to the speaker in the corner.

'Op Minimise, Op Minimise,' said the disembodied voice. 'All personnel are to be aware that Op Minimise is now in force.'

'Fuck,' said Chrissie. 'Gotta go, Lee, we may be needed. Come and find me, when you're up again. I'm with the MERT,' she called over her shoulder, because she was already legging it down the ward with Phil racing behind her.

When they arrived back at their HQ, they found that it was an American team that had been tasked.

'Not one of ours,' said Chrissie, panting but relieved.

'No,' said Phil, 'but it doesn't make it any better, does it?'

Jenna stared at the email. *Going 2 try to skype this evening. Xxx.* She wondered why. They'd only spoken on the satphone the previous week, and Lee didn't seem to have had much news then. What else was there to tell her about the minging place he was in, or the rubbish food he got to eat? And she didn't have much to say to him. Besides, what news she did have was hardly good: that the housing commandant had tried to shut her business down, she'd burned her bridges with Zoë, and all the appointments she had had in her diary had suddenly been cancelled – all the snotty officers' wives who used to queue to get their hair done with her had suddenly decided they couldn't make the dates they'd booked and didn't know when they'd be able to come back. Jenna knew who to blame. Sodding Milward. He was at the bottom of this. He would have put the word out and the wives would have followed like sheep. She'd seen enough of the military to know that wives thought that if they didn't toe the party line, they could wreck their husbands' careers. Frankly, Jenna rather doubted that this was really the case, but they seemed to think it was so. Baa-baa.

So did she really want to break the news to Lee that she was effectively unemployed and unemployable? All that time, money and effort to set everything up, and then one inter-fering little Hitler and it had all come tumbling down.

Jenna sighed heavily and looked around the sitting room. The payments on the furniture weren't cheap, and the TV had rinsed what was left of Lee's savings after she'd paid for the bathroom. She wondered how she'd be able to juggle the finances so she could honour the credit agreements, and what if she couldn't? She wasn't even going to think about the cost of restoring the bathroom back to its original state – not that she had to face *that* expense till they moved out, but even so. Yes, indeed, a Skype call from Lee was the last fucking thing she needed tonight.

She considered not switching on her laptop, but Lee would just phone her mobile, using the satphone, so one way or another, she'd end up talking to him. She sighed again. She was being unfair – of course she wanted to talk to him, but she just wished *she* could pick the times when they did. Not that that was possible – she understood that. Damn the army, she thought for about the umpteenth time that day. And damn Lee Perkins for being a part of it. It didn't cross Jenna's mind that she'd been the one so keen to marry a soldier and get a quarter that she'd practically frogmarched Lee to the altar.

She reached forward and pressed the button on the side of her lappie and watched the machine wind itself up. When the screen had settled down, she hit the Skype icon and made sure the volume was switched on, so she'd hear the notification when Lee called. Then she went into the kitchen, got a bottle of Chablis out of the fridge and helped herself to a large glass. So what that it was only three in the afternoon? There was sod all else to do.

Chapter Twenty-Three

Maddy answered the doorbell and found Caro standing outside, a sheaf of paper in one hand and Luke grasped firmly in the other.

'Hi, Caro, hello, Luke, what can I do for you?'

Caro let go of Luke, who instantly pushed his way into the house. She peeled a sheet of paper off the top of the pile and handed it to Maddy. 'Wives' Club ad. Put it up in your window, would you, hon?'

'Of course,' said Maddy, without looking at it. 'Cuppa? I mean, you might as well now that Luke has already made himself at home,' she added with a grin.

'Oh, go on,' said Caro. 'It'll have to be quick though as I want to hand out the rest of these.'

Maddy led the way into the kitchen where Luke was already playing with Nate's toys. She put the piece of paper on the counter and filled the kettle.

'Changing the subject,' said Caro. 'Fancy going shopping over the weekend?'

'I dunno,' said Maddy. 'I mean I'd love to, but Seb's got a regatta on Saturday.'

Caro shook her head. 'Hello… shops are open on Sundays, too, now. He can't be rowing all weekend, can he?'

'No,' Maddy conceded.

'So isn't it time he did a bit more bonding with his son?

Look, tell you what, I'll cook up a giant shepherd's pie – enough for my three, plus Seb – and Seb can spend the day here with Will, they can have a couple of beers together, watch the Six Nations rugby or whatever while we bugger off and have a girls' day out.'

'God, that sounds so tempting.'

'So why not? What did you have planned for Sunday?'

'Honestly? The ironing.'

'No-brainer, then. See you Sunday, around ten. And tell Seb he'll have me to contend with if he says no.'

After Caro had gone Maddy looked at the flyer. 'Talk by local stylist,' she read under her breath. Shit, Caro was going ahead with the talk on hairdressing with Jenna. Maddy sighed. Why did she have the feeling it was going to cause trouble?

Eight thousand miles away, Chrissie made her way for the second time that day to the ward where Lee was being treated.

'Hi, Lee,' she said when she got to his bedside. 'I brought you these.' She chucked a couple of magazines on the locker by his bed. 'I'm afraid there wasn't much of a choice in the NAAFI. Phil suggested I might be able to see if there are some mags in the welfare packages that may have been finished with. I'm going to have a scout around tomorrow and see what I can get you.'

'Thanks, that's kind,' said Lee, but he didn't look that chuffed. In fact, he looked completely down.

'No worries.' Chrissie gave him a long stare. 'You all right? Your knee isn't giving you gyp, is it?'

'No, the knee's fine.'

'So what is it? You look shagging miserable. I thought you said you liked it here: decent scoff, nice bed, proper bogs...'

'I said, I'm fine.'

Chrissie sat on the chair beside him. 'Want to talk about it?'

'Not really.'

'Want me to go?'

Lee shook his head. 'Not really,' he admitted.

'Then what *do* you want?'

He sighed. 'It's Jenna,' he admitted finally.

Why doesn't that surprise me? thought Chrissie. She forbore to ask *What's she done now* and instead said, 'What's the matter?'

'I know it's tough for her, I know she's been left all by herself, but I've just Skyped a call to her and firstly, she was pissed, and it could only have been about six o'clock UK time.'

'It's not a crime, Lee,' said Chrissie. 'It's not like you've never been pissed, is it?'

'Lots of times, but she must have been drinking all afternoon. Why wasn't she working?'

'Day off?'

'Maybe, but she was really cagey about what she'd been up to. Chris, I think she wasn't levelling with me. And it wasn't just that, she's spent a fortune on the quarter. I could see new sofas and a big flat-screen TV, there was a rug on the floor... It must've all cost a mint.'

'It *was* pretty grotty before,' said Chrissie.

'I know, but... oh, Chrissie, what do I know about interior decorating, but does it really matter if the place is in clip-state, when it's an army quarter?'

'Maybe it does to her. You know how much she likes to look nice herself. Maybe she wants her house to reflect that.'

Lee looked at her. 'That's what I really like about you, Chrissie. You like to find the good in people.'

Chrissie pulled a face. 'Listen, hon, Mother Teresa I am *not*. I can bitch with the best. Honest.'

'Nice to know you're human, then.'

'Very.'

'Maybe you're right. Maybe I'm just worried, because I've got nothing better to do.'

Chrissie nodded. 'For a bet. I'm sure everything is fine. Honest.' She smiled at Lee and he smiled back. Her heart did that little flick-flack and, not for the first time, her resolve to stay completely independent wobbled a fraction.

'So what's it like on the MERT?' Lee asked.

'Either it's mad excitement and adrenalin and we're rushing about like headless chickens, or I'm bored to sobs, hanging around waiting for a call. Of course it's better to be bored, we all know that, but it gets you down after a bit.'

'So what do you do?'

'Mainly I watch films with Phil.'

'Phil?'

Was she imagining things, or did Lee sound jealous? Of course he didn't – why on earth would he be? 'He's a nice guy, and he's into old movies, like me. We have a right laugh, watching some of the really ancient ones.'

'That's nice. What's wrong with *Avatar*, then, or *Resident Evil*?'

'Nothing, if you like that sort of thing, but I just like the old ones. You know, *Gone With the Wind*, *Citizen Kane*, *Meet Me in St Louis*...'

Lee shook his head. 'Chrissie, I haven't a shagging clue what you're on about.'

'Really? You don't know what you're missing.'

'I think I do,' he said. 'I think I do.'

After Chrissie had gone, Lee lay in his bed and thought

about her. He was glad she had Phil, who seemed genuinely fond of her. The two certainly seemed to have a lot in common, and he had no right to feel jealous, but for some unfathomable reason he did. Chrissie was *his* mate, not Phil's.

Chapter Twenty-Four

Chrissie gave Lee a friendly hug. He was out of bed, fully clothed and hefting his day sack. 'I'm glad you're all fixed up,' she said, 'but I'm *not* glad you're going back to the front line.'

'It's my job, Chrissie.'

'I know, but all the same… And remember what I said about looking where you put your feet. I see what IEDs can do and it's not pretty.'

'I'll be all right,' said Lee, with bravado.

'It's what they all say.' Chrissie reached into her pocket. 'Tell me to naff off but…' She pulled out a tatty little teddy bear attached to her key ring. 'This is Fred Bear. Mum gave this to me when she got too ill to get me from school and I had to do the journey on my own. He's kept me safe till now and now I'd like him to look after you.' She told herself that Lee was the only soldier on the front line that she knew really well – well enough to worry about. If she had enough talismans for every single soldier she'd cheerfully hand them all over, but she didn't, so Lee got first dibs. That was all it was.

'I can't take your mascot, Chrissie.' Did Lee's eyes look suspiciously bright or was it just a trick of the light?

'I'm not taking no for an answer. If you don't, I'll just send him up in the post. And anyway, the ring attached to him is just perfect for the chain with your dog tags.'

Lee gave in. 'That's really kind, Chrissie.'

'I don't mean for him to replace any token Jenna gave you,' said Chrissie, as she took the little bear off her key ring. 'He's an *as-well-as* lucky charm, not an *instead-of* one.'

'Jenna doesn't believe in that sort of stuff.'

'She didn't give you...?' Chrissie couldn't believe it.

'Nah, well... I rely on skill anyway.' Lee threaded Fred onto his dog-tag chain and tucked him inside his combat jacket. 'He'll be safe in there till I can give him back to you.'

'You'd better look after him. I shall be really cross if you let him get hurt.'

Lee grinned. 'We'll look out for each other.' He stared at her. 'Well, I'd better get going. My carriage awaits.'

'Yes. Take care then.'

'You too.'

And without warning, Lee dived in and planted a big kiss on her cheek. Before Chrissie could say anything, he'd turned on his heel and walked away, down the canvas corridor that led out of the hospital. Chrissie watched his retreating back till he turned a corner and was lost from sight. She wasn't the least bit religious, but all the same she offered up a prayer to any god that might be hanging around and feeling benevolent, to look after him. As she went back to the MERT ready room, she wondered if Jenna bothered with prayers. Probably not.

Maddy opened her front door, laden with carrier bags. What a day, she thought, as she struggled into the house. Really, she ought to get out more. It seemed an age since she'd had such fun.

'Hello,' she called. 'I'm back.' There was silence. Maybe the boys had gone out for a walk. She put her bags down in the hall and shrugged off her coat, before abandoning her shopping and going into the kitchen to make tea. She'd forgotten how knackering tramping round the shops could be, or maybe it was lack of practice. She'd just got the kettle filled and a mug out, when she heard Seb's key in the lock.

'Hi, guys,' she called. 'I'm home.' She ran out of the kitchen to meet them.

'So I gathered, when Caro came back,' said Seb pushing the buggy into the house.

'Did you and Will have a good time?'

'Yes, thanks.' No smile, no emotion. Something was up.

'Good. And Nate?'

'I think so.'

Maddy narrowed her eyes. Something definitely wasn't right. Was this Seb being antsy with her, for not staying home and playing the dutiful wife? Or was it because he'd had to look after his own kid, for the second time in as many months? God, how childish! Well, she wasn't going to rise to the bait. If he was going to act like a two-year-old, he could get on with it. She wasn't going to join in. She left Seb getting Nathan out of the pushchair, while she went back into the kitchen to finish making her drink.

'Tea?' she offered brightly, as Seb followed her carrying his yawning son.

'No, thanks.'

'And talking of tea, has Nate had his?'

'Yes. At Will's.'

'Good.' She grabbed her mug and pushed past them. 'Then you don't need me, do you? I'm going to put away my shopping,' she said. 'And I may have a lie down on my bed with my tea and read some of my book afterwards.'

If Seb was going to be sulky, he could be sulky on his own. Awkwardly, she gathered up her half-dozen big carriers and stomped upstairs. She'd wanted to show Seb the lovely clothes she'd bought for her and Nathan, but she wasn't going to bother now. The fact that he had managed to put a downer on her day irritated her. It hadn't killed him to look after *his* son for six hours. God, she'd done it, day in day out, for months now and hadn't had any thanks; he did it for one day and was now acting like a total bloody martyr. Well, stuff him.

She began hanging up her purchases, trying to put her annoyance behind her, and was thinking about that, rather than anything else, when she shut the wardrobe door.

Seb was standing behind it.

'Shit,' she shrieked in fight. 'Jeez, Seb, don't creep up like that!'

'I've got a bone to pick with you.'

'So I'm not allowed to have a day off? You can go out and row whenever it takes your fancy and I never complain, but can I have just one day, doing what I want to do? Apparently not.' If he wanted a fight he was going to get one. 'And what's Nate doing? You can't just abandon him like that.'

'He's in his playpen, he's safe, and it's not about you going out for the day.'

'Oh no?' She didn't believe that last bit.

'No. It's about something Will said.'

'Will?' Had she said something indiscreet about Seb to Caro which had been passed on to Will? Something Seb might take offence at? Sure she'd bitched about his endless rowing, but it was hardly likely to be that. So what the fuck was it?

'Yes, he told me Caro's planning on getting Jenna along to the Wives' Club to do a hairdressing demo.'

Maddy rolled her eyes and shrugged in utter incomprehension. 'What?'

'You heard.'

'So? Do you want an invite, is that it?'

'Don't be flippant.'

'Seb, I'm not, but I honestly haven't got a clue what the hell you're on about.'

'He said that Caro says you're going to be there.'

Maddy shrugged again. 'Well, yes, maybe. I'm a wife, I go to the Wives' Club. Is that so wrong? It's hardly like I'm standing around on street corners, touting for trade, is it?' She glared at Seb, daring him to accuse her of being flippant again.

'I don't want you to go.'

She'd just known this talk was going to be trouble. What she hadn't expected was for Seb to forbid her to attend – like he was some sort of Stasi official, bringing a dissident into line. Well, she wasn't having that! She wasn't in the army, he couldn't order her about. 'What? What on earth has it got to do with you?'

'Everything.'

'Come off it. All the wives are going to be there – or most of them will be.'

'But they don't know it'll be *Jenna* doing the demo. *You* do.'

So that was it. It was about being forewarned. It was about her turning up to the demo, *knowing* in advance that Jenna was going to be there. Oh, for fuck's sake! How petty could you get? 'And I'm going to pretend that I don't,' she snapped.

'And supposing Caro tells other people that you did? After all, she told Will.'

'For God's sake, Seb, she won't, she's a mate. Shit, if it means that much to you, let's get her to sign the official fucking secrets act!'

Seb stared at her angrily. 'You just don't get it, do you? Jenna is trouble. Jenna has been told to cease trading—'

'Yes, she has. But doing a demo at the Wives' Club is hardly trading. I just don't get what your problem is.'

'The CO knows what she's been up to, and her husband is in my platoon. If this woman causes real problems, then it might reflect on my next confidential report. If I want to make it to Staff College, it isn't just a question of passing the exams – I need the recommendations too. That woman could really screw up my career and I don't need *you* giving her a helping hand.'

'So that's it. You're giving me the gypsy's warning that I'm not to step out of line, not one inch.'

'Not exactly.'

'It's what it looks like from here.'

'It's just...'

'"It's just" what?'

'Caro and Will don't care. He's not ambitious like me. He joined the army for the sport and the adventurous training and all sorts of reasons, but I don't think making it to the top was one of them.'

No – Caro had pretty much admitted that to Maddy herself. 'So?'

'Well I *do* care. And I thought you did too.'

Maddy took a deep breath. 'I do, really I do. Seb, I know that whatever you do you like to try to win. Shit, I know how cut up you were about not making the Olympic squad – or rowing in the Blue Boat – and I'll support you where I can to get any other goals you want. But *I've* got to be allowed to have my own life too, as much as I can. I've pretty much given up on the idea of having a proper career – the best I can hope for is a succession of jobs. I've got to get used to the idea of moving all the time and worst of all, if we do that, I've got to accept that Nate, and any brothers or sisters he might have, will have to go away to boarding school, but Seb, I am *not* going to have you tell me who I may or may not be friends with, or who I can see or what I can do with my free time. Understand?'

Seb glared at her. 'Only too well.'

Maddy heard him clatter downstairs, and then the front door slammed.

Chapter Twenty-Five

'Cheer up, Perky,' said Johnny. 'It might never happen.'

'I think it already has.' Lee was staring at the picture of Jenna which he kept in his wallet.

Johnny Flint hunkered down next to Lee, his back against the mud wall of the compound in the only slice of shade. The worst of the winter weather seemed to have cleared away while Lee was in the field hospital and now the sun was gaining in strength again. It was almost hot and without sun protection it was easy to get burnt – something to be avoided, because sunburn was classed as a self-inflicted injury.

'So what's the matter, buddy?' asked Johnny. 'You haven't got no fucking reason to be in the dumps – you've just been back to Bastion. All those Gucci facilities to enjoy, plus women, you jammy sod.'

'I'm married.'

Johnny pulled the photo from Lee's fingers and looked at it. 'Your missus?'

Lee nodded.

'I can see why you wouldn't be interested in anyone else.' He whistled. 'How did an ugly git like you pull a bit of top-totty like that?'

Lee took the picture back. 'You know, I have no fucking idea.'

'She a soldier too?'

'Civvy. Local girl, works in the garrison hairdresser's.'

'So did you meet her there?' Johnny ruffled Lee's number two buzz cut. 'You big ponce.'

'Nah. Her car broke down in the barracks, I sorted it out, we went on a date and then the next thing I knew we were getting hitched.'

Johnny shook his head. 'Prat.'

'It seemed the right thing at the time. She's got a good job, she's a beautiful woman, like, her mam lives local...'

'But?' said Johnny.

Lee sighed.

'But?' prompted Johnny again.

'But, maybe I should have got to know her a bit better, before I said "I do".' Lee picked up a tiny stone and threw it at the toe of his boot. He missed, and it plinked into the dust to one side.

Johnny stared at his comrade. 'So what's wrong? Want to talk about it?'

Lee sighed. Did he?

'Hey, you know what else they say, don't you?' cajoled Johnny. 'A friend in need...'

'Is a pain in the arse?' finished Lee.

Johnny grinned. 'Too fucking right. However, I don't mind listening if you want to get it off your chest.'

Lee considered the offer. He knew what his mate presumed. 'She's not playing away, if that's what you think.'

'So what's your problem?'

'It's the bank account. I Skyped a call when I was at Bastion and I could see there was all this new stuff in the house. So I went online and had a look at my bank account. She's rinsed the lot, Johnny. In fact, more than the lot; she's two grand overdrawn. I reckon she's got through eight grand in about six weeks. I mean, I know there's a risk the Taliban might do my legs physically, but I didn't expect Jenna to do them financially. Eight grand, Johnny!'

Johnny whistled. 'Fucking hell, Lee. Have you asked her what she's spent it on? The crown jewels?'

'I tried but she didn't pick up her mobile. I reckon she was blanking me.'

'That doesn't sound good.'

'And I daren't ask for compassionate leave to go back and sort it.'

Johnny shook his head. 'They wouldn't give it to you for that, anyway. It's got to be something really serious – life-threatening.'

'The way I feel right now, it might be life-threatening, all right. Honestly, Johnny, I could kill her. How could she? I mean, I know she's got to have money to live, but eight grand?'

'Shit, Lee, I don't know what to say.'

'Yeah. What is there to say? Total bummer, isn't it?' Lee got up and shrugged. 'But thanks for listening.'

'It's what pals do,' said Johnny.

And pals don't rob you blind as soon as your back is turned, thought Lee. Unlike your wife.

Jenna twisted her glass and watched the bubbles rise in her drink while she waited for Immi to arrive. Tommy's Bar was quiet, even for a Monday evening.

'Penny for them,' said Immi, sitting down beside her and putting her own drink down on the table. She pulled a heavy bag from off her shoulder and dumped it on the bench seat beside her.

'Hi, Immi,' said Jenna. 'And thanks, I could do with the money.'

'How so?'

Jenna turned to face her friend. 'Because the bastard army has put the skids under my business.'

Immi bit back the urge to say 'I told you so' or 'What did you expect?' and instead said, 'Bastards indeed.' She thought for a moment and said, 'But they can't stop you doing hairdressing in peoples' own homes.'

'No, but the wives have to ask me to do it in the first place.'

'And they don't?'

Jenna shook her head. 'Not one. The officers' patch has blackballed me and the soldiers' wives don't like me.'

Immi looked taken aback. 'What? None of them?'

'Not really. I fell out with my next-door neighbour on day one, and I went to one of the coffee mornings and all they could talk about was kids and getting marks out of carpets.' She sighed. 'Honest, Immi, none of them seem to have lives.' She took a swig of her drink. 'And is it a crime not to like kids? I had a basinful of babies when I was growing up, Mum was always making me look after my brothers and sisters, and I don't need any more right now – and certainly not other people's.'

'You'll still do my hair for me? I'll pay, obviously,' Immi added, quickly. 'And not mates' rates, the proper deal. You've got to be businesslike.'

Jenna snorted. 'Businesslike. Ha, ain't that the joke, when I've got no sodding business. But thanks, babe. It's going to be a drop in the ocean, though, the debts I've got.'

'Poor you.' Immi decided to change the subject. 'How's Lee?' she asked brightly.

'OK, I suppose.'

'You suppose?'

'Haven't spoken to him for a bit. You know how it is.'

Immi nodded. You couldn't ring the guys out there, as no one was allowed mobiles, so you had to wait for them to ring you on the satphones, which was frustrating. But you could send blueys – airmail letters – as often as you wanted, and anything else for that matter. Which reminded her... Immi hauled the bag she'd put beside her up onto the table. 'I nicked these from the medical centre, when I went for my annual check-up. Well, that's not strictly true, they were about to chuck them out, so I nabbed them.' She opened the bag to reveal a dozen glossy lads' mags.

'Not my sort of thing, babe,' said Jenna, tapping a copy of GQ with a beautiful red nail.

Immi laughed. 'Not for you. For Lee. I though you could send them out there to him.'

Jenna's shoulders slumped and she turned to look at her friend. 'Listen, hon, I can barely afford to keep myself fed at the mo, what with not having any business, having a monster overdraft and having to pay the instalments on the furniture. I can't afford to spend a fortune on posting a few second-hand mags out to Afghan as well.'

'But... but...' Immi was at a loss for words.

'No buts, Immi, these'll cost a mint to send.'

'But care packages to Afghan go for free. Surely you know that?'

Jenna looked stunned. 'Free?'

Immi nodded, her forehead creased. 'But haven't you been sending him goodies?'

Jenna looked a bit shamefaced. 'I've been busy, you know, setting up the hairdressing. Fat lot of good that was, though.'

Immi remained silent. Everyone sent little parcels of treats out to the soldiers, didn't they? Even complete strangers sent boxes addressed to 'a soldier'. How long did it take to wrap up a couple of mags or some Pot Noodles or a jar of peanut butter and pop them in the post? And in all the weeks Lee had been out there, Jenna hadn't sent him *anything*? She just hoped Lee's mum was making up the shortfall, and maybe other friends were too. Immi made up her mind to send him a few bits and bobs. Everyone loved receiving surprises, didn't they, and if Jenna wasn't doing the biz – well, it was up to everyone else to rally round, wasn't it.

Jenna pushed the mags back towards Immi. 'Kind thought, though.'

So she wasn't going to send them; she just couldn't be bothered. And Lee was her husband, for fuck's sake!

Immi pushed her irritation back down. Lee and Jenna's marriage was none of her business, and how Jenna behaved was entirely between herself and Lee. She sipped her drink moodily, while she wondered why she was letting Jenna's selfishness get to her. Because Lee deserved better, that was why. She might have met Jenna long before she met Lee, but it didn't mean she was blind to Jenna's faults. Immi didn't feel like talking, so she sat and simmered and wondered if Jenna would get the hint that she was bang out of order.

Jenna broke the uncomfortable silence. 'Think I might have to go and get myself a job. Don't know what I can do, though. I can't work at Zoë's no more, can I?'

Immi shook her head; no, she couldn't. She'd dug herself a fucking great hole and jumped into it, and now she was stuck good and proper. She softened. 'There's loads of things you could do if you're not picky. How about something like bar work? I did it before I joined up and it's dead easy. It helps that you're a stunner.' Jenna shrugged. 'No, seriously, it does.' Immi jumped up and went over to the rack in the corner of the bar and picked out the local paper amid the jumble of

TV listings magazines and tabloids. 'Let's see if there's anything in here.' She licked her finger and flicked through the pages. 'Here we go.' She turned the paper inside out and folded the page. 'Situations vacant.' She ran her finger down the column. '*Care home assistant*?' she read out.

'No way. Wiping other people's bums? I don't think so.'

She had a point. Immi looked at the next ad. '*Receptionist, busy local garage*?'

'Maybe.'

'*Basic knowledge of cars essential*.'

'No. I can start one and drive one – that's me lot.'

'*Teaching assistant*?'

'Kids,' said Jenna with a dismissive snort.

'*Truck driver*?'

Jenna just raised an eyebrow.

'Perfect,' said Immi with a whoop. 'Look at this one. *Waitress for local catering company*.'

Jenna took the paper out of Immi's hand. 'It's a possibility.' She scanned the ad. '*Irregular hours* – well, that won't matter being all by myself. *No transport required*. Better and better, means I won't have to fork out for petrol.' She ripped the page out of the paper. 'I'll get the drinks in and then I'm going to ring them.'

'Now?'

'It's a catering company – I bet they're working. Stands to reason, evenings will be their busiest time. Same again?'

Immi knocked back the last of her Bacardi and handed her glass over. 'Please.'

'And I suppose, if I work for a civvy firm, no one will care how I get on with the army or my neighbours. What a result that'd be.'

Chapter Twenty-Six

Maddy got the meal out of the oven: lasagne, Seb's favourite. It looked and smelt delicious. She glanced at the kitchen clock; six thirty. Across the kitchen Nathan was in his high chair, bib on, waiting for the pureed vegetables he was getting for his supper. So, she wondered, was she going to be eating on her own, or would Seb deign to make an appearance? Not that she had much of an appetite; worry about the rocky situation between her and Seb was making her feel quite sick. What if... what if he didn't come back? What if he moved back into the mess permanently? After he'd gone, she'd discovered he'd taken his Rapid Reaction kit – the kit he kept packed, in case the regiment was deployed in an emergency. He had enough kit in that bag to last him for weeks. Maddy couldn't bear to think about what that might mean. She'd sent a text, apologising, but there had been nothing but silence. Had she gone too far? Had Seb been forced to decide between his career prospects and her – and decided on his career? Maddy felt another wave of nausea lurch through her.

A key clicked in the lock of the front door. Abandoning her cooking and Nathan, she raced to the door and flung herself into her husband's arms.

'Oh, Seb, oh, Seb,' she cried. 'I was so afraid you mightn't come home.' She realised that she had two tears trickling down her face. She dashed them away. Relief and love flooded through her, in a huge surge of emotions.

Seb gave her a big hug and kissed the top of her head. 'Shhh. I'm sorry, maybe I overreacted.'

'And I'm sorry, I was stubborn.'

'I missed you,' said Seb, moving back a step so he could look at her.

'The bed was too big without you.'

'And Nate, did he miss me?'

'Sorry.' She gave him a watery smile. 'I'll have to disappoint you there.'

'Where is he?'

'In the kitchen, waiting for his supper.'

On cue, there was a squawk of protest. The pair moved into the kitchen, where Seb hunkered down by the high chair. 'Hey, buddy. Did you miss me?' In response, Nathan bashed the tray of his chair with a plastic spoon. 'I'll take that as a yes.' Seb smiled at Maddy. 'That was a horrible twenty-four hours.'

'It was. But you're back now.'

Seb nodded. 'Let's not fall out again like that. I promise I won't bitch about who you keep as friends. Not even Jenna Perkins.'

Maddy rolled her eyes. 'She isn't my friend, I keep telling you, but let's not talk about her.'

'No, fine. I wouldn't mind about her, if she'd just caused trouble for her poor bloody husband, but she caused trouble for us, too.'

'Yeah, well, as I said...'

'He's well out of it.'

'Not sure being in Afghanistan is better than living at home with his wife, even if his wife is Jenna.'

Seb snorted. 'Personally, I think it would be.'

Maddy let the subject drop, as she zapped Nathan's vegetable puree in the microwave. 'There's a bottle of white in the fridge,' she told Seb, bustling about her kitchen.

Seb took the hint and opened the wine, pouring it into a couple of glasses.

The microwave pinged. 'Feed Nathan, while I dish up,' said Maddy, starting to cut the lasagne into squares, then taking a slug of her wine.

Seb tested the temperature of the green mush and settled down to feed his son.

'And I did some thinking over at the mess. Maybe I'm expecting too much of you. What you said about being an army wife... I know it's not easy and I know some of the other women can be pains in the arse, and I know you feel you live in a bit of a goldfish bowl, with Susie and Mrs N peering in at you. Maybe you should stop stressing quite so much about my career and let me worry about that. You just get on with being Nate's mum and being yourself. I love you and anything you do is just fine by me.'

'Oh, Seb.' Maddy felt another surge of love for him. 'Thank you. And I promise I'll try hard not let you down. Truly. And even if I'm not the perfect military wife, I'll do my best.'

'I know you will. That's why I adore you.'

'Lee. *Lee.*' Johnny shook his mate's shoulder.

'Sorry, mate, I was miles away,' said Lee.

'I could tell that. You had your thousand-yard stare on. Thinking about the missus again?'

'Can't help it, Johnny.'

'Well, you'd better start trying to help it. Listen to me:

going out on patrol with your brain somewhere else'll do no one any good, least of all you. And, frankly, I don't want you with us if you aren't concentrating.' Johnny gave his mate an angry glare. 'Understand?'

Lee nodded. He did. Going out on patrol was teamwork, and everyone relied on everyone else. He had about twenty minutes to get his head in the right place. He stood up from the table, where he'd been loading rounds into magazines, and went to his bed space to get ready. Like many soldiers, he had his rituals – rituals that had no rhyme or reason, but which he believed *were* the reason he'd been kept safe so far. Them and the bear. He fingered the little teddy which still hung on his dog-tag chain. Maybe he'd be better off thinking about Chrissie than he would about Jenna.

No. He needed to think about going out on patrol. Period.

He stripped down to the skin and began to put his military kit on. First up, his bomb-proof pants. Well, they were supposed to be bomb-proof, although Johnny reckoned they weren't up to much. He said he'd already shredded his with farts. But then that made sense – that time he'd let rip in the ops room Johnny had been warned by Sergeant Adams that he was in breach of the Geneva Convention on chemical and biological warfare. Given the toxicity of Johnny's wind, Lee reckoned he had a point; even Kevlar would be hard-pressed to survive close contact with it.

Having got his pants on, he put on his socks, first the left then the right, then his T-shirt and jacket, then his trousers, then his boots, left then right and laces tied in a double bow, and finally his body armour. He picked up his belt kit and fastened it round his middle and then clipped his combat nappy into place. There, he'd got dressed in the right order to keep the luck good. He knew he was being irrational, he knew it was mad, but it kept him sane. Shit, he had more than enough to worry about, without stressing whether his luck was about to run out. He grabbed his Bergen and his helmet and made his way over to the old shipping container they used as an armoury. He signed out his weapon and made sure it was still squeaky clean, before going over to the table and helping himself to half a dozen magazines of bullets. He clipped one into his rifle and put the rest in his ammo pouches. Finally, he shoved half a dozen plastic bottles of water into his Bergen. He was ready.

Ten minutes later, he and the rest of the multiple, minus the guys left behind to guard their patrol base, made their way out of the big metal gate for the umpteenth time. Lee had lost count of the number of patrols he and the rest of the guys had made. Five dozen, six? He didn't like to think that, with every patrol, their luck was being spread just a shade thinner. He tried to think more positively: that they were getting more experienced, less likely to get caught out, but it was tough keeping upbeat. Only the week before, Op Minimise had been activated twice: once for a Canadian soldier who'd fallen foul of an IED out on patrol, and another for a Mastiff armoured vehicle that had been blown up. Luckily the guys inside had mostly been all right – just superficial injuries – but the Canadian had died and it had sobered everyone up. But it wasn't just the death that had been a worry; the Mastiff had been on the main supply route and, given how that was guarded and patrolled, the fact that the Taliban had managed to mine it was a real worry. If they'd done that, where else could they manage to plant IEDs?

Once out of the gate, they tabbed along the berm before they raced across the bridge over the canal, their boots clattering on the metal surface of the prefabricated span. The sun was even hotter today and Lee could feel the sweat trickling down his back under his heavy body armour as he ran. And they all knew what hot sun meant, apart from the fact that the patrols would become ever-more knackering. The snow on the passes would be melting, and as soon as it had gone and the rivers in the valleys began to dry up, the fighting season would start in earnest. The Taliban based in Pakistan could come down from their winter quarters and back up their Afghani counterparts, bringing with them new supplies of explosives and ammo and, more importantly, replacement fighters. Soon, thought Lee, they wouldn't just have the local bandits to cope with; they'd have a whole bunch of reinforcements, plus one-hundred-degree heat. Between the heat, the Taliban and Jenna, his life couldn't get much more shit.

Jenna pressed 'send' on her phone.

Got interview. Fingers crossed.

She hoped Immi would be as pleased as she was. The catering company wasn't her idea of perfect, but it was a job and, frankly, any job would be welcome. And anyway, as a lot of the work would probably be in the evenings, she could do hairdressing – if anyone wanted her to – during the day.

Brill, Immi texted back.

Now all Jenna had to do was think about what she ought to wear. When she rang about the position the guy who had answered the phone had sounded quite young, so should she go looking hot and sexy, or neat and tidy? Jenna pottered upstairs to the spare bedroom and began leafing through the clothes hanging on the rails. Maybe she could do a combo of both looks.

Later, she drove into town, to the little industrial estate

in the old station yard. She found the company easily enough and parked up in the space reserved for visitors. Before she got out of the car, she checked her appearance. Perfect. After all, she was sure they didn't want mingers handing round the canapés – it would put people off their food.

Smoothing her skirt down, she sashayed over to the front door, plipping her vehicle locked with a casual wave of her key. Three minutes later, she was in the MD's office, looking at a guy with the worst case of acne she'd ever seen. Surely his skin condition had to be against food hygiene regs. Not that she knew anything detailed about food hygiene regs, but common sense said that putting him in a kitchen had to be just plain wrong.

She had, of course, prepped answers to the sort of questions she expected from Barry Carlton, which the plastic name plate on his desk told her was his name: why did she want the job, were there any dates she couldn't work, any health issues that might prevent her from working... So she was a tad surprised by the first question.

'When can you start?'

Jenna tried not to look too surprised. 'Erm, now?' Shit, she hoped not. This dress was dry-clean only and she had nothing to change into.

'This evening will do.'

Phew.

'Can you do silver service?'

Jenna shook her head. The ad hadn't mentioned that as a requirement.

'Never mind, we can probably teach you how to do it before you'll need it. Luckily tonight is just handing around platters of food and drink.' The guy looked frazzled.

'So what's the event tonight?'

'Engagement party at the football club.'

'You're leaving recruitment a bit late, aren't you?' blurted out Jenna.

Barry shook his head. 'I was planning on expanding anyway, hence the ad you saw, but last week three of my staff went down with norovirus.'

Jenna shrugged. 'In English?'

'It's also called winter vomiting disease.'

'Euw.'

Barry nodded. 'Exactly. It's just what it says on the tin. It spreads like wildfire, so there is no way any of the staff who were in contact with the infected staff can work, until we're sure they're in the clear.' He rubbed his hand over his face. 'It's been a nightmare.'

'I can imagine.'

'So, I'll give you a paid trial tonight, if you're any good I'll take you on and you'll have a contract. I pay ten pounds an hour. If the client pays a gratuity, I split it equally between everyone. I expect the waitresses to wear black, but I provide you with an apron. Your hair must be pinned up and no nail varnish, unless it's clear. Oh,' and he glanced across the desk at Jenna's feet, 'you might want to wear flat shoes.'

'OK.'

'Right, follow me.' He stood up and walked around his desk, before leading her along a corridor and through a pair of double swing doors. Behind the doors was a massive kitchen, all stainless steel and huge industrial ovens. There were lots of pans clattering, but very little in the way of other noise, despite the fact that there were already five people working there. Maybe music and chatter were not allowed.

Barry moved about the kitchen efficiently, loading up a tray with glasses filled with water, which he then gave to

Jenna. 'Walk up and down the corridor a couple of times,' he ordered her.

'OK.' She managed to shoulder her way through the big doors without spilling the drinks or dropping the tray, aware that Barry was watching her. She felt a bit like a fashion model, but reckoned he wasn't watching how she walked as she returned into the kitchen; he was watching to see how steady she was.

'Now walk around the kitchen.'

'But there's people rushing about here,' she protested.

'And they'll be standing still at a party?'

Jenna sighed and began to move between the two rows of big steel counters. It was a bit like *Total Wipeout*, she reckoned, as she timed her run in order to avoid the chefs bustling about.

'Good,' said Barry. 'Now do it again and hold the tray on one hand.'

Fuck, what was this? She was angling for a job as a waitress, not a circus performer. Once again, she circled the kitchen, only this time one of the cooks stepped back suddenly from a stove and Jenna, dodging her, managed to tip over two of the glasses. The tray was awash with water.

'You can't serve the rest of the drinks now. The glasses are wet and they'll drip on customers.'

'I know, sorry.'

'You'll probably find it easier in flat shoes, too,' said Barry.

'So have I still got the job?'

Barry nodded. 'Although we may just ask you to serve food. Canapés don't tip over so easily. Maybe drinks next time round.'

Four hours later, Jenna arrived back at the industrial estate as instructed by Barry. Outside the business were several vans, some designed to carry people, some to carry trays of goodies. A stream of workers were lugging boxes of glasses, cases of wine and platters of food to and fro.

Jenna spotted Barry. 'What do you want me to do?' she asked.

'Keep out of the way at the moment. We'll give you some proper training tomorrow. Tonight just take in the food that Karen tells you to.'

'Karen?'

'I'll introduce you at the venue. Now, if you'll excuse me...' and with that Barry disappeared back into the building.

Feeling like a spare part, Jenna went and sat in one of the minibuses. It wasn't her fault she couldn't help; she hoped the other wait staff understood why she wasn't.

A few minutes later the vans were loaded and ready for the off.

A severe woman climbed into the driver's seat next to Jenna. She swivelled around in her seat.

'You must be the new girl.' Jenna nodded. 'I'm Karen. I'll show you the ropes tonight. I expect you to listen, ask if you don't understand what I say and do as you're told.'

'OK,' said Jenna. And nice to meet you too. But she told herself she didn't have to like these people in order to earn money; all she had to do was work for them.

Ten minutes later, they drew up at the football club on the edge of town. It was a new building which proclaimed in a large banner across the front that it had been funded by the National Lottery. Jenna wished they spent less money on stuff like this and more on the prizes so the punters had a bigger chance – she felt her finances were just as good a cause as a poxy game of football.

After half an hour of toing and froing, lugging, carrying, running back and forth, she was knackered and her feet ached.

'Chop, chop,' shouted Karen, glaring at her, as Jenna took a breather.

'Fuck off,' muttered Jenna under her breath, grabbing yet another box of glasses to put out on the snowy cloths on the tables ranged along one side of the big club room. By the time the father of the affianced arrived, with his wife and daughter, the room was just about ready.

Jenna stood at the side of the room, with a plate of mini Scotch eggs made from quails' eggs, while he inspected the arrangements. A tweak here, a taste of the canapés there and then he nodded in approbation.

'He must be worth a bit,' whispered Jenna to another waitress called Helen.

'Ex-mayor,' confided Helen. 'His daughter's marrying a soldier.'

'Stupid girl,' said Jenna.

'I think it's romantic.'

'It isn't. Trust me, it's a shit life.'

Other guests began to arrive and Helen and Jenna moved off to circulate with their trays of food. As they moved through the party, the guests swooped on their trays like seagulls, and Helen and Jenna almost spent more time going back and forth from the kitchens to get new supplies than they did handing the food out.

'Jeez, I've walked miles,' said Jenna to Helen, as they picked up yet more nibbles. She'd only been working for around an hour, but she hadn't imagined it would be as knackering as this – which came as a surprise, considering that being a hairdresser had involved being on her feet all day. But mostly standing still, which presumably made all the difference.

By the time the party was drawing to a close, Jenna's feet were caning. She felt as if she had broken glass lining her shoes, not kidskin, and that someone was trying to saw off her little toes with rusty wire. She tried really hard to keep a smile on her face and to walk normally, but in reality it was almost impossible not to hobble or keep wincing.

'It's Jenna, isn't it?' said a man in a sharp suit, taking a mushroom vol-au-vent off her platter.

She stopped dead. 'Might be.'

'Thought I recognised you. I've seen you in the Spar, haven't I?'

Jenna nodded. But it still didn't explain how he knew her name. Her face must have reflected this.

'My wife.' He stopped and corrected himself. 'My *ex*-wife used to go to Zoë's.'

'Oh. Did I do her hair?'

'She was Trudy Armstrong and yes, you did. And I'm Dan. Dan Armstrong.'

'Nice to meet you, Dan.' But 'ex-wife'. That was interesting. She wondered why Trudy, whom she remembered vaguely, had dumped such a hot guy? And didn't she remember Trudy had wanted her hair done specially for a dinner in the sergeants' mess. Was Dan a sergeant? If so, he got paid a pretty decent wedge. Even *more* interesting.

'So, are you a soldier?'

Dan nodded. 'REME.'

'What's that then?'

'Royal Electrical and Mechanical Engineers. We fix stuff. Although other people say REME stands for Reck Everything Mechanical Everytime.'

Jenna laughed. 'I bet you don't.'

'We try not to.' Dan gave her a slow smile before he added, 'What are you doing after this shindig?'

Jenna grimaced. 'Getting these shoes off.'

'How about slipping them off in a bar somewhere?'

Jenna considered the offer. It was only a drink. Didn't she deserve the chance to go out occasionally? Lee need never know and anyway, Dan seemed pleasant. And if he was a sergeant, he could afford to take her somewhere nice. 'Cool. I've got to go back to the company offices to get my pay and pick up my car, though.'

'OK,' said Dan. 'How about we meet in the Six Bells, in an hour? We're not likely to run into any squaddies there. Nothing against soldiers, but they're a bit rough for my taste.' He gave her a smile.

Did he know she was married? she wondered. Was that why he didn't want them to be seen together by guys from the camp? Or was it really that he didn't like soldiers? Either way, so what? It was only a drink, she repeated to herself. She made up her mind. 'Yeah, great.' And the Six Bells – swanky. Her hunch about his pay was right. 'Now I'd better get on, or the boss'll chew me out. Laters.' As she circulated around the few remaining guests with the last of the party food, her feet suddenly didn't seem to hurt so much.

Chapter Twenty-Seven

The hot sun was low and the sky was turning a coppery orange as the ten-man patrol headed back to base. They were tired, the heat had been relentless – how could it have been so Baltic just a couple of weeks ago and now it was baking? – and their supplies of water were almost exhausted. It wasn't an issue: in less than an hour they should be back in the safety of the compound, tucking into their evening meal and with as much water as they could drink, but until then they were all aware that maybe it would be wise not to be too profligate with what water they did have in their Bergens. Lee tabbed along behind Sergeant Adams and Johnny, keeping his mind on the job as much as he could. Even so, every now and again he caught himself drifting into thinking about his bank account. Could he, he wondered, make it so that Jenna couldn't access it? But if he did, how would she pay the bills? Was he being unfair? After all, he was going to qualify for an end of tour bonus and that would pay off the debts. He'd planned on buying a nice Audi, but that could wait. Except why should it? He'd earned it...

Stop it, he told himself.

Up ahead, Johnny's mine detector let out the occasional squeak or squeal, as it passed over odd bits of rubbish on the dusty track that led towards the last village before the Neb Canal: cans, horseshoe nails, spent cartridge cases from other encounters, detritus you'd never normally notice, but you did now the Vallon picked it out. The pale surface was in contrast to the fields on either side, which now had thigh-high plants growing in them. Opium poppies. In another few weeks they'd be flowering, and by the time that happened it would be almost time for 2 Herts and the rest of the soldiers on this phase of Operation Herrick to leave and the new batch of troops to take their place.

Lee watched the tall green foliage swaying. It all looked quite peaceful: the neat fields with crops, the irrigation canals flanked by reeds and trees, with a few goats tethered to stakes in the ground, nibbling on the foliage. It was hard to believe how blood-soaked the soil of this country was. Lee watched the foliage move again. It was then he realised there hadn't been a breath of wind all day. It wasn't the breeze moving the plants...

The reality of what he'd spotted jolted him into action. Someone was lying in wait in the plants. Ambush!

'Take cover,' he yelled, as he threw himself to the ground.

As his comrades followed his lead, there was the most almighty explosion. Lee, flat on the ground, felt the shock wave ripple the length of his body like a wave under a lilo. A chemical, just-lit-sparkler smell wafted past as dust, stones and other shit pattered down on his body armour and his helmet. The shock of the explosion at such close proximity left him feeling unbelievably shaky and his ears were ringing so much that the sound of someone shouting was muffled.

'Man down, man down!' he managed to discern. He raised his head. Sergeant Adams was already up and running forward. Shit, it was Johnny. Despite feeling as though his legs weren't properly under control, Lee also raced forward. As he ran, he could see that Johnny's left leg was horribly shortened. Fear and panic nearly took control before training began to kick in.

'Send a nine-liner,' he yelled at the radio operator. 'We need a MERT.'

'Get Ryan up here,' screamed Adams. Ryan was the patrol medic, the guy with the specialist training and kit.

Lee threw his Bergen off his back and crouched behind it. He was sure the IED had been detonated from the poppy field. The terrorist was probably still in there, lying low or leopard-crawling his way to safety. In your dreams, you fucker, thought Lee. His fear was now morphing into anger – white-hot rage that his mate, his best buddy, had been catastrophically injured.

His hunch was vindicated when a crackle of automatic fire spat through the air. Once again the soldiers dropped to the ground. Lee, emboldened by the slight protection his Bergen afforded, watched to see where the shots had come from. He had a rough idea anyway; he knew where he'd seen the poppies moving. He could get this bastard. He *was going* to get this bastard. If it were the last thing he did, he owed that much to Johnny.

And over his anger and his desire for revenge he felt guilt. Maybe, if he'd been just a bit more on the ball, if he hadn't been thinking about bloody Jenna and his finances, he'd have made the connection about the movement in the field before Johnny had got too near the bomb. Fuck!

Lee opened fire on the area of the poppy field he was sure would hold the terrorist. But then he could hear the bullets zinging in from another direction. Shit, the ambush was even better organised than he'd first thought.

'Nine o'clock,' he yelled, hoping his voice would be heard over the noise and confusion of the firefight.

Other members of the patrol joined Lee, also sheltering behind their own Bergens, and followed Lee's direction of fire. It was difficult to tell if they were having any success as bullets, lit by red tracer, poured back and forth. Had they hit any of the gunmen?

'Get air support,' screamed the sergeant, from where he was helping Ryan tend Johnny. The radio operator jabbered instructions into his set.

The firing from the centre of the field seemed to have died down.

'I'm moving in,' said Lee. 'Give me covering fire.'

His comrades began to let rip with their SA80s, the bullets skimming over Lee's head as he ran, half crouched, into the lush green crop. He felt a tug at his jacket. He dropped to his knees, hiding in the plants. He had a hole in his sleeve. Shit, that was close. He hoped to fuck it was the enemy, not his own side. He didn't want to think that one of his colleagues couldn't aim a gun properly. Not a good thought.

He popped up, meerkat-like, to get a quick bearing. Twenty yards away, the poppies were swaying again. He brought up his rifle and pumped a magazine's worth into the area. Ducking down he rapidly unclipped the spent container, reached into his belt kit, and replaced it. It only took seconds. Then he ran forward a second time. Slumped in the plants was the body of a young lad. He could only have been about fifteen. Lee felt for a pulse but he could tell the boy was dead, and he didn't care. By the boy was the switch that had detonated the IED – the one that had injured, maybe killed, Johnny.

'Live by the sword,' said Lee to his dead opponent, 'and you're going to get fucked.'

Without thinking, he stood up to make his way back to

the rest of the patrol and as he did so pain exploded. He collapsed while the sky darkened and all he could hear, before he passed out, was the sound of someone screaming – himself.

The nine-liner came into the crew room and instantly papers were thrown on the floor, books dropped, as the immediate readiness crew exchanged board games and reading materials for emergency medical equipment, and headed for the helipad. Shit, Chrissie thought, as she grabbed a bag of medical equipment, her body armour and her helmet and raced from the air-conditioned cool of the crew room into the oven-hot heat outside, another poor bastard maimed.

Like everyone, she watched the newscasts beamed to them by the BFBS, and was bemused by how little from Afghanistan ever made it onto the British news. Deaths did, sometimes repatriations if it was a slow news day, but injuries? Not a chance. The British public, she thought, had no idea what the attrition rate was. Not a Scooby-doo. And now another soldier was down and the knowledge made her feel sick. Another young man whose life had changed for ever. The soldiers could joke all they liked about how they would be going to Rio to the next Olympics, the humourless reality was so very different. Maybe, when the guys got back to England, got to the rehabilitation stage, got their prosthetic limbs fitted, they found life looking up; but here at the field hospital, it was pretty grim. There was bloody little joking on the major trauma ward.

When she got to the helipad and ran up the rear ramp of the huge helicopter, the rotors were already starting to spin. There was no mucking about getting MERTs off the ground. Pre-flight checks on a normal mission could take twenty minutes; now time was of the essence, and everything, except the absolute basic safety procedures, was jettisoned in favour of gaining precious seconds. The stabilisation of casualties was still largely carried out on the battlefield and might have become the platinum ten minutes, kicking the idea of a golden hour right down the line, but the speed at which the injured could be got to the operating table was still crucial, and the pilots did all they could to help.

The speed of the rotors and the noise of the engine increased as Chrissie found a seat. The entire aircraft began to shake and, through the open tail ramp, the dust around the helipad began to kick up. One of the Force Protection Unit, the soldiers who guarded them on the ground at the sharp end, was busy strapping himself to the safety lines at the side of the helicopter and then kneeling behind a heavy machine gun, which he'd positioned on a tripod, at the very edge of the ramp. As if the body armour and helmet weren't enough to remind you this trip was really dangerous, *that*, thought Chrissie, surely left you in no doubt. That, and the Apache which would fly alongside providing some even more serious fire support.

She and the others were settling into their webbing seats hooked to the sides of the Chinook, when the news was relayed to the MERT medics that it wasn't going to be one casualty. There'd been a second incident in the battle now raging. Nervously the medical team smiled at each other, trying to convince both themselves and their colleagues that they weren't actually shitting themselves. The soldiers flying with them, the guys who would deploy as soon as they landed, to secure the LZ, looked pumped up and full of adrenalin. But then, this was what they'd been trained for; this was their primary role.

The second nine-liner was passed back down the helicopter. Chrissie scanned the proforma: *one patient, T1*, *stretcher case, urgent surgical, UK soldier, area under sustained enemy attack, flares to mark the pick-up*, she read. She didn't like the phrase 'area under sustained enemy attack'. Still, the worry over what might greet them when they landed at their destination took her mind off the discomfort she was feeling right now. The body of the Chinook was a metal box, which had been sitting in the desert sun the whole day – it was now oven-like and Chrissie felt her whole body prickling with sweat. She could feel rivulets of perspiration trickle down her spine, pour off her forehead, down her neck. Jeez, and she was only sitting still. What must it be like for the poor bloody infantry on the ground, fighting for their lives?

Her heart jolted up a notch as the shaking of the helicopter changed into a more violent trembling, and then everything suddenly swayed as the wheels lifted off the ground and they were airborne. She checked her lap strap and glanced out of the window. On the horizon, the sun was a blood-red disc as it slid behind the dust-laden air. Below, the camp was already flooded with light but, beyond the perimeter fence, away to the east, where night had already fallen, the darkness was Stone Age. Not a flicker, not a glimmer of light for as far as she could see. She turned back to look into the cabin and tried to keep her nerves under control.

Ten minutes later, she could tell they had to be near their destination. The movement of the Chinook had altered and once again they were swaying and bobbing in the air, not thrusting forwards. And then, bump, they were down.

The soldiers raced down the ramp into the hot, black night, guns cocked and ready, to form a defensive ring around the Chinook, while the medics waited on board for the casualties to be brought to them by their comrades. They were ready, the drips were set up, the kit had been unpacked around the stretcher in the centre of the helicopter, and they waited. Above them the rotors spun; inside, the noise was still intense.

From where Chrissie was, she could see the surgeon talking into the head mic which connected him to the pilots. She could tell from his body language that something deeply frustrating was going on. A message, like Chinese whispers, was passed down the line.

Phil punched her arm. 'Come on,' he yelled in her ear. 'We've got to get him.'

Chrissie stared at him, not quite comprehending, but Phil was getting two other medics on side.

'Come on, Chrissie.'

Suddenly she understood what he meant. They had to go out, into the battle, to retrieve the soldier. Fuck! Scared, adrenalin pumping, she unclipped her belt and followed Phil off the chopper, thundering down the ramp into the dust kicked up by the Chinook and the smoke from the flare which had guided the pilot to the LZ. Even with the noise of the rotors and the whine of the engine, she could hear the crackle and pop of gunfire. Suddenly she was back on Exercise Autumn Armour, scared of what she might see, scared of what might happen. Only this time it was for real: real bullets, real injuries. She pulled herself together. She'd come a long way in six months – this time she'd cope, she knew it.

Ahead, she could see four soldiers racing towards them, weighed down by a shape being carried in a poncho. The ambushed patrol could spare guys to get one of the casualties on board but it would be quicker for Phil and his team to grab the second man down while the first casualty was lifted into the helicopter and into the hands of the surgeon. The soldiers ran past them and into the Chinook while Phil led his team off to one side, towards a field of some sort of crop. Phil was in comms with the troops and the pilots and was obviously receiving instructions from someone with night vision goggles as, barely pausing, he led them through the tall plants.

Chrissie followed him, keeping as close as she could, trying not to admit to herself that she was using his body as a shield. She could see red tracer, arcing lazily through the sky, like a low-grade fireworks display. She breathed a sigh of relief that the bullets weren't heading their way. Then Phil stopped, so suddenly she almost cannoned into him. At his feet was a youth in a dirty white kaftan, eyes wide open and obviously dead. T4, thought Chrissie, and not a priority. But beside him was a soldier being worked on by the patrol's medic. If the medic was still working, the lad was still alive. The old adage – where there's life there's hope – was never so true as when the MERT arrived.

Phil whipped off his backpack and extricated a lightweight aluminium collapsible stretcher. In seconds it was assembled and the soldier was rolled onto it. It was then that Chrissie saw his face.

Lee!

Oh my God, Lee. And suddenly all her professional detachment, all her training went by the board as her insides went into freefall and two fat tears of love, fear and shock rolled down her cheeks.

And then someone punched her hard in the arm. What the fuck? And as the pain set in she realised it wasn't a punch – she'd been shot.

Chapter Twenty-Eight

It was the doorbell that woke Jenna. She rolled over in bed to look at the digital alarm beside her. Seven o'clock? Give it a rest. She rolled onto her back and decided that going on to brandy after the best part of a bottle of wine might have been a mistake.

The bell rang again.

For fuck's sake. What could be so urgent?

'Are you going to get that?'

Jenna froze. Uh-oh. Cautiously, she turned her head. Shit. How did that happen? What the *hell* was Dan doing in her bed? She shut her eyes as the bed spun and tried to think back to the previous evening. She'd driven back to Coronet Foods, she'd collected her pay and some half-decent praise, been asked to report back tonight at five for another job and then she'd driven to the Six Bells. So far so good.

Dan had been waiting for her there and he'd suggested dinner. Great idea, she was starving, and there was nothing wrong with sharing a steak and chips and a bottle of wine with a friend, she remembered thinking. He'd suggested ringing for a taxi and collecting her car the next day, which was also a good shout. And the brandy after had seemed a good plan. But maybe not the second one. And that's when it became fuzzy. No, not fuzzy; after that second brandy it was a total fucking blank. She couldn't remember how she'd got home or anything, and she certainly couldn't remember inviting Dan into bed. Fuck!

The bell rang again. Feeling shaky, she clambered out of bed, dragged on her dressing gown and made her way downstairs. She glanced out of the landing window and her heart stopped. A black saloon car was parked outside.

No! Dear God, no! Every wife knew what that meant. Every wife lived in fear that a strange unmarked black car would stop at their door and now one had. And across the road were a couple of wives, staring out of their open front doors, their faces frozen with the shock that bad news was being delivered so close to home.

Even more shakily, Jenna got to the bottom stair and crossed the hall to open the door. Captain Fanshaw was there with Major Milward. Her heart was thumping and her mouth was dry; she opened the door wide enough to let them in. She knew with certainty what this was about. All she needed to know was how bad the news was going to be. If Lee was dead, she'd lose this house; with no military husband she'd have no entitlement to stay in it – and she hadn't finished paying for the improvements yet.

'Mrs Perkins...' began Milward.

'Tell me,' she said. 'Just tell me.'

'Let's sit down,' said Seb.

'Just fucking tell me,' screamed Jenna.

'Lee's injured. He was shot. He's critical.'

Jenna stumbled into the sitting room and slumped on one of the new sofas. 'So he's still alive.' She saw the look exchanged between Milward and her husband's platoon commander. 'Is he or isn't he?'

'As far as we know,' said Seb, cautiously.

'What does that mean?' Jenna felt terrified. If Lee died,

her security was completely gone; she'd have no income, she'd have nothing except debts. It was all a terrifying prospect.

'It means that the last update we had is that he's back at the hospital in Bastion, he was alive when they got him there, and because of that, his chances are good. They'll stabilise him and then, all being well, he'll fly back to the UK.'

Jenna looked up at Seb angrily. '"All being well"? Does that mean, if he doesn't die?'

Seb nodded. 'Jenna, there's no easy way of putting this: he's very ill.'

The awfulness of everything on top of a crippling hangover made Jenna's gorge rise. She swallowed the sour bile back down.

'Shall I make some tea?' asked Milward.

'Good idea,' responded Seb, when Jenna didn't answer. Milward made his way to the kitchen.

'Is there someone you'd like to come and sit with you?' asked Seb. 'Your mum lives locally, doesn't she?'

Jenna nodded.

'Shall I ring her for you?'

Jenna shrugged. 'She'll have to get the kids off to school first,' she said tonelessly. Besides, what good would her mum be? She would just flap and fuss. And anyway, she needed to get Dan out of the house before any more people piled in. Shit, what a mess – Lee getting injured on top of everything else. The sodding icing on the fucking cake.

Captain Fanshaw was saying something to her.

'Sorry?'

'Jenna, we ought to tell Lee's mum.'

'Must we?' She couldn't bear the thought of ringing that old cow. She'd probably blame her for what had happened

– Jenna was in no doubt what Sonia Perkins felt about her, and she had enough on her plate without coping with that old biddy's snide comments.

'She has a right to know. Lee's her son.'

'He's my husband,' she shot back. Silence fell. Jenna considered how shit everything was and how it was all the army's fault. Her business was ruined, she was in a crap house, and if Lee died, she wouldn't even have that. Bastards. And Captain Fanshaw was as bad as any of them. The only person in the army she didn't hate right now was Immi. 'Ring Immi,' she decided, suddenly. 'Ring Immi for me.'

'Immi?'

'Immi Cooper. She a clerk somewhere. In some office in the battalion.'

'I'll get onto it. Maybe she can make the necessary phone calls, if you're not up to it. But, Jenna, we have to tell people: other relations, close friends...'

Major Milward appeared in the door. 'Can I have a word, Seb?'

'Sure,' said Seb.

'In private,' added the major.

Jenna watched Seb leave her sitting room. In a vague, detached way, she wondered what they were going to talk about. Maybe they'd had an update about Lee. Oh God, she hoped it wasn't even worse news. What would happen to her if he died?

She dragged herself off the sofa and followed them; she needed to know what was going on, and anything they had to say, they could say in front of her.

She stopped dead in horror at the door to the kitchen. The floor was strewn with clothes – hers and Dan's. There was absolutely no doubt what had gone on the night before and she was caught bang to rights – with the emphasis on the bang.

Lee felt rank. Worse than he ever had. Everything ached: his head, his body… and his mouth…! He'd had some hangovers, but this was dire. He tried to open his eyes, but they seemed gummed shut and, honestly, he couldn't really be bothered. And he was so tired – completely, utterly wiped. How could he feel so tired, when he'd been asleep? Nothing seemed to make sense. Everything was blurry, his brain didn't seem to be functioning properly. Maybe he'd just lie here, till he felt a bit better, and frankly, he didn't think it'd be possible to feel any worse.

He tried to marshal his thoughts but everything seemed so woolly. What the hell had he got up to? Drinking? No, that wasn't right. Ah – Afghan… he remembered, he was in Afghan. He wouldn't have been on the lash, this couldn't be a hangover! And then it all came crashing back. Johnny, the firefight, the dead Taliban and then… nothing.

Oh shit, was he dead too? Was this being dead? And if he was, why did he feel so fucked? Surely dead people were out of it completely. Maybe they weren't. Maybe this was how it was only no one could come back and tell you being dead was a shit option. And then a wave of wooziness overwhelmed him and grey fuzz clogged his mind, and he sank back into oblivion.

He could hear voices. In the swirling muddle of some dream, he could hear Chrissie. What was she doing out in the compound? She wasn't allowed on the front line, she was a medic. But she was here, chatting. She had to leave. If Sergeant Adams found her, he'd go mental. He tried to tell her to get out, get out of the compound, go back, but no words came out. Instead he felt a cool hand on his forehead. What the hell was going on? This was such a nightmare. He had to wake up, he had to open his eyes.

He managed to crack the left one open and the light was so bright, he screwed it shut again immediately, but not before he'd glimpsed strip lights and a ceiling. This wasn't the compound.

'Lee? Lee? Are you with us?'

But that was Chrissie's voice all right.

He cracked his eye open a second time, just a smidge, so he wasn't blinded. Through the fuzz of his eyelashes, he could see her, bending over him.

'Lee, you're in Bastion, in the hospital. You're going to pull through.'

Pull through what? He croaked, 'What?'

'Water?'

That wasn't what he'd meant, but it'd do. He nodded his head a fraction and regretted it. His neck and shoulder felt as if someone was trying to bayonet him. He shut his eye again till the wave of pain subsided.

He felt something against his mouth – a straw. He sucked and cool water squirted into his mouth. He let it roll around and wash across his teeth and gums before it trickled down his parched throat. He felt his tongue unstick from his palate. That was so good. No pint of beer after an exercise had ever felt as good as this sip of plain water did right now. He took another sip and another.

'Better?'

This time he managed to open both his eyes. There was Chrissie, her big brown eyes filled with concern and care for him, her curly hair framing her face like a halo. The last time he'd seen her bending over him was when they'd first met, way back on that exercise. Back then he'd thought that was what an angel would look like. Now that feeling was even stronger; now he knew how kind and thoughtful she was; now he thought he loved her. Even if it was wrong, even if he was married to Jenna, he couldn't help how he felt.

'Thanks.'

'You need to rest some more,' she said. 'I'll be back later.'

She patted his hand and left. It was only when she had gone that Lee realised that her right arm and shoulder were bandaged and in a sling.

Jenna sat in her sitting room nursing a cup of tea. Immi sat beside her.

'So,' said Immi, 'shall I make those phone calls?'

'I suppose.' She was still reeling from the awfulness of the morning. First the news, then the look on the two officers' faces, when they'd seen the evidence of her infidelity. Milward had guessed what had been going on when he went into the kitchen to make tea, and had made sure Fanshaw realised, too. Well, wasn't that typical of the nasty little man. But, jeez, what a mess. All she'd been able to do was swoop on the clothes and scoop them up, as if it was the leavings of a wayward child and not the result of two sex-crazed adults who'd torn each other's clothes off, rather than make it up the stairs. She'd slammed the evidence into a cupboard and stared the two men down, silently daring them to make a comment. Hiding the clothes didn't solve the problem of what they knew, nor the other, worse, problem of getting Dan out of the house, but she'd decided to cross that bridge later. The fact that all her neighbours were gathering in knots on the grass outside, waiting like vultures to pick over the news, wasn't going to make the latter problem any easier either.

If Lee hadn't got himself injured, thought Jenna angrily, she wouldn't be in this mess now. It was all his fault.

Still, she thought, as she sipped her tea, she'd finally managed to convince both Seb and Alan Milward that all she needed was Immi for company and that she didn't need either the commanding officer or the padre to see her. And eventually, she'd managed to shove them out of the house. As soon as they'd gone, she threw Dan's clothes through the bedroom door and told him to get dressed and out *right now*. They just both had to hope that the other wives would be keeping an eye on the comings and goings at the front door and he'd be able to slip out the back unnoticed. Not that she cared, Jenna told herself. She didn't care a jot what the other wives thought of her – the cows.

'The calls,' repeated Immi.

Jenna sighed. It had to be done. Lee's mum had to know, and her own mum, and if those two felt there were any other relations who needed to be in the loop, then they could pass on the news. She reached across to the phone and called up the speed dial for Lee's mother. 'She's called Sonia,' she told Immi.

Immi nodded and said 'I remember', and hit the dial button.

'Hello, it's Immi here, we met at Christmas. Yes, it was lovely. Sonia... no, nothing like that. Sonia, I'm ringing on behalf of Jenna... Yes, I'm afraid it's bad news... No, not that bad... Yes, he's been injured... No, no, a bullet and he's been operated on...'

Jenna could hear the wails and sobs down the other end of the phone. What a drama queen. He was going to live, that's what they'd said. Sonia didn't have to make such a fuss.

She saw Immi put her hand over the phone. 'She wants to come down.'

'Give me the phone.' She grabbed the receiver. 'There's no point,' she told Sonia bluntly. 'He'll go to a hospital in Birmingham when they send him back – whenever that happens. There's a place there relations can stay, so there's no need to come here.' She handed the phone back to Immi and left her to deal with the spluttering and livid mother-in-law. But she didn't care; if Lee wasn't around, she wasn't going to put up with his mother, no way.

Chapter Twenty-Nine

By the time Seb had finished recounting to Maddy what he'd seen in Jenna's home, her jaw was almost down to her neckline.

'But you're not to breathe a *word*,' warned Seb. 'I shouldn't have told you myself, but I just had to share it with someone.'

'I won't,' promised Maddy. 'Not even Caro.'

'Especially not Caro,' said Seb. 'Honestly, if you tell her, you might just as well make a banner and trail it across the sky behind a plane.'

'She's not that bad,' protested Maddy.

Seb just raised an eyebrow. Maddy didn't argue. Well, maybe Caro could be a tad indiscreet.

'The really worrying thing is, though—' said Seb.

'What, apart from the fact that she's being unfaithful while he's fighting for his life?'

'Apart from that. The worrying thing is that she seemed to feel that Lee had got injured to make life tricky for her. It was as if she was blaming him. That somehow he'd gone and got shot deliberately.'

Maddy frowned and shook her head. 'Surely not. I'm sure you read her wrong. It was probably just panic and worry that made her seem a bit off key.'

'You think?'

Maddy shrugged. 'Maybe I should pop round and see if

she's OK. I could take her a casserole or something. I imagine if she's worried, or in shock, she won't think about eating properly.'

Seb snorted. 'If that's what you want to believe.'

'I'll give her the benefit of the doubt. Any news about Lee?'

'Not yet. They're going to get him back soon – just as soon as he's stable.'

'Poor lad.'

'The whole incident was a mess. One of his section got his foot blown off and then a medic, going in to rescue them, got shot. She's going to be put forward for a gong.'

'*She?*'

'They have women out there.'

'I know that. Just the thought that they're getting shot at is a little disconcerting.'

'But they're soldiers,' said Seb, 'so why not?'

He had a point, thought Maddy. She just hoped they had the means to shoot back!

Seb suddenly grinned again.

'What's so funny?' said Maddy. Frankly, she couldn't see much to laugh about in the situation. A wife having sex while her husband was away, three soldiers injured, two of them catastrophically – yeah, a barrel of laughs.

'I was just remembering Alan's face, when I met him in the kitchen. He told me on the way back to the battalion that he'd seen the insides of dozens of quarters, so had just assumed the kitchen was a mess, that Jenna hadn't bothered to tidy up the washing or something. It was only when he realised it was a bra hanging off the fridge door that he spotted that the clothes were his and hers.'

Even Maddy could see the funny side to this. 'And he's such a humourless old fart.'

Seb's eye twinkled and crinkled. 'And then of course we both realised that the bloke had to still be in the house, unless she'd bundled him out the back without a stitch to wear.'

That was too much for Maddy and she collapsed with laughter. 'God, it's a French farce,' she said, rocking with mirth. Then she sobered up.

Except it wasn't for poor Lee Perkins. Injured and with an unfaithful wife... for him it was all crap, really.

Chrissie sat at the desk in the NAAFI and typed her password, one-handed, into the shared computer. Then she hit the Skype icon. Was Immi online? Whoo hoo. She hit the call button. The ring tone blipped from the computer speakers. And then up came Immi's face.

'Hi, Chrissie,' said Immi. 'How's things?' Then she noticed the sling. 'You've been in the wars. What happened?'

'Got shot,' said Chrissie. She relayed the story.

'You're joking me,' said Immi. She sounded completely stunned. 'And you were rescuing Lee?' Chrissie nodded. 'Bloody hell. And you ended up getting shot.'

'It's just a flesh wound. They're going to send me back too, though. I'm not much use now I can't work, and they want to do some surgery on it to reduce the scarring.'

'Bloody hell, Chrissie, that doesn't sound like nothing to me. It must have hurt.'

Chrissie nodded. 'It did a bit, but I didn't notice properly till the excitement died down.' But she hadn't called to talk about herself. 'How's Jenna? How did she take the news?'

'Not brilliantly. No,' said Immi, 'that's not quite what I meant. She was really quite calm about it. OK, so poor old Lee hasn't lost a limb or anything, but it was a shocking bullet wound. Old Milward told me she wanted me to be there to

277

make the phone calls and everything, but it was almost like she couldn't be bothered, not that she couldn't cope because she was so upset. Honest, Chrissie, I know shock takes people different ways, but Jenna was really weird. She says she's had it with the army. She says she doesn't want anything to do with the welfare system here and isn't sure about accepting the army arrangements to go and stay at the hospital so she can visit Lee. I'm worried about her, Chrissie, I really am.'

'And if she's in a bad way, it won't help Lee. It's a bit of a mess, isn't it?'

'When do you think you and Lee'll be coming back?'

'I'm scheduled on the next medevac flight and if Lee's lucky, so will he, but at the mo he's not too clever and they're keeping him pretty sedated.'

'That doesn't sound great.'

'The bullet that hit him made a real mess of his shoulder – smashed his shoulder blade, apparently, and punctured a lung, plus it caused huge blood loss. Actually, he's bloody lucky. The bullet stopped up against his spinal cord – another inch and it doesn't bear thinking about.'

'Shit, that's awful.'

Chrissie nodded. 'He's going to need lots of physio when he gets better if he wants to get full movement back in his right arm, but the medics here are hopeful.'

'So some good news, then.'

'I'll keep you in the picture. I'm going to go now. I want to pop over to the hospital and see Lee.'

'Give him my love,' said Immi.

'And you tell Jenna he's getting the best treatment.'

Chrissie flicked off Skype and logged off. Time to visit Lee. She felt happy at the prospect. She walked out of the air-conditioned NAAFI into the suddenly searing heat. It had gone from winter to 'blast-furnace' in about ten days, and Chrissie found it exhausting. How ironic, she thought, as she tramped the mile or so to the hospital, that she'd come out here to get away from Lee and yet events had conspired to drive them even closer together.

'Hey!' A familiar voice stopped her in her tracks.

Chrissie turned round. 'Hey, Phil. Off duty?'

He nodded. 'Just been stood down. Where are you off to?'

'Thought I'd drop in on Lee – see how he's doing.'

'Cool. Want some company?'

No, she didn't, she'd like to have Lee all to herself, but how could she tell Phil and not have eyebrows raised? 'Sure.'

'And I've got something to show you.'

Phil fell into step beside Chrissie as they stomped over the grey, dusty ground, between the rows of prefabs and tents with an arc of cloudless sky above them. 'Oh, what?' She had to raise her voice as a helicopter took off and clattered overhead.

Phil waited for it to thunder off, over the perimeter fence, before he hauled his day sack off his back and pulled out a netbook. 'I've got a new film downloaded.' He waved the little computer at her enticingly before they set off again.

'Great, what is it?'

'*Top Hat.*'

'Oooh, one of my favourites.'

'Thought it might be.'

'Although I loved *Flying Down to Rio.*'

'Did you? Now, I preferred *Shall We Dance.*'

They strode on, pausing in their discussion of Fred Astaire and Ginger Rogers films only when aircraft and helicopters thundered in and out of the base, deafening them both, until they reached the field hospital. Inside, the air con brought the temperature back down to something approaching normal, although it was so cold compared to the outside that Chrissie's skin instantly broke out in goose pimples.

They made their way through the myriad tented corridors joining together the prefab buildings, till they got to Lee's ward. He was still lying motionless on his bed, his eyes shut, the drip delivering pain relief still connected into one arm, a drip of saline going into the other, and electrodes and monitors connected to other bits of him. Around him, machines beeped and blipped intermittently.

'How is he?' Chrissie asked a passing nurse.

'Much better,' was the reply. 'We're bringing him off a lot of the medication. I think he'll be flying back to the UK on the next medevac flight.'

'Him and me both, then,' said Chrissie.

'And me. I've volunteered to be an in-flight medic,' said Phil. 'Someone's got to do it.'

'Really?'

'Why not? Spending a day and a half on a round-trip to the UK is my idea of heaven.'

Chrissie pressed her good hand to her chest in mock excitement. 'Ah yes, the glamour of in-flight movies, duty free, departure lounge shopping opportunities...'

'And,' added Phil, 'most of the passengers get lie-flat business class travel. Only the very best customers for me.'

They pulled up a couple of moulded plastic chairs and sat next to Lee's bed. His colour was certainly better. Chrissie cast a professional eye over the chart above his bed and noted that his temperature and blood pressure were almost back to normal. Phil got out his netbook and opened up the media player.

'Fancy a bit of Fred and Ginge while we wait for Sleeping Beauty to come round?' asked Phil.

'Wouldn't say no,' responded Chrissie. After all, what else did she have to do? She was on light duties, couldn't do her day job, her admin was up-to-date... Fred and Ginge sounded a perfect way to while away some time.

Phil plugged his headphones into the jack and passed an earpiece to Chrissie. 'Sorry,' he said, 'we'll have to share. Not exactly stereo.'

Chrissie laughed. 'I almost don't need to hear the soundtrack. I think I know most of the words to this and I know *all* the words to the songs. Not getting the movie in Dolby surround sound will *so* not spoil it for me.'

The film started and they both watched the black and white classic unfold on the screen, engrossed in the story.

Lee began to feel the fog lift. He was used to it now and it didn't make him feel so panicky. As the fuzz drifted out of his brain like mist rising off an autumn field and he realised that consciousness was returning, he knew now what to expect. First the vague sounds of activity in the ward: the sound of rubber-soled boots squeaking on the polished floor, voices, maybe the beep of a pager going off, and then, from outside, the incessant sound of aircraft engines, winding up, winding down, full-throttle on take-off with a heavy load... Then he'd become aware of light on the other side of his eyelids, of the feel of the cotton bed sheets under his finger-tips, of the throb in his shoulder, of the thirst in his throat. And then he'd remember Johnny and the sight of his hideously foreshortened leg. And then he'd open his eyes to lose that image.

Usually all he saw was the ceiling and the strip lighting of this prefab ward. But this time he could see people next to his bed. Visitors. He blinked a couple of times. One was

Chrissie, he'd recognise that halo of hair anywhere, but she was bent so close to this other visitor she completely obscured who it was, although he could see enough of the haircut to know it was a bloke. Whoever she was with they had a shared interest. He could tell by their body language they were totally relaxed with each other. The best of friends. Maybe more.

Suddenly he felt ridiculously emotional; he didn't want Chrissie to be with someone else. He wanted her himself, although he knew it was all wrong, all madness. Why was he feeling like this? It had to be the fault of the drugs, there could be no other explanation.

He watched them for a few moments until Chrissie flicked a glance in his direction. She smiled, her eyes softening with real pleasure, which made Lee's feelings get into an even bigger turmoil.

'Lee! Hi, how are you feeling?' She ripped her earphone out and leaned forward to kiss him on the cheek. His aches and pains vanished as other, stronger emotions washed through him. If she could do that to him with a kiss what the hell could she do to him if they really got it together? No! He *had* to stop thinking like that.

'Hi, Chrissie,' he croaked.

'You need water,' she told him, as if he didn't know. Instantly she picked up his beaker and pressed the straw against his lips. He could feel the warmth of her hand against his chin.

He sucked on the straw and felt his mouth unstick, un-gunge. Bliss.

'So.' She smiled at him. 'How are you feeling now?'

He couldn't tell her the real truth: he was as horny as hell, despite everything. 'Better. Not so dusty. But what about you?' He stared at her sling. 'What happened to you?'

'She got shot, rescuing you,' said her friend.

Lee looked past Chrissie and recognised her companion. Bugger, it was Phil, he might have guessed. But then the significance of what Phil had just said hit home.

'Shot?'

'It's only a scratch,' said Chrissie. 'It's not like your wound.'

'It's nothing of the sort,' said Phil. 'And I'll have you know that despite her wound, this woman still managed to help carry you back to the Chinook.'

She'd done what? Lee felt a total rush of love for Chrissie.

Chrissie punched Phil's arm with her good hand. 'Will you stop bigging it up? It was nothing serious and I still had an arm that worked.'

But she gave her medical colleague a smile that Lee would have walked over fire to have won. But he had no right to that sort of smile, and it seemed Chrissie was obviously mad about Phil, lucky guy. Instead he said, 'Yeah, sounds like it. It must have still killed.'

'To be honest,' said Chrissie, 'I was so fucking wired with adrenalin and anger, it was only when I got off the Chinook back here that it really began to smart.'

'Smart, my arse,' said Phil. Lee noticed the dopey expression on his face. So Phil was equally potty about Chrissie. He wanted to be happy for her, but all he could feel was an unbelievable sense of sadness. 'You almost passed out,' finished Phil.

'Exaggerating again,' said Chrissie, grinning.

The sadness and self-pity Lee was feeling was suddenly too much. He didn't need to see how loved-up Chrissie was. He couldn't blame her for being with Phil, and he was just being selfish – wanting what he couldn't have – but he'd had enough. Their banter didn't involve him. He wasn't a part of this conversation, he didn't have the energy to keep up, and it didn't matter what his feelings were for Chrissie, because nothing was ever going to happen between him and her – the way she obviously felt about Phil had seen to that. And of course he himself was in the wrong for even thinking about Chrissie when he had Jenna waiting for him.

But if she wasn't around...

And suddenly he realised that he actually resented Jenna's presence. He blamed that on the drugs too; the drugs had to be really messing him up, because to feel like that about his own wife was bang out of order.

Chapter Thirty

'Come to tell me I had it coming to me? Because that's what the wives around here think,' said Jenna, leaning insolently against her door jamb and staring hard at Maddy.

'No... I... not at all,' said Maddy, utterly disconcerted. This wasn't what she expected, although she wasn't quite sure what she *had* expected; someone distraught and worried, maybe. 'I made you this.' She thrust a heavy carrier bag at Jenna. 'It's a cottage pie. I thought it might come in useful. I don't expect you feel much like cooking, with so much shit happening, what with Lee and everything.' Jenna still just stared at her. 'And you need to eat. There's enough here to see you through the weekend,' she ended.

To Maddy's surprise and amazement Jenna stood back and invited her in.

'Sorry,' said Jenna, even more surprisingly. 'It's just the other wives have been a bit shitty. I was expecting more of the same.'

And why wouldn't they be? thought Maddy, but she kept her views to herself. 'I'm sorry,' she said. 'Maybe you're just being sensitive, because you're in a bad place. Because of Lee.'

'And maybe my neighbours are bitches, who only want to see the worst in me,' Jenna snapped back.

'Oh, hon.' She put her arm around Jenna's shoulders. 'Would a cup of tea help?' She felt Jenna shrug her off, so she pushed past her into the kitchen so she could dump the pie. She forced herself not to check the floor for discarded men's underpants as she plonked the cottage pie on a counter and grabbed the kettle.

'Tea?' she asked. Jenna nodded. 'Tea bags?' Jenna pointed to a canister near the kettle. 'Mugs?' Wordlessly, Jenna fished two out of a cupboard and handed them to Maddy.

'So what's the matter?' she asked. 'I'd heard that Lee is out of danger. That's got to be good, hasn't it? He'll be flying back soon.'

Jenna nodded. 'I suppose. And thank you for being kind. I appreciate it.'

'It's only a cottage pie,' said Maddy, trying to lift the mood. 'I'm not donating a kidney.'

Jenna shook her head. 'No, well, it's appreciated. And unexpected,' she added.

She suddenly looked vulnerable and Maddy's attitude softened a little. 'But the other wives, your neighbours…'

Jenna shook her head. 'We don't really get on. Nothing in common.'

Maddy was astounded. Just the fact that they were all army wives – that they'd all been through separation and moves and worry and lived in crap quarters and had had to give up careers and faced sending their kids off to boarding school and goodness knows what else because of the army – made them a sisterhood. How could Jenna say they had nothing in common? They had *everything* in common. Even Kipling, a century before, had got it right:

> *the Colonel's Lady an' Judy O'Grady*
> *Are sisters under their skins.*

But she kept shtum. If the other wives were keeping their distance, then something was seriously wrong – and Maddy reckoned it had to be with Jenna. Which was a worry.

She made the tea and handed Jenna a mug, pushing the sugar bowl towards her. Jenna shook her head.

'Shall we go and sit somewhere more comfortable?'

'Suppose.' Jenna led the way to the sitting room. Listlessly she flopped onto one of the big cream sofas.

'Have you a date for Lee's return?' asked Maddy.

'There's a medevac flight leaving next week sometime, they think. I've been told that if he's well enough, he'll be on that.'

'Well, that's good.'

'Is it? Life's utterly shit at the moment so having to trek up to Brum will be the icing on the fucking cake.'

'Why? At least it means he's home and safe.'

'Huh. It means seeing his mother. She'll be there, won't she?' Jenna glowered. 'She hates me, always has done.'

'Maybe you can stagger your visiting times, try not to see too much of her.'

'You think?' Jenna shook her head. 'She'll be all over him like a rash. I've a good mind not to go.'

'You can't do that!' Maddy was aghast.

'Why? Sonia'll only make my life a misery.'

'But Lee'll want you there.'

'Yeah, well… and anyway, I've got a new job. Only got it the other day. If I start wanting time off I can kiss goodbye to it, can't I?'

'I'm sure the company would understand.'

'You think? I haven't even signed the contract yet.'

'Oh.'

'Yeah – oh. It's only a little firm, they're short-staffed, if I don't turn up they'll get another waitress in.'

'It's a restaurant?'

'Catering company. Look, Maddy, it's not like jobs are two a penny, and I need the cash. Lee'll understand.'

It sounded very much to Maddy that what Lee might or might not understand was a long way down Jenna's list of priorities. Poor Lee, she thought. What with Jenna's views about his mother, her fling with this other bloke and now her reluctance to visit her wounded husband, Maddy felt herself starting to side with the other wives. And what's more, she didn't rate this marriage with much chance of survival; and frankly, even though it was none of her business, she felt Lee was probably going to be better off without Jenna.

After Maddy had gone, Jenna went into the kitchen, stuck the cottage pie in the fridge and picked her car keys off the hook by the door. She couldn't sit around here all day, feeling sorry for herself, she needed to get down to Coronet Foods and see if she still had a job. Immi had phoned them to explain why she wouldn't be in for a bit and, give him his due, Barry the MD had been very reasonable. But the fact remained that she still hadn't signed a contract, and if he decided to show her the door she wouldn't have a leg to stand on, so she really needed to go and tell him she was still keen to work for him and hope he still wanted her. However, her car was still at the Six Bells right across the far side of town. Who could she ask for a lift? she wondered.

Dan. Dan was responsible for half of this mess; the least he could do was help sort her out, and since they had exchanged mobile numbers over dinner, she knew how to contact him. She scrolled through her phone and tapped the screen.

'Jenna?' he said, sounding surprised. 'After the way you

got rid of me the other morning, I wasn't expecting to hear from you again.'

She nearly retorted that his expectations were dead right, but decided that pissing him off wasn't the best way to get him to give her a lift.

'Yeah, well, you could see how awkward it was. And if Lee hadn't got injured...'

'You would have got away with having a bit of a fling? No one would have been any the wiser? Is that what you mean?'

'Yes. And your point is?' she sniped at him.

'It's none of my business. So how is your old man?'

Just rub it in that I'm married, why don't you? 'He's out of danger, thanks. Look, Dan, let's not bicker, I need a favour; my car is still at the Bells.'

'And you'd like me to give you a lift over there, is that it?'

'Please.'

'When?'

'As soon as possible?' she asked hopefully. She could really do with having her car back for the weekend.

'You're in luck. I've just fixed a staff car and I've got to take it out for a test drive, give it a good run.'

'Ace. Only best you don't come to the house. Meet me at the bus stop near the tennis courts. Ten minutes?'

'See you then.'

Dan was waiting for her when she got to their rendezvous, the engine of the sleek black car purring.

'Hiya,' she said as she climbed in.

Dan leaned across. 'Is that all I get? Hiya?'

'Don't be daft, Dan. This is hardly private, is it? Someone might see.'

'Bit late to be prudish, isn't it?' said Dan, giving her a

disappointed glance as he slipped the car into first gear and pulled away.

'Why are you saying that?'

'Because, Jenna, what you and I did is all over the garrison.'

Jenna could have sworn her heart actually stopped for several seconds and that her temperature plummeted. 'No!'

''Fraid so.'

For all her bravado about not caring a jot what her neighbours thought of her, she suddenly discovered that she did. She felt tears of self-pity pricking her eyes. Shit, what a label – the battalion scarlet woman. How the fuck could she hide this from Lee when he got back? 'This is all your fault, Dan.'

'Mine?' His incredulity rang in his voice.

'If you hadn't got me drunk...'

'I didn't force the drinks on you. You were the one knocking it back like it was water. And you were the one who suggested bed.'

'So what are we going to do?' she asked.

Dan shrugged. 'Depends on you, I suppose.'

'How do you mean?'

'I'm not the one with a partner, remember. I'm the one with an ex. I can do whatever I like.' The lights ahead changed to red, so Dan stopped the car and pulled on the handbrake.

'Thanks a bunch.'

'Jenna, you have to decide if you want to keep your marriage going.'

'Says the bloke with an ex-wife.'

'Exactly, and I didn't.' The lights changed and they moved forwards again.

'Why?'

'Because she ran off with another bloke.'

'Oh.' Silence fell. They'd reached the town and the traffic

had increased significantly. Dan drove carefully along the busy street as Jenna took in what he had said. 'If she'd come back and apologised, would you have taken her back?'

Dan sighed. 'I don't know.'

'Do you reckon Lee'll forgive me?'

'Why are you asking me? I'm not your husband and I don't know your Lee at all. Never met him.'

'You're a man. You're a man whose wife was unfaithful.'

'Which makes me an expert?'

'Makes you more of an expert than me.'

Dan stopped the car again to let people across a zebra crossing. Jenna hoped to God that none of her neighbours was in town and might recognise her and Dan. Although maybe it was a bit late for that, if the whole garrison really *did* know. Talk about wanting to shut the stable door.

'I think,' said Dan carefully, 'if you really want to make your marriage work, if you want to keep Lee, then it might be possible. You're a stunning woman, and if you were mine, I'd be inclined to give you a second chance.'

'You really mean that?'

'That I'd give you a second chance? Yes.'

'No, that you think I'm a stunner?'

Dan laughed. 'Shit, Jenna, what are you like? But I've got to say, I admire you.'

'What? Why?'

'You really are totally brazen, quite apart from being out for Number One and not caring a toss about anyone but yourself. You are going to be one of life's big survivors, which is quite admirable in its own way.' Dan pulled into the car park of the Six Bells and parked beside Jenna's car. 'Let me know if I can be of service again,' he said.

Jenna had a nasty suspicion that he was laughing at her,

but said thank you for the lift, rather than flouncing. If things went badly with Lee, she might need another string to her bow, and Dan would fill that role very nicely. What's more, she reckoned that he'd be very happy to do so. In the meantime, she needed to get her arse over to Coronet Foods and get Barry on her side, too. She flexed her fingers as she got into her car. Nice to know she could still get men to pretty much do what she wanted, but the thing was, did she want to work her magic on Lee? Or might she be better off just cutting her losses?

Chapter Thirty-One

'Maddy, Maddy.'

Maddy, on her way back from buying a carton of milk at the Spar after delivering the pie to Jenna, stopped and turned and saw Caro panting after her, dragging Luke by the hand.

'Hiya, Caro.'

'I can't believe you didn't tell me about Jenna,' Caro said accusingly, not bothering to greet either her or Nate, in his pushchair.

'Tell you what?' lied Maddy. She knew *exactly* what Caro was on about.

'You must have known, given that Seb was the one who caught her with her knickers off!'

Maddy feigned innocence with a small shrug.

Caro gave her a hard stare. 'Sorry, Maddy, that just won't wash.'

'Seb swore me to silence.'

'So? Some friend you are. Juiciest bit of gossip on the patch for years and you don't share. Pah.'

'Anyway,' said Maddy, refusing to rise, 'how on earth did you find out?'

'It's the only topic of conversation at the nursery school. One of the wives saw a strange bloke hightailing out the back of Jenna's quarter, just after your husband left by the front door, having broken the bad news about Lee. You were right all along, what a piece of work she's proving to be.'

Maddy made a moue of agreement. 'I feel sorry for him. As if it isn't bad enough to take a bullet, he's got a wife playing fast and loose.'

'The word is she's trading up. Someone said the new guy is a sergeant.'

'Nothing but ambitious, is Jenna,' said Maddy, shaking her head in disapproval. 'Wouldn't surprise me if she didn't aim for an officer next.'

'Ha. Well, if she sets her sights on Will she'll regret it. And to think I offered her a chance to talk to the Wives' Club. I cancelled that.'

Maddy wasn't surprised. Even Caro wouldn't keep championing Jenna after *that* incident.

When Seb got in at lunchtime, Maddy told him that Caro knew. 'And before you blame me, I didn't say a word.' Seb gave her a disbelieving lift of an eyebrow. 'No, I didn't,' insisted Maddy.

'If you say so.'

His tone infuriated Maddy. 'She heard it down at the school gate.' She repeated the gist of the conversation.

'God, the wives' grapevine. I swear, when it comes to broadcasting you lot could teach the BBC a thing or two.'

'I'm just telling you, so that I don't get the blame for spreading rumours.'

'Perkins is due back soon. I heard this morning he's being medevaced out next week sometime.'

'Then it's good news. He's on the mend?'

'Apparently. Don't envy what he's coming back to. Alan says Jenna is refusing to go to the hospital in Birmingham because she got a new job, and his mother sounds like a total dragon. I just hope his recovery is really good, because the poor bugger is going to need all the strength he can muster.'

Jenna pulled into the car park of Coronet Foods and hoped that Barry was in. He should be, as it was coming up to the weekend, and if she knew anything about the catering business – which admittedly wasn't a great deal – the weekend ought to be their busiest time. She'd considered phoning ahead, but as the company wasn't much of a detour away from her route home, she'd decided to risk it. She climbed out of her car, locked it and made her way towards his office. Tentatively she knocked on his door.

'Jenna,' said Barry. He didn't look particularly pleased to see her, but then she'd let him down over the job. She'd promised she would be available for the next gig after the engagement party at the football club and then, because Lee had gone and got himself shot, she'd had to cry off.

'Just wondering if I've still got a job?' she asked.

'It rather depends,' said Barry.

'On?'

'How available you are.'

She nodded. Well, that didn't come as a surprise. 'I need the work, Barry.'

'And I need the staff, and I'm really sorry about your husband, but I can't operate if I can't rely on having waitresses around when I need them. How is he, by the way?'

'On the mend. Well, out of danger at any rate. And I *can* be around.'

Barry looked at her with raised eyebrows. 'And what about your husband? What about when he's convalescing?'

'He's supposed to be flying back, but not till next week,

and then he'll be in hospital for a while and then he'll need all sorts of other treatment, they say...'

Barry shook his head. 'So how will you be available?'

'There isn't anything I can do for him, is there? It's not like I can nurse him, is it?'

'But don't you want to be there, by his bed? Stay with him? I thought that was what army wives were allowed to do these days.'

'If they want.' She stared coolly at Barry. 'And I don't, not really. His mother'll be there, vile old bat, making out that I'm not good enough and being sarky, giving me evils all the time.'

'But...' Barry looked completely nonplussed.

'So as there's nothing I can do, till he comes home I might as well make myself useful and earn a bob or two.'

'I suppose. If you really want to.'

'I do. So, can I have that contract?'

Barry nodded and slid his office chair across the floor to a low filing cabinet. He pulled open a drawer and fished out some paperwork. 'But if you sign this, I won't be able to let you have a mountain of leave when your husband does come home. You do understand that, don't you? I'm not being hard, but I've got a business to run.'

Jenna nodded. 'I'm sure he'll be able to manage on his own for a few hours while I'm out working. Well, he'll just have to, won't he?'

'If you say so,' said Barry. Although his face was still a study in incredulity.

Taking off, thought Lee as the Globemaster roared into the air, wasn't half as scary as landing had been, although it was still done in pitch darkness, and the angle was so steep he reckoned that the pilot was trying to escape the pull of earth's gravity rather than just get airborne. However, he felt pretty relaxed because on take-off, there was nothing solid to hit – like the ground, which was what they'd been aiming at when they'd landed. He reckoned Chrissie would have no need for the sick bag this time, which would be a relief for everyone who knew her. After about ten minutes, the lights came back on and the medics on the flight unstrapped themselves from their seats towards the front of the cavernous space and came towards the back of the aircraft to check on their patients. The stretchers were stacked like bunks, three high along the sides, with the medical equipment for the sicker patients lashed to the metal frame of the aircraft. It might look Heath Robinson, but there was no reduction in the level of care between Bastion and the hospital in Birmingham, regardless of how intensive it needed to be.

To start with, Lee felt quite lucky to be on the top stretcher. He wasn't claustrophobic, but from up here he could see what was going on – well, he could now the lights were on again – and he watched Phil as he checked the patients he'd been allocated to make sure they were all comfortable, that those who were connected to monitors were still stable, that nothing untoward had happened during the previous twenty minutes. Then he saw Phil go and sit next to Chrissie – who, as an ambulatory patient, wasn't stretcher-bound. Suddenly he wasn't quite so happy to have a grandstand view.

Once again, he felt a spike of jealousy stick into him. And once again, he bashed it down. Wrong, wrong, wrong. Why did he feel so attracted to her? She had done nothing to encourage him; he was married and yet he'd found himself wondering what his life would have been like if he'd met Chrissie before he'd got hitched to Jenna. He realised he was staring at her again. He really had to stop this obsession; if he didn't he'd turn into one of those spooky stalkers. He looked away, trying to feel happy for Chrissie that she'd found such a good bloke, for he had no doubt that Phil was. Surely, the fact that Chrissie really rated him was endorsement enough.

Thankfully, over the previous week, although Chrissie had been a regular visitor, she'd come along on her own, so he hadn't had to witness again the Chrissie and Phil Show at his bedside. While Chrissie waited for her flight to the UK and cosmetic surgery for the scar on her arm, Phil had been on duty and had rarely dropped by to see him. Lee had been tempted to tell him, on the few occasions he had visited, that he didn't have to bother, but couldn't bring himself to be quite that brutal. The guy hadn't done anything wrong, had he? Instead Lee'd concentrated on trying to be indifferent to his feelings for Chrissie. And if it made him seem a bit cold towards her, then so be it. What the hell did it matter *how* she viewed him? It wasn't going to make any difference; she had Phil, and he was stuck with Jenna.

Yet again, he pulled himself up. He was *so* out of order, thinking of Jenna in those terms, but he was still mad at her for rinsing his savings. And she hadn't answered her phone when he'd rung – so where was she? What was she doing that made her out of contact *every* evening? He didn't want to think badly of her, but what else *could* he think?

Slowly, almost all the activity on the aircraft came to a halt. As with all passenger flights, as opposed to cargo ones, they'd taken off well after dark, to minimise the chances of an enemy attack, and now that it was gone midnight the patients and non-essential staff were grabbing some sleep. The white noise of the giant jet engines was kind of soothing and the dim green light was restful, and soon Lee found himself slipping into a doze and then sleep. But it was a sleep dogged by weird dreams, involving Jenna and Chrissie, and when he awoke again, as the plane was buffeted by turbulence, it was almost a relief.

Phil was also awake and came over to check if Lee needed anything.

'A drink would be good,' he said.

'Water?'

'I'd rather have a beer.'

Phil shook his head. 'Sorry, buddy, no can do – even if you weren't on meds, this is a dry flight.'

'Water it is then.'

Phil went to fetch a cup and a straw and brought it back to Lee. He held the cup while Lee slaked his thirst.

'I've been meaning to ask,' said Lee. 'Is there any news of Johnny Flint?'

'Flint?'

'Yeah, the guy who got his foot blown off, same time as I picked up this.' Lee glanced down at his bandaged shoulder.

'Oh, him. He was stabilised and sent back almost immediately so, sorry, I can't help. But there's been nothing to say that he isn't all right.'

'Being minus a foot is hardly all right, though, is it?' It came out harsher than Lee intended.

'He's in the best hands,' said Phil placatingly. He offered Lee more water, and then went to check on some other patients, before sitting down next to Chrissie again.

Lee watched them chatting, wishing that it was him in Phil's place. Maybe Chrissie picked up his thought subliminally, for she suddenly turned and looked back at him. Even across the width of the aircraft, he could see her blush. Lee made a private bet they were talking about him. The thought made him even crankier.

What was the matter with me? he wondered. He put it down to lack of sleep, but he knew it wasn't just that. No matter how much he tried to deny it, he knew he'd fallen for Chrissie and he didn't want to go home to Jenna.

Chapter Thirty-Two

Jenna crawled into her quarter at about eleven thirty at night, dead on her feet. The job at Coronet Foods might pay reasonably for casual work, and the tips were a nice bonus, but it was knackering. How come her feet had *never* ached like this when she was a hairdresser? Now she had to move around all evening, not stand in one place, they killed her. And she had another job tomorrow, so by the time she got to the weekend, her feet were going to be in tatters. Maybe she'd pop into town in the morning and try and buy some shoes that didn't pinch anywhere. She'd hoped she'd get used to being on her feet, rushing around for hours at a stretch, but it wasn't getting any easier – worse, if anything. She was pleased she had this work, really she was, but it was playing havoc with her social life. How was she ever supposed to get out and have a good time if she was going to have to work every weekend?

Wearily she took her phone from her handbag and switched it on again. While she waited for it to connect and find a signal, she grabbed a bottle of white wine from the fridge and poured herself a large glass. On the counter her mobile gave a series of chirps. Six missed calls – all from the same number, a number she didn't recognise. But she also had voicemail. She hit the screen to call up the messages. If it was some spammer she'd be livid.

'Hi, sweetheart. Just to say I've landed safely at Birmingham. I'm now in hospital. Mum's here, Captain Fanshaw's coming up in the week, but it's you I really want to see. I guess you're busy, that's why you're not answering…' Well done, Sherlock, what a bit of deduction that was. There was a pause. Lee was obviously trying to think of something else mind-blowing to say. 'I'll ring again tomorrow. Take care.'

Jenna chucked her phone onto one of the sofas. Oh God, as if she didn't have enough on her plate with this job, now, to cap it all, Lee expected her to hike all the way up to Birmingham. But Lee's direct request was going to be harder to ignore than Alan Milward bleating to her that she had a duty to welcome him home. Milward had phoned twice earlier that week, telling her about Lee's flight and almost ordering her to go and see him. As if it was any of his bloody business. And the more he'd badgered her, the more stubborn and contrary she'd felt. Eventually he'd got the hint and hung up, but he'd left her feeling even more angry with the army. They had *no* right to order her about, tell her what she should and shouldn't do and tell her how she ought to behave towards her husband.

And now Lee had joined in. She sighed heavily. The thought of his mother *and* a hospital visit was almost more than flesh and blood could stand. She hated them both with equal intensity, and the thought of both activities being joined into one fuck-awful day trip was too much. Well, she couldn't do it tomorrow – she had to be back for an event starting at six, so she'd be needed for the set-up from around four thirty. No way was she going to drive all that distance for just an hour or so of playing Florence Bloody Nightingale. And the next day would be no better. The M25 and the M6 on a Friday...? He had to be joking. Maybe she'd think about going up there on Sunday. Or maybe not.

Seb strolled into the military wing of Queen Elizabeth hospital and gave his name to the receptionist. He'd been astounded by the hospital's architecture as he'd driven into the car park – three towering, oval, shiny glass-and-steel buildings – and he just hoped, as he waited to be told where to find Lee Perkins, that the inside was as good as the outside. The area he was in, while still recognisable as part of the NHS, with blue signs directing patients and visitors to every conceivable type of clinic and treatment centre, was more like a military unit when it came to the dress code, and he was far from out of place in his combats. All around him were medical staff, in various types of services uniform: army QA nurses, discussing notes with air force doctors, naval consultants talking to injured soldiers, with some dressed in multicam and some in barrack dress. Only the number of civvy staff made it more like a normal hospital, which, Seb supposed, it was. It certainly sounded and smelt like one: squeaky clean floors, low voices, blips from machinery, the clang of trolleys being moved about...

The receptionist directed him to the military trauma department – follow the yellow line painted on the floor – and a couple of minutes later Seb was strolling onto the ward. The beds were in a mixture of single bunks and four-man bays, and Seb tried hard not to stare at some of the more grotesque injuries as he passed: the burns, the missing limbs, the scars, the disfigurements... Partly because he didn't want the guys to think he was enjoying some sort of freak show, but mostly because he'd witnessed a couple of dreadful incidents on his own tour out there and had spent the past twelve months trying to crowbar the images out of his head. He didn't want to stuff new ones back in. It always amazed him how the medics coped – the things they saw, the things they treated and the pain they witnessed. How on earth did they manage to sleep? He knew he couldn't. He knew, in the past, he hadn't.

He found Lee looking surprisingly bright and chipper. On the other side of the bed was a large woman with a mouth like a steel trap and glittering eyes which looked as if they rarely missed anything. If this was Lee's mother, Seb could see exactly why she and Jenna were hardly likely to see eye-to-eye.

'Hiya, buddy,' he said easily to Lee. Now was not the moment for parade square formality.

'Hello, boss. Good to see you.'

'I don't want to interrupt...' Seb glanced at Lee's mum.

'Sorry, boss, this is my mum, Sonia – Sonia Perkins. Mum, this is my boss from the barracks back here, Captain Fanshaw.'

'But call me Seb,' said Seb, holding out his hand to Sonia Perkins.

She shook it. 'I don't think that would be right, Captain Fanshaw,' she said in a broad Geordie accent. 'I'm old-fashioned that way. My late husband was military and he wouldn't have approved.' Then she stood up. 'I expect you lads want to talk shop, and I need a tea and some fresh air, like.'

'Please stay,' said Seb, 'I don't want you to feel you ought to go.'

'No, I need to stretch my legs. It's no bother.' She strode off.

Seb grimaced at Lee. 'I really don't want to disturb you.'

'Seriously, boss, it's good to see you. Don't get me wrong, I love me mam, but...' He paused and gave Seb a lopsided smile. 'Let's just say, this is the third time she's visited me in about twelve hours and I'm running out of things to say.'

Seb nodded in sympathy. 'Mums, eh? How are you? How's the shoulder?'

'I'm good, the shoulder is a mess. The surgeon's had a look, says they're going to have to operate to get it to mend properly. Apparently there's a lot of bits of bone messing around where bones shouldn't be. They need to clean all that out and then try and fix what's left with pins and plates. Sounds like it's in clip state.'

'But they think they'll be able to sort it out?'

'They say they can. Don't suppose you've seen anything of the missus, have you, boss?'

Seb felt his heart sink. What could he say? He took a deep breath. 'It was me who broke the news to her. And Maddy, my wife, has been round since. She was very upset, naturally.' But not half as upset as she was about being caught in flagrante delicto.

'I was afraid of that. Poor old Jen. And not much fun for you either, boss. Not a great job to have to do – breaking bad news.'

'It's sort of what I get paid for,' said Seb, trying to make light of the task.

'It must be worse for the wives – getting the visit, not knowing the details.'

Seb nodded. 'Well, we gave her as much detail as we knew. So,' he added casually, 'she's not got here yet?'

'Boss, I don't know what's going on. I've left voicemails, I've tried Skype, I can't get hold of her. I'm worried, sir.'

'I think she's got a new job. That's what she told Major Milward and my wife. Some work with a catering company. Maybe she's having trouble getting time off.'

'Maybe, although the job's news to me. What happened to her hairdressing?'

'Um,' said Seb, 'I think she and Zoë had a falling out.'

'Jenna can be a bit of a firecracker. Bonny, but tricky like.' He sighed. 'I wish I knew what was going on.'

Believe me, chum, thought Seb, you don't.

Lee studied the end of his bed morosely. 'Still, I've got to look on the bright side – I'm better off than my mate Johnny Flint. He lost a foot.'

Seb nodded. 'I heard that ambush was a total clusterfuck. And the medic rescuing you got wounded too, didn't she?'

'Chrissie Summers.' Lee nodded.

'You knew her?'

'She was from 1 Herts too, boss. She worked in the medical centre. The one who raced the RSM and won,' added Lee, helpfully.

Seb knew about her, the woman who had already gone down in regimental legend. He nodded. 'Small world.' There was a pause while they both considered the unlikelihood of coincidences and the fact they happened regardless.

'Sir?'

Seb knew this form of address didn't bode well. 'Yes, Lee.'

'Sir, can you tell me something?'

Seb looked dubious. 'Well, I will if I know the answer.'

'It's a bit tricky, to be honest.'

Seb nodded sympathetically. 'Am I the right person? I can get a padre if you'd rather.'

'Fuck… Sorry. Erm, no. I think you'll be much more help, if I'm honest, boss.'

Seb's heart was so low it was down in his boots. So had Lee heard rumours about Jenna already? 'Shoot.'

'I got to look at my bank account a while back. I had to

go back to Camp Bastion from the compound so I managed to get online.' Lee looked at Seb, a crease of worry over his nose. 'Sir, my bank account has been rinsed. And I don't think it's fraud or anything, I think it was Jenna. Do you know what she's been up to? It's just... Shit, sir, my bank account is overdrawn and all my savings have gone.'

Even Seb wasn't expecting that and he almost felt relief until he realised just how much more destruction Jenna Perkins had wrought on Lee's life. An affair *and* taking his money. Shit. 'Bloody hell, Lee. How much?'

'About five grand in savings and then there's a two grand overdraft, plus all my pay for about a month.'

Seb was stunned. Seven grand? Eight? Sheesh. He took a deep breath. 'Look, I don't know the details, but I do know she wanted to set up a hair salon in your quarter. I think she might have paid to have some alterations done.'

It was Lee's turn to be shocked. 'Alterations? In a quarter?'

''Fraid so. But she didn't get permission first, so the housing commandant wasn't best pleased and her venture upset Zoë, and I think the wives decided to side with Zoë, sort of out of loyalty, I suppose...' Seb looked at Lee sympathetically. 'It's been a bit of a mess, I think.'

Lee rolled his eyes. 'Nothing like a bit of understatement. And that sounds *nothing* like *a bit of a mess*. Total fuck-up, more like, if you'll pardon my language. No wonder the wife doesn't want to face me. And to be honest, boss, I'm not sure I want to see her. Not at the moment, anyway.'

Chapter Thirty-Three

Chrissie stood at the door to the ward and watched Lee and Captain Fanshaw talking earnestly. Bloody hell, she thought, if Lee didn't have one visitor he had another. First his mum, now his platoon commander, when was she going to get the chance to have a chat with him?

Her heart was in tatters, she thought, as she watched him. She'd fallen head over heels, and for a married man at that, and she'd given up fighting it. It had started in the field hospital at Bastion and the slide from friendship into love had been inevitable. After all that determination not to get involved, not to get into a relationship... how had it happened? She sighed. She didn't have a clue, but it had. Except falling for a married man was totally wrong and she was not, *never*, going to be a home-wrecker, so that left her in a pretty bleak place. She sighed. That'll teach me, she thought, teach me to get involved. She turned away, resolving that, if nothing else, Lee must never know.

Miserably, she trundled off to the café, where she saw Lee's mum sitting morosely on her own, supping tea and reading the *Mirror*. She thought about saying hello but decided against it, as she wasn't sure she could chat about Lee and give nothing of her own feelings away. In her limited experience, Chrissie felt that mothers had an uncanny knack of picking up on sub-texts, where their own children were concerned.

Instead, she grabbed a cup of tea for herself and took it to the opposite corner of the café and got her phone out. She needed cheering up and knew just the person who could do it.

'Hi, Immi, how's tricks?' she said as soon as Immi answered.

'Same old, same old,' answered Immi. 'And I miss you, hon. There's no one here that I get on with like you.' Chrissie felt better already, Immi was instant sunshine. 'I mean, the others are OK,' continued her friend, 'but Keelie and Gillie never seem to be about, certainly not at weekends, and although I appreciate having the room to myself—'

'I bet you do,' said Chrissie with a dirty laugh, remembering the succession of male friends Immi had entertained there.

'—but I get lonely,' finished Immi.

Chrissie giggled. 'Really? That's not what I remember.'

'I do, honest. I get lonely for *female* company. Blokes are OK, but you can't share the goss with them like you can a girlfriend. Well, not unless they're gay, and there aren't many of those around here.'

'Well, there are a few gays,' said Chrissie.

'A few,' conceded Immi, 'but being a soldier is a pretty macho thing, isn't it? It can't be your default career choice if you're gay, can it? I mean, I can't see the lovely Gok Wan in a tin hat and multicam.'

Chrissie giggled again. 'No, I see your point.'

'Anyway, talking about gossip, do you want to hear a really juicy bit? I feel a bit disloyal passing it on, but it's *all* over the garrison here, and if you were around you'd know.'

'Ooh, tell me then.'

'It's Lee's missus. You know I went round to hers, to hold her hand after she got news that Lee had been injured?'

'Yes.'

'Well, it seems that, as I was going in the front door to do my Good Samaritan bit, there was a random man legging it out the back.'

'No!'

'Truly.'

'Poor Lee. I mean, how could she?' Chrissie felt a wave of disgust well up inside. Lee didn't deserve that, and they'd hardly been married five minutes – well, a few months, but it was hardly the seven-year itch. More like the seven-month itch. 'He doesn't know?'

'Not unless Jenna's told him herself. Although, when he gets back here, I can't see how he'll avoid finding out. Honestly, the world and his dog is in on the news. He's going to be heartbroken.'

Chrissie wanted to cry for Lee. Shit, he didn't deserve this, not on top of everything else.

After their conversation ended, Chrissie went back to her own ward and waited for visiting time to end and the next ward round to start. She had been promised that, when the doctor saw her next, he'd be able to tell her when the op to tidy up the wound on her arm would take place.

It wasn't until later that evening, when the hospital was finally empty of outsiders, that she got her chance to go and say hi to Lee. Although, as she approached his ward, she worried about how on earth she was going to talk to him and not let slip what she knew. She would just have to put out of her mind that she'd had any news at all from the barracks.

'Hi, Lee.'

Lee looked away from the TV screen at the sound of the familiar voice. He hadn't really been watching it, anyway.

He'd been thinking about what Captain Fanshaw had told him about Jenna and her failed business plan, and the alterations to the quarter, and the way she'd blown all his savings, and it was all such a fuck-awful mess and he couldn't see any way out of it and... and...

Round and round it churned and churned, and with each circuit the problem became bigger, knottier, more intractable. But now, thank God, Chrissie was providing a distraction.

'Chrissie. Good to see you. How's the arm?'

'They're going to operate on Monday. The medics told me it's really simple and they can do it under a local anaesthetic. What about your op?'

'I'm down for Monday, too. Must be their day for patching up soldiers.'

'Or maybe the golf course is shut on a Monday so the surgeons have to come in,' said Chrissie. 'Anyway, as soon as they've sorted me out I'll be good to go. Lucky old me, eh?'

'That's great news. I'll be stuck here for a bit and then I'll be off for rehabilitation. Lots of physio and exercise. And I've heard the place they send you to is gleaming. Like a holiday camp: pools and tennis courts and gyms and everything.'

'That's good. I think I'll get some sick leave and then it'll be back to work for me.'

'But the sick leave'll be ace, and won't you get some post-tour leave too? Just think, days and days of being paid to loaf around.'

Chrissie shrugged and sighed. 'Think I'd rather go back to work. The trouble with having no family is I don't really have a place to go to. It's not like I've got a mum who's going to spoil me rotten. I suppose I'll just hang around the barracks for a couple of weeks.'

'Chrissie, that's a rubbish plan.'

'It is, isn't it, but, you know, when you don't have a better hole to go to...'

Lee was about to suggest that maybe Chrissie would like to stay with Jenna, when he realised that it was an even more rubbish plan than the other one. He changed the subject.

'So how's Phil?' he asked.

Chrissie shook her head. 'No idea. He's back in Bastion.'

'Bastion? You mean, he went pretty much straight back?'

Chrissie nodded.

'I thought maybe he came back on the flight because he was going off on R&R or something.'

'No, he just came along for the ride. I don't think he's due R&R for another month or so, right near the end of his tour. That's the trouble with the draw for rest and recuperation, isn't it? Some people get it right at the front end of their tour, when they've hardly begun, some get it right at the arse end and only the lucky few get it slap bang in the middle. I doubt even bloody Goldilocks would strike lucky.'

Lee laughed. 'Mind you, she was one picky moo.' He gazed fondly at Chrissie. She was so grounded and normal. Lucky old Phil. 'Will you be seeing him when he gets back?'

'I expect so. Why shouldn't I? I mean, he works at the medical centre.'

'Of course he does, I'd forgotten.'

'You were hardly a regular there, though, were you?'

'I will be now.' He glanced at his shoulder. 'Do you give out loyalty cards?'

Chrissie smiled and shook her head.

'Well you should, think of all those gifts I could earn: coffee maker, toaster...'

'Cuddly toy.'

'Blow-up dolly.'

'Lee!'

'Sorry.' He grinned. 'One of me mates in Nad-e Ali got sent one with a puncture repair kit. It still went US in a matter of days – or so he said. We reckoned even she didn't fancy him.'

Chrissie giggled. Lee is so lovely, she thought, and he has so much shit going on. She hoped that when he found out just how bad things were back home it didn't make him all bitter and moody, but how could it not. How could he stay so nice when he found out the true extent of what Jenna had done?

Jenna swung her little car into the visitors' car park and got out. She sighed heavily and hoped Lee appreciated her visit. What a journey – over four hours of stop–start traffic and she was probably going to get the same on the way back. What a waste of a Sunday, for just a couple of hours at his bedside. All she needed now was for bloody Sonia to be there and her day would be complete.

She sashayed into the hospital, aware of the admiring glances from the patients and staff as she made her way to reception and then along the corridors, her stilettos click-clacking on the polished lino.

And there he was, his shoulder swathed in bandages. A lot of bandages. But no Sonia. That was something to be thankful for.

'Hiya, babes,' she said as she neared the bed.

Lee looked up. 'Jenna. You made it.'

'Of course, hon.' She leaned over and gave him a kiss on the lips. 'I'd have come earlier,' she lied, smoothly, 'only this new job of mine is a bugger to get away from. Anyway, how are you?' She put on her concerned face – she was good at looking as if she cared. She used to do it all the time in Zoë's when her customers were telling her about their badly behaved kids or their battles with getting repairs to their quarters.

'Not so bad,' said Lee. 'I'm pretty much off the painkillers, although I expect I'll be back on them again for a bit tomorrow.'

'How come?'

Lee gestured with his good hand to the sign over his bed that read *Nil by mouth*. 'They're going to operate on it tomorrow. Pin it together with a whole bunch of metal. It'll make getting through airport security a bastard.'

Was that a joke? She smiled just in case. 'Poor you. Still, at least you're in the right place and getting the best treatment.'

'Yeah, the treatment's been Gucci from start to finish. And after the op, I'll be getting moved closer to you, to this rehab centre in Surrey.'

'Rehab? What, like the Priory?'

'Not like that. This is for the guys who've got to learn to live with their injuries. I mean, I'm lucky, I'll just need physio. Most of the others will be learning to walk again or how to use false hands, stuff like that.'

Jenna wrinkled her nose. 'It all sounds a bit gross to me.' Lee gave her a funny look, but she couldn't help how she felt, could she? People with bits missing *was* gross. 'Where's your mum?'

'She's gone back home. She's coming down again next week again, to see how I am after the op.'

Good, thought Jenna. No chance of running into the old biddy. 'I'll see if I can get up again, only this new job means it might be tricky.'

'Catering, isn't it?'

314

She nodded.

'Sorry, Jen, but what the fuck do you know about catering? I mean, you couldn't even cook a turkey.'

'I don't have to cook, I do waitressing at events. I can even do silver service now.'

'So what happened to your hairdressing business? The one you set up after I left.'

So how did Lee know? Had that interfering busybody Alan Milward said something? 'How do you mean?'

'Captain Fanshaw told me. He said you'd tried to start your own business.'

'Did he now.' What was it with army officers that they felt they had to interfere with every sodding thing? First Milward had pretty much put her out of business and now Fanshaw was telling tales to Lee.

'He said you've had work done on the quarter.'

'So?'

'So, you didn't have permission.'

'And?' God what was this – the Spanish Inquisition?

'Jenna, you can't do stuff like that. It's not our house.'

'Really? So we don't pay the rent or anything? Of course it's our house, Lee – we pay for it, we live there.'

'The army doesn't see it like that.'

'Then they bloody well should.' She sighed. She hadn't come here to argue with Lee, and there was no denying he'd obviously been in the wars. Duh – the Afghan war! 'Anyway, let's not talk about stuff like that.'

'Why, because you think I might ask about what happened to my savings?'

Jenna went cold. How the hell...? She swallowed. 'I don't know what you mean,' she lied with a bright smile on her face.

'Jenna, I've seen my bank statement.'

315

'But…'

'But… you never sent them on to me, so how could I? Is that what you mean?'

Jenna nodded, weakly.

'Internet banking, Jenna. The internet is grand. I could see all those lovely new things in our quarter when I Skyped you, so I had a look at my account – or what was left of it.'

Horror struck, Jenna felt her mouth open, but nothing came out. Not a sound, not a lie, not an excuse… nothing.

'All my savings, Jen. The savings that I thought, together with my Afghan bonus, we might use to get a foot on the property ladder – or a nice car. Nearly eight grand, Jen, that you've blown, and you've spent it on what?'

'I was going to pay it back, Lee,' she whispered, 'honest, but then Milward ruined everything.'

'As I said, Jen, the army has rules about what you can do in quarters. You waited till I'd left, didn't you, so you thought I wouldn't find out. How could you, Jen?'

Again her mouth opened and shut, as her heart thundered with guilt and her blood pooled down in her ankles.

Lee was looking at her so coldly and Jenna knew with total certainty that she'd completely fucked up her marriage. Lee wasn't going to listen to excuses and if she was honest with herself, she didn't have any. She'd thought she could have things her way, that she could fight the army, but she'd made a complete mess of things.

Finally she found her voice. 'I'll make it up to you, Lee.'

'How?'

'I could sell the furniture on eBay. And the telly. They're still almost new.'

Lee sighed and shook his head. 'Drop in the ocean, but if you want to you can try.'

'I'm so sorry, Lee.'

'Are you? Really?' He stared at her till she lowered her eyes. 'Go away, Jenna. Please just go away.'

'You don't mean that, babes, do you?'

Lee nodded. 'I do. Just go.'

Chapter Thirty-Four

'Chrissie.' Immi's shriek could have been heard by dolphins in the Mediterranean. 'Chrissie, babes!' Immi hurled herself across the barrack room at Chrissie, who neatly sidestepped.

'Immi – watch me arm, Ims.'

'Shit, Chris, I forgot. How is it? How are you?' Immi gazed at her room-mate, her eyes glistening with tears. 'And you were so brave. Everyone says you should get a gong.'

'What the fuck? Don't be daft.' Chrissie screwed up her face. 'You don't get a gong for being a twat and getting in the way of a bullet.'

'No, you get a gong for getting in the way of a bullet and still lugging a stretcher three hundred yards to the bloody chopper.'

'It wasn't three hundred yards.'

'Oh, who *cares*? You're back, that's the main thing. Come on, let's go to Tommy's for a celebratory one.'

'One?' said Chrissie horrified. 'I want a bloody sight more than that.'

'You mean you haven't had anything to drink yet – not since you got back?'

'Immi, I've been in hospital. Since when did the NHS serve a nice Chianti with the liver and fava beans?'

'What?' Immi's face was a study in bafflement.

Chrissie sighed. 'Sorry, I forgot you don't have a thing about classic films like I do.'

'No – I have a life. Now, come on, girlfriend, get your arse in gear.'

When Chrissie got to Tommy's Bar, she found she was a bit of a celebrity. Soldiers she'd never clapped eyes on were offering to buy her drinks, asking her about her tour or her injury.

'Told you,' said Immi, smugly.

'Told me what?' as Chrissie sipped her first Bacardi in nearly ten weeks and felt the hit of alcohol instantly.

'That you're a celebrity.'

'Just don't get me out of here. Well, not till I have had a couple more.'

'Just a couple.'

'I'm going to be such a cheap date tonight. I'm going to be pissed in no time.'

The two girls managed to escape from the attention of their fellow soldiers and find a table in a relatively quiet corner where they could catch up with each other properly.

'So,' said Immi, cradling her drink. 'What are your plans?'

'I can't go anywhere for a bit. I was allowed to leave hospital on the absolute understanding that I report to the medical centre daily to have my dressing changed and my wound checked. Once the MO gives me a clean bill of health, I can take my post-tour leave.'

'And?'

'And?'

'And where are you going to go? Club Med for a wild time partying, or chill in some exotic retreat? You've got all that fantastic tour bonus to spend.'

'God, I don't know. Neither, probably.'

'What?'

'It's not much fun going away on your own, is it?'

'I'll come!'

'I know, hon, and I'd say yes, but haven't you run out of your leave entitlement for this year?'

'A minor detail.'

'I don't think Sir Bates or Sergeant Wilkes'll see it like that. And to be honest, I don't think I'll be going anywhere. After all, all my mates are here.' And Lee will be back in the garrison before too long. But she couldn't mention that, not even to Immi.

Immi shook her head at Chrissie. 'All that leave, all that money from your tour bonus, and you want to kick around the barracks. Boy, Chrissie, you really are a lost cause.'

Lee lay on his bed, his arm throbbing, despite the painkillers, and wondered what he was going to do about Jenna. He knew he could never trust her again and he knew he didn't love her. In fact, he was pretty sure he never really had. He'd been besotted, swept away, and the sex had been great, but in love? No. His mother had been right all along about her. What was the phrase – marry in haste, repent at leisure? He sighed. What a sucker he'd been, he could see that now. He'd been Jenna's means of escape from an overcrowded council house and having got away her next goal had been to achieve her ambition of having her own salon. And he'd bankrolled it. What a mug.

Jenna lay on her sofa and wondered what she was going to do. She was pretty sure Lee was never going to trust her and she was pretty sure he didn't love her, not any more. She'd fucked up good and proper and the mess she'd caused was epic. She felt a bit sorry for Lee, but he'd be all right. He had a good job, he'd get a bonus for his Afghan tour, and someone said he'd get another payout for getting injured. He wasn't going to starve, was he? So, she was the one she had to worry about now. She didn't want to be here when he got back and she wasn't going to move back in with her mum, no way, so she had to find somewhere and fast. She drummed her fingers on the coffee table as she considered her options, which didn't take long. She had no money and no job so she needed somewhere to crash. Dan.

She picked up her phone and called his number.

'Dan? Remember me...?'

The flowering cherries were dropping their petals and the daffodils were well and truly fading by the time Lee got out of the cab. He'd been given a final clean bill of health from the army's rehabilitation centre at Headley Court that morning and had been issued with a travel warrant back to his unit. Part of him had been thrilled that he was finally fully fit, but part of him had dreaded going back home, dreaded facing the mess that Jenna had left behind. Not that he thought it would be a physical mess; she wouldn't have trashed the house out of spite, but he had the bathroom to sort, all that expensive furniture to get rid of, the house to hand back... God, how much sleep had he lost over recent nights just thinking about all he had to do? And over and above everything, he had to decide what to do about Jenna. Divorce, he supposed, but that was more expense.

He paid the driver and then eased his shoulder, rolling it back and forth, more out of habit than necessity. The weeks of physio and therapy had sorted it out and it was almost as it was before the injury. He hauled his kit bag out of the boot and made his way up to the front door. He noted the changes in the neighbourhood since he'd been away: Gary, the snotty kid from next door, had graduated from a trike to a bike with stabilisers; the neighbours opposite had a new car – or maybe they were new neighbours; and the mothy grass had been recently cut and looked almost lush.

As the taxi drove off he walked up the path and let himself in. He looked about him. So, she hadn't lied when she'd sent him a text to say she was moving out. And she'd left it clean, he'd give her that. He dropped his holdall on the carpet and wandered into the sitting room. He noticed the expensive furniture and huge TV had gone. In their place, in the middle of the carpet, was a square of paper and with it a cheque.

I sold the furniture and the telly on eBay. This is what's left after I paid off the finance company. Afraid it's not much. Jx

That was a turn-up, he thought, although it was no more than fair. He glanced at the amount on the cheque – bugger all compared to what she'd taken, but he supposed it was better than nothing.

But there was still the matter of the bathroom. He needed to see for himself what the damage was, he thought, as he climbed the stairs, so he'd better see what he'd paid for.

He opened the door and peered round it cautiously. Well, he could see why it had cost what it had. Gleaming. And he'd always preferred a shower to a bath, but his views weren't going to wash with the housing commandant. The sooner he got this quarter handed back, the sooner the barrack damages could be squared away and the sooner he could put this whole miserable episode behind him.

And the sooner he could tell his mother to shut up about Jenna. *I told you so* seemed to be her only words. She was right, of course, which didn't help matters. He leaned against the counter by the shiny new backwash unit and wondered why he'd been so blinded by Jenna's looks and had never seen the real person underneath the false nails and hair extensions. His mother had seen through her, had tried to warn him, but he hadn't wanted to listen, he supposed. The idea of having Jenna, with her luscious looks, to himself had been too seductive. He snorted. And what a fool she'd made of him.

He made his way back down the stairs. He wondered idly where she was these days, not that he cared. And that was the spooky thing – he really didn't. Back in the hospital in Birmingham, after he'd told her to get lost, he'd wondered if he might have a change of heart, but... nothing. Not a sausage. Zip. Zilch. Nada. He supposed it was infatuation that had got him caught up in Jenna, and once that had worn off there was nothing left underneath to prop up their relationship.

Lee left the quarter and walked through the married patch towards the barracks. He might as well go and see Captain Fanshaw and get his personal admin sorted out. There was no point in putting things off – his situation wasn't going to get any better.

Half an hour later, he was knocking on his platoon commander's door.

'Perkins,' said Seb, looking up. 'Good to see you back. How's the shoulder?'

'Gucci, thanks, sir. I've got a whole Meccano set holding everything together, but it all works properly. I'm still on light duties but I'm hoping the MO is going to pass me fully fit in a couple of weeks.'

'Glad to hear that.'

'Not sure I'll be able to try for the SAS again, though.'

'That's a blow,' said Seb.

'But being at Headley Court puts things in perspective. There's a lot worse things that can happen to a guy.'

His platoon commander nodded. 'That's a commendable approach to have.'

Lee shrugged. 'Sir, the thing is, I'd like to move back into company lines.'

Seb stared at him before saying, 'Ah. It's come to that, has it?'

Lee nodded. 'I can't forgive what she did to me.'

'How did you find out?'

'Online banking, sir, but I told you… at the hospital.'

Seb looked perplexed. 'Sorry, I meant about…' He stopped and looked embarrassed.

'Sir?'

'No, it's nothing.'

But his boss was squirming with embarrassment. 'There's something else, isn't there?'

'Look, Perkins…' Captain Fanshaw paused. 'No, it's nothing.'

'Shouldn't I be the judge of that, with all due respect? Sir.'

Seb stared momentarily at the ceiling. 'You're going to hear about it, anyway, I suppose. It's pretty common knowledge.'

'And?'

'Your wife had a fling, while you were in Afghan. With an REME sergeant. I don't know if it's over, or still going on. Of course, the army posted him out of the garrison quick-sharp but it doesn't mean…'

Seb faltered, and Lee could hazard a guess at the implication. If Jenna and the sergeant wanted to carry on a bit of distance wasn't going to stop them.

Lee waited for the anger or the hurt to kick in, but again,

nothing. 'I see, sir. I suppose it'll make the divorce easier.' And it might explain why she'd moved out – she'd found somewhere else to go. Typical Jenna, that.

'Is that what you want? A divorce? Taking eight grand out of your account without asking was a big breach of trust, and I suppose this other business... But it's a drastic step.'

Lee nodded. 'It's not the money – or this other business. To be honest, boss, as I said, when I was in Headley Court I got to realise that there's stuff that's a lot more important than cash. Being somewhere like that kinda puts a lot of things in perspective. And as for her having a fling... I don't think I was the right man for her. Let's just say, I think we both made a big mistake.'

Jenna waited till she heard the front door slam and then got out of bed. She padded across the bedroom of Dan's new flat and took a packet out of her handbag. There were, she thought, as she made her way to the bathroom, a lot of advantages to living with Dan. For a start there was plenty of money, lots more than when she was with Lee, and secondly they were living in their own place, not a grotty quarter. But on the downside he kept banging on about how they could start a family once the divorce was out of the way. As if.

Jenna sat on the loo and opened the box. She didn't need to read the instructions; this wasn't the first time she'd had to do this. Wee on the stick, wait a bit, and then look to see what the result was. She was pretty sure she knew what the outcome was going to be but she had to be sure and if she hadn't been so preoccupied with getting away from her old quarter and moving in with Dan she'd have noticed she'd missed a period. And now the next one was late.

The result was as she thought. Bugger. Only one thing for

it, then. Really, she thought, as she Googled the number for the Pregnancy Advisory Service, she ought to put it into the memory of her phone. It would save her a lot of time, in the long run. She knew exactly when she'd got pregnant – that drunken night just before she'd heard about Lee's injury – so there was no time to waste or she'd start to show and Dan might notice. As it was she was sure she could get away with getting rid of it, quietly. She'd tell Dan she was going to visit her mum for a bit, and he needn't be any the wiser. A tiny part of her felt a bit sorry for him; it was obvious that he was longing to be a dad, but having kids wasn't the be-all-and-end-all in life, was it? And if he stayed with her he'd just have to get used to the idea, wouldn't he?

Seb shovelled in another forkful of mashed potato, while Maddy fed Nathan some steamed fish.

'I saw Perkins today,' said Seb.

'Really?' Maddy was genuinely pleased. She knew he'd been sent off to Headley Court and that his wife had done a bunk but since those two bits of intelligence had whizzed around the patch, Lee Perkins and his troubles had rather disappeared off everyone's radar, including Maddy's. 'How is he?'

'Surprisingly good, all things considered. He's going for a divorce, though.'

'I would have been surprised if he didn't.' Maddy shook her head as she remembered Jenna and her shenanigans. 'You've got to hope there's some nice woman out there who would make him a proper wife. He deserves it.'

Seb nodded. 'He's a good soldier and I'd like to see him do well. He's a bright lad and he should have a good career ahead of him.' He returned his attention to his supper.

'Seb?'

He glanced up. He knew that tone; it was Maddy's wheedling voice. 'Hmm?'

'Talking of good careers...' She paused. 'How would you feel if I got a job?'

'A *job*? But what about Nate?'

'What about him? Lots of mothers work and their kids cope.'

'I know but...'

'But you said I wasn't to worry about your career and I was to think about being me. Well, I have been and I need to use my brain.' She looked pleadingly at Seb, willing him to understand her point of view. 'I've got a plan and I've discussed it with Caro.'

Seb threw down his knife and fork. 'So you've talked about this to Caro before you go over it with me? Well, thanks very much.'

Maddy rolled her eyes in exasperation. 'Yes, because she's part of the plan. Caro is a trained nanny and I asked her if she'd be Nate's childminder. You know how brilliant she is with him and Nate adores her and her boys.' She stared at Seb. 'Happy?' But she could tell from the look on his face he wasn't really.

'But why do you want a job? I earn enough to keep us.'

'It's nothing to do with the money, and by the time I've paid Caro, there won't be a lot left from anything I earn. Seb, this is about me.'

'You?'

'Yes, me.'

'But aren't you happy?'

Maddy stared at him. He just didn't get it, did he? 'Darling, I love being your wife and Nate's mother but that's all I am these days. I'm not... me. Not like I was at uni. Not like I was when you met me. I don't have a role that's just mine. God, I've even found myself introducing myself to people as Captain Fanshaw's wife or Nate's mum, not Maddy or even Maddy Fanshaw. And I feel as if I'm disappearing. Seb, I've got a degree from Oxford and I'm wiping bottoms, mopping floors and shopping for groceries.' Seb stayed silent. 'You've got a career, why can't I have one too?'

'What'll happen when we move? We're bound to, you know.'

'I'm not stupid, Seb, I know this. I'll just get another job.'

'So when is all this going to kick off?'

'Depends if I get the post.'

'You've already applied? For what?'

'There's a little company that does lab work outsourced by charities researching cancer treatments – it's on the science park. No commuting, right up my street, it's perfect.'

'And you didn't tell me? You deliberately kept me in the dark till you could present me with a fait accompli?'

It was Maddy's turn to get cross. 'No, I didn't. I thought what's the point of having a row if I don't even get an interview?'

'We're not rowing.'

Maddy snorted.

'So you'd already made your mind up to go back to work and asking for my opinion was just an afterthought?'

'No, that's not it. But you've got to see it's a bit chicken and egg.'

'I suppose,' conceded Seb, but he still sounded put out.

'Anyway, cheer up, I mightn't get it.' But she hoped against hope she did.

Chapter Thirty-Five

Chrissie gazed at the morning's appointments list on the computer. Sick parade was over, and now it was the turn of the soldiers who had appointments for check-ups or jabs or ongoing treatment for their ailments to see the MO. Her eye lit on a name: Lee Perkins. She had to steady herself against the counter in reception. Lee! He was back. She could feel her heart thudding in anticipation of seeing him again, and she noticed her hands were shaking.

Since Immi had told her the news about Jenna's affair, she'd longed to ask more about it, but Immi's response to a bit of gentle questioning didn't encourage further prying.

'You shouldn't want to know, Chrissie Summers. Jenna's a cow. I mean,' Immi's voice had risen in indignation, 'why would either of us care what happens to her? Considering what she did to her husband – *and* while he was in a war zone – sheesh, words fail me. Honestly, Chrissie, I don't know why we were friends with her. We should have seen through her.'

Chrissie didn't contradict her and point out that it had been Immi who had been Jenna's mate, not her. Nor did she dare tell her quite how close she'd got to Lee in Afghanistan and how much she felt for him now. Not that it mattered, she thought glumly, as she gazed at Lee's name on the computer screen, she was never going to have a chance with him. She didn't know why but he'd made it perfectly obvious that whatever he'd once felt for her was over. Since his second injury, his attitude had changed completely. She sighed. She just wished she could flick a switch on her feelings like he had, because inside she was dying.

It was almost lunchtime when Maddy rang the bell of Caro's quarter. She was dressed in her smart interview suit and couldn't wait to get home and change into something more comfortable.

'So?' said Caro, as she opened the door, a squirming Nathan cradled in her arms.

'I'm really, really sorry, Caro.'

'Oh, hun. You didn't get it? The stupid people have no idea what they've let slip by them.'

Maddy sighed. 'No, it's not the job I'm feeling sorry about, it's something else.'

Caro's forehead creased. 'I'm not with you, Mads.'

Maddy couldn't keep her smile suppressed any longer. 'I'm sorry but you're going to be stuck with Nate for the foreseeable future. I got the job!'

Caro's shriek of delight not only reduced Nathan to instant tears but was heard halfway across the patch.

'Only pretend I didn't tell you first. Seb's got to believe he's the first one to hear the news.'

'God, men!' Caro handed Nate over to Maddy. 'By the way, do you want to hear some gossip?'

'Caro, I'm a woman. *Of course* I want to hear some gossip.'

'Well, apparently Susie and Mike have been hauled into their kids' prep school and there's a risk their girls might have to leave.'

'No! Why?'

'It seems the girls have been sharing porn with their classmates.'

Maddy's eyes goggled. 'But that's awful.'

Caro nodded. 'It seems they found their dad's stash of dodgy DVDs, copied them and then sold them.'

Maddy's mouth twitched. 'I know it's appalling but you've got to admire their enterprise.'

It's not how their head sees it.'

'I can imagine. But how come you know? I mean it's hardly the sort of thing Susie would post on the Wives' Club noticeboard.'

'Most of the kids there are army ones, so it's courtesy of the wives' grapevine. Of course, it may not be true but I've heard from Philly that as a result Susie's signed the pledge.'

'No!' Somehow that seemed almost as shocking as the other bit of gossip.

'It sort of adds up. Maybe, what with one thing and another, she and Mike had their eye off the ball a bit too much when the kids were home. If she was out for the count on the sofa, weekends and evenings, no wonder the girls were running a bit wild.'

As Maddy took Nathan back to her house she felt even more glad that she was going to have a life of her own, a life off the patch and that didn't involve anyone from the army. It had just been made even more apparent to her that there was no such thing as a private life where the other wives were concerned. It made her wonder, fleetingly, what they knew about her.

'Hi, Lee.'

'Chrissie?' He sounded surprised.

OK, she had the advantage because she knew he was

going to turn up to the medical centre that morning but even so, surely he would have known he might see her there. 'I *do* work here. It can't come as *that* much of a shock to see me.' She tried to sound light-hearted but she was angry that he seemed to have forgotten all about her. Did she mean that little to him?

'No, no... sorry, I wasn't thinking.'

You certainly weren't thinking about me. She felt her heart crack just a little more. 'How are you?' she said brightly to cover up her feelings.

'Better. Look.' Lee swung his arm in an arc like a bowler.

'Impressive. And no aches and pains?'

'Some, but not often, and I've got lots of exercises I can do to ease them.'

'Good.' A light flashed on Chrissie's desk in reception. 'OK, the MO is free. Go on in.'

She watched Lee head down the corridor. He hadn't shown any sign of emotion apart from surprise. So that was that, then. And her heart broke completely. She busied herself with filing patients' notes, tidying up the reception area and any little tasks to keep herself from wondering about what might have been, to keep herself from crying. But despite her self-set tasks, she still couldn't avoid spotting him leaving the medical centre – leaving without even a glance in her direction.

The intercom went on her desk. 'Summers,' said the MO's voice. 'Come to my office, please.'

She blew her nose and got herself in check before she made her way to Major Rawlings' surgery.

'File those, please, Summers,' he said, pointing to a tottering stack of buff-coloured medical files.

'Of course, sir. Anything else?'

He shook his head. 'Nope. When you've done that you

can go for lunch, if you want. That is, unless there's anyone else for morning surgery?'

'No, sir, Private Perkins was the last.'

'Good. Thank you, Summers.'

Chrissie took the manila folders to reception and began to put them back in the filing cabinets. She glanced at the top one – Lee's naturally, as he'd been last to see the MO. She noticed that his personal details had been altered. His address was no longer given as one of the married quarters – he was down as a single soldier, living in. He mightn't be divorced in law, but as far as the army was concerned, as soon as a marriage broke down and the soldier moved back into barracks, he or she was single again.

So, he and Jenna had separated? They must have done. Lee's docs said so. She needed to speak to Immi to see if she knew more.

As quickly as she could, she stuffed the remaining notes back into the filing cabinets and raced off to the cookhouse, texting Immi as she went, demanding that her friend meet her there for lunch.

She was waiting by the door, tapping her foot with impatience, when Immi put in an appearance.

'You never told me,' said Chrissie to Immi, as soon as she was within earshot.

'Told you what? For fuck's sake, Chrissie, I'm a clerk, not a clairvoyant.'

'That Lee and Jenna have split up. That he's moved back into company lines.'

Immi looked bewildered. 'Not being funny, Chrissie, but why should I have done? You knew Jenna'd had an affair, so her and Lee breaking up can hardly have come as a shock. It isn't exactly hot off the press, is it?'

'No... but...'

The pair joined the queue for the salad bar. 'So what would you care?' said Immi.

'It doesn't matter why, I just do, OK?'

'But why?'

Chrissie remained silent. She didn't want to answer that one.

Immi stopped. She stared at Chrissie, and Chrissie could almost see a cascade of pennies dropping. 'Oh my God. You and Lee. *You* and Lee? You and *Lee*! In Afghan. Oh my God, you and Lee.'

Chrissie held a hand up to stop Immi speculating any more, as their queue shuffled forwards. 'No! I mean, yes, we were out there together, but that was it. He was out in Helmand and I was in Bastion. Yes, our paths crossed once or twice, but that was it. Honest, Immi.'

'But you wanted more to happen?'

'No.'

Immi gave her a look which couldn't have said 'pull the other one' more clearly if she'd had it tattooed on her forehead.

'All right, yes I did, but it didn't. Really. Truly, Immi. You must believe me. He was married and I respected that.'

Around them the other soldiers stopped shuffling forwards to get their meal and began to openly eavesdrop on the developing row.

'So did you and he plan to go out to Afghan together?' Immi's eyes widened again. 'Of course you did!' she said triumphantly, as she made the connection. 'That's why you didn't want me to mention your posting last Christmas, in case anyone else managed to put two and two together.'

'No! No, Immi, it was just coincidence. When I saw him at Brize, I was as surprised as anyone.'

'Who was surprised?' Lee's voice stopped both of them in mid-flow.

Chrissie jumped, guiltily. 'Nothing.'

'Doesn't sound like nothing to me,' said Lee. His gaze flicked questioningly between the two women.

'No, it certainly isn't,' said Immi.

'Immi,' said Chrissie, a warning note in her voice.

But Immi took no notice. 'I was just about to say to Chrissie that, while everyone in the garrison was having a right go at Jenna for shagging that REME guy, you and she were playing fast and loose out in Afghan. Well, I hope you're proud of yourselves.'

'What?' Lee looked gobsmacked. 'Me and Chrissie? Screwing? Oh, get real, Immi. As if.' And the look on his face was the final straw.

Obviously, thought Chrissie, feeling her already damaged heart finally shatter into a million tiny shards, he finds the idea of screwing me utterly ridiculous and repellent. Stifling a cry she fled from the cookhouse, cannoning into soldiers as she fought against the incoming tide, half-blinded by tears.

'Now what have I said?' said Lee to Immi.

Immi gazed at Chrissie's fleeing back view before she switched her attention back to Lee. 'So you and she didn't...?'

'When? Immi, just how on *earth* do you think we got it together out there? Shit, I spent most of my time on the front line.'

'I dunno.' She thought about her own love-life. 'But where there's a will there's a way.'

'Exactly. And I was happily married – at least I thought I was,' he added bitterly. 'And Chrissie's got a boyfriend. I wasn't about to muscle in, when she was in a relationship.

Just because my life was going shit-shaped, I wasn't going to screw up hers too.'

'What?' It was Immi's turn to be completely bewildered. 'Relationship? Who with?'

'That medic, Phil Johns.'

'Phil?' Just when Immi thought the day couldn't get any more surreal, it just did. 'Phil and Chrissie.' She started to giggle.

'Now what have I said?' Lee sounded annoyed.

'Oh come on, Lee, surely you know how unlikely that is?' She was actually shaking with laughter now.

'No.' Lee's irritation was starting to morph into anger. 'What's the joke? What have I said?'

'Phil's gay.'

'A poof?' Lee's eyes popped.

'I don't think that's very PC,' said Immi primly, her laughter gone, 'but yes, totally, 100 per cent, dyed in the wool... poof.'

'So he and Chrissie...?'

'Not for an instant.'

'So why's she so upset, like?'

Immi repeated Lee's words back to him: '"Me and Chrissie? Screwing? Oh, get real, Immi. As if."' She gave Lee a significant look. 'If you ask me, Chrissie thought you'd rather shag a gorilla than her. And as a result, I think you've just broken her heart.'

The colour drained from Lee's face. 'What have I done?' He began to head for the cookhouse door.

'Top floor, Duchess of Kent block,' Immi called after him. 'Room three hundred and ten.'

Chapter Thirty-Six

The door was shut fast and Lee opened it with trepidation. As he did, he could hear muffled hiccuping sobs. Quietly he shut the door behind him and tiptoed across the room, the square of carpet in the middle muffling the sound of his boots, but Chrissie was crying so hard, he doubted she would hear anything anyway. All he could see was a little ball huddled under the duvet.

He sat down at the foot of the bed.

'B-b-bugger off, I-i-mmi,' came Chrissie's indistinct voice.

Lee stayed put.

'I s-s-said, *b-bugger off*!'

Still Lee didn't move.

The bed erupted as Chrissie, mad with grief and anger, threw back the duvet to lash out at her room-mate. Her mouth opened and shut and then she said, 'Lee!'

Her face was puffy, flushed and tear-stained, but Lee didn't think he'd seen anyone so lovely before.

'Chrissie—'

'Get out,' she screamed at him. 'Get out!'

'Chrissie—'

'Out!' she yelled again, and hauled the duvet back over her head.

Lee stood up and pulled the covers off her.

'Listen to me,' he yelled back, his face inches from hers.

Chrissie was so stunned her sobs ceased. She just lay there, staring up at him, huddled into a foetal position, the epitome of misery.

'Listen to me,' he repeated more gently. 'Chrissie, I had no idea you had feelings for me.'

Inelegantly Chrissie wiped her nose on the back of her hand and glared at Lee. 'Well, you've made it quite plain how you feel about *me*.'

Lee walked across the room, picked up a box of tissues from a nearby dressing table and brought back a handful of handkerchiefs to Chrissie. She snatched them and blew her nose.

'You have *no* idea how I feel about you.' He glared back at Chrissie, daring her to contradict him. 'And shall I tell you why?' He sat down on her bed again.

Chrissie snorted. 'If you must.' She pulled herself into a sitting position, against her pillows.

'I backed off. I could see – at least I thought I could see – your heart was elsewhere. So I didn't want to complicate things for you.'

'Complicate what *things*?' she sneered.

'You and Phil.'

Chrissie's jaw slackened.

Lee held his hand up. 'Yes, I know all about Phil *now*, don't I? Immi's just put me straight.'

'Which is more than Phil wants anyone to do for him,' said Chrissie, sniffing and dashing away tears off her cheeks.

Lee smiled at her. 'That's more like it, bonny lass. So that is why I got so cross when Immi accused us of getting it on in Bastion. Talk about unfair: screwing you – which isn't the nicest way of putting things but hey – was the one thing I'd wanted to do and hadn't been able to; and then I get blamed for it anyway.'

Chrissie gave a wan smile. 'You wanted to?'

'God, Chrissie, I spent half my waking hours thinking about you. Which was wrong of me, I'll admit, 'cos at the time I thought I was still happily married.' He shrugged. 'Well, we all make mistakes.'

'Said the hedgehog climbing off the hairbrush,' murmured Chrissie.

Lee chuckled. 'But then when I got injured and you and Phil were always together, I thought, well, I've missed me chance.'

'We just liked the same films.'

'*Brief Encounter*.'

'You remembered.'

'I've watched it.'

'Really?' She was impressed.

Lee nodded. 'Not really my style, like, and I didn't think much of the soundtrack.'

Chrissie laughed. 'No, I don't have you down as the classical music type.'

'Is that what it was – classical music?'

'Rachmaninov.'

'Bless you.'

Chrissie giggled again. 'That's the name of the composer, silly.'

'So do you forgive me?' he asked. He leaned forwards a little and Chrissie saw something nestling in the V of his open combat jacket neck. She hooked the object out with her finger. It was Fred Bear, still on a chain round his neck.

'You've still got him.'

'He's the most important bit of kit I've got. I've been keeping him safe.'

'He didn't do a very good job, though, of keeping you safe, did he?'

'Who cares? That injury meant I got to see lots more of you than I would have. I think, all in all, your little bear did a cracking job.'

'I think,' said Chrissie, 'if you wanted to, you could see a lot more of me yet.'

'That goes without saying, now we're both back here.'

'Not that sort of seeing *a lot more of* me,' said Chrissie as she began to unbutton her combat jacket.

'You mean…?'

'I most certainly do.' And she pulled Lee towards her and kissed him.